FIC   Laker, Rosalind.

The silver touch

cop. 1   16.95

THE SILVER TOUCH

THE SILVER TOUCH

Rosalind Laker

DOUBLEDAY & COMPANY, INC.
GARDEN CITY, NEW YORK
1987

Library of Congress Cataloging-in-Publication Data
Laker, Rosalind.
The silver touch.

1. Bateman, Hester, 1709–1794—Fiction.
2. London (England)—History—18th century—Fiction.
I. Title.
PR6065.E9S56   1987   823'.914   86-24199
ISBN 0-385-23745-6

To Nancy, Paul and Jenny

Acknowledgment

For advice on silversmithing I am indebted
to Grahame White, who first introduced me to
Hester Bateman through one of her spoons
washed up on the seashore of my home town
from some long ago shipwreck.

R.L.

THE SILVER TOUCH

Chapter 1

All they had allowed her to keep as a memento was the silver thimble. In a corner of the cottage room, Hester Needham sat out of the way on a stool. Twelve years old and country reared, she watched bleakly the ransacking of her home by her half-brothers and -sisters. They had come to the funeral of her mother, the third wife of their late father, mainly to recover family possessions, and were picking over the spoils like so many vultures in their mourning attire.

No one had appeared to consider that the offspring of the marriage might have a right to anything, and she was too proud and independent by nature to beg, once her initial protest had been ignored. Even some pretty china, which she knew had been part of her mother's dowry, had disappeared into one of the wooden crates that they had brought along. Gone as well were the herbal distillations at which her mother had been expert, the assorted little bottles of green, blue and amber glass with their healing contents annexed with everything else. At least she had inside her head the instructions she had received in this skilful craft, and nobody could take that from her.

It was only when Ann Needham's sewing box, which nobody wanted, was opened for casual inspection that the thimble had come to light. Even in their greed they had not liked to remove it after agreeing among themselves that Hester could have the sewing box; for her it was a special treasure. Her first memories were of the thimble catching the light on her mother's finger. Star-bright; a thing of beauty in a precious metal that had never touched her life in any other way. It would always mean much to her.

"Now what is to become of you, Hester?"

There was a look of compassion on Jack Needham's ruddy face as he crouched on his hunkers to peer into her grief-pinched visage, his breath pungent with ale imbibed earlier that day. Of them all he had been the only one not to lay claim to anything in the cottage. His domineering wife had done that, and he had simply obeyed her out of habit.

"The parson's wife has offered me domestic work." She was thankful not to have to be beholden to anyone present. "I'll be living in there."

He shook his tow-haired head solemnly. "No, lass. That's not good enough. As head of the family, I can't allow a Needham to make a home with outsiders. You shall come to us and be welcome. Martha and I have plenty of room in our tavern for a young 'un."

With a gulp that was almost a broken cry, Hester flung her arms around Jack's neck from where she sat and buried her face in his huge shoulder. He had always been kind to her and her mother, calling-in whenever he was in the district to make sure that all was well with them. Probably his wife, Martha, had never known of his gifts of a piece of bacon, a sack of flour or some other such item that had been more than welcome in their meagre circumstances. Big and generous, he had never come without a new hair-ribbon for her in his pocket, or a simple fairing. Now, benevolent as ever, he was not going to desert her in her new and terrible loneliness.

A silence of relief had fallen on the room. The child had been on everyone's conscience in that respect, each waiting for someone else to offer. None of them had approved their father's marriage to a woman less than half his age, but she had been a harmless creature who had looked after him well for the remaining years of his life. Nobody had anything against the child either, even though family hearsay was that she had been troublesome in the past and her russet-coloured hair was warning enough that troubles of another kind might occur in the future. Only Martha looked displeased by the solution, glaring at the back of her husband's head.

"You'll not regret taking me in," Hester promised fervently, her choked words muffled against the coarse serge of her brother's coat. "I'll work hard."

Martha's voice cut sharply across the room. "You shall indeed. Fetch your cape. It's time to leave. I want to get back to London before it's dark. It's not safe to be abroad on the road after dusk."

Everybody was leaving, exchanging farewells. Jack picked up the sewing box to put it into the wagon before he hurried off to the parsonage to explain the change of arrangements. Hester took her cape from a peg and put it on. The moment of departure from home had come and it was hard not to cry out in anguish for the love and happiness she had known there. In spite of herself there came the sting of tears again and she blinked them away, gathering the bundle that held her clothes before tucking under her arm a battered leather holder that had been leaning against it. Nobody asked her what it contained, it being too shabby to be of any interest, and she was intensely relieved that it had been ignored. She could not have borne to have shared anything of herself with any one of them, not even Jack, and the folder held the best results of what she believed to be her only talent, an ability to draw and paint in a simple way.

"I'm ready."

"About time, too." Martha's hands were rough as she hustled the child out before her. Not in the least maternal, she had always been thankful that motherhood has passed her by. Now she was saddled with this new and unwanted responsibility when she could least do with it. Her life was the tavern, its comings and goings, the jokes with patrons old and new, and the happy conceit that as a fine-looking, amply-built woman with a witty tongue, she was as much an asset to the high reputation of the Heathcock Inn as the good ale and food it served to travellers and local folk alike. Jack was an oaf and always had been, too easy on those in debt to him and too lenient generally to be landlord of the best tavern in the Strand. Yet he could be as stubborn as a mule if he set his mind on something, which was why she had known better than to query his decision over Hester, particularly in front of the others. She had respect for him in a rage, although not at any other time.

As she took her place beside the driving seat at the front of the loaded wagon, Jack returned in time to help Hester up into the back of it. He thought her a thoroughly plain little thing at the moment, with her freckles dark against her pallor and her large grey eyes sunken in grief in her oval face, the swollen lids weighed down by the long, tear-damp lashes. She might easily have been a changeling he was settling into his wagon, for there was no sign today of the vital, lively young creature he knew her to be. But she would recover. There was no doubt of that.

"You'll be all right with us, Hester." He jerked his chin in hearty reassurance. "Never fear."

In the wagon seat his wife twisted around impatiently to address him. "Come *on,* Jack. We've been away from the Heathcock too long already."

With a suppressed sigh he went to swing himself up beside her, taking whip and reins into his hands. The wheels rolled forward. Hester sat amid a huddle of furniture and other remnants of her home, watching the cottage draw away along the rutted lane. She was leaving everything that was dear to her; the familiar clean wide countryside, the birds that came to her window and the nuthatch that had fed from her hand. Disappearing from view were the woods where she knew every path and the bluebell dell she had painted in all its azure tints. Gone forever were the meadows where she had run through the golden cowslips in spring and lain, drowsy with sunshine, amid buttercups under summer skies. A tearing pang went through her as she was driven past the churchyard where the new grave had been covered over, holding to itself the wild flowers she had thrown into it. The first part of her life had gone beyond recall, left behind already with its gentle memories. Now she was on her way to London where she had been born, although she had no recollection of the city. She had been only a few months old when Ann Needham had left it in early widowhood to return to her roots, having been a country girl. By then Ann's parents were dead and Hester could just remember the day when news came that her mother's only brother had been lost at sea, leaving them no kin on that side of the family.

There was no knowing yet whether she herself would like London in this year of 1721 any better than her mother had done. Probably not, but that did not mean she would not make the best of things. She was young and strong and healthy, unafraid of hard work as she had promised Jack, for she had done a full share of potato digging and fruit picking and harvesting in her time. Unexpectedly the numbness of sorrow, which had been with her for many weeks since it had first become apparent that Ann Needham was not going to recover, was pierced by her natural resilience. It spurred her into lifting her head and shifting her cramped position to turn and watch for the first sight of the spires and roofs of London.

When the market-town of Islington had come and gone along the road, the wagon rolled on to pass the Charter House and rumble through Smithfield before crossing the boundary of the Old London Wall at Newgate. They skirted the prison and came by way of Ludgate Hill into the Strand. Hester, who had been kneeling up ever since the crowded buildings and busy streets had begun to close in on all sides, caught a full glimpse of the new St. Paul's Cathedral. It's great dome shone like a gigantic pearl, dominating the whole skyline and visible from far afield.

She was dazed by the noise and stench and bustle of the city, the number of carriages and carts and sedan chairs and the streams of people on foot. Brightly painted trade signs swung over every shop door, and the barber-surgeons' striped poles gleamed red and white in the grim colours of blood and bandages. From everywhere there came the individual sing-song cries of the street-vendors, male and female, who carried baskets of lavender, oranges or fresh cherries, balanced trays of muffins on their heads, or bore creels of fish or mussels and cockles for sale on their stooped backs. Dusk was falling as Jack drove along the Strand, where the lamp-lighters had been at work and the hanging lanterns, suspended by chains or slung from iron wall-brackets, gave a glow as if a hundred moons had been captured there.

"Here we are," Martha announced with satisfaction, glad to be safely home.

Hester stared up at the tall gabled building with black timbers, its name proclaimed by the swinging sign of a male black grouse against a green ground. All the windows were bright with lights. Although a door led into the tavern from the street, Jack turned the horses into an archway at the side and they entered a cobbled yard where a second and larger entrance was conveniently located for arriving passengers. While a groom took the horses' bridles, two porters in fustian jackets came to unload the wagon. Jack lifted Hester down from the back and handed her possessions to her. She was quick to follow after Martha, who was already disappearing into the tavern.

It was like stepping into another world, where the air was blended of savoury aromas, pipe smoke, the scent of beeswaxed wood and the strong smell of ale. Hester had thought the street noisy, but here was another kind of din. A rumble of voices and bellows of laughter resounded from the taproom; cutlery clattered in the eating rooms and waiting maids scuttled across the entrance hall weighed down by trays of food and drink for those in the private parlours. Following Martha into the kitchen, she was assailed by the heat of the cooking fires where poultry and joints of meat sizzled on the spits. Pan lids clanked in turn as Martha lifted each one to inspect or taste the simmering contents. All turned their heads to stare at Hester when she was introduced as their employer's half-sister, and even the little scullery boys paused in their work to gape at her.

Leading the way upstairs, Martha talked over her shoulder in her sharp, articulate tones. "Jack and I have our own parlour on this upper floor. The rest of the rooms are bedchambers and it is the same on the floor above. Female servants sleep in the attics and the men in the stable lofts. Since you are family, I shall put you in a small bedchamber near ours. Apart from eating with us, you'll have no other special privileges. We're on the go from morning to night in this place and sometimes during the night if a late coach comes in and passengers need to be fed. You'll be up at five every morning and you'll be thankful whenever you manage to get to bed." She flung open a door. "This is your room."

It was tiny and the ceiling sloped sharply. The furnishings consisted of a narrow bed, a corner washstand, some wall-pegs for clothes and a three-legged stool. Hester had no complaint. She would have privacy, and she was sure that in daylight she would have a splendid view of the London rooftops from the dormer window.

"I'll like it here," she said genuinely, looking about her.

"It makes no difference to me whether you do or don't. You have come to the Heathcock to work, not to air your opinions." There was an underlying savagery in the words. "In return you'll have a roof over your head, food for your belly and clothes for your back. You'll also obey the general rules of good behaviour laid down by me for this house as well as two more for your own safety and well-being." Martha wagged a warning finger. "You are never to set foot in the taproom, linger in any dark corridor, or enter any of the private parlours when they are occupied by gentlemen on their own. Second, you'll not venture outside the grounds of the establishment unless accompanied by me or some other responsible person. I've seen country innocence come to a fall too many times to risk disgrace being brought on the good name of Needham." Her lips curled back thinly as she saw Hester's face tighten. "You can wipe that mulish look away right now, miss. Looking after yourself in the countryside is a far cry from the evil ways of the city." The finger wagged again threateningly. "Now mark well what I have said. You'll have a hard time if you get on the wrong side of me!" Swinging back to the doorway, she paused to issue one more instruction. "Come down for something to eat when you have unpacked. I shall allot your duties to you in the morning."

Hester, who had been holding her possessions to her all the time like a shield, set them down on the bed and began to untie the knot of the bundle. Curiously, there was hope in her again after weeks of sadness and despair. It was rising to course through her veins in the most curious manner. She had a feeling that however much Martha might seek to suppress and restrain her, the means of shaping her life by her own choice lay waiting for her in this great city.

In the weeks and months that followed she was kept as busy as Martha had predicted, taking a turn at every task within the domestic regions as part of her training to be useful in every sphere. She scrubbed and cleaned and polished, washed up tankards and glasses until sometimes it seemed to her that the whole of London must be imbibing at the Heathcock. Daily she trimmed the candles in their broad-based chamber-sticks that stood on the hall table for guests to light their way upstairs at night. She made up beds and humped dirty linen down to the washhouse in the walked kitchen yard at the rear of the tavern. Sometimes she spent days there at a stretch, pounding down with a blunt-ended poss stick, the linen boiling away in the tubs amid steam and suds. The best days were when Martha took her to market. Holding the baskets, which were soon to be filled with purchases, she would stare around her, taking in the sights of the streets, fascinated by the fashions of the richer folk and wishing she could read the pamphlets that were sometimes thrust into her hand.

Reading and writing were skills she had never mastered. Illiteracy was common enough, the charity schools being too few in number to educate all those unable to pay for schooling. Local lessons were sometimes arranged by high-principled men and women, who did their best for the children who attended. She herself had been given such a chance in her village, although nothing had come of it. Unlike her fellow pupils, most of whom were far from being as quick-witted as she knew herself to be, she found she confused letters, particularly those that were similar, such as *b* and *d, p* and *q,* and small words such as *of, for* and *from* completely defeated her. As a result, she was ridiculed by the grim-faced woman who took the class, called a dunce and had such a sense of shame at her own stupidity instilled into her that at times she vomited behind the church wall when the hateful lessons were over. At home she became wild and difficult, half-mad with frustration, and a climax was reached when one day she ran away and was not found for two days. After that there were no more lessons for her. The teaching dame would not have taken her back in any case. She had found comfort in what she could do, which was to draw, and birds were her favourite subjects.

She missed them and their swooping patterns of flight more than anything else in her new surroundings. There were plenty of sparrows that came to peck in the yard, some blackbirds and a goldfinch or two, but it was the shyer birds that had flown in from the woods and meadows to the cottage garden that had been such a joy to her, appearing in almost every one of her sketches. She thought of them frequently, the corn buntings and the yellow-hammers, the skylarks, lapwings and woodpeckers and the darting blue flash of the kingfishers across a stream that lay at the end of the herb garden. How did her mother's herb garden look now? Was it already overgrown with weeds or had the new tenant taken care of it? At this point she always shook her head to drive away the homesickness threatening to overtake her, as it still did sometimes in unguarded moments, and got on with whatever chore she had in hand.

Martha had little to complain about in Hester's work, but her resentment never eased and she found fault constantly out of general irritation. Moreover, Hester was growing up. An exuberance for life and a quickness of spirit had remanifested themselves in her not long after her arrival at the Heathcock. Sometimes wilful, alarmingly fiery-tempered when roused and frequently exasperating, she was nevertheless always conscientious about the chores she had to do. "I've finished that task," was often a reply when asked why she was not washing pots, or folding linen, or cleaning cupboards.

Martha found such youthful vitality increasingly irksome, especially when her back ached and her feet were tired. It was impossible not to notice that Hester was blooming, a new lustre giving highlights to the rich colour of her hair, her brows and lashes darkening while there was an added translucent quality to her alabaster skin. Soon she had grown quite tall, and her fuller, softer curves meant the expense of new dresses that suited her, for Jack insisted she be well-clad as a young woman should be, with an end to hand-me-downs from Martha's clothes-press. For the first time Martha became conscious of her own years and the lines that paint and powder could no longer hide. Bitter jealousy of a young girl's charms began to take over from her long-held resentment until it bordered dangerously on hatred.

With restrictions long since lifted on going out alone, Hester had come to know London well, usually on errands for Martha. Much of the oldest part had been re-designed as well as re-built over the decades since the Great Fire, and the city had expanded widely in all directions with beautiful architecture, new long streets, parks and leafy squares. In contrast there remained ancient alleyways and slums where thousands lived in squalor, their misfortunes a shadow across a prosperous land where roast beef was the daily fare of the middle classes and vast fortunes grew on commerce at home and abroad.

There were few highlights in her hardworking existence, which was why an exhibition proved to be an event of some magnitude for her. One of the Heathcock's patrons was a goldsmith named Harwood, a big portly man with a florid complexion and one of the most prosperous master craftsmen in his field in London. He was also a powerful voice in the Worshipful Company of Goldsmiths, which dated back to the twelfth century and, with strict rules, maintained the rigidly high standard of work in English gold and silver. He was in the habit of inviting fellow master craftsmen and merchants to discuss business matters over dinner at the Heathcock, quite apart from having a tankard of ale on his own in the taproom at regular intervals. Now and again he and his wife brought friends to supper there in a private parlour after the theatre and Martha took their orders herself, putting her best waiting maids to serve them. Recently his daughter, Caroline, his only child and the apple of his eye, had been included in the supper parties when the theatrical entertainment attended beforehand had been deemed suitable for a young girl, her age being no more than Hester's.

One evening when there was only male company present, and a profitable business deal had gone through over the food and wine, Master Harwood, bloated and flushed from all he had eaten and drunk, issued an invitation to Jack and Martha to attend an exhibition at the Goldsmiths' Hall where some of the objects displayed were from his own workshop.

"I've enjoyed the best that you can produce in the good wine and victuals that my guests and I have been served this evening. Now it is your turn to come and see the best that I can produce, which will surely measure up to your pigeon and mushroom pie." He laughed heartily at his own joke, which was an indication of the success of the evening and the amount of wine he had drunk, for he was by no means jovial by nature and his face was granite-like and harsh-jawed in repose. But he spent lavishly, never questioned the Needhams' honesty by querying the bill, and those whom he introduced to the tavern invariably came back to be regular patrons of the Heathcock themselves, spreading its good name still further.

"You do us much honour, sir." Jack bowed low and Martha curtsied. It was expected that those in a lower position should be obsequious, and Jack would have had no qualms about kneeling to polish a patron's boots if it meant increased trade and money in the coffers. Martha had her limits, but she was highly flattered by the invitation.

"We shall attend, sir," she said, quite pink in the cheeks and curtseying again.

When the day came she had developed a streaming cold and was unable to venture out. Jack, who had no interest in the exhibition, still felt obliged to go. "You can come with me," he said to Hester. "We needn't stay long. It's just so I can say I was there."

The Goldsmiths' Hall was a distinguished building with fine windows, a grand entrance and crystal chandeliers shining on carved and polished woodwork within. It was to this place that new goldsmiths came after completing their seven years' apprenticeship to register their individual punch-mark, or the "touch," as it was known in the trade, which would indentify their work for all time. Once granted the Freedom of the Company, they were able to work for any master or set up on their own, and certain privileges went with their position that were denied ordinary craftsmen in what was one of the most aesthetically rewarding trades that any man could follow.

"Don't be nervous, lass," Jack said to her, thoroughly uncomfortable himself in such a grand setting. Footmen were posted at intervals to bow the visitors through to the great chamber where the gold and silverware were on display. To add to the magic for Hester, everybody present was extremely well-dressed, many in silks and brocades. Yet all else paled before the sight that met her when the exhibits came into view. Set on velvet-draped stands, tasselled cords dividing them off from the public, were gold and silver articles of such magnificence that she was captivated instantly by the dazzling spectacle. In contrast to the utensils used at the Heathcock, here everything that could possibly be used at a table or sideboard was fashioned out of the two most beautiful metals in the world.

"Hell's bells!" Jack exclaimed, struck only by the monetary value of the display. "Whatever would this lot be worth then?"

Hester was beyond speech. She had seen beautiful church plate, although never at these close quarters, and there had always been glass between herself and displays in goldsmiths' shopwindows. Here, with plenty of sunshine pouring through the tall windows, neither the gleam nor the radiance could hide the intricate results of superb craftsmanship.

Jack began craning his neck to see where the Harwood exhibits were located, intending to view them briefly and leave again. Hester pulled at his sleeve. "Let's look at everything," she implored.

He always wore a fob watch on a gold chain and he cupped it in his broad palm to study the time. "I can't stay more than another five minutes. Not with Martha in the state she is and only one barman in the taproom. You may stay as long as you like, as far as I'm concerned."

"Then let me stay."

"Very well then. But don't let anyone else know I let you have the time off." He placed a finger beside his nose and winked to cement their little conspiracy. She knew full well that by "anyone" he meant his wife, and she gave a nod of endorsement.

He left her in front of the Harwood display. In the centre of it was the paraphernalia needed for the growing fashion of drinking tea, all of it arranged on a rosewood tray-top table. Since tea was vastly expensive, teapots were small and this one was octagonal in shape, which was quite beautiful. The kettle on its lampstand, from which the lady of the house would pour boiling water onto the tea-leaves, was the same unusual shape, with an ivory swing handle, its silver sides reflecting the matching jug, slop basin and sugar vase. In addition there were the spoons on a spoon-tray, a sweetmeat basket and a tea canister, which was in silver gilt with a flower finial and could be locked against servants' thieving fingers. Hester had tasted tea a few times, for Martha had to cater to guests who could afford it, and she had been allowed to share what was left in the teapot when more hot water had been poured over the leaves. It was a palatable drink and she liked it, although she thought it would taste even better if served from such a handsome octagonal teapot of silver.

Flanking the tea table, which was drawing attention, was a magnificent wine fountain with a high domed lid, the handles mounted on two rampant lions. On the opposite side was a presentation cup and cover in gold, of a size and splendour she thought fit for a Lord Mayor of London at the start of his year's service to the city.

She wandered from display to display. Everything was here, from tureens to chocolate pots, candlesticks to huge centrepieces that would grace some long dining table, and smaller items such as snuff-boxes, salts, casters and nutmeg graters. When she finally left the exhibition she felt dazed by so much beauty. If she had been a boy she would have followed that marvellous craft. There were women goldsmiths, the work of two having been on display, and it was her guess they were goldsmiths' daughters, which would have enabled them to take a full apprenticeship within the family circle. Such opportunities did not come the way of ordinary girls like herself.

When she reached the tavern, she went upstairs to her bedroom and took the old silver thimble out of her sewing box to view it in a new light. She was filled with pride that she owned something in the precious metal that had been displayed in such splendour at the Goldsmiths' Hall.

On her sixteenth natal day Hester was allowed in the taproom to serve at the tables for the first time. Martha was vehemently against it, but Jack insisted, knowing the effect that a pretty face could have upon a gathering. "She's old enough to know her way about, and nobody would dare put a hand on her in my presence."

To Martha's anger, it had happened out of his presence, although he chose to forget the trouble it caused. Once, in the private rooms, Hester had punched a travelling gentleman in the eye and another time had kicked an alderman. Both occasions had caused an uproar, with Jack acting like a madman and throwing the men out on the cobbles for having made unwarranted advances to his half-sister. Why could he not see that those laughing grey eyes, narrow waist and the tantalising grace of a candle flame would always be a natural invitation to the opposite sex? Martha felt strongly that he should try to make her responsibility for Hester lighter instead of heavier, for it was still her particular cross to protect his precious relative from harm. She had never been one to shirk a duty once it was laid upon her, and it galled her that her untroubled husband knew that only too well.

Hester enjoyed her new position as waiting maid. She viewed it as a promotion. It could not have come at a better time. She had had earlier stints at sharing the cooking in the kitchen, but for the past three months she had been baking without respite the pork pies for which the holstery was famous. Martha had discovered she had a light hand with pastry, and Hester had begun to fear she was never going to be allowed to do anything else again. In the taproom there was jollity, laughter and singing, and during her past four years at the Heathcock she had received enough cheeky chaff from brewers delivering ale and from stable lads and grooms to know how to stem good-temperedly any customers' remarks that threatened to go too close to the bone.

Tips were a welcome, if infrequent, part of this new rôle. Sometimes only a halfpenny during a whole week, but there were the more generous among the better-off who now and again gave her a silver sixpence. It was the first time she had ever had money of her own in her pocket. Jack, who had thought of everything else concerning her well-being, had never considered how much a few pence now and again would have meant to her. Instead she had had to rely on Martha's doling out for necessities with never a farthing over, which was hard when the shops amd stalls were full of pretty things.

Her first shilling tip in the taproom came from a sergeant in the Grenadiers. She looked at it shining in her palm. "It's a freshly minted one," she exclaimed in awe, for it was embossed with the head of the new king, George II, which she had not seen before.

The sergeant closed her fingers over the coin, not wanting too much attention brought to his generosity. By rights such shillings in his possession were currency to cement the recruitment, often by wily means, of young men into His Majesty's army, and for once he had a few in hand. "Buy yersel' some fripperies," he advised splendidly, munificent in his drunkenness, "an' bring me another tankard of that black ale as quick as you did before."

The next time she was out on an errand she bought herself a drawing tablet, some paints and other requirements to replace the worn-out sketching materials she had brought from home so long ago. She could not remember when she had last done any sketching, except with a fingertip before dusting furniture or in steam on a window pane, and she wondered if her skill had deserted her. But it came back as if no more than a day had elapsed. Her first subject was a flight of geese winging across the London sky, observed from her bedchamber window.

In spite of having drawing materials to hand once more, often weeks and even months went by before she could use them again. Life at the tavern continued in its hectic routine, enlivened at times by brawls, organised pugilistic bouts in the main yard, and once a duel with rapiers when two drunken gentlemen fell out, fortunately both too unsteady on their feet for either to do the other any harm.

Another natal day came and went for her. With Martha's watchful eye, there was little chance of forming romantic liaisons, and in any case she had not met anybody who was of interest to her. Her only regret was that time to herself was so limited, but she had learned to snatch whatever was available and to take advantage of any lull, however short, usually with her drawing tablet on her knees. When she was out and about in the city there was so much that caught her eye and was tucked away in her memory to be set down at the first opportunity.

Her artistic ability had always been a private matter to her, something not to share with others, although naturally her mother had known of it. Maybe the old disgrace of failing to read had stunted any wish to sketch her fellow human beings, or to let them into her own special sphere. Whatever the reasons, she made sure that her drawing materials were kept out of sight in her room and only ever brought downstairs when she could be sure of being unobserved.

There was a corner of the kitchen yard where she could conceal herself and have plenty of warning should anyone approach. It was on some steps that led from a little-used rear door away from the kitchen entrance. If she locked it behind her, nobody could come upon her unawares, and the balustrade wall of the steps hid her from view. She welcomed the rare moments of solitude in the open air that this retreat afforded and was blissfully happy as she sketched from memory the swans on the river or a ship in sail, or anything else that had a lovely line.

She was sketching the tavern cat, its face squashed in sleep, on a hot August afternoon when someone entered the yard by the kitchen gate, the only spot from which she could be easily seen. If it had not been left ajar, the screech of the hinges would have warned her of an approach. Instead she continued drawing, her bodice strings loosened against the heat of the day, her skirts up to the knees of her bare legs in a tumble of petticoat frills, and her head, free of the white cotton cap that was everyday wear, bent over the work in hand. The cat's tabby fur was downy in the sun, light as spun gold and as difficult to capture in pencilled lines. She was totally absorbed.

What made her look up she never knew. Maybe the strange alchemy that can exist between a man and a woman set a spark flying in the quiet, sun-baked yard. A tall young man stood there, slender and wide-shouldered, his shadow foreshortened by the high sun that blazed into his fair hair, which he wore caught at the nape of his neck with a black ribbon tie. He was staring at her as though magnetised and for a few seconds she was held in the same spell, registering the planes and hollows of his keen, energetic face, the thin aristocratic nose, the well-shaped mouth and the handsome chin. His clothes were shabby and ill-cut, those that any poorly paid worker might wear, and his buckled shoes were worn. One part of her mind judged him to be about nineteen to her eighteen years, while her gaze continued to be held by alert eyes that were as river-blue as the Thames on a summer's morning and with equal depths to drown in.

The drawing had been slipping from her lap unnoticed. Its sudden flutter as it skimmed down the steps to rest face downwards on the cobbles brought her back to her senses. She sprang up, remembering her disarray, and clutched her bodice together, her skirts swinging into place about her ankles. The fixed look in his eyes broke and suddenly he appeared to be as startled by the whole encounter as she. Her voice burst from her on a higher note than was normal.

"Why are you here? What do you want? Most people go to the coach-yard entrance."

"I came by way of the alley, taking a short cut." He spoke in what she recognised as educated tones. "My master sent me to pick up a watch-chain from Master Needham, which is in need of repair. I am expected. Should I find the other entrance?"

"No," she insisted hastily, not wanting anyone else to take up his errand for him. "Wait here. I'll let Jack know you've called." Turning, she hurried up the steps and unlocked the door to let herself in.

He came to the foot of the flight and called after her: "One moment!"

"Yes?" She looked down over her shoulder. The serious set of his face, which she guessed was normal to him, had relaxed into a quick, leaping smile, showing teeth that were white and even.

"I haven't asked your name or told you mine," he said, leaning an arm on the stone balustrade.

"I'm Hester Needham."

"Are you the landlord's daughter?"

"No, his half-sister. I came to live and work here six years ago. And you?"

For some reason his smile widened, illuminating an extraordinary kindliness in his features, making her feel that here was a good man in the true sense of the word, one without cruelty or baseness. "My name is John Bateman."

In the cool, flagged passageway within, she drew a deep breath to recover herself, pulling the strings of her bodice tightly together and tying a bow. John Bateman. It had a ring to it like that of a fine wineglass, and she was sure he had given his name more for her benefit than for Jack's. Her heart was pounding as if her whole world had been turned upside down. Nobody had ever had this effect upon her before, although maybe the circumstances of their meeting had something to do with it, for she was not used to being caught at a disadvantage.

As he had come for a watch-chain, it was her guess that he was an apprentice goldsmith. Apprentices of every trade were always in the Heathcock, usually in the rougher taproom frequented by travelling coachmen, servants and similar folk, and if they made a drunken nuisance of themselves they were soon thrown out by Jack. Whipping her white cap from her pocket and popping it on, Hester did not think that John would ever make a public exhibition of himself. He had a quiet air about him.

Smoothing her apron and satisfied that her appearance was orderly again, she went in search of Jack and failed to find him anywhere. "Where is he?" she asked Martha, who was doing accounts in the office, seated at the high desk.

"Out," Martha replied abruptly, her pen still scratching across the open page of the ledger in front of her. She never wasted words in conversation with Hester.

"A messenger has come for his broken watch-chain."

"I've no idea where it is, although I heard the arrangement being made." Martha dipped her pen into the ink again. "In any case I'm too busy to look for it now. Inform the fellow you'll deliver it to

Master Harwood's workshop tomorrow." She failed to see the flash of delight that passed across Hester's face.

"I'll tell him."

Going downstairs, Hester almost danced down the flight. She had been handed the chance to see John Bateman again, to further the unusual encounter, and she would make sure that she delivered the watch-chain to him personally. As for Master Harwood, whom she had waited on many times, she had always thought he would be a hard master to serve.

Emerging into the sunshine again, she halted abruptly with a sense of deep shock. John Bateman was holding her drawing of the cat and studying it intently. "That belongs to me!" She made an involuntary rush down the steps as if she would have snatched it from him.

He looked up from the drawing, his expression intrigued, his eyes narrowed. "You're extremely talented. This is a fine drawing. I assume you're self-taught."

She was trembling in the aftermath of shock, but there washed over her an intense joy that he liked what she had done. It was like a benediction, his approval a balm, sweeping away the rejection and scorn she had always expected others to pour upon her efforts. Her mother had always praised them, but that had been different altogether, part of the security of home, an extension of herself.

"Yes, I am." She felt unusually vulnerable. "I have always liked to sketch, but I have little time these days."

"That's a pity." He handed the drawing back to her. "Do you have the watch-chain?"

"No. Jack is out and his wife doesn't know where it is. I'm to deliver it to you tomorrow at Master Harwood's workshop." She noted that he smiled again, as if inwardly he was as pleased as she that they were to have another meeting.

"Do you know where the workshop is?" he inquired. "No? It's easy to find." He gave her clear and precise directions. It was in Cripplegate, not far from St. Giles's Church. Many goldsmiths had workshops there, it being common practice for those of one craft to set up in close proximity.

"Are you going to do the repair?" she questioned.

"I expect so."

"Then I'll ask for you."

He nodded, those river-blue eyes dwelling on her. "Please do that, Miss Needham. Now I'll bid good day to you. I have to get back to work."

"Good day, Mr. Bateman."

She watched him stride across the cobbles to reach the gate. There he paused to look back at her with a wave. The hinges screeched as the gate swung closed after him. She stood lost in her own happy thoughts until Martha, shouting from an upper window, caused her to go scuttling back indoors.

Her one fear that evening was that Master Harwood would come into the tavern and then Jack would hand over the watch-chain to him directly, curtailing all chance of her expedition the following day. Fortunately Master Harwood did not appear, and during the clearing up in the taproom at the evening's end, Hester seized an opening to tell Jack about John Bateman's call.

"I know the lad," Jack said, turning chairs upside down on the tables ready for the sweeping out of the old spittle-soiled sawdust and the spreading of the new. "John Bateman is Harwood's senior apprentice. He comes of good Staffordshire stock but has no money. It's the familiar story of gentlefolk impoverished by the gambling of previous generations. Both his parents died young, and he was reared by his grandfather, who paid for his education at Westminster School and settled him in his present apprenticeship, which was the limit of what the old fellow could do, being almost in penury himself."

She was surprised to have learned so much in a short time, even though Jack was typical of most landlords in being affable and talkative with a fount of information gathered about people and events far beyond the range of their own taproom bars. "Did Master Harwood tell you all this?" It struck her as odd that a master craftsman, even in his cups, should discuss a humble apprentice during a social hour.

"He did. About six or seven months ago when his daughter became betrothed to young Bateman."

"Betrothed!" She was wiping beer rings from the oaken surface of the bar and swung round to look towards him, her face dismayed. Not only had she waited on Caroline Harwood during supper parties and knew her to be good-looking in a cool, elegant way, but by repute Master Harwood's daughter was educated and well read, having been tutored from the age of seven until her seventeenth natal day as if she were a boy. Moreover, it was said that she played two or three musical instruments with remarkable talent. Wildly in her racing thoughts, Hester remembered pitying Caroline for not having been given the chance to serve a goldsmith apprenticeship and for being subjected to book-learning instead. Now it was she herself who was in need of pity, having no cultural attributes to compete with this paragon for John Bateman's attentions.

Jack did not notice her state of distraction, being occupied with his task. "The betrothal is not official yet. It can't be until the lad has served out what time remains of his indentures and gains the Freedom of the Goldsmiths' Company. In the meantime the young couple have an understanding. You'd better take the watch-chain to the Harwood workshop tomorrow morning before we get busy."

She plucked absently at the washcloth she held, her words coming bitterly. "I wonder that Master Harwood should consider a man without means suitable as a husband for his daughter."

Sensitivity was not a quality in Jack's blunt nature, and he continued to be oblivious to her tension as he clattered another chair. "Ah, it's skill that is young Bateman's fortune. The lad is a born goldsmith and will be the mainstay of the Harwood workshop in time to come. What better for a master craftsman without sons than that he should train a future son-in-law into his own ways. It's a unique chance to ensure that the business remains sound, even when he himself is gone."

Finally he realised how long Hester had been standing at the bar and looked across with a frown. "Ain't you finished that cleaning yet?"

Hester, galvanised into action, rubbed away at the bar in a furious burst of energy as a silent outlet for her pent-up feelings. Later, as she prepared for bed, her optimism returned and she shook off the dismay that Jack's information had caused her. What did her lack of education really matter? She could always keep her secret that she knew nothing of books or writing by talking of other things to hold John's interest. Neither was it important that she could not play the lute or a harpsichord, for she had a sweet singing voice and was never out of tune. As for John's prospects of a future governed by a father-in-law, she did not think that any man of initiative would take kindly to that. Surely John with his skills would be more than ready to make his own way and harvest his own successes once the Freedom was his, which is what she would have done in his place.

Finally, and most important of all, she refused to believe he had ever looked at Caroline Harwood as he had looked at her that day, staring as if she were Venus rising from the sea. Few women could have seen a man so transfixed.

Chapter 2

Ever since he had come to the workshop that morning John had been watching for Hester. Common sense told him she would not appear at too early an hour, but then common sense seemed to have abandoned him since that moment yesterday when he had stepped into the yard of the Heathcock Inn and seen her sketching on the steps, a total innocent in her disarray, her long hair holding all the hues of a late sunset against the warm red bricks behind her.

It was an image impossible to put out of his mind—the lowered scoop of neckline revealing the shadowed cleavage and the length of beautiful leg amid white frills with ankles he could have encircled with finger and thumb. Then, when she had looked up, the impact of startled eyes, caught breath and parted lips had touched some chord in him that seemed to arouse an instant rapport in her. Their conversation had paled before that other language of mind and body. He was as impatient as a madman to see her again.

His shirt, which had been clean that morning, was soiled already due to the grimy conditions of a goldsmith's workshop, where smelting, alloying and manufacture took place. The floor was swept meticulously every night, and the dust and dirt sieved afterwards to catch any *lemel,* the old French word given to the grains of precious metal that flew from the impact of a tool or escaped the leather aprons of the craftsmen, which were permanently attached to the workbenches and tied with tapes behind their waists. The dirt was then bagged and sold at the door to those who still thought it worthwhile to purchase the sweepings from a goldsmith's floor.

Wherever possible the workbenches with their semi-circular cut-outs, which gave a convenient edge to work against, were placed under windows to catch the maximum amount of light; hanging candle-lamps gave extra illumination when needed. John's work-

place was at an end cut-out in a bench occupying a favourable position, and his own tools were conveniently at hand, many of them on
wall-racks. Communal apparatus, such as extra stakes and heads—
the names given to cast-iron shapes over which the precious metals
were beaten into the required forms—crucibles for melting, hammers and vises and many other tools, were racked or shelved and
formed a strangely proud mural that ran the length of the long
workshop on either side.

On the floor as well as on the benches were large elm tree stumps
into which the stakes and heads were set for stability while a piece
was worked on; they also had another use, the old wood having
become worn through time, often over two or three or more generations of goldsmiths, into marvellously smooth indentations suitable
for beating workpieces into shape. A good stump was as much an
heirloom to be passed on to a goldsmith's son as a set of tools. At
the darkest end of the workshop were the charcoal hearths, their
strategic position making it easier to see when an article was approaching red heat in soldering or annealing.

The working area occupied the whole of the ground floor, with
the Harwood living quarters above. In all, Master Harwood employed thirty journeymen and three apprentices, in addition to half
a dozen women engaged in filing, polishing and similar routine
tasks. It was to be expected that apprenticeship in such a thriving
workshop would be eagerly sought after, and John had been aware
of his good fortune from the first day.

He was engaged that morning on an interesting workpiece he
had begun three days ago. It was a magnificent tankard formed of
thin sheets of silver soldered together while the mouldings of the
spreading foot were most finely beaten. With a scroll handle and a
domed cover, operated by a corkscrew thumbpiece, it would never
hold ale for a poor man's lips. Although usually two and a half days
were allotted for the making of a tankard, this was an elaborate one
that had involved many extra hours.

As John worked, he tried to rationalise his intense desire to see
Hester again and bring it to a sensible level. He blamed it on the
monastic rule that governed all apprenticeships, together with a ban
on swearing, drunkenness, gambling and even marriage. Being
young, strong, healthy and virile, was it any wonder that such a

lovely sight as Hester should have stirred him as it did? That was all there was to it.

If only there could have been a full relationship between himself and Caroline he would have been less susceptible to another girl's appeal, for he was not by nature easy in his loyalties or commitments. As it was, he could number the kisses and embraces from Caroline on the fingers of one hand. She was no less eager than he, but since she had made it known to her father that they were in love, new restrictions on her movements had curtailed all chance meetings on the premises, which had been such a pleasure to them both. Instead, he was now invited to the upper regions of the Harwood establishment, previously a barred area, for dinner at the fashionable hour of two o'clock twice a month, on alternate Sundays, at which her parents always presided. Before the first invitation had been issued, Master Harwood had called him into the office.

"I understand from Caroline that you and she have developed a sincere affection for each other."

"That is so, sir."

"Well, no more can be said on the matter until you have been admitted into the Goldsmiths' Company at the end of your apprenticeship. Then you may make known to me your honourable intentions towards my daughter. Is that understood?"

"Yes, sir. I look forward to that day."

That had been the end of the interview. It had told him clearly that he was approved; no barriers would stand in his way.

After rising from the Sunday dinner table, he and Caroline would talk together in a corner of the room, able to forget to a degree that they were being observed, for they had much in common, her interests being as wide as his. If they became too absorbed, her mother would interrupt by asking Caroline to play the harpsichord, particularly if there was other company present. In fine weather there was occasionally a sedate walk, he and Caroline proceeding in front of her parents, which meant there could be no lingering behind their backs. He thought sometimes it would have been more agreeable for Caroline and him if she had kept their love a secret for a while longer, but she had always been close to her parents and could not hold back the joy of telling them.

When the Sunday afternoons were over, he always returned to the dank basement room below the workshop that he shared with the two other apprentices, Tom Nicholson and Robin Pomfret. It was here they slept on straw-filled wall-beds and ate the meagre victuals doled out to them three times a day from the household kitchen. He did not resent the conditions, because it was the lot common to most apprentices, and he and his companions were better off than those who actually had to sleep under their workbenches. Since they received little pay, cash was always a problem. Luckily there was plenty to do and see in London that was without charge. Unlike either Tom or Robin, who were a noisy, boisterous pair, he read a great deal. Whenever the small allowance came from his grandfather, he would put a few pence aside from that needed for shoe repairs and other necessities, and then comb the market stalls for any volumes of interest that could be picked up cheaply, plus some candles to read them by.

In the activity of the workshop, he did not hear Robin's approach or know he was there until he was tapped on the shoulder. "There's a young woman to see you, John. Says she has a watch-chain that can't be handed over to anyone else."

He nodded, straightening from his work, and untied his leather apron to hook it forward against the workbench with slow deliberation to subdue the sudden churn of excitement in him. It would not be as yesterday. That had been a moment out of time. Today everything would be commonplace. He must prepare himself for that.

In the entrance hall Hester waited. At the far end, by an office door, a massive staircase led to the rooms of the Harwood residence above. She was impressed by the size of the establishment and its obvious prosperity. Brasswork had shone on the porticoed door and here inside there was a waxed sheen to the dark floorboards. From this place went an outflowing of handsome gold and silver items, all bearing the Harwood hallmark.

A gilt-framed looking-glass with candle-sconces that would reflect the light at evening-time was hanging on the wall near the staircase. By taking a few steps to the right, she was able to check her appearance in it. She was wearing a lace-trimmed cap with floating ribbons of primrose yellow; her hair was dressed back smoothly in its customary style of glossy, well-brushed swathes high across the back of

her head. Her dress was grey-striped calico and her apron, part of
the fashion scene even among high-born ladies who had them made
of silk and lace, had a pleated edge. She was looking her best and
she waited neatly, the watch-chain wrapped in a piece of white
linen in her hand.

A door opened and John came into the hall. A flat, guarded look
across his face dissolved immediately at the sight of her. Any doubts
she might have harboured about how it would be when they met
again were completely banished. There was nothing to worry
about. It was as she had believed in her heart it would be. He came
hurrying towards her.

"Miss Needham! You found this address without too much difficulty, I hope."

"Yes, it was easy." She glanced about admiringly. "And what a
grand place it is. You are fortunate to be working here."

"I am. Unlike some establishments, this one is large enough to
give me an extensive training in every branch of goldsmithing."

Her glance flicked over his grimy attire. "What work do you like
doing best?"

"Anything in silver. It particularly appeals to me, and the results
can be as beautiful as anything in gold."

His preference for silver seemed to send an echo ringing through
her veins. "What do you make?" she questioned keenly.

"Salvers, punch-bowls, coffeepots and tankards." He spread his
hands to indicate the wide range. "Spoons and forks and all the rest
of it. Orders come in all the time and there's always work ahead of
us here. I wish I could show you round the workshops, but that's
not permitted."

She shook her head to show she was not disappointed. "It
wouldn't be safe to let strangers in among all those precious metals.
Jack is equally vigilant over the keys to the wine cellar. That re-
minds me. He wants to know how long it will be before he gets his
watch-chain back again." Carefully she unfolded the linen and held
it out, the watch-chain gleaming in its folds.

He took it and examined it. "This won't take long, although at
the present time I have some other work on hand. A link has been
lost, that's all." Then, against all wisdom, he heard himself say, "I'll
return it personally. Just as soon as I can."

Her heart pounded and her breath seemed to leave her. "I'll tell him that." Then she added merrily, "Don't expect to find me sketching again. That only happens rarely. I'm usually waiting at tables in the main taproom."

"I wouldn't leave again without finding you there."

Although her instincts had told her that, it was still satisfying to hear him say it. She moved towards the door and he sprang in front of her to open it. No man had ever opened a door for her before, except by chance. She hesitated for a moment in the patch of sunlight, savouring the experience, her smile radiant. "Farewell until our next meeting, Mr. Bateman."

On her way home she no longer had the least doubt that she had fallen in love. What else was this extraordinary happiness that made her want to dance instead of walk, sing instead of talk? The confines of the tavern and the city streets beyond had never seemed more restraining. She would have liked to be back in the countryside, to throw her arms wide and run down a hillslope, which was the nearest any human being could come to the lovely flight of birds.

She did not expect to see him for several days. The repair would not be done until he had time, and even then Master Harwood might set a priority on some other work.

A few days later, as she was beginning to expect his arrival, she was taken suddenly aback to see Jack's fob-watch dangling on its chain from the broad expanse of his crimson waistcoat. "When did you get that back?" she demanded in bewilderment.

"Yesterday evening. Harwood brought it when he came in for a tankard of ale."

She guessed it must have been when she was on duty serving in the private parlours, for the sight of Master Harwood would have alerted her. Telling herself it was only a temporary disappointment and that John would soon come anyway, she picked up four brimming tankards, two handles in each hand, and continued serving the thirsty customers.

Two weeks went by before John came to the Heathcock. He was wearing his one good coat of stout brown cloth, kept for his leisure hours, full-skirted with flapped pockets, his waistcoat a lighter shade, his knee-breeches black and his hose white.

When the chore of delivery of the watch-chain had been taken from him, he had decided it was all for the best, because it had saved him, at the last minute, from running uncharacteristically into folly. Nothing could come of furthering an acquaintance with Hester, and the wild attraction he had felt for her had left unchanged his feelings for Caroline. Their last Sunday meeting had been an especially happy one, with a few unsupervised minutes in which he had been able to kiss her, startling her with the pent-up violence of his mouth, but instantly she had melted against him, eyes closed and trembling ecstatically. Why then, when all was going well for him, and against plain logic and reasoning, had he allowed himself to be inexorably drawn back, in his best clothes, to the place where Hester was to be found? He refused to consider what the answer might be as he strolled into the main taproom.

She did not see him at first. The place was crowded and pipe smoke was hanging in the air thick as a winter fog off the river. Taking a seat at one of the oaken tables along the wall, he waited until she should come near, feasting his gaze on her as she darted to and fro serving customers, every one of whom seemed to have a vast thirst to be quenched.

He could only afford a small beer himself, but it would give him a chance to talk to her and arrange to see her later when her duties were done. She was wearing the customary cotton cap, as were the other waiting maids, a few escaping tendrils of her red-gold hair dancing down the back of her white neck, and her smile was quick as she took orders. Now and again some quip would make her throw back her head in laughter, and to his dazzled eyes all the enjoyment of life seemed concentrated in her. How had he managed to stay away so long?

When finally she saw him her eyebrows arched and her colour came and went in pleased surprise. Then instead of crossing over to him, as he had anticipated, she whirled about and returned to the bar. Moments later she set a tankard of frothing ale down in front of him and one of the Heathcock pies, hot from the oven.

"It's on the house," she said quickly. "Eat up. You look half-starved."

He grinned as she darted away again, apron ties flying. Taking up the pie with both hands, he bit into it, the rich juices running into his mouth, the meat tender, the pastry crumbling in its golden-brown lightness. It tasted better to him than all the Harwood Sunday dinners he had eaten. When it was finished, he took up the last crumbs from the pewter plate with the tips of his fingers just as she swirled onto the bench beside him.

"I can only stay a minute. This is our busiest night of the week."

"I'd like to wait until you've finished your duties."

She looked doubtful. "That will be late. I thought apprentices had to be in by what is deemed to be a Christian hour, even on a Saturday night."

"So they do, but there is a grid that my fellow apprentices will pull aside for me to get back in unobserved."

Her eyes danced with amusement. "You are the last person I would have expected to break rules."

He frowned at her perception, not altogether pleased by it. "What makes you say that?"

She put her head to one side, studying him. "I don't know. It's just an impression I have." In her own mind she supposed it to be a basic seriousness she sensed in him, for whenever he was not smiling that kindly, fleeting smile that illumined his whole face, there was a deep-thinking, composed look to his features that she had absorbed at their first meeting. She spoke quickly to reassure him. "I'm not deriding you for it. It gives more value to your coming here to see me this evening than a visit from anyone else in similar circumstances."

His eyes dwelt on her. "I'm pleased to hear you say that."

Briefly she touched his hand where it rested on the table. "I'll give you a sign when I can get away. Then go round to the kitchen yard and wait for me there. We can have a little while together."

She left him again to return to her duties. As he made the ale last, savouring the full-bodied flavour, he thought over what she had said. His quiet temperament was disturbed by disruptions and still more so by lawlessness and violence. He had no stomach for bear-baiting, cock-fights or similar pastimes when animals were set upon each other for the pleasure of spectators. He always avoided the huge crowds that gathered for a hanging at Newgate prison, once having been enough for him when he had been trapped by pressure in the street and unable to get past until the event was over. Yet none could call him weak-kneed, for like most people slow to anger, he had a fierce temper when it was aroused, and if he made a stand on a principle, nothing could shake him from it.

There was no doubt that his preference for a peaceful existence came from his beginnings. He could scarcely remember his parents, and his childhood had been spent in country pursuits with his grandfather, fishing and rambling and riding, the two of them always together. Books had been another part of that secluded existence, a rich world within that dilapidated old house, servantless and dusty, where they had eaten their meals at a long kitchen table, watched by waiting dogs and with hens pecking about at their feet. No boy ever had a happier existence, but being reared by an old man had made him staid for his years and old before his time.

When, following in his father's footsteps, he had gone to Westminster School, life had been a nightmare until he had floored a few bullies with his fists and asserted himself. As for his apprenticeship, he saw it in the terms of the last gold coins taken from a box to pay for his seven years' indenture, bringing poverty right over the threshold into that Staffordshire house where one old man now lived alone, with the last of the dogs and horses gone from the stables. To have done less than his best in his training would have been to betray everything from his past, which was also why his apprenticeship had been singularly free of the reckless escapades usually indulged in by young men bound by restraining circumstances. His plan to slip back into the Harwood building by way of the grid was new to him and full of risk, a measure of how much it had meant to him to see Hester again.

She came to collect the emptied tankard as a sign that she was ready to meet him, although the taproom seemed no less busy. He went out into the night to follow the Strand to a side street that would give access to the rear of the tavern.

Not possessing a sword, he walked with fists balled in readiness as he entered the darkness of the alleyway, not knowing who might be hidden in the blackest shadows. A few rats scuttled out of his path, making him start, but he met nothing else.

Hinges screeched as he entered the Heathcock's kitchen yard. Rectangles of golden light, thrown down by the tavern windows, lay across the cobbles. He passed swiftly through them and sat down on the steps where he had first seen Hester at her sketching. Almost at once she came from the door leading to the flight and dropped down onto the step beside him, smiling into his face.

"I thought it wasn't fair to keep you too late. One of the other girls is covering for me until I get back. If you like I'll see you tomorrow instead. I'm almost always free on a Sunday afternoon."

"Much as I should like it, I'm afraid that's not possible." He was uncomfortably aware of the Harwood Sunday dinner looming on the morrow. "Would next Sunday do instead?"

She had looked down at her hands in her lap at the first shake of his head at her suggestion, as if to hide any disappointment in her eyes. Now she raised them again, her expression eager. "We could walk by the river; I always like that."

They arranged where they should meet. She thought they would have about three hours together. "You work hard at the Heathcock, don't you?" he said, thinking that her days were even more taxing than his. At least he had no work on Sundays.

"I suppose I do. I'm so used to it that I think nothing of it." She told him a little about her daily routine and then how and why she first came to live at the Heathcock. When he heard that she had had a country childhood similar in some ways to his own, they were on common ground. It was something stable between them to anchor still further the intense physical attraction that each felt for the other.

When it was time for her to go, he rose to his feet with her and they stood facing each other on the step. The night all around them was warm and full of stars. He had wanted to kiss her the first moment he saw her. Not at all sure what her reaction would be, he reached out to draw her nearer. To his surprise, her cool palms immediately cupped his face and she raised herself on tiptoe to press her lips softly against his. It was over in a matter of seconds, the brush of her breasts against his chest, the feather touch of her fingers and the whip of her skirt against his legs as she turned to run up the steps and into the tavern out of sight. He smiled to himself, slapping his hand deliberately against the stone balustrade as he descended the flight. There was a spring in his tread as he went out of the gate to make his way home.

As Martha made ready for bed, brushing her hair vigorously with a tortoiseshell brush, she looked across at Jack, who was already tucking down in the pillows of their four-poster. "Who was that young fellow that Hester sat at a table with this evening for a while? She knows it's not permitted to sit with customers."

Jack, tired as he was at the week's end with its frantically busy Saturday night as a climax, thought to himself that Martha missed nothing with her sharp eyes as she moved constantly from taproom to dining room and into the private parlours and the kitchen to ensure that everything was running smoothly and well.

"Perhaps she has a sweetheart. It's about time she settled on one. There's been enough lads after her."

"Then it's your duty to find out about him. He looked neat and clean in his appearance, but not grand enough to court your sister."

The rasp of sarcasm in her voice, directed against his fraternal fondness for Hester, grated on him. He had given up long ago wondering why he had ever married Martha, resigned to her being the way she was. Now and again he reminded himself doggedly of her good qualities, especially when her nagging began to reach a danger point with him. He had struck her more times than he cared to remember in earlier days, blacking her eyes and once knocking a tooth out, for which she had never forgiven him. Eventually she had learned just how far she could go with him, and she used that knowledge with a skill that was deadly in its own way.

He grunted wearily. "Hester will tell me when she's ready to seek my approval of her swain. Come to bed. I ain't able to sleep with candles burning."

In the morning he had forgotten the incident. Martha had not and she observed Hester closely, able to recognise the state of being in love, even though she herself had passed through it and left it behind years ago.

Dinner at the Harwoods was as usual. John arrived on the stroke of two o'clock and was greeted by Caroline in the presence of her parents. She was quite small in stature and had to tilt her dark curly head slightly to look up at him. Her serene, porcelain looks, almost fragile in their delicacy, gave no hint of her will and strength of character. Totally self-assured, with tranquil depths in her soft brown eyes, she smiled warmly, pale pink lips parting, and moved towards him, elegantly attired today in maize sprigged lawn over rustling petticoats.

"I trust I find you well, John."

As he made the conventional reply, he found himself extraordinarily relieved to see her. Her calm presence seemed to wash over him. Everything was always orderly and settled when she was near, which was how he liked things to be. He was certain Hester's call to his senses would fade after he had seen her a few times to get her out of his system. Nothing could compare with Caroline's intelligent companionship, her unique understanding of his pride in his work.

"I hear from Father that you are to do much of the work on the Presentation gold piece for the retiring Worshipful Master of the Goldsmiths' Company," she said in congratulatory tones. "I haven't seen the design yet. What is it to be?"

He had anticipated her enquiry and from the inside pocket of his coat he took out a copy of the design, spreading it on a nearby table for her inspection. Together they bent their heads over it. "As you can see," he said, "it is a shaped circular salver supported by four ball-and-claw feet." His hand followed the border. "This will be chased with the flower, London Pride."

"Most appropriate. Was that your idea?"

"It was my suggestion," he admitted, pleased by her perception. Her enthusiasm for his work was always a great encouragement.

She leaned both arms on the table to peer closer. "What is the figure to be engraved in the centre?"

"St. Dunstan."

"Ah! The patron saint of goldsmiths. What could be better?"

"A final touch will be the arms of the Company with their motto: *Justitia virtutum Regina.*"

She was full of admiration. "It will be a magnificent piece."

"I shall do my best."

"You always do," she whispered proudly, drawing back to let others in the room have space to look at the design, too.

It was due to there being an extra number of dinner guests that he did not get a chance to talk to Caroline on her own again. If the rest of the time dragged as a result, it was not the case for the remainder of the week, for the following morning he began work on the salver and was absorbed from the moment he took the required disc of gold into his hands. It was from such flat sheets of metal, sometimes called blanks, that every conceivable shape could be raised by skilful beating with a hammer. He began by cutting the disc to the right size and filed the edges smooth to prevent cracks developing from any nicks or scratches. He marked out the centre to preserve the area that needed to remain flat, and then, taking a dome-headed hammer, he rested the disc over a shallow depression in his wood block and began to strike the edge. He grinned to himself. He and the salver were now on their way. Gradually, as he turned the disc slowly, the first saucer curve, which would eventually become the rim of the salver, began to rise under his skilful beating.

By the time Sunday came the work was well advanced and he was satisfied with the progress made. Before he could reach the gate of the Heathcock's kitchen yard Hester came through it, having been watching for him. She had decided that nobody should know about this meeting, or any other, until he and Caroline had dissolved the understanding existing between them; otherwise Jack was bound to be difficult if he discovered she was seeing someone supposedly in line as a future son-in-law to one of his most esteemed patrons.

"Here I am!" she announced, poised with her arms spread wide at her sides.

He gazed at her joyous face framed by the mass of tawny hair and everything else was obliterated. There was no Caroline, or workshop, or presentation salver, or even the dire consequences that awaited broken indentures. Hurrying forward, he caught her by the hand.

"And there was never a prettier sight, Hester! Believe me."

She did believe him—and he had called her Hester. What a start to their time together! "There's not a minute to be lost, John," she urged enthusiastically. "Let's make our way to the river. All London will be afloat on the Thames today."

They went there hand in hand, talking all the time, each wanting to know more and more about the other. Now and again they broke spontaneously into a run, as if their pleasure in each other's company could not be contained without an outlet of energy, and once making an archway of their arms and linked fingers for an old woman hobbling along with a basket, her eyes on the ground. Their pace slowed to a leisurely stroll when they came within sight of the Thames, the city's highway and lifeline, along which sailed a continual host of tall-masted ships coming and going to all corners of the globe. They turned their steps to follow the river eastward to London Bridge, which, with its collection of ill-shaped buildings, stood high on the skyline not far from the Tower and spanned the gleaming water across to Southwark. Since it was the city's only bridge, thousands of little ferry-boats plied their trade to and fro, making an ever-moving pattern in each direction as far as the eye could see.

Hester perched on a wall to watch for a while, John leaning his arms on it beside her. What she most liked to see were the gilded and marvellously decorated barges of the rich livery companies that dated their origins back to the craft guilds of medieval times. They gave an almost Venetian touch to the scene, oars rhythmic and flashing colour, the oarsmen themselves in handsome crimson, yellow, purple or blue jackets according to which individual coat of arms was located high for all to see. One of the most spectacular was that of the Goldsmiths' Company, although that was not to be seen today. Instead a barge of the Apothecaries' Company, painted ruby and gold, was making its way leisurely upstream.

"Have you ever wished to go far afield to foreign places?" she asked John dreamily.

"As a boy, I thought once of going to sea." He shifted his position onto one elbow, looking up at her. "I'd read so much about the strange mammals of the deep and the mysteries of ancient lands that I wanted to see everything for myself."

"What made you change your mind?"

"My grandfather gave me a book on the treasures of the Incas, and that sparked off an aim in me to work with precious metals."

She wanted no more talk of books and reading. It was a dangerous subject as far as she was concerned. "Have you made plans towards the day when you'll be admitted into the Goldsmiths' Company?"

If he'd been asked that question before today, he would have answered at once that he expected to remain with Master Harwood, where the opportunities for fine work were manifold and he could do no better elsewhere. Moreover it would please Caroline that he should continue to work for her father. But now everything that was orderly and well arranged in his life was under the threat of disruption by the magnetism of this lovely girl looking questioningly down at him, the breeze from the river playing tricks with her hair and flapping the frill of her neckline against her white throat. Desire for her surged up within him with such force that he answered her abruptly, turning his gaze back to the river, angry with his own madness.

"Time enough for decisions when I've been granted the Freedom. Master craftsmen are always in demand whatever their trade."

She sensed that her question had unsettled him, and she wanted nothing to infringe upon the happiness of the day. Slipping down from the wall, she scooped her arm through his, her face bright with optimism. "One thing I do know, and that is that one day you'll be the most famous goldsmith in the whole of London."

"Only London?" he teased mildly, his fleeting smile returning to enliven his features.

"Of course not. They'll speak of you all the way from China to the American colonies."

"How can you be so sure?" He was enjoying the experience of sustaining the little joke. "You've never yet seen anything I've made."

"I don't have to." She could tell she had dispersed whatever it was that had suddenly threatened the day. It gave her an insight into the power she might possess to lead this serious young man into lighter frames of mind whenver he was troubled. "I think that here, on the banks of the Thames, I've suddenly developed second sight!"

She enjoyed seeing him laugh and laughed with him. Her arm remained tucked into his as they continued their stroll, aware only of each other.

After that day they met regularly, not only every two weeks on a Sunday but occasionally on weekdays when some of her free time in the evenings gave them the chance to talk for a little while in the kitchen yard. Without actually bringing Caroline's name into the conversation, he had told her about the Harwood Sunday dinners. She, in turn, had said enough for him to understand she must have heard something of his involvement with his master's daughter. For the time being, by unspoken consent, they left the matter there.

On his part, to avoid any chance of running into Master Harwood in the main taproom, he took ale sometimes in the rougher end of the tavern. Although Hester did not wait there, she always managed to spend some time sitting at a table with him when her brother and his wife were safely elsewhere, which gave them the chance to hold hands. She had to face some good-natured chaff from the rest of the staff about her swain, but she shrugged it off, knowing it would not be voiced in either Martha's or Jack's hearing, for in spite of being related to them, she was very much a lowly member of the staff and therefore belonged to the confederacy of the kitchen regions.

John often looked back to that first afternoon with Hester at the river as the start of a new pattern of living that tore daily at his conscience. The Harwood Sunday dinners became unbearable to him. He was frequently abstracted and lost to the conversation until jerked back into it by a direct question. Now and again he took stock of the situation as if miraculously a solution might suddenly present itself. On the one hand there was Caroline, still lodged in his affections, still secure in an understanding that they were to share a future together. Nothing had been stated categorically in their love-talk—even her father had forbidden mention of it until a later date—but for someone of his outlook an unvoiced promise was as binding as any other. He was in it up to his neck!

On the other hand there was Hester, drawing him to her by day and filling his dreams at night with images of her as Caroline had never done. The bachelor's adage of a good girl to woo and a bad one to tumble did not even apply in this case, for Hester, honest and generous and warm-hearted, held herself in respect and commanded it in others. The thought of abusing her never occurred to him. On the contrary, she awakened in him such tender feelings, combined with the longing to possess and cherish her, that eventually he came to the stark realisation that he was in love with her as he had never been, or ever would be, with Caroline.

It became more difficult with every meeting to hold back what he wanted to say to Hester. He could tell she knew his feelings and was waiting each time for him to speak, particularly after they had kissed when she was pliant and yielding and breathing softly within the circle of his arms. Again and again he had to choke back the words, realising that he could easily plunge them both into depths from which it would be impossible to draw back.

Yet eventually the moment came. They were taking a Saturday afternoon stroll along the Mall. As with everywhere else in the land, the high and the low had equal rights to all public places, and it was here that the latest fashions of both men and women were to be seen, which made the Mall one of Hester's favourite walks. Although the cooler weather meant that capes and cloaks now shielded or partly hid the grander garments underneath, there was an abundance of rich velvets, feathers and fur trimming.

Suddenly, when heavy drops of rain began to fall from a darkening sky, people hastened in a swirl of colour towards waiting carriages or scampered, like Hester and John, for whatever shelter the trees could afford. By chance nobody else came to the oak they had run to and they huddled close together against the rough bark. Holding his cloak across her for added protection, he looked down into her rain-wet, wonderfully inviting face and the words burst out of his heart.

"I love you! I'll love you all my life."

She turned pale with joy. "I love you, too," she whispered. "I have ever since that first day." Her arms went tight about his neck as he caught her still closer and they kissed as never before, heedless of the drumming rain.

It was the same afternoon that Martha, listening at the kitchen door, finally overheard in a snatch of conversation the name of the man that Hester appeared to be seeing at every opportunity. She went at once to Jack.

"It won't *do*," she stated firmly. "You must put a stop to it at once or you'll be in danger of losing Harwood's custom."

"How could that be?" Jack was cynical.

"My! You can be senseless at times! He is not going to think well of your sister dallying with his daughter's betrothed. If Harwood should turn against us and the Heathcock, his acquaintances would soon follow suit. You've said yourself he's not a man you'd wish to cross swords with."

Jack accepted her reasoning while at the same time concern for Hester came uppermost in his mind. He tackled her about the matter that evening. She had known that sooner or later she would be challenged and she answered him in a forthright manner.

"Yes, I am seeing John Bateman. Is he to be denied all other company because the Harwood family have staked some claim to him? You told me yourself that nothing was officially settled."

"That's beside the point. I ain't going to allow anyone to trifle with your affections when he's under other obligations, official or not. Stay away from him, Hester. No good can come of it." He became irritated and exasperated by the whole business. "London is full of young men. You don't have to hob-nob with one already spoken for." His forefinger with a grimed nail pointed sternly at her, his scowl matching his action. "I mean what I say. You'll not see young Bateman again!"

Hester ignored his instructions completely and kept her next appointment with John as arranged. She told him of this new development as they sat side by side on a wooden bench overlooking the river. Dark clouds were streaking a sky already grey, and the wind made whirlpools of the fallen leaves from the trees around them.

"It's happened as I feared. Until you are free of all previous commitments, Jack will continue to oppose my seeing you." She knew he had attended a Harwood Sunday dinner since she had seen him last. "Have you told Caroline about me yet?"

It was the first time Caroline's name had come into the open between them. Until now she had been a shadow that they had both chosen to ignore in their deepening love for each other.

"Not yet," he replied hoarsely. At her news he had leaned forward to stare towards the river, elbows across his knees and his hands clenched, his right thumb working across his left knuckles, the skin strained over them. "It's a difficult situation."

She was disappointed that he had not taken the chance when he had it to explain matters to Caroline. Deliberately she tested her own power of attraction. "Perhaps it would be best if we didn't meet again for a while."

"No!" He turned to grip her hands in his. "I can't say how long it's going to be before things are straightened out. How could I go two or three, or even six months, without seeing you?"

"Six months!" She jerked her hand away, aghast. "Are you out of your mind?"

The tension between them was rising. He felt himself being driven into a corner and resented it. "All I'm asking is that you have a little patience."

"You expect me to stay dancing on a string like a puppet for six months?"

"Don't keep throwing the length of time at me." He was thoroughly wretched and feeling guilty enough to be ready to retaliate fiercely in his own defence. To be plagued by too much conscience was as great a handicap in his present opinion as having none. "I used it figuratively."

Her colour flared. Suddenly she had become possessed by an intense jealousy of Caroline that she could not control. Her eyes flashed. "Figuratively or not, it is days you should have listed in any case, not months!"

"Whatever you will." It was a well-intended attempt to extinguish the first dangerous sign he had recognised of his own anger, which was always dreadful to him. In his mind's eye he saw it as the first ominous rising of the curl of smoke that precedes a forest fire.

Hester was not appeased. "It is not my will that counts now, but yours. You have only to tell Caroline that she has to absolve you from whatever understanding once existed between the two of you. No woman of any spirit would want to hold, much less marry, a man no longer in love with her."

Tormented, he retorted sharply: "You don't understand. In her circle marriages are arranged in a practical manner and love is a bonus. I must wait for Caroline's own rejection of me. It's a point of honour—"

"Honour!" she exploded, leaping to her feet, her temper unleashed. "What of your honour towards me?"

He sprang up to face her, his cheekbones standing white. "I should never have spoken of love to you until I was free to do so!" Having admitted his fault, the forest fire was almost upon him. He could feel its awful crackling coming up through his veins to break into flames in his head. "It was a terrible mistake on my part!"

"So you have regrets now!" Deeply hurt, feeling torn inside by his words, she couldn't stop herself from hurting him. "Maybe I have them, too! I can see I've been mistaken about you in every way. You are still fonder of Caroline than you would ever have me believe."

His self-control snapped and his fury burst forth. "What if I am?" He waved his arms about. "She hasn't changed. She's still the same person I admired for her looks, her cultured mind and her educated attitude to life."

For Hester it was too much to be borne. He could not have said anything, however unwittingly, to strike harder at her. All her vulnerability about her own intellectual shortcomings had been delivered a dreadful and humiliating blow. Her pride could not endure it.

"Stay with Caroline then," she raged, backing away from him. "It's what you have really wanted to do all along if you had only dared admit it. It is I who have been in second place, not her. Marry Caroline! Spend the rest of your life with her. I never want to see you again!"

He roared back at her: "If that's your decision, so be it!"

In the heat of his fury he let her run from him. He did not even watch her go, turning instead to stalk away in the opposite direction. That evening he went with Tom and Robin to the Blue Boar Inn where, for the first time in his life, he drank himself into a stupor and had to be carried home.

It took an early morning dousing under the yard pump to get his head clear and ready for work. Still shaky, plagued by a thumping headache and with his face chalk-white, he took his place at the workbench. By ill chance his task that day was to raise a silver bowl by beating on the outer convex side until it was moulded over the steel head from which it was taking its lovely shape. Every tap of the hammer jarred up his arm into his aching head. It was a relief to take a break when he was told that Master Harwood wanted to see him in the office. He felt no trepidation. Both Robin and Tom had assured him that he had not been seen by anyone in the establishment in his drunken state. His guess was that he was to be given something special to do again; the presentation salver had been much admired.

In the office Stephen Harwood paced the floor as he waited, hands clasped behind his back, fingers flicking impatiently. The previous evening he had taken a theatre party of friends to supper at the Heathcock and, when he had settled the bill, Mrs. Needham had invited him aside to put a word in his ear. He had listened without expression, nodded his thanks to show that her considerate warning had aroused no personal ire in him against her or her husband, and mulled over what he had learned going home in his carriage.

"Ah, Bateman," he said when his apprentice stood before him. In his own residential quarters on Sundays he called John by his Christian name, but here in the business regions it was a different matter. He lowered himself into his chair, taking his time and settling his elbows on the polished arms as he put his fingertips together. It would do no harm to let the young fellow sweat a bit.

John's first thought was that his drunkenness was known about after all. He was not unduly alarmed. It would be his first black mark in nearly six years and he would not get booted out for that. "Sir?"

"There comes a time in most apprenticeships when a young man needs to be reminded of the rules governing his behaviour as laid down in his indentures. If they have been flagrantly broken, then penalties are not enough and he must go, his chances of mastercraftmanship lost beyond recall."

"I know that can happen."

Stephen Harwood watched him from under his black brows that were at odds with the brightish hue of his brown periwig. "You're a good craftsman. From the start you showed the makings of an exceptional talent and you've gone from strength to strength. I've never once had cause to be disappointed in you. As you know, I'm not a man to give praise lightly, which should encourage you to grasp fully the significance of all I have said." He shifted his heavy weight forward in the chair and lowered his hand onto the desk in front of him, gold rings gleaming, an emerald blinking green fire. "Since you have such skills in you, it is nothing but folly on your part to put your future in jeopardy by pursuing a tavern-maid."

It was not what John had been expecting to hear. His eyes narrowed and his face tightened. All the rawness of the parting quarrel twisted like a knife in him. As always when he lost his temper, he felt drained afterwards, his equilibrium shattered. And it was that, as much as the after-effects of drunkenness, that was weighing him down today. In his numbed state his loss of Hester had yet to make its full impact.

"That pursuit is at an end," he stated bluntly.

With a relaxed air Stephen Harwood sat back in his chair. Having misinterpreted the cause of the words he had heard, he thought simply that his warning had gone home quickly and effectively. He had been young himself once and remembered the frustration of never being alone with his closely chaperoned betrothed before he had married her. Seeking release elsewhere was natural enough, but the sin was in being found out. In this case matters had reached a peak where the tavern-maid's own relatives had pleaded for him to intervene, being aware, as he was, that girls who lost their heads could make a nuisance of themselves, something that John Bateman obviously had yet to learn.

He was grateful for Mistress Needham's timely whisper. She had understood that at all costs he would want to protect Caroline from gossipy hearsay. His own well-chosen words had brought this otherwise excellent young man to heel. It bore out his conviction that John Bateman, with his even disposition, would always be malleable enough to be guided in all things by his future father-in-law, which in turn would ensure in time that the business never left the solid path on which he himself had set it. Caroline could easily have made a better match if money had been all there was at stake, but this craftsman would always be worth his weight in gold in the workshop—a simile that amused him—and that was not an asset to be easily turned aside, combined, as it was, with gentlemanly origins, which put Bateman on the necessary plane. Nevertheless, an apprentice of any standing could not be allowed to escape scot-free from a misdemeanour without some retribution to drive the reprimand home.

"There's no more to be said then." He could guess at Bateman's sense of relief. "I'll consider the matter closed." Deliberately he checked a gesture of dismissal even as his hand was in the air. "I have just remembered there is a man short on wire-drawing. Leave whatever workpiece you are engaged upon and take the absentee's place until further notice." His shrewd eyes saw he had delivered a sentence that fell hard on its recipient, even though it was received in stiff-necked silence. "Now you may go, Bateman."

As John went to put his tools away and wrap up his half-finished workpiece, he thought he had rarely had a worse day. On top of everything else he was being returned to work he had been through during the early days of his apprenticeship and to which he had never intended to return. It was a branch of goldsmithing that held no interest for him, wire-drawing being the method by which gold-coated silver bars were drawn through dies with each hole being smaller than the last, until finally wire was produced that could be made into gold and silver lace as well as thread for embroidery on ecclesiastical copes, royal robes, elaborate uniforms and the richly ornamented garments that fashion decreed for those who could afford them. It was a noisy process with the rattle of wheels and pulleys, the hammering of the forged bars, the thump of bellows and the grunts of effort that came from the amount of physical pressure needed in the processes. It was no wonder that qualified wire-drawers were sometimes granted admission into the Blacksmiths' Company. He cursed long and loud as he took his place at a pulley. In the general din it went unheard and he felt no better afterwards.

Before the day was out the full realisation began to sink in as to what a future without Hester was going to mean to him. That evening he sat on the edge of his bed, his head in his hands, having refused an invitation from Tom and Robin to go out with them again to cheer himself up. It was not drink he needed now but a clear head to assess what had happened and to find a means by which to accept it. He had never supposed they would be split apart forever by a final and terrible row. Yet now that he was free of Hester, the thought wrenching at him with a force that made him groan aloud, he knew it was going to be easier to speak to Caroline of his self-doubts about their future alliance. Why that should be he could not comprehend, but that was how it was.

On Sunday Caroline, coming to meet him at the head of the stairs, saw at once that there was a change in him. With the sensitivity of a woman in love, she had been able to tell weeks ago that there was some new distraction in his life that had come between them. There had been times when she felt herself to be on a precipice, as if some word from him might plunge her down into emptiness without him, and it had needed all her alertness to keep matters in hand.

Now he was different again; no vagueness in his glance or absentminded smile on his lips, but a purposeful air about him and a set expression in his face that alarmed her far less than all those signs that had indicated he was falling in love with someone else. She felt she could cope with whatever came now.

"I need to talk to you at some length without being overheard," he said at once.

She knew they were being observed through the open door of the drawing room and drew away her hand, which he had caught tightly in his to emphasise the importance of his request. "The chance will come. Not today, I fear, but somehow I'll arrange it."

It came about the following morning. When her father was out, she went down to his office and sent for John. He answered the summons with some misgivings, wondering if further trouble awaited him, and his whole face lit up at the unexpected sight of her.

"This is a pleasant surprise!"

"We have our chance to talk now." Her ravishing smile gave nothing away of the turmoil of anxiety within her. She could guess what he planned to say and needed to gain the advantage while there was still a chance. "I should like to speak first."

"Say whatever you wish," he encouraged, resting his weight on the edge of the desk.

She did not sit herself. Instead she stood a little distance from him, the linking and unlinking of her tapering fingers the only sign of some stress. "You have fourteen months of your apprenticeship left," she began; her voice firm. "I should like to suggest that once you have been granted the Freedom we start to know and love each other all over again. The restrictions imposed on your Sunday visits have put unnatural fetters on our relationship. I would go so far as to say I feel we have lost each other along the way."

His expression of relief confirmed her deepest fears. "I see what you have said as yet another example of how well we have always understood each other. Remember how often we have thought alike on many matters."

"Then you agree to my idea of making a fresh start?" She gave him no chance to reply, hurrying on with what she had to say. "Once you are a master craftsman in your own right, my father will no longer control your life, even though you'll still be in his employ. Everything will be quite different for us." As he opened his mouth to speak, she put a hand forward. "Let me say just one thing more. I'm asking you to release me from all understandings of the past, just as I'm willing to release you. Only in that way can we begin again."

He shook his head in wonderment that she should show such wisdom, and yet it confirmed once again what an exceptional person she was in every way. "I agree to all you have said." His face was etched deep with the seriousness of his mood. "Much has happened to me in the past weeks. I have to tell you that at the present time I can't see that anything can ever be between us as it was before."

It was all she could do not to cry out in anguish. Somehow she kept her expression under control. "That will sort itself out one way or another." Inwardly she was sick with dread that she might have made a terrible mistake in releasing him, but to have held him to old ties would have strangled whatever feelings he still had for her. Now at least she had a fighting chance. "There shall be no looking back for either of us, and the future will be allowed to take care of itself. Is that agreed?"

"Agreed." The sensation of being liberated swept through him, bringing a wave of warmth and admiration for her. She saw it in his face and knew then that she had made the right move.

Their subsequent meetings were always pleasant for him, for they met as good friends. No longer troubled by his conscience towards her, the Harwood dinners lost their strain and he was back to lively participation in the conversation. In the workshop he was soon back again at his own workbench and engaged daily in the intricate work he enjoyed.

Everything would have been agreeable for him if the loss of Hester had not persecuted him every hour of the day and night. It seemed as if there was a grinding emptiness in his existence, the pain getting worse daily instead of better. She was never out of his thoughts. Even at the workbench she was always at the back of his mind, ready to leap forward at the slightest reminder. Knowing her strength of pride and independence, he doubted whether she would consider letting him back into her life. There were times when he tried to be rational and think it was all the better for him that it was over. In the end, after several weeks of agonising, he took a pen and wrote to her.

My dearest Hester,
   Although I have no idea what your feelings might be for me after all this time, I am writing to tell you that nothing has changed with me except my circumstances. All that stood between us has gone. I love you now as I did then and long to see you again. Just let me know when and where I might meet you. If nothing else, allow me to give you my apologies in person for the distress I caused you through my angry words, which have been much regretted.

John

Robin delivered it for him, simply handing it to a porter in order not to bring special attention to it from Jack or Martha Needham. In retrospect John had made the guess that one or the other of them had spoken to Master Harwood about Hester's association with him, probably directly after the quarrel when she had been seen to be upset. At least now he could be sure that Hester would know he still loved her in spite of everything, and he was certain she would write to him. Feeling more cheerful than he had for a long time, he began to wait optimistically for her letter of reply.

Hester, who had watched daily for John in the desperate and gradually declining hope that he would come back to her, did not see the letter. If she had she would have passed it by, not being able to read her own name. Martha had found it when she was alone in the office as she sorted through the postal delivery that had come with the coach, John's letter having been put with it. Without the least compunction she broke the seal and read it through. Then she lighted a candle from the tinder box and put a corner of the letter to the flame. It curled and burned right away, the last scrap almost scorching her fingers.

Chapter 3

Hester pined during the winter to the point that Jack, not normally observant, noticed that all was not well with her. Failing to get a satisfactory answer on several occasions, he questioned Martha.

"What's wrong with her? There's no life in her anymore."

Martha, on her knees sorting wine bottles on a low shelf, grimaced. She herself could drop from fatigue and Jack would barely notice, but Hester, always Hester, could claim his attention. She had come to believe he saw the girl as the daughter they had never had. "She's winter-sick, that's all."

"Maybe she should see a physician."

"Nonsense!" She rose to her feet, a bottle under each arm. No helping hand under her elbow from Jack, who had become more bull-like in his ale-ripened appearance and build and habits with every passing year, the agreeable looks that had once attracted her long since swilled away in a pint-pot. She thumped the bottles down on the bar, thinking it was as well he knew nothing of the part she had played in the cause of Hester's loss of weight and shadowed eyes. "Winter-sickness touches every one of us at times. She'll be better when the spring comes, you'll see." Then, seeing he remained unconvinced, she added, "I'll advise her to make up a herbal potion for herself. She's skilled at that sort of thing. A syrup she made cured the linen-maid's cough, and cook's rheumatic pains were much improved after some other concoction she devised."

Jack continued to keep his eye on Hester. It seemed to him that she did improve when the spring came, but she lacked sparkle and remained far from her usual self. He came to the decision that Martha had worked her too hard over the years and it had finally taken a toll on her health. He pondered which of his brothers or sisters would take her for a short holiday and dismissed each in turn, deciding that since he would never want to stay with any of them, he could not see that Hester would benefit either. Eventually he hit upon a solution. She should have more time off until she was herself again.

"You shall have a full half-day off twice instead of once a month," he told her without consulting Martha. "Get out and enjoy yourself. I want to see some roses back in your cheeks."

It was a measure of her low state that his kindness brought a swim of tears to her eyes. "Thank you, Jack."

He took her face between his big hands, rumpling her hair and speaking to her as if she were still a child. "Cheer up, then! Let's have a smile instead of those tears."

She managed to smile for him and he was pleased, thinking her as good as cured already from whatever had ailed her. For herself, the hollow ache inside her persisted unabated, as it had since she had finally forced herself to accept that John had made Caroline his choice and was never coming back to her.

Martha did her best to baulk Hester's new liberty, but Jack put his foot down. "She's no good to you or herself or the Heathcock if she's under par. Just let her be for a while. I believe that's all she needs."

Hester found the extra time to herself healing in its own way. On fine days she went to St. James's park and sketched the birds that flew between the trees and hopped on the grass around her. For a while she was able to forget her troubles, and at the end of the afternoon she would pack her drawings away in the same battered leather folder she had originally brought from home.

With an extra evening free as well, she saw more of the friends she had made over the years. They were mostly daughters of shopkeepers and merchants in the Strand area. With them and their beaux, she began to attend the open-air dancing, which had been resumed with the milder weather, and she was never without an escort on these occasions. London boasted of over seventy pleasure gardens, some quite small, others spread over several acres, and the price of admission was within the means of most working people not weighed down by too many children or drunkenness in the family, which was the lot of many.

On any expedition beyond the tavern she wondered if she would see John. Large though London was, and it was said to be the most populous city in Europe, the chance remained that one day she might meet him face to face, and she both longed for and dreaded such an encounter, knowing it would rip her to shreds all over again. There had been many weeks when she had wanted to die, all meaning gone from life, for she had loved him—and still loved him —with a passion that possessed her completely. Since she could not have him she wanted no one else, which was why men amorously inclined towards her met with total rebuff.

There were ten in the party on the June evening of the expedition to Cuper's Gardens. It was one of the city's oldest pleasure gardens and had much to offer in the way of entertainment, with many booths for refreshments, a playhouse and a pavilion of side-shows. People from all walks of life went there, no class barriers existing in these public places, and it gave spice and excitement to the atmosphere, nobility and working folk rubbing shoulders together in the glow of coloured lanterns and leaping flares. Hester's escort that evening was Alan Marshall, a friend's brother, who was betrothed to a girl who lived in Cornwall, which meant she could enjoy his company in the knowledge that there would be no unwelcome tussles to fend off. They often paired up for these occasions, both missing someone else in their lives, his common knowledge and hers secret.

"I feel like dancing this evening until I have holes in my shoes," she declared gaily as they arrived, music floating out to meet them.

"Then let's waste no time," Alan said with a smile, leading her ahead of the rest of the party along an illuminated path that led to a rotunda, which was one of several centres in the wooded and gladed spread of the garden where dancing took place.

It came into sight like a vast lantern, all doors and shutters folded back to make the rainbow lights outside one with the brilliance of the chandeliers suspended from the tentlike ceiling within. The liveliest of country dances was in full swing, the bows of the fiddlers flashing in unison as the merry music set the pace for those whirling around the floor. Alan took her by the hand to run her up the steps and into the maze of dancing couples. He was a good dancer and she was feather-light on her feet as they rotated together, the billowing of her skirt and her fluttering ribbons keeping time with his swirling coat-tails. In the next dance they parted to cross and counter cross before linking hands again. Several times during the next hour they changed partners with others in their party. Then they were back together for a riotous square for eight with high arm movements that had her laughing with him when, her head flung back, she saw John looking down on her from the crowded gallery. The visual contact was no more than a second or two, for Alan was twirling her under his arm, and when she looked again John was gone.

"What's wrong?" Alan asked her as the final steps of the lively measure came to an end. All the laughter had gone from her. She looked taut and distracted.

"I saw someone I used to know. If you don't mind I'd like to go home."

Thoroughly good-tempered, he was willing enough to oblige her, able to see she was in a state of distress. Then, as she turned with him to leave the rotunda, she saw that John had descended the flight from the gallery and was waiting in her path, a tall figure against the multi-coloured lights in the gardens beyond. She reached out a hand and pressed Alan's arm without taking her eyes from John's gaze, which was fixed on her as if willing her to him.

"Go back to the others, Alan. I thank you for bringing me here this evening. All is well now." She could not be entirely sure about that. This was simply a reunion that had to be between John and her on their own.

"If you're sure . . . ."

She nodded and he drew back to watch from a distance. As she covered the remaining stretch of floor between John and herself, she felt as if she were walking on ice that was cracking all around her. When she reached him she might be plunged down into icy depths. She had to be prepared.

"I'm pleased to see you well, Hester."

A conventional beginning. She was thankful for that. Within a few short months there had been a change in him. He looked taller, if that was possible, and had filled out as if he had been better fed; the boyish looks had hardened into those of a fully mature man. She put a guard on her voice out of fear of betraying herself.

"I trust it is the same with you?"

"Never better. Will you stroll a way with me? I should like to talk to you."

She nodded and they went down the steps together. As if from a distance, she heard herself remarking on the mildness of the evening and how good the summer promised to be. In desperation she commented on the beautiful roses bordering the path they were following, which was one of several score that threaded the whole area, some leading to sheltered arbours and secluded gazebos. It was not for nothing that Cuper's was also known as Cupid's Gardens. He made brief replies to all she said. Although he kept giving her long glances, it was as if she were side by side with a stranger, the brief space between them as wide as the Thames. When a silence fell between them it was an awkward one. They broke it simultaneously.

"How is your work progressing?" she asked.

"Why didn't you reply to my letter?"

She came to an abrupt halt, and he stopped in turn to face her. "I have never received a letter from you," she exclaimed in astonishment.

"Then what happens to the mail at the Heathcock?" His surprise was equal to hers. "Do they throw it away?"

She shook her head absently. "When did you write?"

"A few weeks after we quarrelled, which incidentally happens to be something I have deeply regretted."

Turning her face away to hide whatever he might read there, she began to stroll on again. "I was equally guilty of losing my temper and I'm sorry for it. We should have accepted that there were matters that could never be bridged between us and parted amicably to remain friends."

"I could never have endured mere friendship with you," he declared swiftly.

She blushed, feeling it rise up her neck and into her cheeks. Such talk belonged to their past association and not to the present chance meeting. She decided to ignore what he had said. "What was the reason for writing to me? Was it to express that unnecessary apology?"

"Much more than that. I wanted you to know that the situation had changed between Caroline and me. I still attend the Harwood

Sunday dinners twice a month. I had intended to withdraw from them, but Caroline wanted us to go on meeting as friends, which I appreciate. Otherwise these occasions hold no importance for either of us. I'm free of all obligations towards her. That is what I wanted you to know. That is why I wrote the letter."

She kept her head high, looking straight ahead. Her curiosity was sharply aroused. The fact that he was continuing to dine with the Harwoods led her to deduce that so far his master knew nothing about this change of feeling towards Caroline. What was more, Caroline obviously had no one else yet, or John would have been replaced at the Sunday table. It was an odd state of affairs. At least he had been frank with her, but as yet, she was not prepared to give an inch. "How was that to interest me?"

"Only in that I hoped you would agree to forget our quarrel and see me again. I'm putting the same request to you now."

Her pace did not change. She felt she had to keep walking to give herself time to think, to accept, to cope with all the sudden joy that had gushed into her heart. It was as if she were coming alive again after a long and terrible sleep. Like a butterfly emerging from a chrysalis, her wings were still tender, too vulnerable yet to allow a move in any direction. "Let us enjoy this walk for a little longer. There's plenty of time to talk later."

The soft cadences in her voice gave him no doubt as to what her answer would be. He wanted to take her into his arms, but it was too soon yet.

It was not by chance that he had chosen the particular direction they were following, for he knew that before long they would reach one of the secret corners where he could be quite alone with her. The music and the noise of merry-making faded away behind them, shut off by the trees. She did not draw back when he led the way from the path, holding aside branches for her, to reach a bower entwined with rambling roses, the scent fragrant in the still air. They stood looking at each other in the moonlight, her beautiful face as pale as the blossoms. He could sense a lovely trembling in her and he lifted his hands, letting them hover, not yet daring to touch her. This was for them as it had never been before.

"Hester," he breathed, "every day away from you has been like a year. You are and always will be everything to me."

"As you are to me." Her eyes shone and her lips were slightly parted. She seemed scarcely to breathe in the electric atmosphere.

He reached for her and she swayed against him to receive his arms about her. "Is the past behind us then?" he asked her.

"All that made us sad. Not the happy times."

"My love!" His mouth closed down over hers and instantly they were both ignited by an explosion of passion that no amount of kissing could assuage. Being in each other's arms again after the long months of miserable separation propelled them irrevocably towards a point of no return for which she yearned as frantically as he did.

She was weightless against him as he bore her down onto the dry grass. His eager hand loosened her ribbons and spread them wide as his kisses travelled from her lips to her eyes and temples and down her neck to the wonderful fullness of her breasts now revealed to him. Her back arched with the desire he aroused in her. He felt her shudder with sensuous delight as his caresses defied the encumbering petticoats to travel up her silky thighs and discover the sweet, moist core of her. What he was exclaiming to her he did not know. It was an outpouring of love such as he had never uttered before. With a deep gasp he entered her, his passion-swept face above hers, and he held her tightly through her moment of pain before loving her with all the force and power of his whole heart and body. When her unleashed ecstasy broke upon him like a wave it completely matched his own, convulsive and abandoned.

For a while afterwards they were beyond speech. It was as though in their union all their promises had been made, every vow taken. He was drunk with love for her and held her gathered to him, her head resting in the hollow of his shoulder. Some rose petals had caught in her hair and he brushed them away with his fingertips. All the wonderment of lovers was upon them and they kissed, smiled with velvet looks and kissed again.

"If only we could stay here, away from the world forever," she whispered yearningly.

He cupped her face tenderly in his hands. "I should like any place where I could be alone with you."

"There must be other havens," she breathed, feeling exultant and utterly shameless.

He was deeply moved, such vistas of love-making with her filling his mind that his voice became choked. "Say you'll be mine for ever. Just as you were tonight."

"Always, John." Her tone was fervent, her expression rapt. "Until the day I die!"

Before they left the glade he picked one of the deep pink roses and gave it to her. She held it as he escorted her home through the lamp-lit streets. Her fear that he might be sighted by Jack or Martha caused her to insist that he let her cover the last few yards to the Heathcock by herself. He waited until he saw her turn safely into the tavern before making his own way homewards. His thoughts ran over the evening at Cuper's and all it had brought him; it seemed a lucky chance he had gone there with Tom and Robin out of restlessness, never suspecting what the outcome would be.

He had a twinge of misgiving when he recalled his lack of any precaution in making love to Hester. The tumult of passion had driven all practical matters from his mind. Fortunately it was always said that conception rarely occurred the first time. However, he would be more careful on future occasions. She should never come to any harm through carelessness on his part.

Hester pressed the rose between two pieces of drawing paper and set a weight on top before going to bed. To have put it in water would have been to keep it for only two or three days before the petals dropped away, and she wanted to keep it for ever.

Her new happiness, reflected in her face and in her laughter, soon brought its own unforeseen penalties. Martha had been seeking an excuse for some time to curtail the extra half day off that Jack had decreed. Hearing Hester singing as she worked gave the necessary opening.

"I can hear there's nothing the matter with you any longer." Martha smirked with satisfaction, knowing that Jack was within earshot and he had remarked only a few days previously that he thought Hester had never looked bonnier. "It's back to the same hours as everyone else for you now, my girl."

Hester breathed deeply, fighting back an angry retort. She wished she could have retaliated by accusing Martha of tampering with John's letter, for there was no one else likely to have interfered, but she had to hold her tongue. On no account must she let either Jack or Martha suspect that she was seeing John again. She cast a look in her brother's direction, hoping he would rescind the change that Martha had made. He simply went on filling his clay pipe, tamping down the tobacco with care as if he had nothing else on his mind. He had heard and she knew it. Her extra liberty was at an end.

As a result, her meetings with John were all too brief and had in any case to be arranged as far as possible away from the Heathcock, which in turn cut their time together still further. They snatched hours on the river banks, in parks and in the garden of a little tavern where neither of them was known. Nowhere were they able to be entirely alone. Then, as if some kindly quirk of fate had turned in their favour, her long-awaited half day coincided with a Sunday when he did not have to attend a Harwood dinner. Through a girl whom Robin knew, John was able to arrange a lift out into the countryside with her father, who was a market stall holder, on the day he went to collect eggs and other produce.

"How shall we get back?" Hester asked when they were settled in the back of the empty wagon, a picnic basket covered with a check napkin beside them.

"Our driver always takes supper with a sister in the village before he starts his return journey. It's there we'll meet him in the early evening."

It was wonderful for Hester to be back in the countryside, which she had not seen since the day she had left her childhood home. The environs of the village of Hampstead were much like those she had once known, and she was full of stories to tell John as they wandered through buttercup-carpeted meadows and shady woods. He helped her over stiles and led her across stepping-stones when they met a stream. They settled for their picnic on a hillock under the side spread of a great oak tree. She unpacked bread and cheese and slices of beef, pickles in a jar, seed cake and oranges and a flagon of ale, all of which the Heathcock cook had given her from the pantry.

After they had eaten and repacked the basket, John, already in his shirt-sleeves, stretched out and slept with his head in her lap. She watched over him with love, flicking away with a blade of grass any insect that threatened to settle on his face, utterly content and protective.

Later they found a corner of a hayfield. The shimmering, sun-dried grasses were waist-high and hid them where they lay together, she naked to his nakedness in the summer heat. He made love to her slowly and tenderly, prolonging every delicious sensation until the same high passion swept through them like a great tide. Tears ran from the corner of her eyes out of love for him, and he kissed them away.

The sun was setting when they made their way back to the village and the cottage where their driver was downing a final tankard with his brother-in-law. The wagon was full of produce piled high, including three crates of clucking hens. Hester declined a seat beside the driver and sat with John at the back of the vehicle, their legs dangling over the passing road all the way back to the city, his arm about her waist, their heads together. It had been a perfect day, unspoiled even by a tiny private worry that had been troubling her for the past two weeks and more.

There was a hitch to their next planned meeting. At the last minute she could not go due to the sickness of one of the waiting maids. That proved to be only the beginning, for the next day several more members of the staff as well as Jack himself succumbed to the strange illness. It had been Hester's suggestion to John that Robin or Tom, neither of whom was known to her brother and his wife, should be asked to act as messengers if ever she failed to keep an appointment or he was prevented from getting away. She had made the excuse that she did not want another letter lost on its way in or out of the tavern and thus saved herself once again from confessing to illiteracy. It was a relief to her when Robin, whom she had never met, made himself known to her in the taproom. She explained the situation.

"I've no idea yet when I'll be able to see John again."

"Never mind," he said obligingly. "I'll look in at intervals until you're able to let me know when it will be."

When she was finally able to get away from the Heathcock, she met John outside a hosier's in Lombard Street. He flung out his arms exuberantly when he sighted her and she ran the last few yards, her little red heels tapping. Laughing with pleasure, he embraced her and she buried her face in his shoulder as if she had come home to refuge before she raised her lips to receive his ardent kiss, his mouth warm on hers.

"I've missed you," he said when they drew breath. "It was a worry to me that you might fall ill, too."

She was encouraged by his concern for her. "Could we sit and talk somewhere? I can't stay long and I've something to tell you."

He patted his coat pocket jokingly. "My allowance from my grandfather came yesterday. We shall drink coffee grandly today while we talk."

Taking her by the elbow, he escorted her into the coffee-house next to the hosier's, where they followed a passage to mount the stairs into the large coffee room, which was quite busy. It was divided into boxes by high partitions, which was the usual furnishing, for each trade and profession had adopted certain coffee-houses as individual centres in which to discuss business, and privacy was welcome. This establishment, known as Lloyds, was a place of financial exchange and insurance matters. She was glad of the seclusion that the partition box gave John and her as they sat down opposite each other at the table. He ordered a pot of coffee from the waiter and it came almost at once. While she poured, he told her the news of his grandfather and his village.

"Now," he said when she had handed him his cup, "what is it you have to tell me?"

She thought how unsuspectingly happy and carefree he looked, joyful at being with her again and proud to be treating her to coffee. Taking up her cup, she took a sip to sustain herself before setting it down again. Then she drew a deep breath.

"I'm going to have a baby."

There were a few terrible seconds of silence in which his whole face changed as if a smiling mask had been whipped off. In despair she watched shock and anger contort his expression, hollowing his cheeks and giving a hard brilliance to his eyes. "You can't be!"

His reaction was worse than she had feared. Somehow she found the strength to go on with what she had to say. "There's no longer any doubt about it. At first I refused to believe it myself. I found all sorts of reasons as to why things were not as they should be." There was a kind of tragic innocence in the tremulous line of her mouth.

"I hadn't realised it was so easy to conceive the first time. It must have happened at Cuper's Gardens."

There was a greyish tinge to his pallor, and he shook his head vigorously as if refusing to accept this unbearable turn of events. "Perhaps you have been affected by the sickness at the tavern! Surely that is possible?"

"My nausea has been in the mornings with no doubt about its origins. There were enough among the sick suffering similar symptoms for it to be thought I was going through a minor attack of the same malady. Otherwise my condition would almost certainly have been discovered."

He looked utterly bleak and drained, finally submitting himself to the situation. "Damnation! Of all the misfortunes that could have happened, this is the worst." He set his elbows on the table and dropped his head into his hands with a heartfelt groan.

She stared at him. Even in her own distress she could understand fully his state of mind. His whole apprenticeship, his long years of hard work learning his craft, would be forfeit if it became public knowledge that he had made her pregnant. That was why she had not come looking for a speedy marriage, because for an apprentice to wed bore the same penalty. But she had expected him to say they should marry as soon as he gained his Freedom, and she herself had been prepared to shield him from discovery as her baby's father until that time. Now she was remembering for the first time that in all his love talk there had never been any definite mention of marriage. He had used the words "always" and "forever" and she had put her own interpretation on them. How wrong she had been! This, then, was the outcome. It was a situation as old as time.

"Very well," she said shakily, the muscles of her face feeling stiff and awkward, as if her throat were trying to reject what she was about to say. "There are ways and means of ending this kind of trouble. Nobody need know. I have heard talk in the kitchen of a woman—"

He did not seem to have heard her, his face still hidden as he uttered another groan. She pressed the back of her hand against her quivering lips to keep back the gulps of misery threatening to burst from her throat, and sprang up from the seat as if propelled. In the general hub-bub of the coffee-house he did not realise for a few seconds that she had gone.

Someone opened the door from outside as she reached it and she darted through to run away down the street, her heels flying. She sobbed as she ran, the huge tears pouring from her eyes, her ribs racked by choked breaths. Far worse than anything to be faced on her own in the future was that in the end he had not loved her enough to offer a minimum of comfort when she had never needed it more.

In her tear-blinded haste she bumped into people as she ran, some shouting after her and others tut-tutting in her wake. Turning to cross the street, she hardly looked for traffic and caused a few bystanders to call out in alarm when a coachman was forced to haul on his reins as she slipped and almost fell in his path. Escaping the flailing hooves, his bawled obscenities ringing in her ears, she reeled to safety onto the pavement and sagged in exhaustion against a brick wall, her hands pressed tightly over her tear-wet face, heedless of the stares of passers-by. She had failed to hear footsteps running in her wake.

"Why did you dash off like that?" John's breathless voice was close at hand. "I had the devil's own task to keep you in sight and then I saw you almost kill yourself under those horses' hooves! Were you hit at all?" When she failed to respond, he pulled her hands down sharply by the wrists and then took a handful of her hair to jerk her face upwards to his. "Merciful God! I thought there in the traffic I had lost you."

She saw he was stricken, his pupils still dilated from the fright she had given him. Fiercely she snatched herself free. "It would have made no difference. You had lost me already in the coffee-house."

When she would have pushed past him, he seized her by the shoulders and sent her thudding back against the wall, almost knocking what breath she had left from her body. He thrust his face within an inch of hers, his jaw jutting. "It is my baby as well as yours that you nearly destroyed! And understand this! I'll have no talk of you risking your life at the hands of one of those dreadful women."

Her expression crumpled and she collapsed against him, to be

held hard in his consoling embrace. "Why did you let me think you
didn't care?"

"You took me by surprise, that's all. Of course I care. What sort
of man do you think I am? It's just come at a deuced awkward time
when I'm on the last lap of my apprenticeship."

"Do you think I don't know the penalty that would be yours if
this trouble came to light?" she exclaimed desperately, pulling
away from him.

"Don't get upset again," he urged. "We'll solve this problem
somehow." Noticing they were not far from a square, he put a
supporting arm about her and led her the few yards into it. Tall,
elegant houses stood on all four sides, with a flower garden, a lawn
and trees in the middle. He sat her down beside him on a stone
bench under a chestnut tree. "We must marry sooner than we intended. How and when has to be settled."

She dried her eyes. "It can't be until you have completed your
apprenticeship."

"By my reckoning that would mean our baby bearing the stigma
of bastardy for the rest of his or her life even though we married
afterwards. That is entirely out of the question." He was leaning
forward, arms resting across his knees, his brow concentrated in
thought. "If we could just keep my master from hearing of it until I
obtain my Freedom, all would be well. Perhaps if you moved out of
the Heathcock to Hampstead village or somewhere like that, we
could be married in a country church where the banns would be
read out without much chance of news of them reaching as far as
London."

"That wouldn't do. It would mean a secret departure, and even
though I'm sure I could find work to give me a roof over my head,
Jack would search high and low until he found me, which would
bring the truth out anyway." She paused. "There is another way."

"What's that?"

"A Fleet wedding. No banns are needed there." During many
sleepless nights it was the only solution that had presented itself. At
the Fleet prison for debtors there were always some clergymen
among those incarcerated until their debts were paid, and in their
unfortunate circumstances they were eager to perform the marriage
ceremony for payment in coin or in kind, however small. Some of

them touted for business through the iron bars and hung out adver-
tisements, often marvellously inscribed. No proof of the legal right
to wed was ever asked for and as a result the Fleet had become
notorious. Bigamists as well as runaway couples and outright vil-
lains took advantage of the easy wedlock offered; some drugged
brides, who would have otherwise been unwilling, were known to
have been victims. No self-respecting man or woman would consider marriage there and Hester was not surprised when John
swung round on the seat towards her, outrage stamped on his face.
With a rush of words she forestalled the argument she knew was
about to come.

"I know it's a dreadful place and not what we would have chosen, but it is the only answer for us. Our baby will be born in
wedlock and nobody need know of our marriage until you have
been granted the Freedom."

He lowered his eyebrows grimly. "Are you suggesting I let you
suffer the disgrace of what will appear to be an unmarried pregnancy? No! We must think of something else."

"There is nothing else." She was adamant. "Don't worry about
me. It will be nobody's business but mine who is the father of my
baby. However much Martha may moan, Jack will never turn me
out." Although she could see she had a hard argument to win, she
was determined to get her way. "Mull it over," she advised, getting
up to leave. "And remember it won't matter to me what anyone
says or thinks for a few short months. On the day you register your
own mark of *J.B.* at the Goldsmiths' Hall, I shall shout it to the
rooftops of London that I'm Mistress John Bateman." Her whole
face bloomed with her smile. "How wonderful it will sound!"

"Hester," he said with admiration, walking with her out of the
square, "there can be nobody else like you in all the world."

"Then—?"

"I've decided nothing yet," he stated firmly.

She used no more persuasion, certain that with a little time he
would come round to her point of view.

The marriage was finally arranged for a Saturday afternoon in
late September. Hester was exactly three months into her pregnancy and so far nobody suspected her condition, not even Martha,

who normally missed nothing. She wore her best muslin dress under her long cape and had retrimmed a wide-brimmed hat with blue ribbons. It proved difficult to leave the tavern without being sighted by Martha and questioned as to why she was dressed up in the middle of the afternoon, and she had to linger until the woman was well out of the way. Fortunately she had allowed plenty of time and did not have to hurry too much in order to reach the Fleet prison on time. It was a gloomy, frightening place where the inmates, already in dire straits, had to pay their jailers for food and any privileges. Those without friends outside to help them often died of starvation.

John was waiting for her. He was wearing his good clothes, in which he always looked exceptionally handsome. On his coat he had pinned a flower and he was holding out a small nosegay that he must have bought from one of the flower-sellers who hung about the gates, waiting for wedding couples. She took it from him and inhaled the sweet scent as they smiled at each other in welcome.

"It's lovely, John."

"You look beautiful, Hester."

A guard admitted them through a door in the great gates. In the gate-house they faced a warder across a desk. "Protestant or Catholic?" he questioned in bored tones.

John answered: "Church of England."

"Right. Go through to the courtyard. You won't have long to wait."

It was an ill-smelling cobbled area of some size, surrounded on all four sides by the bleak prison buildings studded with barred windows. A few guards stood about on duty. As John and Hester walked to the middle of the courtyard, faces appeared at all the windows and there was an unruly din as shouts and cat-calls and pathetic cries for alms echoed about them. A chill of horror settled on Hester and she held still tighter to John's strongly clasping hand. Worse was to come when a door opened and about a dozen Protestant clergy burst through, buffeting each other to be the first to reach a chain-barrier that kept them confined to one corner of the yard. Most wore surplices, some of which were in tatters, showing how long the wearers had been incarcerated, and there was a desperate look on their faces as they cajoled and bargained their willingness to perform the marriage ceremony, vying with each other to make themselves heard.

"Wait here," John said, sparing Hester the heart-rending task of making a choice from these men of the cloth brought to such degrading circumstances. She watched him pick out a little man who had been crowded out at the back, and then two more to be witnesses.

The odd little procession came towards her. Composed now, there was dignity about all three of the clergy in spite of their rags. Payment had already taken place; a roll of tobacco for the Reverend Curtis, who was to marry them, and snuff for both the witnesses. A well-thumbed prayerbook was opened and the ceremony began.

" 'Dearly Beloved, we are gathered together here in the sight of God and in the face of this congregation, to join together this Man and this Woman in holy Matrimony . . .' "

At times it was almost impossible to hear his words for the raucous noise continuing unabated from the barred windows. Once she felt quite faint, the prison stench overcoming the perfume of the nosegay she held. But when it came to making their vows, she looked into John's eyes and forgot her surroundings momentarily. He slipped the ring on her finger. It did not matter that it was not gold. With it he had made her his wife. The ceremony was concluded.

John was too private a person to give her a bridal kiss within earshot of the bawdiness being shouted down at them. He waited until they had re-entered the gate-house with the three clergy for the registering of the marriage. It was a short, sweet meeting of their lips that was chivvied impatiently by the warder.

"Plenty of time for that later. Come and sign the marriage certificate." He twisted it round and thrust it towards them across the table.

John drew it to him and signed. Then he dipped the nib in the ink again in readiness for Hester and offered the pen to her. She stood motionless, dangerously close to panic. With writing having no part in her life, she had forgotten completely that she would be expected to sign her name. Now John would know! The old shame seared through her, making her want to throw her arms over her head and hide herself away. Everybody was waiting; all eyes on her. "I—" Her voice faltered and broke.

Then John put the pen into her wildly shaking hand and said in a special tone of comprehension, meant only for her to grasp. "Let me show you where to make your cross, my dear wife."

She did it, making the nib splutter, but that was not important. Those little inkblobs would always remind her of the moment when John had shown no disappointment, no condemnation. Instead he had looked at her with as much love as before. The witnesses added their signatures, sand was shaken over the wet ink to dry it and then, after the certificate was folded, it was handed to her. She put it into her draw-string purse, thinking it of more value than all the Crown Jewels in the Tower.

Outside the gates they had to part, he to keep up the façade of being a bachelor apprentice and she to hide for as long as possible the increasingly visible evidence that she was going to bear a child. They had agreed it was vital that nothing should link them, and for this reason they would not meet unless an exceptionally safe circumstance presented itself. Neither had any real hope of this happening. They continued to hold hands as they slowly drew away from each other to go in opposite directions, until finally the last contact of their fingertips was gone. They both turned constantly, sometimes taking a few steps backwards as they went, until they could no longer see each other in the stream of passers-by.

Before Hester reached the Heathcock she took her nosegay to pieces in order to make it look like an ordinary bunch of flowers, pocketing the lace frill that had held it together, and removed the new ribbons from her hat. Lastly, and reluctantly, she drew the wedding ring from her finger and put it in her pocket until she could find a place in her room where it could be safely concealed. With her dress covered by her long cape, there was nothing to show outwardly when she re-entered the tavern that her outing that day had been different from any other.

Chapter 4

Another month went by and Hester still managed to keep her secret. Full skirts and starched aprons were a good disguise for a thickening waistline, but she was aware of other developments that could not be hidden; an indefinable change in the face that her looking-glass reflected and a growing fullness to her breasts that bands of linen could not quite compress. Once or twice she caught Martha giving her a speculative glance, but the unlikelihood of her being pregnant was a defence in itself and nothing was said.

She was glad she was feeling well because she was being kept busier than ever, her free time quite dispersed, as if Martha was trying to recoup from her those working hours that had been lost. Since she was unable to see John, it was far better to be busy with little time to think. When she did have an hour or two to herself, she sewed baby clothes in the privacy of her bedchamber and hid them away in a drawer.

In the back of the wash-house in the kitchen yard was a lean-to that served as a bath-house for the staff, the guests having hip-baths in their rooms whenever required. Hester was standing in the tub one day, rinsing soap from her head and body with a jug of warm water, when the door to the wash-house, normally locked, was thrown open and Martha entered. She set her hands on her hips and glared at the swollen contours of Hester's body.

"I thought so, you little whore!" she shrieked. "As soon as you're dressed you come immediately to the upstairs parlour. Jack will want to speak to you."

In spite of the outrage of Martha's intrusion, Hester felt calmer than she had expected to feel now that her secret was out. With her hair still damp and pinned under her cap, she mounted the stairs slowly, her hands folded across her waistband, her back straight and her chin high. When she entered the parlour, Jack was waiting. He seized her by the shoulder and half-flung her into the middle of the room. Martha sat on the windowseat with the light behind her.

"Who is he?" Jack thundered, his face congested with rage. "What's the man's name? I'll skin him alive for bringing you to this pass!"

Martha's voice rasped sarcastically: "I don't imagine it was rape."

He rounded on his wife with a bellow. "Keep out of this for the time being! I've seen enough libertines and rakes come through this tavern door to know the tricks they can play on an innocent girl." He swung back to face Hester, his fury directed entirely at her seducer, his ham-like fists clenched as if in readiness to beat the offender to pulp. "Tell me! Come on! I swear to you I'll leave him in a state where he'll never be able to play that kind of trick again!"

"I'm not prepared to tell you anything, Jack."

He gaped in disbelief. "What are you saying?"

"It is my business entirely."

"No, it's not!" Martha had sprung to her feet. "Your disgrace is reflected on us. Answer your brother at once! Tell him the father's name!"

Hester compressed her lips. "I will not."

Martha's head shot forward. "Maybe you don't know whom the father might be. Is that it?"

Hester did not deign to reply, her glance of contempt enough. Jack gestured for his wife to keep silent and peered closer at Hester. "You're shielding the rogue, ain't you? Why? If he won't do the honourable thing and marry you, then you're only being a fool in letting him get away with it." His coaxing was rough and clumsy. "Let me deal with him. He deserves a beating." Then, seeing she had no intention of telling him what he wanted to know, his temper shifted against her, a dangerous glint in his eyes. "Do you want me to turn you out into the street? Do you wish to have your baby in the gutter?"

She did not flinch, although her face was ashen. "You must make your decisions as I have made mine. I'm not telling you who fathered my baby however long you interrogate me. I was a willing partner."

He almost hit her. His raised fist shivered as his fondness for her warred with his rage against her defiance. Martha watched bitterly. He had never hesitated towards her. She swept forward two paces and poked him in the arm. "Ask her if her lover is married already. You might get the truth there."

Jack fixed his gaze on Hester. "Well? Is that the case?"

Hester almost closed her eyes with relief. "He is a married man," she answered. Any chance of John being suspected had been completely wiped out. "That is the last thing I'm going to say."

He drew in his breath noisily. "You're my sister after all and your home is under my roof. In spite of what I threatened, I'll not change that, but what you have said makes me still more determined to find the man responsible for bringing you to this state. If it's the last thing I do I'll see he gets his dues. He'll not escape me —not with the contacts I have in this city and elsewhere." Thrusting her aside, he strode out of the room, slamming the door after him.

A moment's silence followed, Hester looking over her shoulder in his wake, suddenly full of trepidation. Martha folded her arms and watched her with malicious satisfaction.

"You've a right to look alarmed. You know Jack as well as I do. He can be like a bulldog when he sets his teeth into something. However long it takes he'll never let go. Your fancy lover will get his come-uppance before Jack is finished with this matter, I can tell you."

Hester chose to ignore her jibing. "I'm sure you have other things to say to me."

"I have. When is your brat due?"

"My baby will be born in five months' time."

"Right. You'll be in the kitchen and the wash-house from now on. You'll use the back stairs and make sure you're never seen by either guests or regular customers in the taproom. There'll be no going out for you either. The name of Needham has never been shamed before, and I'm going to minimise it to the best of my ability for Jack's sake and mine. Afterwards there'll be no place here for the baby. It will have to be farmed out, but we can meet that hurdle when we come to it."

"Is that all?" Hester demanded coldly. Nothing should separate her from her baby for the last few weeks before John obtained his Freedom.

"For the time being. Now get out of my sight, you slut!"

There was no harder work than that of the kitchen and the wash-house. Hester found it taxed her strength as it had never done in the past and she collapsed into her bed at night. As her pregnancy advanced, she became more and more exhausted. She guessed that Jack would try to find out if the culprit was among the patrons of the tavern and assumed a check had been made on the company she had kept during the period before her reunion with John. Over and over again she thanked Providence that her meetings with him afterwards had not come to anyone's notice.

In early January, Martha voiced a suspicion that had been steadily growing in her mind. "You don't suppose Hester took up with John Bateman again, do you?" she said to Jack. They were alone in the taproom and he had just set up a cask of ale.

"She said the man was married," he reminded her, wiping his hands on a rag.

"That could have been a lie to throw you off the scent. Remember you had her in a desperate corner."

He considered for a moment and then shook his head. "I warned her off seeing Bateman and that put an end to it."

"That's what you *thought,*" she emphasised, her tone half-mocking. "As it happens, she went on seeing him after that, which was why I chose to have a discreet word with Harwood and he thanked me for it. I've no doubt that he called Bateman to heel."

Jack showed mild surprise at the action his wife had taken unbeknownst to him and then he shrugged. "That's it then. No sane fellow in the final stages of his apprenticeship would risk his master's displeasure a second time."

Martha proved persistent. "Suppose Hester was infatuated with him and maybe he was with her. What if he couldn't stay away from her? We know how foolish the young can be."

Jack's brows drew together suspiciously. "I can't say I've ever really noticed the lad. I only remember what Harwood told me and I certainly didn't see him the evening he was in the taproom talking to Hester. What's he like?"

"Tall and broad-shouldered and slim built. Fair hair and good-looking in his way." She stopped, seeing her husband's face had taken on a purplish tinge as his temper soared up in him. His huge fist banged down on the bar, making everything vibrate.

"By God! That fits the description of a man seen with her near Tower Bridge by someone I know. Why didn't you tell me this before?"

"Because you never thought to tell me you had any description," she retaliated. "What are you going to do?"

He threw aside the rag he was holding. "I'm going straight to Harwood before Hester gets wind of this! I want the truth out of Bateman before she has the chance to cover up for him again!" Dashing through to the office, he grabbed his caped greatcoat and thrust his arms into it. Martha followed to take his tricorn hat down from another peg for him, excited by this development.

"You can't be sure about Bateman being the guilty one," she felt bound to advise.

He snatched his hat from her and jammed it on. "If I'm not right, nothing is lost. If I am, then Bateman is going to rue the day he ever set eyes on my sister!"

Left on her own in the office, Martha saw through its window into the side hall used by the servants that Hester was taking a large basket of laundry through to the wash-house. As soon as she was out of sight, Martha left the office and made for the stairs. In Hester's room she shut the door behind her and looked around. Surely somewhere she could discover a chance link with John Bateman in case denials should make Jack's errand fruitless. It was not that she expected to find love letters, Hester being illiterate, but girls liked to keep love tokens, and something bearing a name or initials might come to light.

She began a thorough search. It was not the first time she had investigated Hester's possessions, although the previous time she had had only to open a drawer and turn back its contents to find the store of baby clothes, which had finally confirmed her suspicions and led to the carefully planned denouement in the bath-house. Hester's leather folder lay on the shelf and she took it down to open it, hoping it would contain a sketch of the man in question. Only drawings of flowers and trees and birds came to light, plus some old yellowed papers on which sketches of herbs gave their owner the proportions of various herbal remedies and ointments. There was also a pressed rose among the drawings that gave nothing away. She turned to the chest of drawers and the rest of the room, even standing on the stool to peer at the top of the bed's canopy and shaking its curtains to make sure nothing was concealed in them. Being Hester's domain, there was not even any dust. Stepping down again, her heel caught on a loose floorboard and a new possibility dawned. Nothing was revealed underneath it, but that did not deter her. On her hands and knees, she began a systematic examination of every floorboard.

In the wash-house, Hester remembered she had not brought down one of her own petticoats she had meant to include. A scullery boy was stoking the fire under the copper for her, and she left him in charge as she went back to the tavern. Suspecting nothing, she opened her bedchamber door to find Martha kneeling beside a prised-up floorboard, studying the marriage certificate she had just unfolded.

"What are you doing?" Hester was aghast. "How dare you touch my possessions!" She darted forward to try to snatch the paper away. Martha, scrambling to her feet, whipped it behind her back.

"Why didn't you tell us you were wed?" she rasped, her lips pinched back from her teeth. "You would have saved your brother a deal of misery!"

Hester stooped to pick up from the floor the little purse containing her wedding ring and from which Martha had taken the certificate. She held the purse to her in a protective gesture. "How you have pried!" she accused in disgust. "Why couldn't you have left well alone? John and I agreed to tell no one of our marriage. It was the only way of keeping our secret safe."

Martha tossed the certificate contemptuously onto the bed and set her hands on her waist, arms akimbo. "What makes you think I can't hold my tongue when needs must?" she inquired slyly.

Hester jerked up her head, incredulous and uncertain. "Would you really stand by John and me until his apprenticeship is finished?"

It amused Martha to raise the girl's hopes and then dash them again. "As it happens, the matter is already out of my hands. It's not a quarter of an hour since Jack and I finally put two and two together and decided John Bateman was the one. Jack is on his way now to see Harwood about it all!"

With a choked cry Hester dropped the purse into her apron pocket and rushed for her cape. "I must stop him!"

"You'll never catch him up."

"I'll do my best." She swung a muffler around her neck against the cold she would meet outside. "There's always a chance he'll be kept waiting. Maybe Master Harwood will be out somewhere. All I need is a little time to make Jack listen to me!"

Martha followed her out onto the landing and watched her hasten down the stairs. She shook her head. With the pace that Hester could make in her advanced condition, Jack should be almost home again before she reached the Harwood establishment.

In the workshop John was applying decoration to a silver alms dish. He held the chasing tool almost vertically between his left thumb and two first fingers, his other fingers free to steady his hand on the workpiece while the hammer in his right hand rhythmically commanded a smooth propelling motion, taking the design slowly and meticulously around the rim.

His concentration was broken abruptly when he was told Master Harwood wanted to see him immediately. Untying his leather apron, he hooked it forward into place. Slipping his waistcoat over his shirtsleeves to make himself more presentable, he set off for the office.

When he knocked, Master Harwood's voice bade him enter.

As soon as he saw Jack Needham in the office, apprehension gripped him and he knew something was terribly wrong. He guessed at once that what was to be said had been arranged, because when Jack, whose expression was one of intense rancour, leaped up from a chair to take a threatening step towards him, Master Harwood waved him back to his seat with an authoritative gesture. Jack obeyed, muttering to himself.

"Bateman," Master Harwood began heavily, "an extremely serious accusation has been made against you. I'm hoping to hear it is without foundation, but I want the truth and nothing but the truth. Do I make myself clear?"

"Yes, sir." He could make a guess at what was coming. His

whole future was hanging in the balance, and waves of shock were coursing through him.

"I had to remind you once before of the rules of apprenticeship, which strictly forbid fornication. Do you recall my words?"

"I do."

"Then let me put this to you. Have you any reason to suppose you might be the cause of Master Needham's sister, Hester, being in a state of pregnancy?"

There was only one reply that could be given. John's jaw set rigidly, a nerve leaping on one side. "I am responsible."

The statement seemed to echo in the quiet office. Jack's features congested menacingly and again he shifted his weight, checked once more by Master Harwood, whose own expression had become savagely hostile. "From what I have been told, you have abandoned the girl. Is that correct?"

John felt a rush of anger at whatever twist of circumstances had defeated the conspiracy of silence that he and Hester had hoped to maintain. "Hester is my wife. We were married three months ago at the Fleet."

He watched out of his own fury and despair the reaction of the two men in front of him. Both were astonished, Jack immediately mollified to a degree, Master Harwood developing a gleam of murder in his eyes while he spoke in a controlled and deadly manner.

"Well, Bateman, that information will have changed everything for Master Needham." He turned in his chair to address Jack with no change of tone. "I suggest you return to the Heathcock now. There will be an opportunity for you to talk to your new brother-in-law later. At the present time I want to continue this interview on my own with him. He is still my apprentice."

Jack had no choice but to leave. He stood, looked uncertainly at John and then bowed to Master Harwood. "I trust this affair will make no difference to your esteemed patronage of my tavern—"

"Good day to you."

"Er—good day, sir."

No sooner had the door closed when Master Harwood gave full vent to his wrath. "Not only have you disobeyed me, Bateman, but you have deceived my daughter! You accepted my hospitality under false colours. As a married man, you continued to play with

Caroline's affections, leading her to believe, as I did, that your intentions towards her were trustworthy and honourable. What have you to say about that?"

"Caroline was under no illusion. We are friends and I value that friendship."

"The devil you do! At least there is an end to it now and she'll be the better for being rid of you." Pushing back his chair, he got up and went to a filing cupboard. He took from it a parchment document that John recognised as his contract of apprenticeship.

"I have only a short time left to serve!" he exclaimed hoarsely.

Master Harwood unfolded the contract and held it open wide as he looked menacingly at it. "Three months and two weeks and one day, to be exact." Then deliberately he tore the contract in two.

John gave a furious roar of protest. "No!"

With equal anger, his hard face flushed and nostrils dilated, Harwood shook one half of the contract at him. "By your marriage you forfeited your right ever to be a master craftsman! And I promise you that I shall see to it that the registration of your apprenticeship with me is erased from all records as if it had never been! What's more, I shall personally get you blacklisted from any workshop of renown in the whole of London. Now pack your belongings and get off my premises before I have you thrown out."

John had never felt hatred for another human being before now. Even in the heat of the moment he could accept that the termination had been brought about by his own actions, but the humiliation and further penalties inflicted on him were a sheer injustice, a total misuse of power by a vengeful man. His grandfather's rearing came to the fore without him being aware of it. He bowed as gentlemen did at the time of defeat, his dignity totally unimpaired, untouched and uncontaminated by the questionable tactics of his adversary. Square-shouldered, he went from the room.

Anyone glancing up as he went through the workshop was able to see by his gaunt expression that some disaster had occurred. Opening his tool-box, he began to pack away his tools, taking them from his workbench and from the racks on the wall nearby. They were the most precious possessions of any craftsman, having such meaning to those who worked in precious metals that they were only ever bequeathed to another of equal talent. His had been brand new, a gift from his grandfather at the start of his apprentice-ship, and they had become part of his hands, an extension of his fingers and his brain, the fount of his skills. Now he would be an ordinary journeyman for rest of his life, like thousands of others in his trade, able to register his punchmark if ever he should have the finance to set himself up as a goldsmith, but without the prestige of the Freedom, which he had lost for ever. And for what? An un-timely rush of passion for a girl whom he could have possessed at any later date and whose face he could barely call to mind at the present angry moment, not having seen her for over three months.

"Has the old man really given you the boot?" It was Robin, who had come from another part of the workshop, his broad face bear-ing a look of baffled disbelief. "Why? What happened?"

"He found out that I'm a married man."

"What?" Robin's yell of astonishment was lost in the rattle of treadles worked by the women on nearby polishing machines. He followed John into his living quarters, gesticulating wildly. "Who's the girl? Is it Hester Needham? When did this happen?"

John gave him a short explanation as he packed his clothes and other belongings into a valise. "You'd better get back to your bench," he advised, "or else you'll be in trouble. I can't take my books with me now. There are too many. I'd appreciate it if you would bring them to me as soon as I have an address."

"Willingly, my friend." Robin shook hands with him solemnly. "I know I speak for Tom too when I wish you luck."

"I thank you."

John shouldered his tool-box, and with his valise in his other hand he walked back through the workshop. Everyone watched him go. Tom, unable to leave a piece of work that was at a vital stage, gave him a comprehending nod from a distance. Somebody opened the door for him. Instead of turning for the flagged pas-sageway that was the route out of the house used by those em-ployed in the workshop, he went on into the main entrance hall. Since he was leaving after nearly seven years, it should be with some grace. He would write to Caroline later. Her shock over this turn of events would be as great as his, for she had his well-being at heart.

It was for this reason, in spite of Hester's decision that nobody should be told, that he had disclosed his marriage to Caroline. He had not felt able, in all honour, to let her go on believing that something might come eventually from their close relationship. She had reacted with extraordinary courage and without spite or vindictiveness of any kind, for that was not in her nature and he knew it. He had also known she would keep his secret, for she was an exceptional woman in every way. Another letter he would have to write was one that he dreaded to pen, knowing what a bitter disappointment it would be to his grandfather to learn that after all the sacrifices made on his behalf, he had thrown his whole career away.

He crossed the entrance hall and swung his toolbox down from his shoulder to open the door and lift it through onto the top step outside. Before he had time to close the door after him Caroline called his name, coming at a run from the direction of the stairs. She crossed the threshold in a rush and flung herself against him, full of distress.

"I just heard. Oh, my dearest John! I feel I've failed you somehow. I should have found a home for your wife somewhere in the country and then nobody would have discovered your secret marriage until the time was safe."

He held her by the waist, looking fondly at her. "It's too late to think of that now. Most probably the result would have been the same. The truth has a way of coming out if fate has decreed it."

"What will you do? Where will you go?"

"In spite of your father's threats, I'll find work somewhere."

Her head sank forward onto his chest. "How I shall miss you!"

"I shall miss you."

She raised her distraught face again. "Let us see each other again sometimes."

"That will happen. I don't intend to leave London."

Abruptly she linked her fingers behind his neck and used her weight to jerk his lips down to hers as she propelled herself upwards, her kiss of farewell ardent and abandoned, awakening the same response in him for all that had been between them. Then, with a sob, she flung herself away from him into the house, the door swinging shut after her.

With a sigh he shouldered his tool-box again and took up his baggage to go down the steps and turn right along the pavement. A heavily pregnant young woman was leaning in exhaustion against the railings. It crossed his mind that she must have caught every word that was said even as recognition dawned. "Hester!"

All her hair was hidden under an ugly grey laundry cap, and her face, puffy in her pregnancy, was patchy in colour from her breathless state, her hand pressed to her side. She looked bulky and awkward; the unsightly bulge thrusting out her washerwoman's apron made her appear out of proportion. Throughout their separation he had pictured her as he saw her last. Now it was as if he were viewing her through a piece of distorted glass.

"Jack found out about us," she explained unnecessarily, struggling against the stitch in her side. It had plagued her most of the way from the tavern, slowing her progress. When she had spotted him coming out of the Harwood establishment she had found the strength to run the last few yards, the presence of his baggage showing her that she had arrived too late. Her one thought had been to comfort him. Then she had been stopped in her tracks by Caroline's sudden appearance and all that had ensued. "I had hoped to get here in time to tell Jack we were married. I failed." Anguish twisted down the corners of her mouth. They were facing each other like strangers instead of reaching out their arms. He had not even set down his possessions. She closed her eyes and turned her face away, continuing to clutch the railings for support. "I'm sorry."

"No one's to blame, you least of all." He up-ended his tool-box onto the pavement. "Sit on this for a few minutes and rest. Did you hurry all the way from the Heathcock? That wasn't good for you." He took her arm and helped her to the seat, which she accepted thankfully. "As soon as you feel rested, I'll see you back there."

Her head shot up, her eyes alarmed. "I'm never going back to live in the tavern again! My place is with you." Fumbling in her pocket, she brought out her wedding ring and pushed it onto the finger of her laundry-reddened hand.

Her action made him feel trapped as never before. He tried persuasion. "It would be best for you to stay at the Heathcock until after the baby is born. I have no work, no roof and only a few shillings in my pocket. I may have to sleep rough for days, even weeks perhaps."

She was bewildered. "Why should that be? With your education there will be openings for you in banking, merchandise and insurance and much else that you will know of better than I."

His eyes were steely on her. He was appalled that she should have so little understanding of him. Although Caroline had questioned him, she had known without voicing it that he would continue in his craft along a lower path. "First, I should need letters of introduction and recommendation, and I have neither. Second, I would never desert my skills. They are part of me. I'll live and die a worker in precious metals. Nobody could ever persuade me to do otherwise."

It was a warning to her not even to try, and she accepted it, swallowing hard, aware that she was fighting for her very existence, for if she let him go now they might never come together again. "I'm your wife. I'm going to be at your side always. If we have to sleep in a park, that won't matter to me as long as I'm with you. But it should not come to that. I have a little money saved, which should be enough to keep us housed until you get work."

Immediately she saw she had made another mistake. That curious arrogance peculiar to the upper classes, which she had never previously glimpsed in him, came to the fore. "Do you imagine I should allow us to stay in accommodation for which I was personally unable to pay?"

"But as your wife, everything I have is yours. Think of my small savings as my dowry, since I have nothing else." To her relief, that appeared to be acceptable to him. The stitch in her side eased and she gave him a little smile. "I feel better now, and so will you when we have organised ourselves. Let's start looking for a place straight away, and afterwards we'll visit the Heathcock to collect my belongings."

He was too raw from his dismissal to be touched by her optimism, too ripped apart to be heartened by a few encouraging words. Her determined presence weighed him down, and his lost bachelorhood seemed like a sweet dream. Without intending it, he spoke brusquely. "Let's go then if you're ready."

They found a room with a hearth in a slum street off the London Wall. It was on an upper floor in an old house nudged on either side by Tudor buildings that had escaped the Great Fire, one of them shored up by heavy beams. As with all such streets, a stinking drain ran down the length of it and was filthy with rotting rubbish and slops thrown out by the inhabitants of the dismal dwellings. If Hester quailed at the prospect of living there she did not show it. Instead she looked around the room, ignored the dirty straw left by the previous tenant and pushed aside a broken chair.

"There's nothing here that a broom and soap and water can't put right. Just make sure there's a good sound lock on the door. We don't want your tool-box stolen when we go to fetch my things."

The lock was broken. She left him to repair it and went alone to the Heathcock, where the midday rush was on. It spared her from seeing Martha, who was busy supervising the dining room. Jack, sighting her, left the bar to draw her into his office with the inevitable question.

"Why didn't you tell me you were legally wed?" he blustered, seeking to ward off any recriminations for his blunder and showing himself hurt by her deception.

She could never let him know that although she was as fond of him as a sister could be, his wits were too dull for him to keep anything from Martha, whom she could never trust. "We can talk over all that another time. You are busy and I have to get back to a room that John and I have rented." After telling him where it was and answering a few of his questions, she made a request. "Some surplus furniture from my mother's home has been stored in the attic since I came here. May I have it?"

"I'll get it brought down for you today and delivered in the wagon."

After packing her belongings together, she left them to be transported in the wagon together with some bed linen and other items Jack had told her she might have as a wedding present in addition to his gift of five guineas, which she put in her purse. She left the tavern carrying a bucket, soap and other cleaning utensils. As soon as she arrived back at what was now their home, John went out to look for work before Master Harwood's black-listing should take effect. He had not been idle in her absence. She found that as well as clearing out the straw and litter, he had set a cauldron of water to boil over a fire of sticks from the broken chair and put a stack of more fuel by the hearth. A she began washing down the walls, she thought that they had not yet even kissed each other.

It was late evening when he returned, and he halted in surprise on the threshold of the room as he saw its transformation. Everything was clean and it was furnished with a table and chairs, two cupboards, a dresser with pewter plates and some china. A four-poster bed was made up under a red quilt in the corner and a rug was spread on the scrubbed floor. On the table a savoury meal awaited him.

"I feel I must have come to the wrong address," he said in praise as she came forward to help him off with this greatcoat. She had bathed and changed after her housework, which had caused her considerable tiredness from all she had done. No ugly laundry cap now but the rich tones of her hair catching the candlelight, her figure under a soft white apron no longer as grotesque as it had appeared earlier.

"Did you have any luck?" she asked tentatively.

He nodded. "With a goldsmith named Feline in Rose Street, Covent Garden. He's a registered large-worker, which means he produces tureens, punch bowls, table centre-pieces and other articles of size, some on a really grand scale."

"That's splendid!"

"I was frank with him. He might have looked on me less favourably if he hadn't had a rush of orders to be filled. He said that any man trained by Master Harwood to my length of service should be able to produce the work he wanted. Inevitably he won't pay me a journeyman's wages until I have proved myself, which is fair enough."

"That shouldn't take long," she stated confidently. "Sit down now. Supper is ready."

He was hungry and appreciated the quick and simple dish she had prepared. It helped ease the atmosphere between them as they talked, although an invisible barrier remained in the devastation of his career, particularly when they discussed their financial situation. In view of what he was to earn, every farthing would count, and it would take all her conniving and inventiveness to keep them adequately fed on what could be spared for food.

"I can make a good soup from a nail if needs be," she boasted humourously. Her joke fell flat. He found it too close to a possibility to be amusing. To her everything ahead of them was a challenge. He failed to see it in the same light.

"The five guineas from your brother must be kept for emergencies," he said, looking up from the paper on which he had been jotting down figures. "I shall bank it to gain some small interest by whatever channel is available."

She would have preferred to see the food cupboard full of stores and a new pair of shoes on his feet to keep out the wet, but she supposed his caution was to be commended. And she wished that whenever a silence fell between them it could have been one of harmony and not of awkwardness.

When it came to preparing for bed, a dreadful shyness about her swollen figure overcame her. She thought she would never forget the dismay in his eyes when he had turned after Caroline's departure to see her leaning for support against the railings. The fact that he had not made the least affectionate gesture towards her bore out that in her pregnancy she had lost all her charm for him. More than that was her conviction that in the intervening months since their wedding day, Caroline had reestablished her hold over him. What she had witnessed had been evidence of deep feeling on both sides. No matter what developed in the future, she would never be able to dismiss wholly the conviction that if it had not been for the conception of their baby, John might never have married her.

He was first into bed when she was still in her petticoats, and he lay watching her. She turned away from him but sensed his gaze. "Please snuff the candle," she requested in her embarrassment.

He did as she requested. The rosy glow of the fire engulfed her instead, more than she realised. He watched her last petticoat fall and glimpsed her white back and the lovely curve of her buttocks before her billowing nightgown enveloped her. Then came one of the most seductive actions any woman could make in the unpinning of her hair and shaking it free. Taking up her brush, she gave it a certain number of strokes before coming towards the bed. He shifted over to make room for her, his arm ready to enfold her. She closed the bed-curtains after her against draughts and lay down beside him.

"You can't—" she whispered.

"I know," he said softly. "I just want to hold you. For four months you've been on your own, facing heaven knows what slights and insults. You'll never be alone again. In future I'll always be here to protect you and to provide to the best of my ability for you and our child."

She was comforted to a degree but still yearning for words of love. "I'll always be a good wife to you."

"I'm sure you will. Forgive me for any strangeness I may have shown towards you today. It was the worst day in my life. I think for a while I wasn't quite sane. If I caused you any hurt I do regret it."

She turned to him within the circle of his arm. "That is in the past already. We must look to the future."

"I love you, Hester." He meant it. He had never stopped loving her even though circumstances had convened against it. If Caroline still lingered with him it was in a separate capacity, not for Hester to know or for him to think about. In the warm darkness of the bed he sought her loving mouth with his own, drawing her to him in a close embrace. Suddenly he drew away from her in surprise. "I felt the baby kick against me!"

She laughed quietly. "He kicks me all the time."

"Is it a boy then?" he questioned with a chuckle in his voice.

"That's what a firstborn should be."

There was a long pause. "Let me see."

Another pause. Then almost inaudibly she whispered, "If that is what you wish."

He knelt up and stretched across her to hitch a bed-curtain aside on its rings. The fire's glow was sufficient as he folded back her nightgown. Gently he put his hands on the rise of her belly and felt the life within. "He's strong," he said in awe.

"You see," she mocked gently. "You think it's a boy, too."

"No doubt of it." He leaned forward to kiss her as he drew her nightgown into place again. As they settled for the night, her last thought before sleeping was that somehow she would make up to him for his shattered career and his diminished financial outlook, for he could never hope now for the riches that might have become his as a master craftsman with his own business. She would also try to compensate for whatever else he might have had if she had not disrupted his life by coming between him and Caroline in the first instance.

John worked three weeks at the Feline workshop before Harwood's black-listing caught up with him. As he received his wages, he was given notice.

"I'm sorry to let you go, Bateman," his employer said, "but I owe your former master a favour and I can't ignore his wishes. I'm willing to give you written commendation of the work you have already done for me, which should be of some help to you."

In spite of this reference, given with the best of intentions, John met with a shake of a head at every workshop he visited. Whether there were genuinely no vacancies, or if the black-listing was responsible, he had no way of knowing. Finally he managed to secure work at wire-drawing, the branch of goldsmithing that had no appeal for him.

Yet the work had a curious kind of beauty, for it was often easier to wind the fine gleaming wire around one's body instead of directly onto spools, which gave him the illusion many times of being wrapped about the waist with lengths of gold and silver hair. Unlike Master Feline, who had been prepared to pay journeyman's wages as soon as his skills had been recognised, his present employer was unscrupulous and had not hesitated to take advantage of his position as a former apprentice with broken indentures desperate for work. His wages were miserably low.

One evening Tom and Robin came to supper, bringing his books with them. Hester served a tasty broth and the evening was a pleasant one. Yet he was glad when they went, for what little he had had in common with them was gone. He was married with responsibilities and they were free men set to reach the summits of goldsmithing that were lost to him. After seeing them off the premises, he returned to find Hester contemplating the stacks of books for which they really had no space.

"Why not sell them?" she suggested practically. She was finding their room difficult enough to keep clean, dust forever flying from the cracks around the old beams and floorboards, without having this stack of musty-looking books to look after as well. "If you've read them you surely don't need to keep them, do you?"

"Indeed I do!" He crouched to pick out one and then another at random. It was like welcoming old friends back into his life, something it was impossible to explain to Hester, who had no appreciation of books. He found it sad that her bright and lively mind had been deprived of the gift of reading. At some convenient later date, when her mind was less preoccupied with baby matters, he would teach her himself. He was convinced she would be a ready pupil.

She had drawn away from him, biting her lip at his unconsciously abrupt reply, and busied herself putting away the supper dishes she had washed. It was obvious that books were to him what her favourite sketches were to her. It was extraordinary how marriage highlighted differences that were less noticeable during the passion of courtship. The simple education she had received from her mother was no match for his intellectual grounding. Her love and obedience and caring were not enough, and somehow she must find a way to meet his mind with her own. If not, the spectre of Caroline would continue to haunt their marriage for years to come.

One morning in early March, which happened to be Hester's own natal day, she was setting bread and cheese on the table for their breakfast when she suddenly doubled over. It was as if a knife had been driven into her. She sank down into the nearest chair and managed a lop-sided smile as John peered anxiously into her face.

"You'd better call in at the midwife's house on your way to work."

"I can't leave you today!"

"You must go to work. Don't be foolish. It will be hours before anything happens. I shall be in good hands."

It was the longest working day he had ever known. He came home in the evening to find the door barred against him by the midwife, and Hester in the final throes of her ordeal. He paced the landing, listening helplessly to the agonised sounds within. Finally he heard the baby's cry. Even then he had to wait to be admitted until the midwife finished all she had to do, although she did have the rough grace to shout through the door that it was a boy.

Three weeks later at the end of March the baptism took place at the Church of All Hallows. Hester had wanted their son to be named after John, to which he agreed in order to please her, although it was his wish that his grandfather's name should be given. She compromised by addressing the child as John-Joseph in a term of affection, which was gradually reduced to the diminutive of Joss and the name stayed with him.

Chapter 5

Until the birth of her son, Hester had had no real qualms about where they were living. It was the best they could afford and it was pointless to be depressed by the petty theft and other nefarious activities that went on in the neighbourhood. There were far worse slum areas where every kind of vicious crime took place and it was unsafe to walk abroad by either night or day. At least in her street the beadles, who kept the peace armed only with a stave, were not afraid to walk singly, and even the night watchman would pause at the end house to shout the hour and that all was well. She also had a good neighbour, a middle-aged woman who lived opposite, and they often passed the time of day.

Nevertheless, she was not content. She was fearful that Joss would pick up some infection, for sicknesses could float through the air in such places, and however clean she kept her own room, the surrounding squalid conditions were a constant threat. Where she had been used to the clean-swept length and breadth of the Strand, here the street was narrow enough for those in the overhang of the Tudor houses almost to shake hands from opposite sides if they had wished it, and she often had to wear wooden pattens on her feet to keep her skirt hems free of the rotting refuse. When summer came it was impossible to open a window unless a kindly wind was blowing. At times the stench in the house outside her room was as bad as anything in the street, for some of the other tenants chucked out onto their landings almost as much garbage as they threw with their slops from the windows.

From first moving in she had put bowls of potpourri in the rooms to keep the air fragrant and she replenished them whenever she took Joss to one of the parks, because there were always daisies and buttercups and sweet clover that defied the gardeners in the grass and freshly fallen rose petals for the gathering. These she dried and mixed with fine wood shavings, which absorbed the aromatic oils. Together with lavender, which could be bought for almost nothing from street vendors, as well as sprigs of rosemary, thyme, sage and lemon balm, cloves and juniper berries, it was easy to make up variations that her mother had taught her long ago. She trusted in them to keep disease at bay.

Another worry constantly was that of money. Between them she and John accounted for every farthing. He took nothing for himself out of his meagre wages, and she was often ashamed of herself for speaking sharply to him at times when she was at her wit's end to know how to put enough food on the table to keep hunger at bay. If anything she was even sharper if Joss was at all sickly or had cried at length for some reason she had been unable to define.

Although John bore her outbursts tolerantly, she could see he was harassed by them. At times she almost wished he would shout back at her, giving her full rein to flare up and relieve her tensions, but he never did. She would never have believed it possible that at times it could be difficult living with a peace-loving man, but it was, particularly for one of her fiery temperament. The only time she had ever seen him in a temper was the day they had quarrelled over Caroline and almost lost each other in the process. She never wanted that to happen again.

On the grapevine, John heard of a vacancy for a craftsman in a back-street workshop in Whitechapel. When he applied there it was as he had hoped—too insignificant to have received Harwood's blacklist. On the debit side, he could see at once that the work was not of the style and standard to which he had been accustomed in his days at the good workbench. The goldsmith, who was old and tetchy, was a small-worker, which had nothing to do with the size of his premises and meant his line was in salts, candle-snuffers, snuff-boxes and similar items. The wages he offered were lower by a shilling than those John was receiving as a wire drawer, and he discussed with Hester whether or not he should make the move.

"Take the new job," she encouraged, thinking that it would not be long before Joss was weaned and she would be earning herself, a project she intended to voice when she had found the right kind of work. "It's a good move for you. Far better to advance from your own sphere when Master Harwood's ban begins to ebb elsewhere with time."

"I thought that was what you would say." He was proud of her. There were many times when he wished he could have taken her and Joss to Staffordshire to meet his grandfather, who would have been well pleased with them both, but employers did not give time off for anything except a death in the family and in any case the expense, at present, was out of the question. Fortunately he was able to write at regular intervals, as he had always done since leaving home. The heavy cost of postage would have been restrictive if his grandfather had not always paid it upon receipt of the letters.

Joss was finally weaned. Hester had made enquiries as to what employment was available in the district and was ready with her plans on the winter evening she broached the subject to John. He was smoking his long-stemmed clay pipe on one side of the hearth and she sat opposite him, her head bent over a grey woollen stocking of his that she was darning.

"I know Jack would take me on any time at the Heathcock," she began conversationally, "but Martha wouldn't and I'd never give her the satisfaction of refusing me. I hear there's a vacancy for a waiting maid at the Red Lion. It's not far away and the wages and tips should be good there. Mrs. Burleigh will mind Joss for me."

John lowered his pipe and shook his head smilingly. "You can't do that. It's a brave idea, but not to be considered."

"Why not?" She gave him a quick glance before returning her gaze to her task, hoping he was not going to be difficult. It was why she had chosen what she believed to be a good moment, and now he had made her feel uncertain and ill at ease. "You know we can only scrape along on your wages." It was not the most tactful way to express her long-held concern about money, but it had been building up in her over a long period and now tension had caused her to blurt out the hard truth. "What I'd be able to earn would make all the difference. What is your objection?"

He sounded surprised that she should even ask. "You're my wife, sweeting."

She did not need an endearment to remind her of that. Their bed was a domain of joy and pleasure to them both. She would never have suspected from their first meeting that such an outwardly quiet man could have been capable of such tremendous passion. He had awakened her flesh to delights that just to think about sent a tingle running through her. "The Red Lion is a walk away and a well-run place. I'll be perfectly safe working there, if that is what's worrying you."

"I'm not convinced about that, but it's beside the point. Bateman wives," he explained patiently, "have always contented themselves with their children and domestic duties even after the family fortunes changed for the worst."

Her needle, which had been keeping a regular rhythm across the wooden darning mushroom, suddenly jerked its thread tight. "Dignified poverty is easier to maintain in the country, where a garden yields every kind of vegetable and it's always possible to get cheap meat for salting down in the autumn slaughtering. I know that from experience. London is a different kettle of fish. What's more, it's full of wives allowed by their husbands to bring in extra money by honest toil. The fortunate ones have careers in their own right, such as the female apothecary in St. Martin's Lane and the women goldsmiths with their own establishments, quite apart from those who are shop and tavern keepers or run establishments of lace-making, dress-making, mantus-making and so forth. How would decent widows left with families to support be able to survive if they didn't exert their legal right to take over their late partners' businesses and run them with equal efficiency? Don't speak to me of Bateman women. They were ladies born and I'm not."

"You are to me."

It was lovingly said. At any other time she would have melted and gone across to sit on his lap for the kissing and cuddling that invariably ended on the floor in the firelight. But this evening her ire was up and still rising like the temperature of a furnace that could not be banked down. Her needle dug in and out, cobbling what had begun as a perfect darn.

"That doesn't alter anything. If you don't want me to do tavern work, I'll do something else. There are always openings for confectionery cooks, laundry hands, sewing women and lots more that my training at the Heathcock equipped me for." She was daring him to deny her this compromise and was ready to explode if he did.

"I've been selfish." He tapped out his pipe against the brickwork of the hearth. "No more money shall go on my tobacco."

His self-sacrifice enraged her. Her head shot up and, spoiling for a fight, she hurled her darning down on the floor. "The few pence you use for a pipe two or three times a week aren't going to put beef on our table or clothes on our backs."

His whole face took on a stiff look. "Do you imagine that your earnings would?"

"They would help provide."

"At what cost? Joss at the mercy of a stranger and you making a slave of yourself."

"Mrs. Burleigh is a kindly neighbour who has known better days. I would trust Joss to her implicitly."

"That's as may be. I just won't have it." In spite of himself anger at Hester's hostile persistence had begun its dreaded surge in him.

She threw up her hands in exasperation. "For mercy's sake stop thinking of yourself as a gentleman. That's the root of your argument. I know it's bred in the bone and hard for you to shake off, but try to be practical. We're a working couple with a baby to rear, not landed gentry with servants in a country mansion."

"I don't need to have that said to me." His voice shook on the violence of his temper as it broke forth, carrying with it the pent-up stress that had plagued him over the past months. "You've made a little haven here in the midst of ugliness, but do you imagine a day passes without my wishing I could give you and Joss a better home? I loathe our surroundings!" He jerked himself to his feet and stepped foward into the middle of the room, shaking his fists in frustration at the ceiling and the walls. "I detest this creaking house that is full of noise and drunkenness and brawling. It offends my whole nature to be living in environs devoid of any artistic or aesthetic influence with prostitution taking place under our windows and foul-mouthed language the common tongue of all but a few in this rat-infested slum!"

"A grand statement!" She was on her feet, too. Their raised voices had awakened Joss, who gave a loud wail from his cradle. "Yet you're not prepared to let me help to ease the burden until our fortunes change."

He whirled about to face her. "You once said that you'd take pride in bearing the name of Bateman. Has that gone since I lost all I had originally hoped to achieve?"

"No! That's a grossly unfair suggestion!"

"Then accept that I cannot allow my wife to work in a public place. However much you may decry it, it would go against all the traditions by which I was raised if I did not carry the sole responsibility for you and our son."

She was aghast at his stand, feeling as if she were hammering against a glass wall that made it impossible to get through to him. It made her voice a retort she might otherwise have left unsaid. "You seem to forget you held out no such objection to my working at the Heathcock when your future at the Harwood workshop was at stake. I was as much your wife then as I am now."

He flushed crimson, his eyes sharp and glittering. "That was your misfortune. It remains your misfortune to be married to me. I failed you once, as you have reminded me, but I'll not fail you again. There'll be more money coming into this home soon, I promise you!"

He flung himself out of the room, and seconds later the street door slammed after him. Joss's demanding cries took her to the cradle and she picked him up to hold him to her. She was still fuming as she made all the usual soothing sounds that settle a baby down and was somehow angered still further by John having forgotten to put on his greatcoat on such a cold night. Joss took a long time to go to sleep again, probably because of her tense mood, and when she laid him back on his pillow, anxiety began to set in. Where had John gone? He had seemed to be off on some mission when he left, leaving that wild promise behind him. She retrieved her darning from the floor, but was too agitated to do any more that evening. One hour and then another went by. It was a wild, windy night and the house seemed to be protesting its buffeting in the groaning of its timbers. In such weather it almost swayed under the pressure of neighbouring buildings that were shored against it. She went constantly to the window. Once she heard the watchman cry the hour. It was ten o'clock and everything far from well as far as she was concerned. She undressed and made ready for bed yet did no more than turn back the covers, drawn again to the window.

It was almost midnight when he came home. There was no more

anger in either of them, but he looked drawn and haggard and was a far distance from her.

"Our financial worries are alleviated for the time being," he said without expression. "I went to see someone I know and he has agreed to take me on in his workshop."

"You haven't left goldsmithing?" There was something about this change of work, made abruptly and with apparent ease, that filled her with misgivings.

"Far from it. Now let us to bed. The hour is late."

That night, and for several nights afterwards, a space remained in the bed between them. Eventually, each as miserable as the other in their estrangement, they drew together again and he held her close to him.

"Forgive me, Hester. You were right to say all you did. It haunts me that I virtually abandoned you at the Heathcock for four months of our lives, which we should have spent together. It takes some men time to shake off bachelorhood and I was guilty of that. If I could have my time over again there would be no parting at the gates of the Fleet."

"I don't hold that against you." Her hands smoothed his face and hair and throat and chest, starved of contact with him. "It was my decision too."

They made up with love-making the rift that had been between them. Afterwards, everything was outwardly as it had been before. The cause of their quarrel was not raised again, and he never talked about his work. His wages proved to be double what they had been before, and her relief at being able to buy a few of the things she needed urgently for Joss and for themselves was marred by her feeling that it was in some way contaminated money. She knew from all he had told her that the goldsmithing world had its share of rogues who falsified gold and silver content, dealt in stolen plate that was quickly melted down, found innumerable ways to dodge the duty of sixpence an ounce on silver and were up to all manner of other tricks that reputable craftsmen scorned. If John had not been the man he was, she would have suspected him of having become part of these nefarious dealings, but however desperate she had inadvertently made him about money, she knew he would never resort to such measures.

She had her first inkling as to what his new work involved when she did the laundry. It was his habit to change his shirt every day, and now as she plunged the shirts into the suds it was not the odour of clean, honest sweat that rose from them before they were fully immersed, but a curious, almost acidy smell that she could not identify. When she asked him what new materials he was using, he brushed her question aside with some vague reply, as he did every time she tried to discuss his work. She also noted there was a new kind of stain on his fingers that scrubbing would not remove.

Her worry never left her, which was why enlightenment came at an unexpected moment when she was buying vegetables in the market. By chance a clatter on the next stall caught her attention, and she saw that a stack of cheap metal bowls ornamented with imitation gilding had slipped forward. That was it! Gilding! He had become a gilder. All the evidence immediately added up; gilding was the most dreaded branch of the goldsmiths' trade for health reasons. She felt almost faint and dropped back onto the stall from nerveless fingers the bunch of leeks that she had intended to purchase. Turning away, Joss a heavy weight balanced on her hip, she moved as if in a daze to cover the long walk to John's place of work.

She knew all about the gilding process, for until recently John had encouraged her interest in goldsmithing until there was little she had not learned about it. Thin plates of gold were melted and three or four times its weight of mercury was poured into the same crucible, producing an amalgam of butter-like substance. With the fingers it was smoothed over the workpiece to be gilded, which in turn was held over a charcoal fire until the mercury evaporated, leaving the gold. Then it was cleaned and polished. It was in the fumes of the evaporating mercury that the terrible danger lay. It attacked the lungs with devastating results. Few gilders lived long, and John had taken on this deadly work because she had driven him to it.

If she needed confirmation as to her correct deduction it was on the sign suspended over the doorway of his place of work. *Charles Hardcastle, Burnisher and Gilder.* It was work almost every goldsmith contracted out, for the fumes spread wide. She sat on a wall to wait, keeping Joss satisfied with a baked crust she had carried wrapped in her pocket.

At midday the workers came out into the air to eat their noon pieces. It was a poor street and there was nobody around to object to their lolling about or sprawling on the ground to rest. She was filled with horror and pity. Many coughed as they came out into the air, and some had a skeletal look, as if their days were already numbered. There were some haggard-faced women among them. Recent recruits looked well enough, their time yet to come, and in the midst of them was John. He saw her at once and came to her, resigned that she had discovered him.

"Not this!" she exclaimed imploringly.

As if afraid the fumes might still he hanging about him, he made no attempt to touch her or their son. "Go home, Hester."

"Come with me! Don't return to that hell-hole!"

"We'll talk in the evening." He turned away to rejoin his fellow workers, and she had no choice but to do as he had bidden her.

She was out of sight by the time he went back into the workshop, his noon piece eaten and some fresh air in his lungs. There was no better method of covering metal with a thin film of gold than fire-gilding, and it gave a pretty look to the insides of silver-caskets, boxes, cruets, cups and bowls. Not many people outside the trade knew the high cost of this ornamentation that was greatly in demand.

He picked up his leather helmet and put it over his face and head. It had a breathing tube that went over his shoulder to escape inhaling the worst of the fumes. He found it hot and uncomfortable to work in, and it was his experience that the obnoxious vapour still leaked in. Yet he and his fellow gilders in this place were fortunate to be provided with this innovation; he had seen some pathetic homemade headgear in his time that gilders had struggled with, hoping to maintain their working lives. Therefore he could say he was better off in this workshop than he would have been in most other places in the gilding trade, although he did not think Hester would view it in that light.

She did not. In spite of her heartfelt persuasion that evening, he would not budge in his determination to go on working there.

Rosalind Laker

"The pay is good," he replied doggedly, "and we need the extra money."

They were eating together, and he noticed she appeared to have lost all her appetite, pushing the food around on her plate with her fork. "The wages are only high because it is such dangerous work," she persisted.

"I admit that." He helped himself to another slice of bread to eat with his meat. "It should do me no harm for a while."

"I'm sure every minute of every hour with those fumes is deadly!"

At that moment a crumb caught in his throat, making him cough. Hester, thinking the gilders' malady was already upon him, dropped her fork with a clatter, white to the lips. He took a quick gulp of ale to wash the crumb away and, his breath recovered, made a promise out of compassion to settle the worst of her fears.

"I'll return to some minor goldsmiths' workshop after six months of gilding if nothing better turns up in the meantime. By then we'll have saved enough to tide us over for a while."

She had to be content with that, for he would agree to nothing more. Luckily for her peace of mind, he was spared the gilding work after another month when Robin, fresh from registering his mark, his indentures at an end, called one evening with some good news.

"I'm going to work for a well-established goldsmith, Master Barton, in Holborn, next door to the Cross Keys tavern. There's a vacancy for a worker, not at the bench that I've been given, but with prospects for the right man. I've spoken for you; there was a favourable response. If you're interested, be there tomorrow morning at seven o'clock."

"I'm interested indeed!" John shook his head appreciatively. "There's only one possible snag. I met Master Barton and his wife and daughter several times at the Harwood Sunday dinners. He may have forgotten my name, but he'll surely remember me face to face and recall that I've been banned."

"Have no fear. He does remember you already. If he had you on a black list he must have torn it up. He and his family no longer dine with the Harwoods. Masters Barton and Harwood fell out a while ago through rivalry over certain civic commissions."

"I'll be at the Holborn workshop tomorrow morning and take my chance in any case. Thank you, my friend."

On the first evening he came home from working in Holborn, she heard the difference in his step before he flung open the door, smiling and exuberant as a schoolboy home for the holidays. "Hester! Such splendid pieces are made there. As yet I'm only on routine work, but I'll reach the major benches before long."

She rushed to him and they hugged each other. "I'm so glad," she rejoiced.

It proved to be as he had anticipated. His work as an exceptional craftsman was recognised after a short time, and a range of fine work was put to his creative talent. He was earning twenty-four shillings a week, which meant that a little could be put by again. Just when it seemed they were on the crest of a wave, Hester found herself facing a new turn of events that reawakened old fears.

"By the way," John said one evening, deliberately on a casual note, "Caroline was at the Barton place today. Apparently she visits quite often."

Suddenly alert to every nuance in his voice, Hester continued to search for cotton thread of a certain colour in her sewing-box. "I thought the two families were not on good terms."

"The girls have remained staunch friends in spite of the differences between their fathers."

"Who told you that? Robin?"

"No, I heard it from Caroline herself."

Hester thought her heart stopped. "You've spoken to her?"

"Yes, today, for the first time, although I have glimpsed her a couple of times through an open door. Then this morning she came to speak to Robin and happened to see me."

The thread she wanted had come to light. "You haven't mentioned seeing her before."

"It must have slipped my mind." He opened the newspaper, which he could now afford to buy once a week, and began to read, putting an end to the conversation. Hester found her hands were shaking too much to put the thread through the eye of her needle.

The day came when he was late home and the mutton stew she had prepared, which was one of his favourite dishes, had burned at the bottom of the pot. "I was delayed," he explained, washing his hands and face in the bowl of warm water she always had ready for him. "Caroline happened to come out of the Bartons' residential doorway when I was making for home. We walked part of the way together. She had heard praise of my work in the Barton household and wanted to know more about the set of salvers I'm making."

With supreme effort she held back a retort, biting the inside of her lip until it bled, and her hands tightened their grip on the ladle she was holding until the knuckles turned white. The enemy was moving in. Men were so gullible in such matters, unable to see when a combination of charm and flattery was leading them by the nose. What perfect timing on Caroline's part, not only in arranging a social departure to coincide with the home-going of the craftsmen, but in starting to pick up the threads of a relationship when a marriage was well into its second year and the first flush of romantic passion might have been expected to ease off. Hester did not believe for one instant that a chance call into the workshop to see Robin and thus meeting John again had not been carefully planned. What more natural than that Master Barton's daughter should have mentioned to Caroline that John was now working there. The danger was increased by everything being conducted gradually and without haste.

"I hope the stew won't taste burnt," was all she said with remarkable self-restraint. He appeared relieved that his explanation was not to be dissected and assured her that the stew was delicious. She tasted it and it was; no thanks to Caroline.

About a week later he brought home a little toy that Caroline had given him for Joss. It was a monkey on a stick. Joss played with it for hours, otherwise Hester would have thrown it on the fire. After that day John did not refer to Caroline again. Whenever he was late he gave no explanation beyond having a task to finish. His reticence about Caroline, who was surely just as frequent in her visits to the Bartons as before, became far more alarming to Hester than anything he could have said. Once, unable to restrain herself any longer, she asked him straight out if he had seen her recently. She thought he looked taken aback, for she had caught him off guard.

"Yes, she is well. We pass the time of day whenever we meet. Her father isn't in good health. He had a slight seizure recently."

It gave her a lead for another time. "Have you heard how Master Harwood is now?"

He did not look up from his newspaper. "He is recovered, but his daughter has doubts that he will ever be truly himself again."

It seemed significant to her that this time he did not even speak Caroline's name. Her only comfort was that his loving attitude towards her was unchanged, but even this thread of security seemed to be in danger when at All Hallows one Sunday the rector took as the theme of his sermon the Church's determination to put an end to Fleet marriages, which he declared made a travesty of the marriage ceremony.

"Fleet weddings are an abomination," he thundered from the pulpit. "Let them be abolished and every union already conducted there declared invalid!"

Hester was thoughtful on the way home. "Could Fleet marriages be declared invalid?"

John was carrying Joss on his shoulders, the two of them having fun together, and he answered her without much attention. "There have been reports on the subject in the newspapers for some time, but I can't see it happening myself."

"But suppose it did," she persisted. "We wouldn't be married anymore."

He was laughing with Joss, who had pushed his tricorn hat forward over his eyes, and he had to tilt his head back to look at her, his eyes merry. "I'd be a bachelor again with all the women in London to chose from."

"Would you still want me?" She knew it was a foolish question, since he was not prepared to take it seriously, but it was an appeal from the heart for reassurance for all that.

"Who else would put up with me?" he joked. Then he broke into a jog as he play-acted being a horse for his young son's pleasure.

She followed at an unaltered pace. "I know one who would," she said disconsolately, although he was too far ahead to hear her, "and gladly too."

That night in bed she lay in his arms and said, "Let us be married again, John."

He nuzzled the soft warmth of her neck. "No couple could be more man and wife than we, my love."

"Not if our marriage lines are declared null and void."

He raised himself on an elbow, looking down into her face. "You're not still worrying about that, are you? I daresay Fleet marriages will be abolished in time simply because the Church is making such strong objections, but it is hardly likely that past marriages will be affected. The Church is not going to turn thousands of children into bastards by the stroke of a pen. Far better to let those bigamous liaisons remain unpunished."

"I want to be married at St. Botolph's church over in Bishopsgate," she said, sweeping aside his argument. "My parents were married there."

He groaned, falling back on the pillows. "Don't ask me to go through all that ritual again. It's totally unnecessary. If it really looks as if some move is going to be made against past Fleet marriages, there'll be plenty of time to see about another ceremony then."

"What if abolishment should happen overnight?"

"It won't."

"It might." She moved restlessly. "I don't feel really married anymore."

He refused to take her misgivings seriously. His tolerance became strained when she continued to bring up the subject at tactical moments.

"This nonsense about us marrying again has to stop," he insisted. "Just consider the practical difficulties for a start. To marry at St. Botolph's, which is out of our parish, would mean my having to move into Bishopsgate since one or another of us has to reside there for the time during which the banns are called."

"You could stay with Robin. He lives in Bishopsgate."

"You'd turn me out, would you?"

"It would only be necessary for you to sleep there."

"No."

"John—"

"No! What's behind all this?"

She pressed a hand across her forehead and closed her eyes, a quiver tugging at the corner of her mouth. "I should die if I lost you."

"Have you so little trust in me?" He was wearied by the whole subject. "You can't know me at all if you think I'm a man who would desert his woman and his child. Be sensible, Hester. Put away your foolish fancies."

She struggled to do as he wished, but a yearning for a church marriage had taken such a hold on her that she could barely think of anything else.

Whatever he might have had on his mind was driven away completely when he arrived home one day to find that a prepaid letter had been delivered from Staffordshire. It was not in his grandfather's hand. Anxiety rose in him as he broke the seal. Hester saw by the way his face became drawn as he read that something was seriously wrong. She went to stand close to him, putting her hand on his arm.

"Is it your grandfather?" she asked with compassion.

He nodded. "He's dying. I must go to him."

For two weeks John was away. He sent her a letter, which Robin read to her. The old man had died peacefully the day after he arrived. Now the funeral was over he was arranging the sale of his childhood home and its effects, which was a sad duty, being full of memories.

When he returned home it was to tell her that he had inherited everything. In spite of the broken-down condition of the property, its sale and that of the land had given them a nest egg for the future. He had arranged that a few pieces of furniture, which he knew had been in the Bateman family for two or three generations, should be stored until such time as he was able to get a house large enough to accommodate them.

"Now we can move at last," she exclaimed thankfully.

He shook his head. "Not quite yet. I've had plenty of time to think about the future since I heard the reading of my grandfather's will. I have the means now to set up as a goldsmiths' outworker with my own small workshop."

"That would be wonderful, John! Think of it!" She was thrilled that he should have shown this ambition. It made all their struggles worthwhile. "How soon will it be?"

"I can't say." He saw the disappointment in her expressive face and put an arm consolingly about her. "There's no question of my rushing into it. Before I give up my present employment I must investigate to find out how much work I could expect to come my way."

"I understand."

She could not help wishing he were less cautious. If it had been her decision she would have plunged in right away, confident that all would be well. In the past she would have argued and tried to sway him to a swifter decision, but she would never forget how her sharp tongue had driven him to put his health into jeopardy. Without her being aware of it at the time, that experience had tempered a change in her. She had learned a terrible lesson in that her strength of character was such that she could destroy this loving man if she did not sublimate it. Gradually, since that shattering experience, she had come to see that although his strong will was more than a match for hers, it was the basic gentleness of his nature that she had in her power to torment to some point of break-down if she did not guard against it. For that reason her request for remarriage had been an appeal and not a demand. She did not want to hurt him ever again. To that end she was resolved to let him be the undisputed head of the household, the maker of decisions, and she would cosset him to the best of her ability to the end of her days. His present decision to wait awhile for his workshop would try her patience, but she accepted it.

It had never been easy for her to be patient, and this time it proved to be even harder than she had anticipated. Her longing to get Joss away to a healthier area became more acute now that it would have been possible any day if John willed it. She felt as if she were enclosed in dark shadows and looking towards a door standing open to sunshine that she could not reach. A strange sense of foreboding settled upon her and kept her in an unusually sombre mood that she could not shake off. It magnified all the difficulties and daily annoyances that came from living in a seedy area and that previously she had taken in her stride. Sweeping away other people's garbage from the landing outside her door now aroused her anger, whereas previously there had been resignation. Her back-ache from having to carry Joss along the filthy streets in the neigh-borhood seemed to get worse. There was also the hazard of washdays when she had to keep a watch on her clothesline in case anything was stolen, for on the very first day in the house when she had turned her back on a pegged-out line every item had vanished.

She was hanging up washing in the rear yard, sighing that it was another wash day in this thieving area, when she heard what she thought at first to be a rumble of thunder not far away. Surprised, for the day was bright and sunny, she looked up into an almost cloudless sky. Then there came a reverberating crash that made the cobbles shiver underfoot. She spun about to see that one of the huge timbers shoring up the neighbouring house had fallen away. A great crack had appeared in the wall, spilling bricks and plaster. From within came muffled screams.

"Merciful God!" She sprang for the back door through which she had just come. Joss was upstairs in their room in the middle of a mid-morning nap. Already the house was beginning to shake as its neighbour shifted, black dust billowing out like smoke around the beams. She pounded up the flight, meeting panic-stricken residents from the floor above, and hurled herself across the landing into the room. Joss had been awakened by the noise and sat crying in his little truckle bed. Cracks were leaping up all the walls. She snatched him up, half-choked by dust, and turned for the stairs. When she reached the bottom of the flight she saw that the front door appeared to have wedged while the back door still stood open. Even as she made for it a wall gave way. There was a rumble as if a volcano had discharged, and as the beams descended, she flung herself protectively over Joss. A chunk of plaster hit the back of her head and she blacked out from the pain of it. Rubble and plaster buried the two of them.

In the street people came running from all directions to the scene. The shored-up Tudor house had brought down the greater part of the neighbouring houses on both sides. Those who had escaped at the last minute staggered about in a stunned condition, some nursing injuries. Mrs. Burleigh, who knew Hester was at home that day, sent two of her sons on errands, one to notify John and the other to the Heathcock. Then she rushed to give a helping hand to those beginning to claw aside rubble in the hope of finding survivors. It was not unusual for very old property to collapse in poor districts, often with a high loss of life. She hoped that would not be the outcome today.

Jack arrived first in his gig, the Burleigh boy with him, and used his whip to get through the crowds of gaping spectators. He hurled himself into the rescue work, which two beadles were trying to organise, using his powerful strength to heave and propel aside the fallen beams. John arrived soon afterwards, and Mrs. Burleigh ran to meet him.

"I know she's in there, Mr. Bateman! I saw her at the window not ten minutes before."

He nodded, too frantic for speech, and threw his coat aside to lend his weight and his efforts to burrowing through. People were thick as ants on the ruins of all three houses and an hour later there were sounds of distress from the families concerned as bodies were recovered. Rescuers took turns with others when they needed to rest, but neither John nor Jack let anyone else take his place. It was almost evening when they got through to Hester. She must have flung herself half under the staircase, for what remained of it had kept the heavy timbers from crushing her. She looked dead when she was lifted out, her hair grey with dust and blood on her face and neck. Even as she was moved, Joss, disturbed from a sleep of exhaustion, began to cry. John felt for her pulse as Jack reached to pull Joss out unharmed.

"She's alive!" John croaked. "And Joss, too. Thanks be to God."

He carried her to the gig and lifted her carefully into it. Jack handed Joss to him and then drove them to the Heathcock. A doctor was summoned while Martha and one of the waiting maids bathed Hester clean and made her as comfortable as possible.

She recovered consciousness twelve hours later to find her head bandaged, her right arm in splints and Joss protesting noisily outside her door, angry at not being allowed in to see her. "Let Joss come in," she called weakly.

Martha brought him, keeping a restraining hand to stop him clambering up on the bed. "You'll be well again in a few days," she said brusquely, "but you've lost all your possessions. Jack says you may stay here until your husband finds another home for you."

She made it sound like a concession; Hester guessed that Jack was pleased enough to shelter her and her child under his roof for a little while.

It was six weeks before she and John set up home together again. As soon as she was fully recovered, except for her bound arm, she went house-hunting, sometimes with John at the week's end and often on her own, for in return for a few pence any one of the waiting maids was willing to look after Joss in off-duty hours. John was not unduly surprised when she found a house in the parish of St. Botolph's that she was eager for him to see. He was willing enough to consider it, for it was a good area for him, with plenty of goldsmiths in the vicinity.

It proved to be a plain, unpretentious house at the end of a row at the junction of two commercial streets. To his surprise, she took him past the front door to enter by a side gate. Crossing a small cobbled yard with a well, they reached the rear door. To his increased astonishment, it entered directly into what had once been a carpenter's workshop, with stout benches and shelves and tool-racks still in place, the floor flagged and a blackened hearth in the corner. Immediately he tested the benches for strength and stability and grinned widely at his findings.

"These are splendid." He turned to the window that faced the yard and stood with arms akimbo and feet apart, nodding with satisfaction. "Plenty of light, too."

"You like it then?" she ventured. "You feel you could work here?"

He swung about to her, still grinning. "We need look no further for a house, if the rest of it is to your liking."

"Oh, it is. Come and see!"

The rest of the ground floor was taken up by the kitchen regions and the parlour that looked out on the street. Upstairs were three bedchambers, one little more than a boxroom. When he learned the rent from her he found it was well within the range he had allowed. "Then we can move in as soon as everything is signed," he said when they were downstairs again. She went to take another look around the parlour, and he leaned a shoulder against the jamb, watching her. "This is certainly a good location for business. Apart from the work I've had promised me, I should be able to gather some in from the goldsmiths in this neighbourhood after a while."

She nodded, her thoughts full of furnishings. "I like it because it will be no distance to the nearest shops and markets."

"That's true. We're also far nearer St. Botolph's than we were to All Hallows." His words seemed to drop into the silence of the room. She was already in profile to him and he saw how her hand fluttered to her throat before she became motionless, held in an aura of light from the window behind her, not daring to guess at what he was about to say. Smilingly, he ended her suspense. "I suggest we have the banns read and you become my bride again."

She looked towards him, her whole face suffused with joy. Then with a little cry she darted forward into his arms.

The furniture from his childhood home that had been in store was brought to the new address in two full wagonloads. Hester was overjoyed to find that in addition to some fine carved pieces, which included the four-poster in which several generations of Batemans had been born, there were some worn but still beautiful carpets and several boxes of fine porcelain as well as more humdrum domestic articles, all of which would be put to good use. With everything from her own home lost in the rubble of the collapsed slum house, it meant much to her that there should be links with John's origins.

They moved into their new home on the eve of their second marriage. That day John finally finished fitting out his workshop, which she had washed and scrubbed clean for him as she had done the rest of the house. She was intrigued by the wide variety of tools, the tree stumps with the many indentations, the vises tightened into place on the benches, the oval anvil and the casting moulds. Equally intriguing were the strange names, such as stakes and heads, horses and mandrels, which John told her were as old as the craft itself in England, and the terms that covered the various stages of the work. Having never forgotten the impression made on her by the gold and silver exhibition she had seen as a young girl, she was particularly fascinated to view at last the tools that brought about the creation of such marvellous pieces.

"So many hammers and mallets!" she exclaimed, looking at the racked rows of them in every size, some shaped as she had never seen before.

"Each has its own purpose," he said, unpacking from a box a set of scales for measuring gold and silver.

She came across to watch. The weights were set into wooden boxes. "Perhaps I could weigh for you. As you know, I can count even though I can't read, and it would be easy to memorise these weights."

He was intent on adjusting the scales to a perfect balance. "I could teach you to polish if you like. That would be of help to me."

"Yes! Anything! I'd like to become another right hand to you."

His frown of concentration dispersed as he completed his task and straightened his back. "I daresay there will be several small chores you'll be able to do for me as Joss gets older and you have more free time on your hands."

She closed the lid of the weights box that she had opened, smiling to herself. So he was not averse to her working with him. It did not go against his pride, as the thought of her working for strangers in a public place had done. She could understand that. In his workshop she would be under his direction and protection, his dignity and hers unimpaired by what could be termed a partnership, albeit her skills would never match his. Without his knowing it, he had opened a door for her. Perhaps it was that very door that her premonition about the falling down of the house had made her fear she would never reach. A sweet fresh wind was blowing through it, not scented with flowers but with the strange aromas of goldsmithing that stung her nostrils as if she had already entered that new realm.

"Take a look at this, Hester." He had unwrapped a package that had been delivered to him that day in readiness for his first outwork. It was a dull-looking sheet of metal.

"What is it?"

"A disc of silver. Nothing much at this stage, is it? Gold is no better in a 'blank.' That's why goldsmiths never let a client see a piece in the making, because they would only be disappointed and have groundless fears about the end result."

"What do you look for in a good article of silver or gold?" she wanted to know.

"I don't have to look because it will hit me here." He thumped his chest over his heart. "The honesty and liveliness of it combined with its sense of style in true beauty of form and decoration will reach out to me and declare itself."

She had a flash of insight. He had put into words the instinctive feelings she had had at that exhibition at the Goldsmiths' Hall. She almost caught her breath on the revelation. Somehow it made her feel as much one with him as in their most intimate moments.

All three Batemans had new clothes for the wedding day. Joss wore a manly little coat of red velvet over his blue smock. John sported a dark green coat and knee breeches, his waistcoat gold coloured and his hose white. Hester looked at her menfolk with pride, she herself in cornflower silk with a motif of roses, her hair dressed high under a wide-brimmed Leghorn hat tied under her chin with satin ribbons. In the church she would be receiving a gold ring from John. The metal one had been put away that morning as a treasured keepsake. The long-case clock from Staffordshire chimed half-past eleven in the hall.

"It's time to go." John drew her to him with a smile and kissed her before she linked her arm in his and took Joss by the hand.

Robin, who was best man, met them at the door of St. Botolph's. He led the bridegroom into the church to await the bride at the altar. Tom, who was also there, took charge of Joss. Jack, waiting in the porch, was resplendent in a new coat of ginger-brown cloth with the fashionable cuffs reaching to his elbows.

"This is a good day, Hester," he said to her. "I'm glad to see you truly church-wed."

He bowed to her in the well-practised manner he used towards his most important patrons and offered his arm to take her up the aisle. Several of the pews were occupied by friends, some of long standing, and even Martha was there, although more out of curiosity than goodwill. Afterwards everyone would go back to the house for wine and plum cake.

When the ceremony was over, Hester again signed her cross under John's guidance. The bells rang as they came out of the church. There was nothing to mar the happiness of her day.

Chapter 6

Hester had heard it said that a love-child was always far more like the father than any conceived in wedlock and it was certainly true of Joss, not only in looks but in character. An amiable child, slow to anger, he had John's dogged determination and, if early signs were right, he was going to be another goldsmith. Hester held herself responsible for that, for it was through her that he became accustomed to being in the workshop. It came about gradually.

John, having been compelled by events to start up as an outworker sooner than he had intended, had not secured the amount of orders he would have liked as a beginning. He had plenty of rivals, outworkers long established, and masters of repute did not risk orders with those unknown to them. All that he could hope for was that word of mouth would eventually recommend him. Master Barton had been the first to give him work, a generous man who bore him no grudge for leaving to start as an independent outworker, and a steady order for cutlery, to the designs supplied, resulted while work from other sources remained a trickle. There were periods when if it had not been for the Barton spoons and forks there would have been no work for John to do, and there were times when even that ran out.

He was often silent and depressed in the evenings. Worry hollowed his cheeks and drew out the bones in his face. When the cutlery orders came in again, Hester always wished that Master Barton, who knew John's ability, would give him work more demanding of his skills, although it was natural that any master contracting out would keep the best for his own journeymen.

"Things will get better," Hester encouraged optimistically, polishing away at a plain tea canister at the next workbench to his. From the first week at their new home, she had allotted some part of her day to the workshop. She took her first lessons in polishing during Joss's daytime naps, John showing her how to dress soft chamois leather with compounds and jewellers' rouge to bring a shine to a finished piece. It was rewarding work. Under her hands emerged the gleam and sparkle that gave glory to the simplest piece and sent reflected light shooting over walls and ceilings. When Joss gave up sleeping in the daytime, she had established herself too securely in the workshop to be willing to surrender her sessions there. She overcame the problem by making Joss a plaited harness, which she attached by a lead to the leg of the workbench to keep him from straying under John's feet and, if given a few hammers, he would play happily without being a trouble to either of them.

Daily Hester became more fascinated with silver. Its marvellous malleability after only a gentle heating to release the compressed crystals that made up the metal, no violent fire required, never failed to fill her with wonder as she watched the flat "blanks" rise up and take shape under John's hammer. During the spasmodic workless periods he had time to give her special instruction in his craft and was impressed by the rate of her progress. Intelligence on its own, even when combined with enthusiasm and a sense of artistry, was not enough in goldsmithing; there had to be that special empathy with precious metals before a good goldsmith was made and he recognised that Hester had it in her. What had started out as a means of making her more useful to him whenever work should happen to increase now took on a new significance. With time there was every likelihood that Hester's talent would bloom to the full. His interest in teaching her helped him to weather the times when more than once he was tempted to close the workshop and take whatever other employment was available.

He had been struggling along for more than a year when he received his first order of importance from a totally unexpected source. Master Feline, who had dismissed him after receiving notification of his black-listing, came to the workshop. He was a thin-faced man in a grey periwig with an unprepossessing, dour expression. Yet to Hester, who had admitted him, it seemed as if the sun itself radiated from the gold buttons on his cinnamon velvet coat once the purpose of his visit was made known.

"So this is where you are, Bateman," he said with some irritation, as if he'd been put to trouble finding him. "You did good work for me during the short while you were on my premises, and to my mind the ban that applied there doesn't count here. I'm inundated with work. Will you ease the load for me at the same standard as before?"

"I will indeed."

"Good! Four candlesticks and a pair of matching candelabra in silver. Come with me now to collect the designs, and be as quick as you can with the work. We'll settle the price on the way."

As soon as the order was filled, more work was forthcoming, all of it of the highest quality and of immense interest to John, calling on all his skills. At last Hester was able to see for herself how every kind of workpiece was made, whether it began, as he had instructed her in his teaching, from a "blank" cut to form a cylinder dove-tailed together or raised up and shaped from those same discs. There was some casting work, usually of buttons, spouts, finials and feet, which she was able to do for him.

It was not long before work of similar quality came from else-where. John had a theory about it. "Whereas Master Barton has never mentioned me, I believe Master Feline probably dropped word of a good outworker at the coffeehouse where goldsmiths meet. It may have been deliberately passed on or only overheard— that doesn't matter if I get the work. It seems that the Harwood ban doesn't apply if I don't venture off my own premises to do what-ever I'm given."

As orders increased, some gold work was required where previ-ously everything had been in silver. If it was a matter of gilding he contracted that stage of the work out, grimly reminded of the effect it would have on some unfortunate's lungs. He also contracted out engraving, for although he had received some basic training in the craft while serving his indentures, it was specialised work and had its own long apprenticeship to reach the high standard required.

When workpieces were finished and before the final polishing, they were taken to the master goldsmith for whom they had been made and he would stamp each article with his own punchmark. Next they went to the Assay Office to be weighed and checked before receiving the punched assay marks, which denoted quality, the year of manufacture and gave the city's own lion passant that

showed it was London made. When they were back in the workshop again, the articles would be given a final cleaning and polishing by Hester before she wrapped the most costly in chamois and
the lesser pieces in yellow cloth for final delivery. If John
harboured any bitterness over never being able to stamp his own
"touch" on his work, he never showed it. As time went by, Hester
came to the conclusion that he had shut out regrets about his broken apprenticeship long ago.

It was no longer necessary to keep Joss on a harness in the workshop. He was an intelligent child and understood the reason he
must keep out of the way. Almost from the first his boyish instincts
had led him to imitate his father at work, and by the age of three he
had become adept at copying many of the stages of goldsmithing,
learning from his mother the basics of the craft. When she was
filing the edge of a disc, he did the same with a piece of non-
precious metal; if she was busy dishing a rim, he also tried to raise a
saucer edge by beating, quite unperturbed when his little hammer
had no effect. He liked to help her sift the dust for *lemel,* his fair
curls close to her kerchief-covered head, and his eyes were as quick
as hers in spotting the glint of minuscule fragments that would be
put aside for melting down in a crucible for reuse. He was four
years old and they had been nearly three years in the house when
Hester, who had kept at work for as long as possible in her second
pregnancy, gave birth to a daughter.

The new baby, baptised Letticia after her paternal grandmother
at St. Botolph's, completely disrupted what had become for Hester
a pleasant routine divided between goldsmithing and domestic
chores, with playtimes and outings set aside for family hours. Intensely maternal, she devoted herself to the baby's needs. John,
remembering how it had been after Joss's birth, resigned himself to
a period of never quite having her whole attention, her ear always
tuned for the first note of the baby's cry. Yet she did turn to him
alertly, pausing in the folding of some baby garments, when he
mentioned having heard that Master Harwood had suffered another stroke.

"Who is in charge of the business then?" she inquired swiftly.

"Mrs. Harwood."

"Will she do well, do you think?"

"She did last time he was ill. In any case she has Caroline to assist her."

"Is Caroline not wed yet?" There was a rasp to Hester's voice.

"I hear she is betrothed to a naval man."

"Indeed?"

John was aware of how penetrating Hester's gaze was on him. It was as if she was trying to read in his face what his reactions were to his first love transferring her affections at last. His feelings on that score were too private, too shut away for anything to be revealed on the surface. "I know her father's affliction must be a great grief to her. She has always been devoted to him. Her betrothed is surely some comfort to her."

"If he is not at sea."

"Ah well." He shrugged to show he was not certain about that. "He was the last time I heard talk of the Harwoods before this new development. I hope for her sake he is home again now."

It had not pleased Hester to hear Caroline's name again, and perversely neither did it to know that he had heard news of the Harwoods on another occasion that he had not passed on to her. If she had not been completely absorbed in the baby she might have brooded over their conversation, but somehow outside distractions had lost their impetus temporarily.

When eventually the early demands of an infant began to wane, she returned to the workshop to find John busy on the most elaborate piece that had yet come to him in his capacity as an outworker.

"Who is this for?" she asked, resting her arms on the bench to study the design pinned there. It was a two-handled wine cistern of gigantic proportions, destined for some grand dining-room and elaborate to the point of vulgarity in her eyes. She was not impressed by excessive ornamentation at any time. Simplicity of line and restrained and beautiful decoration were the attributes that counted with her. Too often cherubs' heads, scrolls, shells, swags and foliage weighed down a piece in what was spoken of as the Rococo style, which was charming enough in its way but too fanciful for her increasingly honed and incisive taste.

"Master Feline," he answered her, busy at his work. The wine cistern was taking its shape from a huge stake that had been little used before.

She traced the drawn pen and ink design with a critical fingertip. "I wish I could prune away this abundance of vineleaves."

"I agree with you. It must have been commissioned from Master Feline by a nabob with more money than taste."

"And with a gargantuan thirst!"

He chuckled with her and paused in his tapping to throw her a glance. "Have you come back to work?"

"I can spare an hour."

"Well done." His eyes narrowed at her. "I've missed you here with me."

It was satisfying to know he had come to rely on her at the workbench. After four years of marriage a solid base of companionship and tolerance, combined with their good working relationship, had built up to support their undiminished passion for each other. He was good to her in so many ways. She could not understand why Caroline should still loom as a threat to her. There were even times when she had the uneasy sensation that Caroline lingered close at hand, touching their lives in some indefinable manner. It remained impossible for her to subdue her misgivings, just as she had been unable to suppress the foreboding that had preceded the time when she and Joss had barely escaped death in the ruins of their home.

Her hours in the workshop would have been severely restricted if she had not thought to ask her former neighbour, Mrs. Burleigh, if her eldest daughter, Abigail, could come as house help and nursemaid. Mrs. Burleigh was more than willing to see the girl go to a good home. Abigail, sensible for her sixteen years, able to cook when necessary and thankful to escape the surroundings of her upbringing, arrived with a small bundle of belongings much as Hester herself had done when leaving the countryside for London.

"I hope you'll be happy with us, Abigail," Hester said in welcome.

"I know I will, madam." She was a big honest-looking girl with arched eyebrows that gave her a look of permanent anticipation of pleasant surprises, and with a wide smile to match. Joss, who knew her from times of calling with her mother, went to put his hand in hers and accepted her taking charge of him without complaint.

Letticia was never as easy a baby as Joss had been and from the toddling stage developed a demanding and imperious manner that her parents considered to be an amusing, if somewhat irritating, stage in her development, never supposing it was a stamp she was to bear for the rest of her days. A beautiful child with hyacinth blue eyes and pale copper hair, she had myriad dimples that she often used with effect to get her own way when her tantrums failed. She took advantage of Joss's good nature at every opportunity and was intensely jealous that he was allowed in the workshop while she was not.

"Me come, too," she insisted mulishly when the door was closed firmly against her and flung herself down on the floor kicking and shrieking until borne away by Abigail. There was no doubt in Hester's mind that her daughter had inherited her explosive temperament, and she hoped that time would ease it, although not through the kind of circumstances that had forced her to subdue and sublimate herself.

Inevitably there were times when she snapped, eyes flashing, her whole body taut; if John was involved she would leave his presence at once and shut herself away in the bedchamber upstairs until the rage in her had died down and she could think and discuss rationally again. Whether he understood why she dealt with her temper in this manner she did not know. It was probably enough for him that he was spared what he hated most and could concentrate on his work without domestic upheavals to distract him.

Work was going along steadily. John had established himself as a reliable outworker who could be trusted to do a task well and deliver on time. He still worked long hours, but always finished at noon on Saturdays to be free until Monday morning. It was the time of the week that Hester liked best, for they could be together as a family, taking the children to see the shipping on the river, or to the zoo in the Tower, or to play in St. James's Park where cows grazed and milk was on sale for the thirsty. When John decided that some time at each week's end must be allotted to giving Joss a measure of schooling, Hester was in full agreement, for there would still be plenty of time for leisure pastimes together. What she had not realised was that John intended to instruct two pupils in the subjects of reading and writing.

"You shall learn to read with Joss," he said to her. "It's a splendid opportunity for you to start from scratch and offer competition to him at the same time."

She froze, all her old terrors sweeping back to set her stomach churning. "No! I'm too old to learn now."

He burst out laughing, throwing his head back and showing his white teeth. "You're twenty-five! A slip of a girl! Remember how quickly you did well in the workshop. It will be the same with reading. After all, you have no trouble with reckoning."

She twisted her hands together. "I don't know how to explain. The letters of the alphabet defeat me."

"Only because you were never taught properly. You have a quick brain and a good eye. You'll soon be at home with books. Think how much better it will be for you to write down whatever you want to record instead of drawing all those little symbols that only you can understand."

Nobody could say afterwards that she did not try. She had learned the alphabet by rote as a child, which should have given her a head start over a five-year-old, but she could not relate the spoken letters to those written down for her. She had shut the thought of reading out of mind with such determination over the years that it was harder to learn than it had been before. It was as though something within her that she could not control rejected every effort she made. Why was it she could draw freely, and yet in the setting down of words, even her own name, everything refused to stay level on a line ruled for her? She felt cursed. In no time at all Joss had advanced to reading and writing simple words without difficulty, while all John's patient efforts failed to penetrate the blockage that stood between what she saw on slate or page and her comprehension. Sweat broke out constantly on her palms and upper lip, and at times she reached a peak of tension at which the feeling of nausea rose in her as it had done in childhood. It came to a point that her own son attempted to help her.

"It's like this, Mama. Try to write it with me. Watch what I do."

She developed little tricks of memorising what Joss had read and then being found out by turning the slate over to the other side too soon. She was equally defeated by letters being changed about, which showed that she was only guessing. Joss never laughed or crowed over her as another child might have done, and John never showed impatience, but the humiliation was acute.

"I'm holding Joss back," she insisted after a particularly harassing session. "This can't go on."

John gave a nod. "I agree." Then he dashed away her rise of relief by adding: "I'll teach you on your own."

Where she had always looked forward to the evening hours alone with John after the children were abed, she now began to dread them. After dinner dishes were cleared away he would get out the hated slate and books and the lessons would begin again. By now she could write her name and a few short sentences, but no matter how often she was told, she frequently reversed letters or left them out, as she had done long ago. When he corrected her yet again she could hardly hold back the scream of frustration that rose in her and more than once hammered her fists on the table over an error.

"Don't despair, sweeting," he would say cheerfully, putting an arm about her. "You've made progress, as I knew you would. It is only a matter of time until all goes well."

The main cause of her despair was his stubbornness in refusing to give up the struggle. She longed to be released from her state of purgatory and from the old sense of shame that was as heavy upon her as it had ever been. Then one evening she thought that blessed time had come. Instead of the slate and the rest of his teaching paraphernalia, he put some drawing paper in front of her.

"I want you to design a teapot for me. You're always able to see what is right or wrong in the designs that come with the outwork. Now I should like to see what you can produce."

She felt as though a great weight had slipped away from her. Her increased distress during the past week's lessons must have finally touched him. He was not going to inflict his well-intended teaching on her anymore.

"That's an easy task," she answered happily. "I'm always making little sketches for silverware for my own pleasure."

"I know you are. Now give me one in the detailed style of the professional designs."

She set to work at once with pen and ink. Her guess was that for once he had been given free rein in choosing the design for a teapot and was drawing in her ideas with his. She felt honoured and greatly complimented. He did not leave the table to sit in his wing chair and read the newspaper while she drew, which was what she had expected. Instead he continued to sit near her as he had done throughout his tutoring and watched every stroke that she drew of a pear-shaped teapot, its beauty in its graceful lines, chased festoons its only ornamentation, the lid topped by a cone finial.

"There!" She sat back. "What do you think?"

He studied it. "Charming. It would make up well. Now for the finishing touch I'll help you to write *Teapot in silver* underneath and your name beside it."

Her eyes dilated as she stared at him. He had tricked her! It was all a ploy, a new way to get her to write and read that would tear apart all her joy in drawing and destroy it. She uttered a kind of strangled shriek and swept the drawing and all else from the table with the back of her hand as she leapt to her feet. Nausea gushed up in her. She hurled herself from the room and only just reached the outdoor privy in time. When she came out into the air again, wiping her mouth, she sank down onto a wooden bench. Her vomiting might have been induced by her outrage, but she recognised it for what it portended. She pressed her folded hands across her stomach. Without doubt she was pregnant again. It explained the recent disorder of her moon cycle, which she had blamed on the stress of the lessons.

Tilting her head back, she closed her eyes and drew in a deep breath of overwhelming relief. This was her escape. John would never risk upsetting her during a pregnancy, and there would be no more lessons or humiliation or shame. It did not matter whether she was to bear a boy or a girl, for she would always cherish a special love for this coming child, who had been instrumental in obtaining her release from what had been a loving persecution. Suddenly serene, she rose to her feet and went back into the house to break the news to John.

As she had anticipated, there were no more lessons for her and they were never mentioned again. John, stubborn as he was, had accepted defeat. Perhaps to compensate her for what he saw as his own failure, he gave her advanced instruction in the intricacies of goldsmithing, and her ever-quick ability and talent left him even more puzzled by her resistance to the letters of the alphabet.

Joss continued to make strides in his learning. John would have liked him to attend Westminster School when he was old enough, but the fees put it far out of reach. At least he could give his son the benefit of his own classical education received there and he began to prepare Letticia, who was a bright child, for the time when he would teach her in her turn to read and write and reckon. Although it was never said, it was clear he did not intend to tolerate any illiteracy, other than Hester's, in his family and that applied equally to the child who had yet to be born and any more that might come in the future.

When Hester was brought to bed for the third time the birth proved to be the easiest to date. As she had somehow expected, the baby was a girl and Hester had her own mother's name of Ann ready for her. It was typical of Joss that when he was admitted to the bedchamber, he should welcome his new sister with a rattle he had made for her. Letticia, jealous of this new arrival, hung back from the cradle and had to be pushed forward by Abigail.

"Go and give Baby Ann a kiss."

Letticia did not do that, although her glare into the cradle changed immediately with a coquettish tilt of the head into a smug smile. "She is not as pretty as me!" Then, perhaps seeing a coolness towards her in her mother's expression, she went to the bed and flung herself forward for an embrace. "You still love *me*, don't you?"

Hester stroked back the copper-fair hair from the child's upturned anxious face. "I love you dearly," she said reassuringly. Yet she knew there was a niche in her heart exclusively for Ann, which had been made seven months ago and would always remain there.

Although Hester was never to show favouritism, Letticia continued to be jealous of Ann. For a long time she created trouble at every opportunity to bring attention to herself until gradually she came to realise that Ann, with her plain looks and thin brown hair that seemed reluctant to grow, was never going to outshine her.

Hester could never be quite sure when she began to suspect that some of the grandest workpieces on John's bench were being made for the Harwood establishment. She knew that Master Harwood had never recovered from his second stroke and was a bedridden invalid. Although John never spoke of the Harwood family, she had heard through Robin that Caroline had taken control of the business, leaving her mother concerned solely with the care of her father, who would tolerate no one else to nurse him. What more natural than that Caroline should seek to help John by sending him such work? If that should be the case, then why had he never mentioned it? Equally puzzling was her own reluctance to question him outright. The thought of challenging him brought dread to the pit of her stomach and she did not know why. Constantly she searched her memory to try to settle the time or place or day when suspicion had first seared into her brain, hoping it would bring some light to the matter. Was it that at some time he had given her an evasive answer about a new source of work that she had not paid attention to at the time, but that had lodged in the back of her mind to cause a build-up like a grain of sand in an oyster?

Against her better instincts, she found herself watching and waiting until one grand workpiece or another was finished and ready for delivery. Mostly he delivered in daylight for safety reasons, but there were times when he had to go by night if an article was required urgently. On these occasions he hired a retired army sergeant as armed escort, which relieved Hester of anxiety when he went out with a valuable article in its presentation box under his arm. A piece of rough cloth disguised its importance, and if it was an extra large presentation box, he would carry it in an old sack over his shoulder. Even with the sergeant's good sword arm in readiness, there was no point in inviting trouble. On the evenings he set off with what Hester guessed to be Harwood articles, she found herself timing his absence and comparing it with how long it took to deliver elsewhere. Over a period of many weeks a definite pattern evolved.

On the night he returned home at midnight, the latest he'd been to date, she was waiting for him at the head of the stairs, a light robe over her nightgown, her face pale with stress. Inwardly she was seething with the same heated jealousy she had perceived often enough in Letticia and was as powerless to control it. He hung his tricorn hat on a peg in the hall before he turned for the stairs. Then he looked up and saw her in silhouette against the glow of a candle in its chamberstick on a small table on the landing. The thought occurred to him that the trouble with peace-loving people like himself was that they took wide circles to avoid trouble and still managed to bring it down upon themselves, inevitably at the least prepared moment. He had expected Hester to be asleep and could tell by her face that his secret was a secret no more. He hated to be on the defensive and, due to a traumatic turn of events that evening, he was in no mood for confrontation.

"I didn't expect you to be awake," he said quietly from the foot of the flight.

"How could I sleep knowing that you were with Caroline?" she burst out in pent-up torment.

He sighed and began to mount the stairs, the aura of candlelight holding his drawn face as if in a cameo. "I stayed too long, I know. But it would have been discourteous to refuse supper and a glass of wine."

"What would her betrothed think of your supping alone with her?"

He had reached the last but one stair before the top and stopped there, his eyes on a level with hers. "What makes you think we were on our own?" he questioned sharply.

"Because you have been on previous occasions; you can't deny it!"

"I've no intention of denying it." A nerve began to throb in his temple and his eyes glittered. "But let us talk about this in the morning when you'll be more in charge of yourself."

"No!" She could see the warning signs that his rare anger was rising and recklessly she welcomed it, all resolutions gone momentarily beyond recall. "Guilt is written all over you. Why didn't you tell me you were seeing her?"

"To avoid such a scene as this!" he replied fiercely between his teeth.

She hit him across the face with all her strength. His head jerked back and the ring of her forceful blow seemed to hang suspended in the air. She had caught him off balance just as he was about to step onto the landing. He staggered slightly, reached for the newel post to save himself and thrust out a hand as if to keep her at bay. In her fury she would have hit him again, but he caught her wrists and grappled with her. They swayed together, knocking against the little table that stood there, causing it to tilt. The chamberstick and the table cloth went sailing off the polished surface to land together on the floor. The still-burning candle illuminated them like two actors in the footlights as he bore her backwards against the wall and held her there, his angry face within an inch of hers.

"You want the truth, so you shall have it! When Caroline took charge of her father's business after the second stroke, the first thing she did was to see that the ban was lifted from me, which has helped me in gathering in more work. When some of her best journeymen left, not wanting to stay on under the direction of a woman, should I have refused the fine pieces she wanted me to make for her?" He shook her in his impatience. "Answer me!"

"Yes," she retorted furiously, thwarted by him in her efforts to pull free. "I should have expected you to have more pride than to accept work from that source!"

"I never once connected it with my former master. In any case, I bear that sick old man no malice now."

"What need when you have Caroline in spite of him? Doing work for her gave you the excuse to see her anytime you wished!"

"And glad I was of it!" he responded savagely.

With a shriek of jealousy, she tried to hit him again, her range limited by the pressure of his body against hers. They struggled fiercely together until a first whiff of smoke reached their nostrils at the same time. As he released her, they turned together to see that the candle had set fire to the cloth that had fallen to the floor. He sprang forward to stamp out the flickering rise of the flames while she dashed into the bedchamber to fetch the ewer from the wash-stand. Rushing back, she tossed the water onto the fire, dousing it completely. She cradled the ewer as they stood looking at each other across the mess of water and blackened cloth on the floor between them. The air reeked of the ill-smelling smoke. Shock was in both their faces. He spoke first, his voice intensely weary.

"You had better get to bed. I'll clean this up."

"Very well." She was horrified that their quarrel should have endangered not only their house but the lives of their children. If the wall panelling had caught fire—it did not bear thinking about. In the bedchamber she put on a dry nightgown, the other having been splashed by the water from the ewer. She climbed into bed, hearing him still at work on the landing, and did not snuff the bedside candle, leaving it for him. Twice he went downstairs to empty the leather bucket into which he had wrung out a cloth. Waiting for him, she sat up in bed, her own anger gone and only hurt left. She could only guess at his feelings.

Downstairs John shut the back door after swilling the last of the water into the drain. He turned in to his workshop and put a light to a candle there before sliding his weight onto a stool and resting his arms on the bench as he stared unseeingly at his own reflection multiplied in the leaded panes of the window. Here in the workshop he was always at peace. The difficulties and challenges of a workpiece did not constitute the kind of stress that reared spasmodically in his domestic life. He should have told Hester about Caroline's lifting of the ban and of the aid and advice he had given her whenever a problem with the business had arisen. At first he had waited for the right moment, but that had never seemed to come. Hester, loving, laughing and exuberant, fast filling her ambition to become another right hand to him in the workshop, changed whenever the Harwood name was mentioned. A rigidness came over her, the lovely spark in her damped down by hostility towards a woman who was no challenge to her in her security as his wife. He had not wanted to face that change in her every time a Harwood workpiece was on his bench or a delivery was due, bringing disharmony into the one sanctum, other than their bed, where he and Hester were always in complete accord. To tell her about Caroline would have been to disrupt both.

He had not expected he would have to face two feminine explosions of emotion when he had set out for the Harwood establishment that evening, but as soon as he arrived, he saw that Caroline was nervous and upset. They went first into the office, as they always did, where he set down on her desk the silver casket he had made for her. After payment was made it was their custom to go upstairs to the drawing room, where she would serve him Madeira and they would discuss business matters before closing the evening with some pleasant talk of books or music or plays in which they were both interested. Sometimes she would play the harpsichord or the lute for his pleasure. Her mother never joined them. It was his guess that she disapproved of her daughter renewing a friendship that had once caused such an upheaval in the household, but Caroline was now the one to make decisions and nothing could gainsay her.

"What is wrong, Caroline?" he inquired with concern. She had approved the casket and sat down to draw up a banker's draft for the amount due to him, the pen trembling in her hand. "Is your father failing?"

"No more than the steady deterioration from which there is no hope of betterment." Her voice faltered and broke piteously. "It is my life that is at an end. Richard is home from the sea. He has come into his inheritance in Norfolk and his days aboard ship are over. We are to be married at the end of the month." She dropped the pen in a splutter of ink and covered her face with her hands.

He swung up a chair and sat down to bring his face close to hers. "Don't you care for him anymore? You've been betrothed a long time."

Her elbows slid outwards and her head sank until her brow rested on the back of her hands in a position of abject despair. "He's a good man. I do care for him."

"Then what has happened?" He put a hand compassionately on her shoulder.

"Nothing that hasn't always been there." Abruptly she raised her head and looked at him in yearning, the swimming tears spilling from her eyes. "It's you I love and always will."

"Caroline, my dear," he said huskily. Until now she had shown only that same calm, friendly attitude that she had maintained throughout the time when he had known only relief that she had put an end to promises between them in the hope of a new beginning. Now as then, his fondness for her remained unchanged by everything that had happened throughout the nearly eight years since that day she had set him free. If events had not gone the way they had, he would have married her and loved her with the same depth of feeling to the end of their days.

But Hester had changed everything by getting into his blood and eliminating every other woman for him, stirring him to boundless passion as Caroline had never done and would never have been able to do. Life with her would always have been placid to the extent that it would have been dull—like food without salt, a dry summer without the welcome break of a thunderstorm. He would have suffocated.

She snatched up his hand and kissed it before pressing his palm against her breast, the nipple hard through the fine silk. "This is the last time we'll ever be alone together." Her face had become flushed, a new brilliance in her eyes, and suddenly she flung herself passionately across his chest, breathing deeply. "Make love to me, John! Just once! Nobody will ever know and I'll be able to live the rest of my life on the memory of having been in your arms!"

In the workshop he passed his fingers across his forehead as if to erase what was lodged in his mind's eye. Behind him the latch of the door lifted with a click and there was a creak as it opened. He twisted round on his stool and saw Hester standing there. The sight of her wrenched at his heart. Her expressive face gave away the relief she felt at finding him there. It was obvious that in hearing no sound after he had closed the back door she believed him to have gone out again. The time must have passed slowly for her.

"Can't you sleep?" he asked, although her shadowed eyes told of wakefulness.

She shook her head. "I could ask the same of you."

"It's been a strange night," he said as much to himself as to her, returning his gaze to the window. The first tint of the spring early dawn was streaking pink ribbons across the sky. Somewhere close by birds were chirping.

She pushed the door shut behind her but stayed where she was. "I had thought to make myself a pot of elderberry tea. Will you share a cup with me?"

He seemed not to have heard her, deep in his thoughts. Then he turned his head again and spoke as if there had been no previous conversation. "My life would be nothing without you, Hester." His heart was in his voice. "I should have told you about the work for the House of Harwood, but knowing it was only for a limited period, I decided unwisely to keep it to myself. As it happens, there'll be no more work from there in any case. The business is to be sold."

"And why is that?" She spoke quite steadily.

"Caroline is to be married this month. Then she'll be leaving London to live in Norfolk."

For the sake of her own sanity she knew she must believe that there had been nothing between Caroline and him. If Caroline's decision to marry at last had been the cause of the haunted look in his eyes upon his return home, she would not dwell on it now or at any other time. In that direction madness lay waiting to tear heart and mind and soul to shreds.

"I wish her well," she said with sincerity. Caroline's going was like a bountiful gift that the woman herself had bestowed on their future life together.

His face twisted wryly, as if her words had touched a raw nerve, and looked away from her. She went forward and put a hand on his arm. He covered it with his own and held it hard for several minutes before turning his head to meet her eyes again. She touched his haggard face with the fingertips of her free hand.

"I mentioned a cup of elderberry tea just now," she said almost in a whisper.

He nodded heavily on a silent sigh and slid his weight from the stool. "I'll heat the water for you."

Putting his arm about her shoulders, he kept her close to his side as they went from the workshop together. It was in the kitchen as they sat at the table opposite each other, sipping the fragrant elderberry tea, that she told him she had had the first sign suggesting she might be pregnant again.

"I can't be sure yet," she admitted uncertainly.

He gave her a tired smile, reaching out for her hand across the table and clasping it, although there was no smile in his eyes, only a deepening of the misery already there. "If that should be the case, then it is time we moved. We are crowded here already."

She wondered why she should have chosen this moment to tell him what she barely suspected. Was it to try to emphasise the marital bond between them to the exclusion of all else? On impulse she sprang to her feet, knocking back her chair, and whirled around the table to where he sat. She drove her fingers into his hair and drew his head deep against her breasts. At once he clung to her with a groan, his arms encircling her hips. There was still a breach between them that only time could heal, and she felt as lost as he.

It was from a warning carrier, who visited all workshops regularly with descriptions of stolen gold and silverware and gave the alert on gangs of thieves, that they learned of Master Harwood's death. It occurred only days before Caroline's marriage, which took place as arranged the day after the funeral, quietly and privately without any of the pomp that would otherwise have attended it. The property had already been sold to another goldsmith. Not long afterwards they heard that the widow had left for Norfolk to live with her daughter and son-in-law. The name of Harwood had gone from London as if it had never been, except for what Hester saw as a scar left across her own marriage.

It was summer when they moved into a much larger, three-storeyed house in Nixon Square, Cripplegate, in the parish of St. Giles. To Hester's delight, there was a garden at the rear where the children could play, still leaving ample space for a herbal patch where at last she could plant whatever she wished. The other residents of the sizeable square were mainly outworkers like John with workshops in their own homes, following a variety of trades from cabinet maker to glass grinder. As with nearly all the houses there, the entire ground floor was a workshop, with ample living quarters above and a kitchen basement below. For the first time Hester was able to afford a maid in addition to retaining Abigail, who was looking forward to having a small baby to care for again. Joss was the one who suffered the biggest upheaval through the move. At nine years old he was still a serious child, conscientious and particular, his likeness to his father as marked as it had ever been.

"There is a charity school in the countryside that I heard about," John said to him. "It has connections with St. Giles' Church. After I talked to the vicar and showed him some of the mathematical and other written work from your lessons with me, he agreed to speak to the governors on your behalf. Today I received their reply." He tapped the letter in his hand. "They are prepared to admit you. You are a fortunate lad."

Joss did not feel fortunate. It was unusual for him to show excitement, but he had been really excited about the new workshop. A treadle polishing machine had been installed to relieve the tedium as well as the time taken up by hand polishing, and he and his mother were both looking forward to using it. To be cut away from the workshop was a heavy blow to bear.

"How long shall I have to attend school?"

"Until you are fourteen. Then I shall apprentice you to the best master goldsmith I can find."

It was the bright light at the end of a long dark tunnel and something he wanted above all else. Philosophically he faced his education in between. It was no hardship for him to learn, and books were as much part of him as the goldsmithing he was determined to follow. "When do I start school?"

"On the first day of September."

He brightened. There was still plenty of time left to get used to the new treadle machine and finish making the little bowl for Ann in time for her third natal day. Deliberately he shut the thought of school out of his mind and was then astonished by the speed with which the day came upon him.

Hester packed her son's travelling box with all he would need in his school life. Knowing he would benefit from country air did not negate the fact that he was a home-loving boy and would feel the break tremendously. She dreaded his going, and her misgivings were not aided by John teaching him fisticuffs and how to defend himself against bullies.

When the time came for departure Joss showed the kind of straight-backed courage she would have expected of him.

"We'll say goodbye here, Mama," he said to her in the parlour when it was time for him to leave. He had not wanted Letticia or Ann to be present, and they were waiting with Abigail on the steps outside to wave him on his way. She did not offend him by telling him to be good and work hard or offer any other unnecessary admonishments. Instead she stooped to give him a big hug and put a packet of toffee into his pocket for the journey.

"It's your favourite," she said, patting the flap of his pocket back into place. "I'll make some more for Christmas when you'll be home to see us again."

He hugged her once more, the desperate pressure of his young arms saying more than words, and then broke from her to dash from the room. She hurried to the window. John had shouldered the travelling box and stood on the pavement, half-turned to the door and waiting for Joss to finish saying farewell to his sisters. Then the two of them set off across the square. Had it not been such a poignant moment for her she might have smiled at the similarity of their walk, both striding purposefully, their coat-tails swinging in unison. Two streets away they would board the coach for the thirty-mile journey, and John would return later that same day.

She turned away from the window when she could no longer see them and wiped her eyes with her fingertips. Letticia had not waited for Joss to be out of sight but had scampered back into the house on some business of her own. It was Ann who came running into the parlour to be comforted now that he had gone. "I want Joss back, Mama!"

Hester missed Joss in the workshop most of all. Although he had had lessons set for him every day, he had always finished them in time to do some work at his own section of the bench, his expression absorbed, his silky fair hair falling forward over his eyes. She had only to look across at John to see the familiar resemblance, but he never had time these days to glance up at her with a smile, for he gave himself no rest. When a rush of orders was on he would work late into the night and start again at dawn, something that was happening more frequently all the time. Had Sundays not been sacrosanct, his family time for her and the children, she believed he would have worked seven days a week, barely stopping for food. Yet that lack of a smile was in a way symbolic of the subtle change in their relationship, which had never been the same since the night the candle had caused the fire. She wondered how it was that a man and wife, intimate in every sphere, should find it impossible to communicate in words their own private thoughts and sorrows. Sometimes it was as if she were living with a loving stranger.

Joss did not come home for Christmas. Freak blizzards and heavy snowstorms halted travel and made the roads impassable. The weather was bitter, and in the intense cold every lake and pond in London froze and there was ice floating on the Thames. By now Hester was near her time and the need to rest had made her give up her place at the workbench. To pass the time she often drew designs for pieces she would like to make if ever John could afford to let her have some discs for her own use. As yet silver had no place in their home; their cutlery was of base metal and their dishes of crockery and pewter.

She had allowed the maid to visit a sick parent and was alone in the house on a Saturday afternoon, the New Year of 1740 being only two weeks old, when there came a knock on the door. She was designing a set of spoons for her own amusement and put her drawing aside to heave herself out of the chair. John had taken Letticia to skate on a pond, and Abigail and Ann had gone to watch. She took a little time to get downstairs, but the caller was patient and she opened the door to the handle-maker, who had a box under his arm.

"Good day, Mrs. Bateman," he greeted her. "I've brought those handles your husband ordered."

"Thank you. Come in." She led the way through to the section of the workshop where the handles were stored, and he set the box down on a bench for her. After he had gone, she opened it to examine the contents. The handles were very fine, made of ivory or bone, a few of wood, destined for coffeepots, chocolate pots and other containers for which a silver handle was not required. The intense chill of the workshop without the full warmth of the charcoal burner made her shiver. She turned for the stairs and the cosy parlour above with more haste than she should have done. Clumsily she almost slipped, saved herself from going down by grabbing at the bench and then released it involuntarily as she was gripped by birth pangs of extraordinary ferocity. She fell to the flagged floor, landing heavily on her right side, and lay floundering helplessly.

There was no one to hear her cries. Her attempt to crawl was defeated in the first attempt, the sound of her torment echoing back from the whitewashed walls. Once she almost lost consciousness, caught in a whirlpool of pain, and returned to the realisation that the birth was imminent. It was then that she heard John returning with the children. She screamed his name.

He flung open the workshop door, took one look and drew it almost closed again as he sent the girls upstairs and gave Abigail instructions: "Fetch the woman from next door! Bring her back at once!"

Alone, he rushed to where Hester lay. He just had time to throw off his coat and roll up his shirt sleeves before delivering his second son with his own hands. As he held the bawling infant, the tears coursed from his eyes at the miracle, and yet he could feel a grin on his face that surely stretched from ear to ear.

"He's perfect!" he shouted jubilantly.

"Give him to me," Hester gasped, holding out her arms.

He attended to her, and in looking for something immediate in which to wrap the baby, he took up a square of the yellow cloth in which finished silver was wrapped, only to throw it down again and take a length of the expensive soft chamois instead. Nothing but the best for this son!

When the neighbour arrived at a run, Abigail in her wake, she found John cradling his wife with the baby between them wrapped up like a piece of silver. She was not an imaginative woman, but she was struck by the way the couple were looking at each other. It was as if they had met again after a long time. Impatiently she tossed away the foolish thought and took charge.

When Hester had been carried up to bed and order restored, John found the design of the spoons she had been drawing before the handle-maker's knock had taken her downstairs. He studied it, struck as always by her eye for line, and he smiled to himself. A fourth child was surely cause for a birth gift of some value and in this case he knew exactly what it should be.

Two days later he presented it to her. As she sat up in bed to unwrap it, he went to look in the cradle. Peter was sleeping. He liked the name. It was a good choice. Hester's exclamation of pleasure drew him back to her and he sat on the bed's edge. "Do you like it?"

"It's the best gift I've ever had!" It was a silver spoon for her use made up from her own design. What meant most to her was that it was stamped *J.B.* It was probably the only time his "touch" would ever grace a piece of silver and it was hers.

Chapter 7

Joss finished school on his fourteenth natal day. He had hated every moment of being away from home in a bleak environment where harsh discipline and the frequent use of the birch had been the rule of the day. He was strongly built himself and had withstood in stoic silence whatever punishments had come his way while weaker boys had frequently fainted or collapsed. Remembering how his mother had failed to grasp the fundamentals of reading and writing, he had felt deep compassion for those pupils punished for failing to keep up an educational standard beyond their abilities or comprehension. Now all that misery was behind him. He leaned from the window of the coach to wave excitedly to his mother and sisters who had come to meet him. As the lumbering vehicle slowed to a halt, he flung wide the door and leaped out to run towards them.

"Welcome home, my son!" Hester exclaimed warmly, thinking how he shot up in height during every absence and, once again, his coat sleeves had failed to keep up with his wrists.

"It's splendid to be back in London for good!" He gave Letticia's curls an affectionate tug in greeting. She jerked back, not wanting her hair disarranged.

"You've grown as tall as a maypole, Joss! I've grown, too, don't you think?"

"You have indeed. Quite the young lady." He turned to Ann and chucked her under the chin. "What about you then? Are you pleased to see me?"

Her shy smile confirmed it. He faced his mother over her head and they exchanged a look of deep feeling, all the gladness of his homecoming radiating in his face and hers. The bond between them was strong. She alone had understood what it meant to him to be away from home and family. Without their ever discussing it, he had sensed that she knew he harboured a certain grudge against his father for what he had seen, and still saw, as his banishment from the workshop, albeit that it had been for his own good. She had tried to annul that illogical twist of resentment in him, unable to bear even unspoken criticism of his father; and to a certain extent she had succeeded. He greeted her with his singularly sweet smile, kissing her hand and then her cheek. The charity school had instilled gentlemanly manners.

"You look well, Mother. How is Father?"

"In excellent health and looking forward to seeing you."

"Where's Peter?" He looked around, half expecting his younger brother to come popping out of hiding.

Hester laughed softly. "I couldn't prise him out of the workshop."

"What?" Joss raised his eyebrows in amusement. "At four years old!"

"You were the same long before that age. I think we've another up and coming goldsmith in the family." She drew Ann fondly against her side. "This is the budding scholar among us. Ann has discovered books and loves them now as much as you and your father."

It struck him that Ann only ever came to the fore when propelled there by their mother. He had never been plagued by shyness himself but he was sympathetic towards it. "You'll be able to tell me which stories you like best," he said to her.

She nodded, her head hanging to hide her face. "I will," she whispered.

By then his boxes of belongings had been unloaded from the coach and he called forward a porter with a handcart to arrange its transport to Nixon Square.

As always when he returned home after an absence, he went straight to the workshop. He had almost reached it when Peter emerged, an old pewter plate clasped to his chest.

"I've made a gold dish for Mama," he announced, lost in his own game of pretence, and went past Joss as if they had seen each other only minutes before instead of months ago. Joss grinned and glanced after the stocky little figure going in search of Hester. Then he pushed open the workshop door and smelt the familiar odours of charcoal and pitch and compounds, appreciating once more the cavern colours of this well-equipped place. His father, busy at work on a bowl, turned at the sound of his step on the flagged floor and immediately put down tools with an exclamation of surprise.

Joss could never decide afterwards if it had been a trick of the light or a chance glancing of the bowl's reflection, but for a matter of seconds it seemed to him that he saw the stamp of sickness on his father's face, a momentary revelation of some ailment still lurking and dormant. Then the illusion was broken by the sun's rays through which his father came to greet him, hand extended, the handsome smile wide.

"Joss! The coach must have been prompt for once to bring you home on time." John shook his son's hand heartily and at the same time clapped his shoulder. "Now it all begins, eh? You've done well at school—a good preparation for what lies ahead. Your mother and I expect great things of you, you know."

Joss was experiencing a sense of relief. Now that his schooldays were at an end, whatever had been left of that inner resentment against his father appeared to have gone. Maybe it vanished in that curious, almost eerie moment that still hung in his mind, or more likely it was because nobody, not his father or anyone else, could keep him from a workbench any longer. "When do I start with Master Slater?"

"I'll take you along to his establishment tomorrow for you to sign your certificate of indenture. Then, after a week at home to get yourself organised, you'll be moving there and beginning that apprenticeship you've been long awaiting."

There was a rustle of petticoats as Hester appeared in the doorway. "Come and eat now, Joss. I've prepared a light repast for you, and we'll all dine together later."

Hunger had been with him throughout his schooldays, never quite enough on his plate to fill his stomach except on his visits home, and he turned eagerly to obey the summons. As he did so, his glance alighted on an oval snuffbox not yet fully polished, lying on a workbench. Almost reverently he picked it up and turned it about to examine it, observing closely the decoration of floral swags on the lid.

"This is very fine!" he praised. "One of your best, Father."

"Your mother made it." There had been the slightest pause before reply.

Joss turned to his mother, the snuffbox still in his hands. "I offer my felicitations. It's a lovely piece."

She blushed like a girl and spoke quite sharply. "It was done under your father's supervision. Come now and eat as I bade you."

He put down the snuffbox and followed her.

However much she tried to shift the credit away from herself, it was due to her. During the space of time that covered his schooldays, she had developed her skills to a point that she could have been judged a good journeyman if her position and circumstances had been different. Yet Joss knew, and normally obeyed, the rules of the game she played. No praise in that field must ever go to her. She was always his father's shadow, her craftsmanship only there to support and aid and relieve the pressure of work that fell upon John Bateman's shoulders. How often Joss had heard her say, "Your father taught me how to do that," or "I could never have grasped the method of raising the bottom of a vessel to strengthen it if your father hadn't been patient with me." Today he was glad he had congratulated her openly. He looked forward to the time when he would be able to make unaided such a perfect little piece.

On the eve of his departure to Master Slater's establishment, there was a family supper, even Peter being allowed to stay up for the occasion. It had been a hectic seven days since his arrival home. He had been kitted out with new clothes and his travelling box repacked in readiness. Although he would be no more than three miles from home and within the city, Joss was prepared to be cut off from his family again as if there had been a far greater distance between him and Nixon Square. Apprentices in a local area were discouraged from keeping close family contacts. It set them apart from those who had come from farther afield and sometimes made it less easy to give a full commitment to work. But the situation was different from when he was at school. He would be training for the career he most wanted and would be allowed home some Sunday afternoons, to attend Christmas service with his family or in any emergency if someone should fall ill. On this thought he looked towards his father at the head of the table and wondered why he had misread the healthy countenance of a man of only thirty-six with a well-muscled physique and plenty of vigour.

John caught his elder son's gaze on him and smiled. "This has been a merry supper, has it not? Now let's go into the parlour. There is something awaiting you there."

Joss could guess what it was as soon as he saw the rectangular shape hidden under a cloth. It was what he longed for. At his parents' encouragement, he approached the table on which it stood, savouring the moment, for it was in his nature never to rush at anything. In a way Letticia spoiled it for him. Impatient at the delay, she whipped the cloth away a fraction too soon for him and revealed the tool-box that stood there.

"Turn the key!" she urged. "See! It has a brass lock."

He turned it and slowly lifted the lid. Within lay all the tools he would need as an apprentice. A lump rose in his throat and he gulped it down, his chest tightening with pleasure. Almost wonderingly, he took out one tool and then another to handle and weigh in his hand, thinking of the work that would come to them under his guidance. He managed to express his thanks, more clumsily than he would have wished. "This is a day I'll never forget."

John set a firm hand on his shoulder. "Use them well, Joss."

"I will, you may be sure of that."

Hester, watching the two of them, had long since resolved how it should be for Joss. He was the one who would absolve the last shadow of his father's broken apprenticeship and put the name of Bateman on the map of London where it should have been from the start. All her hopes were pinned on this stalwart, serious son with his deep warm heart.

The house returned to normal routine the next day after Joss left. Hester had never been more content. These days when orders came in, it was taken as a matter of course that she should make whatever small articles were required while John took on the larger work pieces. It was not a question of skills but simply of preference, although she did take on work not truly to her choice whenever John required her help.

What mattered most to her was that as a result of her achievements at the workbench, she and John had at last that special communication that comes from completely shared interests, and the spectre of her illiteracy no longer plagued her. If she had to sign a receipt of delivery at any time, or some other such paper, she did it cheerfully with her cross. The lip-biting, sweat-producing agony of inscribing her name had been shut out with everything else on the day her lessons from John had finished forever. As well as John, she now had Letticia to read to her from the newspapers and she kept well abreast of political and world affairs.

The Jacobite uprising in Scotland and the north of England was a worrying matter. The London mobs, ever quick to flare, exhibited their anti-Stuart feelings with violent demonstrations, burning effigies of Bonnie Prince Charlie in the streets and setting buildings on fire in the process, sometimes accidentally but more often on purpose as an outlet of fury. Looting was an integral part of these events. When the Scots advanced into England on their way south towards London, the demonstrations became riots of ungovernable proportions.

On the evening the rioters surged dangerously near Nixon Square, Hester was alone in the house with Abigail, the two maids and the children. John believing them to be in a safe area, had gone out earlier on a delivery and was long overdue in returning, which added to her anxiety. As the din of shouting and yelling drew nearer, she went up to the attic window and looked out. The wind blew chill in her face and she could see a snake of flares approaching, smoke from some burning buildings in its wake. Even as she watched, she saw the column head into the street that led from some distance away into Nixon Square. Fear gripped her. Her first thought was the safety of the children and those in her charge, her second for the value of the silver in the workshop, which would bring the looters rampaging through her house with consequences she did not dare to think about.

She ran back down the flights of stairs to the kitchen, where the three women had gathered nervously together. "Wake the children and get them dressed without alarming them," she instructed Abigail. "The rioters may reach here." As one of the maids gave an hysterical squeal, she slapped down the girl's hands that had begun to flap in agitation. "There's no time for that, Matilda! Fetch me a ladder at once! I have to get the sign down from outside. There's no sense in advertising that a goldsmiths' outworker lives here."

148

"What can I do, ma'am?" the second maid asked her, more level-headed than her workmate.

"Shut and fasten all the shutters in the house, Joan!"

While they ran to do as she had bidden them, she herself went to the workshop to collect the tools she would need. The ladder was outside when she opened the front door, Matilda having brought it round from the outhouse at the back, and the girl supported it as Hester mounted the rungs. The smell of smoke was in her nostrils and the rioters were smashing windows as they approached, to judge by the tinkling of glass. Afraid that any moment they would come into view, the nails securing the suspended sign defeating all her efforts with a chisel, she took the mallet she had tucked into her sash and with all her strength dealt a heavy blow to the wooden bracket that held the sign. It cracked but did not give. Two more blows and it broke, crashing to the ground below and taking the sign with it.

While the maid returned the ladder, Hester gathered the broken wood and the sign, which she bundled back indoors with her. After shooting home the bolt on the door and turning the key, she dragged and pushed a heavy hall table against it to give further protection. Joan and Matilda came in time to help her lift an oak cupboard sideways on to it.

"Now get my gardening spades. We have to dig a large hole in my herb garden."

It was hard to see her carefully tended herbs being dug aside, but there was too much at stake to think of them. Fortunately, the soil being soft and damp, it did not take long for the three of them to make a sizeable hole. In the workshop she unlocked the chest where the silver materials were secured for safe-keeping and put them into a sack, which was carried away to be buried. Ann and Letticia had appeared with Abigail, and to them she gave finished and half-made workpieces wrapped in a cloth to run out with to the herb garden. Peter ran, too, with some spoons.

By now the rioters were in the square. She flew out the back door, locked it with some difficulty, the last of the silver in her arms, and while Abigail gathered everyone to hide in the outhouse, she buried what she carried. Scooping the earth roughly into place, she pushed back some clumps of herbs and hoped the garden would pass muster in the light of the flames. Then she joined the others in the outhouse. It was where the winter logs were stored and all her gardening tools were kept. The children gathered to her immediately, frightened by the din. She perched on a box, putting her arms around them, with Peter climbing into her lap.

"There's no need to be afraid," she assured them. "Those noisy people will run past our house soon and then we'll go back indoors and have some hot chocolate for a treat before you go to sleep again."

It did not sound as if the rioters were going past. In her mind's eye Hester could picture the swirling mass of maddened people beating against the square of houses like an angry tide. Her heart almost stopped as the side gate crashed open and rioters thundered in over the cobbles of the yard to batter at the back door of her house, yelling and bawling and bent on an orgy of destruction. The glass of the workshop window shattered, but for security reasons the shutters were extra strong and resisted the blows aimed at them. How long the locks on both windows and the door would withstand the onslaught, Hester had no idea, her fervent hope being that those milling feet would not kick up what had been hidden shallowly in the soil.

When a cheer went up she realised that the door must have given. She shuddered at the violation of her home, drawing the children still closer to her. At least the rioters would find nothing in the workshop. Pray God they did not come searching outside to the woodshed.

Musket shots and screams added to the racket in the square. If anything the roar of the mob became louder, like that of a wounded animal.

"What can be happening, ma'am?" Abigail asked her fearfully.

"I don't know. Whatever it is, I think it's bringing those people out of my house."

It sounded as if they were leaving in a kind of panic, departing as quickly as they had come. There were more musket shots and the din began gradually to recede.

"I think it's over," Abigail said, her voice rising on a hopeful note. Then she caught her breath on a rasp as the side gate opened again. One of the men had come back. They heard him go at a run into the house. Hester, straining her ears, could hear him shouting. Disengaging the children's arms and then lifting Peter onto Abigail's lap, she got up and opened the door to look out cautiously.

"Don't go out there, Mama!" Letticia implored tearfully.

"It's all right," she replied reassuringly. "I think I heard my name. Yes, I did!"

She pushed wide the door and ran across the yard into the house. John, coming downstairs from a frantic search for his family, saw her rushing to meet him.

"Thank God!" he exclaimed, kissing and hugging her in joyous relief. "I was afraid you had tried to escape and become caught up in the riot!"

"No! No! We hid in the outhouse. We're all safe." She leaned back in his arms to look at him. His face was bruised and his coat torn. "What happened to you?"

"I had a struggle to reach Nixon Square in the throng, but I managed to get through."

"What was the shooting?"

"The militia was called in. We mustn't let the children look out on the square until the morning. A few rioters were shot and they're being carried away."

"Let's fetch the children now."

They had their promised hot chocolate before they went to bed and so did everyone else, all seated round the kitchen table. Downstairs was a shambles where cupboards had been opened and contents smashed and spilled, but the rioters had not had time to get upstairs and those rooms were undisturbed.

In bed, John decided the time had come to break some bad news to Hester. "I'm afraid tonight has been a financial disaster for us, my love. All the silver from the workshop was looted."

"No, it wasn't." Lying close within his embrace, she turned towards him. "It's all buried in my herb garden. Tomorrow you can dig it up."

Astonishment widened his eyes and then he chuckled at her ingenuity, gathering her to him. "No man ever had a wife like you, my darling!"

At that point passion swept them both away. At dawn next morning when he took a spade to the herb garden the spout of a silver teapot showed him where to begin digging, and by a clump of chives a half-finished tankard had been churned up to the surface by the milling of feet there.

The advance of the Scots ended at Derby and they were driven back across the border, the rebellion crushed, and the city settled down once again. Hester did not. She had believed her family complete. Due to Peter being a most sensible child, she had had more freedom than ever before to work at John's side. Now she was never going to forget the riot and many times in the future she was to wonder if the troubles of that night had left their mark on her fifth child.

Throughout the months of her pregnancy she was sickly and ailed as she had never done before. At first she tried to carry on at her bench in the workshop but her tiredness and lack of energy defeated her and waves of faintness forced her to retreat to a couch upstairs, where she spent most of her days. John could only guess at her frustration in having to confine her hands to sewing and embroidery instead of to the rich craft of precious metals.

There had been times when he had thought seriously of registering his punchmark and opening his own business as an independent goldsmith, but it was a great risk for a family man of moderate means, and now a new threat to his livelihood had arisen. In Sheffield a new and cheap method of making plate had been discovered, a process by which a thin coat of silver was applied by fusion to a copper base. Nobody in goldsmithing knew what effect it was going to have on the trade, and there was plenty of head-shaking and pursed lips in the goldsmiths' coffee-house whenever the subject was discussed. As yet he had no lack of work, which made it harder to have Hester indisposed, and he had had to sub-contract in turn. As for the forthcoming addition to his family, he would welcome the infant when it came, even though he knew from Hester's lack-lustre eyes that this was the one child she could have done without.

Almost as if in revenge for being unwanted from the start, the Batemans' third son, who was to be named William, chose to delay for many pain-racked hours before finally making his appearance, feet first, just as dawn was rising. He almost cost Hester her life. If she had not been a survivor by nature she would have succumbed during her ordeal. As it was, she lay exhausted for hours afterwards, not knowing who came and went at the bedside. William was four days old before she had the strength to look at him and hold him. By then he had become accustomed to a wet-nurse, Hester having no milk, and the vital link that might have drawn them together was lost. He was the first of her children to bear no likeness to John from the start, and that in itself detracted from his chances of arousing love in her. She could only see one of her half-brothers in him, the greediest of those who had been present at the dividing of her childhood home, and she was thankful when he was taken from her and put back in his crib. As she might have expected, he bawled in protest and he had a loud and penetrating wail. She closed her eyes wearily, turning her face to one side on the pillow, terribly afraid she had given birth to a tyrant of the nursery.

Her fears proved to be well founded. When fed, comfortable, warm and newly dry, he would continue to bawl, his tiny fists flailing as if to hit back at all who came near him. Seeming to need sleep only in snatches, he disturbed the nights of the Bateman household and disrupted the days to the best of his ability. Only Ann was able to quieten him. Something in her soft voice, perhaps a recognition of love in her tone, would make him gulp into silence, listening to her intently. It became her greatest pleasure to care for him and, although she was a child herself, she treated him as a little person and not as a doll.

Abigail, who had become larger and rounder and plainer in the fourteen years she had been with the Bateman family, was full of praise for Ann. "She's a real little mother, madam," she said often enough to Hester. "Young William would nearly have driven me out of my wits at times if it hadn't been for her."

Privately Hester felt the same. At least William had done something for Ann that nobody else had been able to do, for by accepting responsibility for him she had come out of her shell. Her pride in being the one most able to comfort him had given her an awareness of herself as an important cog in the family wheel. She would always be the quiet one, for nothing could change that reserve inherent in her, but she no longer hung her head when she was the focus of attention, and the worst of her shyness seemed to have left her.

Although Hester was never able to feel the same depth of love for William as she did for her other children, she eventually overcame her initial withdrawal by reminding herself that he had been fathered by the man she loved. With time he lost the look of her relative that had helped to turn her from him and became a handsome child with a mop of dark chestnut curls, his smile mischievous and merry, and he had a fount of laughter in him.

He was also strong-willed and destructive. Unlike his brothers and sisters when they were small, he wrecked whatever came into his path. Toys hoarded from the past were broken the moment they came into his hands, and whatever he was unable to destroy he tossed from him, invariably causing some damage in the process. When he was reprimanded, he would focus a melting appeal for forgiveness that invariably caused all hostility towards him to fade away. Hester alone failed to be moved by either his open, hazel-eyed gaze or his lisping words. She recognised, as nobody else in the family appeared to, that he had been born with the most devastating power that any human being could have over others, which was the gift of charm. Ann had been the first to succumb from his crib days and was his constant champion, ever trying to conceal his misdemeanours and making excuses for him. It was she who wept when Hester punished him, while he received a slap or a locking in his room without a tear, merely puzzled that his mother alone could never be won over and retained that hard glint in her eye.

"At least we know there's not going to be a third goldsmith among our sons," John said with amusement after some latest mischief by William had been reported to him. "To my mind, he shows all the signs of becoming a pugilist when he's grown."

"I trust not," Hester replied wearily. William had run riot once again in the workshop. Since then the lower half of the door was kept permanently bolted while the upper half stood wide. He freqently escaped Abigail and Ann to come to the door and hammer on it for admittance and, if ignored, would throw whatever came to hand over the top. Again and again, Hester had to interrupt her work to drag him back to whoever happened to be searching for him.

With her concentration at the workbench frequently broken by these tussles with William, or by the need to investigate an uproar of his making in another part of the house, she was far more tired at the end of the day than she would have needed to be. John's arms at night were always a comfort to her. It was through tiredness and sleepy warmth that she failed to take her own simple precaution against further conception.

Her sixth and last child, another son, was born in the second week of November, 1747. It was a quick and easy birth, a contrast in every way to William's delivery. Unexpectedly, William did not resent this new arrival on the scene. Only the baby's name defeated him. He could not manage to say Jonathan. " 'thon," he called his brother. But it was typical of him that he did not give in until eventually he had mastered it. "Jonathan!" he shouted triumphantly. Then he shouted it daily about the house until those around him clapped hands over their ears.

It was always said in general conversation afterwards that it had been Jonathan's arrival that had created the need once more for a larger house and caused the move from Nixon Square. Letticia, an observant, quick-witted fourteen-year-old, held another opinion. Her father certainly appeared to think he had been the instigator, but the evidence was against him. Already Letticia had discovered, through taking note of her mother's tact, that a clever woman could manipulate a man into doing her will if she had a mind to it and, what was most important, letting him believe he had thought of it first. To the best of Letticia's knowledge, her father had been perfectly content at Nixon Square, but suddenly there was a great uprooting and the Batemans moved to the northern outskirts just beyond the city boundary to a house on a route out of London known as Bunhill Row. She was certain it was her mother's wish that had been fulfilled.

Letticia's deduction was close to the truth, although it had not been as hasty a decision as she supposed. In fact, it had involved much discussion between John and Hester, he seeing the threat of Sheffield Plate as a reason against a move from Nixon Square; she convinced that a step towards greater independence was long overdue. John was sufficiently established now as a dependable outworker to take himself beyond the city boundaries, where he would no longer be tied by many of its laws that restricted those, such as himself, with the skill in his craft to match any man but without the qualifications.

He was not, and never would be, an ambitious businessman, as she had discovered long since. His sole aim was security for her and the children, which in itself was highly commendable and far more than countless women received from their husbands. She was grateful for it, but nobody could advance without some risk and to avoid it was stultifying. She truly believed that if he had attained his freedom of the Goldsmiths' Company he would have been content to jog along as he did now, leaving the fame and glory to others. At least with Joss it would be different. Joss would bring renown to his father's name.

There was also another reason, no less important, that she had favoured a move. John worked extremely hard, as he had always done, and she was convinced that to be on the outskirts of the city and away from the river fogs when his day's labour was done would be immensely beneficial to him. Now and again he was subject to a slight cough, and although her herbal mixture of horehound, honey and egg-white soon banished it, she felt that the sweeter, cleaner air of the countryside would prevent further recurrence. It was an enormous relief to her when the move took place.

Bunhill Row ran right through the parish of St. Luke's, the southern end being mainly commercial due to its nearness to the hub of the city. There many prosperous businesses stood shoulder to shoulder, including the House of Whitbread, renowned for its ale. Towards the northern end it was mainly residential, although there was an armoury house in a large artillery ground and the residences, all well built and occupied mostly by well-to-do tradesmen and successful artisans, thinned out gradually into open countryside with Bunhill Fields rich with wooded groves and the glint of streams.

It was this open view that stretched beyond the windows of Number 107, the Batemans' new home in a row of three houses standing quite alone with gardens to the rear. Part of their garden was taken up by a light, airy workshop, solidly designed where the windows could be opened to the balmy country air.

John and Hester were soon to become acquainted with their neighbours, and Peter made friends the first day with the twin brothers of the Beaver family who resided at Number 84. They brought along some other boys, nearly all of them around the same age, and Peter was immediately absorbed into the group. Elizabeth Beaver, who happened to be his age exactly, had trailed in after her brothers. She stood staring at him with large sapphire-blue eyes, her fair hair tied up with a pink ribbon, and offered him one of the sticky toffee pieces that she had with her in a twist of paper. He took a piece and thanked her as best he could. It almost filled his mouth.

"I helped my mother make it," she informed him.

"It tastes good."

By then the others had fallen on the toffee and taken every piece. She did not complain, simply licking off whatever sugary fragments remained on the paper. Hester, sighting her from the window, invited her into meet Letticia and Ann. There was nothing tomboyish about her, quite the reverse, there being something almost ethereal about her looks, but although she became friendly with the girls she was to remain one of the boys' group, always on the outskirts, mostly ignored, but steadfastly attempting to join in the games and climb trees and run races. Hester took to her, admiring her spirit, and was pleased whenever she came to the house.

On her own first day in her new home Hester had seen again birds she had not fed since childhood, and Peter, who was clever with his hands, made a little bird table for her in spite of unwanted help from William.

"Leave that saw alone! Put down that hammer!" Exasperated, Peter finally dealt his brother a harder clout then he had intended and shoved him away. "Go back indoors."

William withdrew a few steps. The blow had hurt but he did not cry easily. He fixed his eyes on Peter in unspoken appeal and waited. It did not take long. He saw his brother glance towards him reluctantly and sigh.

"Oh, very well. You can hold the nails for me."

William beamed. "I won't drop them, I promise." He did, of course, quite accidentally, and they had to search for them in the overgrown grass of what would soon be a lawn again.

Hester had plans for the garden. There was room here for flowers and vegetables as well as her herbs. Already everything had run wild in the interim when the house had stood empty, waiting to be sold, and she would have to call in a gardener. The herbs she would sow herself when the spade work was done, and she would replant those brought from Nixon Square. She felt she had never been happier. She had loved the house from first sight. It was solid and unpretentious, not as large as its neighbours on either side but roomy and spacious, with softwood panelled walls, dentilled cornices and pleasing fireplaces. There should never be any need to move again. Here she could put down her roots once and for all.

John was also pleased with the new location when his last doubts about the wisdom of the move finally vanished. It was a far better area in which to bring up the children, Hester was happy as a lark to be back in the countryside and he and his workshop were still within convenient reach of the city. He could walk to his favourite coffee-house to talk shop with other followers of his craft in less than an hour and, although he was not much of a drinking man, there was a tavern, called the Royal Oak, within a few yards of his new home. Lying back from the street, which at this far end of Bunhill Row had petered out into a country lane, the tavern stood wall to wall with a large mansion, presently closed, which belonged to a London banker, James Esdaile. The forecourt of the tavern ran parallel to the well-kept flower garden that fronted the mansion, separated by the high garden wall that surrounded the Esdaile property. In the tavern, he heard more about the absent owner from local residents and he related what he had learned in turn to Hester.

"He is a widower with a twenty-year-old son and two younger daughters already wed. He rarely comes to the Bunhill Row residence."

"Why is that, do you think?"

"It's not his only home. He has a house in the city and another country seat at Great Gains, which he obviously prefers to Bunhill Row."

"I've looked through the gates. Everything is in perfect order. It must be a considerable expense to keep up a property never used."

John smiled. "From what I hear, it wouldn't matter to him. He's a wealthy man whose father began supplying accoutrements to the army from the building that is now the Royal Oak, which explains its cheek-by-jowl position to the house. It was a family business, but James Esdaile himself founded and is head of the Bank of Esdaile, Hammet and Company in Lombard Street."

Hester sat back in her chair and tapped her cheek thoughtfully with a forefinger. "Such a grand house must have a herb garden somewhere in its grounds, and mine is not going to be properly established until next year. Do you think there would be any objection to my taking what I needed if I speak to the Esdaile gardener?"

"I should suppose none at all."

"Then I'll seek out the fellow tomorrow."

He was not difficult to find, for he lived in a cottage along a lane that branched off Bunhill Row. Thomas Cole was a thin-faced man in his early thirties with the ruddy complexion of those whose living keeps them outdoors. His wife, who had a toddler at her skirts and a baby in her arms, proved to be the cleaner at the Esdaile mansion.

"Tom does the outside and I does in," she informed Hester cheerfully. "You take whatever 'erbs you want. We've a patch of our own 'ere and so those at the big 'ouse never gets picked."

"I shall appreciate having them." Hester put some money on the table as a sign of appreciation. Mrs. Cole promptly scooped it up and popped it into her apron pocket. She was undoubtedly the dominant partner.

"Do you want a gardener at your 'ouse, Mrs. Bateman? The garden there looks a real jungle."

That was the other reason Hester had called. "I was about to ask your husband if he would like to take it on." She turned deliberately to him. "Would you?"

"Yes, ma'am. I'll start whenever you like." He looked pleased at getting some voice in his own affairs. It was short-lived. His wife elbowed him out of the way.

" 'E'll chop wood and put up shelves or anything you want done. 'E's real 'andy."

Hester was glad to get away from the cottage. She thought Tom a pleasant, quiet man who would be an asset to have around the place, and she pitied him for his loud-talking wife.

Over a month passed before she had a chance to get to the Esdaile herb garden, because the hold-up in work due to the move meant that John was in urgent need of her at the bench. Fortunately Abigail, while still keeping the children in her charge, eased her mistress's domestic yoke by taking on the training and supervision of two local girls whom Hester had engaged as house-servants to replace those they had employed at Nixon Square who had not wanted to leave the city.

It was a warm, sunny day when Hester, a basket on her arm, eventually pushed open one of the tall ornamental double gates that led to the Esdaile mansion. She had notified Tom the day before of her coming, and he had left them unpadlocked for her. The lawns on either side of the short gravelled drive were like velvet, not a wayward daisy to be seen, proof in plenty that Tom was both a watchful gardener and a conscientious man. She paused to look up at the house, which was built substantially in rosy brick with moulded stone architraves to the tall windows that were shuttered from within. The entrance, which owed the shine of its brass door furniture to Mrs. Cole's polishing, was sheltered by an elegant porch supported by Doric columns, three steps leading down from it to the gravelled drive where she stood. It looked a good family house, one that should have been alive with the movement and vitality it must have known in the past. The shutters gave it a sad, lifeless look, and there was a tomblike stillness to it in contrast to the bustle of the tavern fettered to its north end.

A path led from the drive, and she followed it past the south end of the house to meet a vista of more lawns, shady trees and colourful flowerbeds. It was like entering another world, no sound reaching here from the tavern yard or the wheels along the lane. Only the birds broke the stillness, giving full throat to the glorious day. The fragrance of roses and honeysuckle hung in the air. She made her way to a stone seat and sat for a while savouring the beauty and peace of her surroundings. Curiously, she had the sensation of time being suspended in this place, and she smiled at the illusion, for many matters awaited her attention at home where the hands of the clocks would be whirling on. With effort, she bestirred herself and after a little exploration found the path behind a box hedge that would have allowed servants to pass between the kitchen garden and their own regions without being seen by anyone at leisure in the grounds.

The muted scent of the herbs reached her before she saw them, and then suddenly they were there in orderly profusion, the variations of colours giving the look of a patchwork quilt to the section of the kitchen garden they occupied. She was not surprised that another hedge made this a private place, because often the lady of the house would let nobody else have access to her herbs, dealing them out herself when they were needed for cooking, and making her own selection without witness for her distillations if she were a true herbalist.

Hester threaded her way slowly and carefully through the herbs, stooping or kneeling to gather what she required, snipping carefully with scissors and laying her harvest into the basket set down beside her. She marvelled at the lush growth of each herb. Butterflies fluttered about her, and bees came and went. Nothing gave warning when suddenly the peace was shattered.

"Who the devil are you?"

Startled, she looked up with a gasp and sat back on her heels. A large man, tall and broad, had bellowed at her in a blend of fury and astonishment, a resonance to his deep voice that could have belonged to a baritone in opera. Aged about forty, with a determined set to his head and shoulders, he had an astute, powerful face, large-nosed and strong-jawed, with greenish eyes that glinted at her from between narrowed, hooded lids. Guessing his identity from the little she had heard about him, she rose to her feet in a dignified manner, highly conscious of being pin-pointed as a trespasser—she a mature law-abiding woman of thirty-seven years. The additional adage of being a wife and mother did not come to her then for a reason she was only to comprehend later.

"You must be James Esdaile," she said evenly, dispensing with prefixes. "I'm Hester Bateman, new to the neighbourhood from the city. I never expected to see you, much less meet you, in such angry circumstances. I'll leave at once." She picked up her basket and turned to cross to the verge on the opposite side of the herbal patch, away from him.

"How near a neighbour are you?" His tone had eased. "Surely not at the tavern?"

She paused to glance in his direction. With the anger gone from his face, he was still a dramatic-looking man, and his settled features now gave the impression of one who would be prepared to reason and consider whatever was brought before him. There were even creases at the corner of his eyes that could only have come from laughter in happier moments, and for the first time she noticed that his lips had a sensual fleshiness indicating a fondness for the pleasures of life. But the situation had taken a turn-about. She was the hostile one now.

"No, I am not from the tavern. My husband has removed his goldsmithing workshop from the city to Number 107, Bunhill Row, and the reason I am here is that I'm still without a cultivated garden and was in need of some herbs." She tilted the basket to turn out what she had picked onto a small compost heap. Nothing would make her keep anything to which she was not welcome.

"Wait! Don't do that!" He came hurrying around the edge of the herbal patch to reach her where she, halted by his concerned shout, stood uncertainly with the basket at an angle. He grabbed it from her and held it away protectively. "I don't begrude you the herbs. My outburst had nothing to do with that. The truth is you gave me a great shock—no fault of yours. My late wife used to tend this place. Coming across you so unexpectedly touched a raw nerve of grief that I thought had been eased by time. I beg you to pardon my abruptness and my rough speech."

Pity moved her. She could understand what it must have meant for him suddenly to discover her there, and her aggravation with him melted away. "I accept your apology and I'm not offended. Your gardener told me there would be no objection, but I realise I should have obtained written permission from you before coming here."

"Not at all. What are neighbours for if not to oblige one another? Have you gathered all you want? Come and take what you need whenever you wish. If there are cuttings or seeds that you require for your own garden when it is ready for them, I should be pleased for you to transplant from mine."

"You are most kind." She was conscious of how he was assessing the woman she was, something close to a twinkle having come into his eyes, as if he was extraordinarily satisfied with the outcome of their encounter. He was without doubt an intensely physical man, and in the hushed and scented solitude, his maleness assailed her senses disturbingly. "I must go. I'll not interrupt any longer this rare visit you've made to your property. I'm sure you have company waiting for you."

"There's nobody with me." He fell into step at her side to escort her at a strolling pace back through the flowerbeds and across the lawn towards the path at the side of the mansion. "I came along to cast an eye over my property and decided to do a round of the grounds first. Everything out here appears to be in perfect order. Now I shall take a look indoors and hope to find all is well there."

"I'm sure you will." She was unable to hold back what had been in her thoughts since she had first seen the mansion and heard it was unoccupied. "It seems a great shame that there's no life in that beautiful place."

"You like the look of the house, do you?"

She nodded, surveying it sweepingly as they approached. The back was as full of fine windows as the front, and a flagged terrace was enclosed by a stone balustrade with the enhancement of potted urns from which green plants cascaded their foliage. "I don't know how you can stay away from it."

"Maybe I won't for much longer."

Some undertone in his voice held a meaning she chose not to think about, but it rippled within her like fingertips drawn across a harp. She spoke coolly as a defence. "Indeed? I heard that you have a country residence at Great Gains that you prefer to this one."

"Only because the city has encroached more upon this area and as a result the hunting as well as the shooting is better now at Great Gains." He threw her a sideways glance as they passed the south end of the house to enter the drive. "However, last week I made a marriage gift of the place to my son and his bride. So I'll not be going there again except by invitation."

She thought it a generous gift, not so much from a monetary value, since he was reputedly a very rich man, but because there had been an element of self-sacrifice involved, surely unspoken and therefore not known by the recipient. "Your son is young to wed," she commented.

"Following in the Esdaile tradition. I was only eighteen and my wife a year younger."

She refrained from saying that with John and herself it had been almost the same. "I believe I can guess why you've come to Bunhill Row today."

"Oh? What is your guess?"

"You're going to open up the house again," she ventured.

"I have it in mind."

"That's excellent news!" A little laugh of sheer pleasure at the mansion's forthcoming release from isolation rose up in her.

"I'm delighted that it pleases you." He was intrigued that it should matter to her. While they were speaking, they had reached the steps of the porch, and by coming to a halt himself he brought her automatically to a standstill when she might have expected him to see her right to the gates. She held out her hand to receive her basket of herbs, which he still held, and they exchanged a long smile indicative of friendship.

"My feeling is that you have known happy times in this house and you will again," she said sincerely.

He kept the basket at his side, leaving her hand still extended. "Why not come and see indoors for yourself?" Then, in case she should imagine he had any ulterior motive, he continued: "I happen to be considering remarriage. I should appreciate a feminine opinion as to any changes or alterations that should be made to suit a second wife before I bring her here."

She did not hesitate and inclined her head. It was a reasonable request, and she was curious to see if the interior of the mansion lived up to the promise of its handsome exterior. "I'll willingly give you any advice I can."

"That's most amiable of you." He took a key from his pocket. She followed him up the steps as he unlocked the door and flung it wide for her.

On the threshold she paused, looking over her shoulder at him. "How long is it since you lost your wife?"

"Ten years. It is a tedious length of time to be on one's own, although it seemed no more than ten minutes when I came upon you in the herb garden."

She was full of compassion. "Am I like her personally at all?" she inquired with interest.

His eyes hardened on her in a disconcerting stare. "She had the same free spirit in her that I see in you."

It was as if he had probed deep into her. She felt thrown by it. If she had not already stepped inside the house, she would have drawn back. But it was too late, even though he left the door open behind them to give light. She saw they were in an entrance hall of some grandeur, with a gracefully balustered staircase sweeping up to a gallery above. He put her basket down on a chair as he crossed to some double doors and opened them to disappear into what she supposed to be a drawing room. She followed him into it. Everything was shrouded in dust sheets. As he opened the interior shutters of the first window and folded them back on either side, flooding the long room with light, tapestry panels leapt into shades of emerald, cobalt, crimson and gold. A ceiling-high chimney piece was carved handsomely with what she guessed to be the family crest of a demi-lion rampant holding a mullet in its claws. On impulse, she darted forward and opened another of the windows herself, something she had wanted to do since she had first seen the blank, unseeing expanse of glass. James, who moved on to the one beyond her, laughed approval. They criss-crossed each other in turn until all eight windows had been unshuttered. Then they stood at a distance from each other in shared amusement. Not taking his eyes from her, he grasped a dust sheet covering a sofa and ripped it away, revealing its rich brocade.

"Pray be seated, ma'am."

She swept across to it and looked about as she settled herself. "This room is large enough to hold a ball in."

He sat down in a wing chair opposite her, not bothering to remove the dust sheet first. "Many have been held here in the past, both in my time and that of my father before me. Our family name was originally D'Estaile and it became anglicized when my Protestant grandfather fled from France to escape persecution after the revocation of the Edict of Nantes."

"Was he a military accouterer in France?"

The corner of his mouth lifted wryly. "Far from it. The comtes D'Estailes enjoyed a leisurely life on extensive estates for many generations. All of them were confiscated, and it was my father who had a commercial frame of mind and recouped our fortunes here. I'm proud to have followed in his footsteps and made my own contribution to the financial life of London."

She glanced again at the carved crest, which was linked to a French title no longer used and a heritage that went deep into the soil of France. Her gaze returned to him. He did not look particularly French except romantically across the eyes, for he had a dangerous way of looking at her—and probably at any woman attractive to him—that made her feel beautiful and intensely desirable and quite unique. It was impossible to remain immune to it and it was flattery of the most perilous kind. Firmly she brought her thoughts back to the purpose for which she had entered the house.

"From what you have said, I assume that much of the furniture dates from your father's time in residence here?"

"Some of the rooms are virtually unchanged, although my late wife did quite a lot of refurnishing, including the brocade sofas and chairs as well as the tapestries in this salon."

"Then I should advise you to remove anything that was personal to her. Give the items to your son or your daughters, who will treasure them. From what I know of remarriages, a second wife often finds it extremely hard to live with the first wife's possessions. It is as if she cannot make her own mark on the house or her husband's life with reminders of her predecessor on all sides."

He seemed less than pleased by her advice, his arched black brows drawing together. He had looked for no more than suggestions about the changing of faded drapes or the restuffing of upholstery. Yet he saw the common sense of what she had said, and on a sigh of acceptance he gave a shrug of resignation.

"You are right, of course. I shall do what you say. Any marriage involves a difficult enough adjustment without inviting disharmony. As it happens, the lady I'm to wed has the gentle name of Mary and none of the characteristics expected of it." His grin spread slowly and widely across his face. "Your wise counsel is most timely and I thank you for it."

"I'm gratified to have been of help," she replied smilingly, her curiosity about the future Mrs. Esdaile strongly aroused. He had spoken of her with fondness and respect, but the inference implied she was quite a firebrand. What effect would such a woman have upon this quiet house? It would be interesting to see. "How soon shall you be married?"

"Not until the spring of next year."

"There's no better time to tie the knot." She recalled her own wedding at St. Botolph's on a fine spring day.

"Would you like to see the rest of the house now?"

"I should be delighted."

He led her from room to room upstairs and down, entertaining her with tales of his father's time and of his own boyhood. She asked him about his daughters, for she wondered why he had not brought one or the other with him to look the house over. She learned that both lived with their respective husbands far out of London. That brought his city residence to mind.

"Shall you have to rid your London home of many things?" she asked.

"No. It was always very much a place of business. It was here at Bunhill Row and at Great Gains that my late wife turned everything to her liking." They had reached the entrance hall once more, and she had supposed the tour to be at an end when he added, "There's one more place of interest I'd like you to see."

He led the way along a corridor towards the north end of the house until they came to a thick studded door. She was intrigued as to where it led and wondered if he was going to reveal an entrance to something mysterious, such as an underground passage linked to some long-ago ruins on the site before his house was built. He was smiling to himself as he took a key from his pocket and inserted it in the lock. It clicked, and he threw the door wide for her.

She was astonished. There was nothing mysterious here. All that was revealed was a mundane little parlour furnished with simple comfort. Suddenly she had a clue in the rumble of voices resounding quite clearly through an ordinary panelled door opposite to where they were standing. She rushed across to climb onto a chair at the wall and look out the high and partly bottle-paned window.

"We're in the tavern!" she exclaimed.

He was buoyant with the success of his surprise. "That's correct. I could have had this part of the building pulled down when it was no longer needed for offices and storage, but it appealed to my sense of humour to let it become a tavern and to keep a door into my own private parlour. You see, I have a deep thirst and a great liking for good ale."

Looking down at him from where she still stood on the chair, she felt the joke of it rise in her. She threw back her head in a peal of laughter, and he bellowed into mirth with her. With her eyes almost shut with merriment, she pressed a hand against her chest to try to check her helpless laughter and swayed with it.

"Don't fall!" he guffawed, which seemed excruciatingly funny to them both at that moment, and he clasped her about the hips to let her slide down through his arms until her feet were on the ground. Still supporting her, he stared hard into her eyes for a matter of seconds and then plunged his mouth down on hers. It was a devouring kiss of extraordinary passion, driving mirth from them both, for he forced open her lips and crushed her to him until she thought her ribs would crack in his embrace.

When he released her, to his relief, she did not make the kind of stupid protest of outrage he might have expected from a respectable married woman caught off guard. Instead she filled her lungs and released a long breath. Straightening her cap and tucking some wayward tendrils of russet-bright hair back behind her ears, she regarded him quizzically.

"I think a small tankard of that same ale you mentioned earlier would be extremely acceptable now."

Their gaze held potently. This new friendship of theirs remained unimpaired, but he understood her silent communication that what had happened must not occur again. He chuckled his appreciation of her unruffled state.

"At once, ma'am. I've rarely heard a more timely suggestion." He made for the parlour door. Alone, she sank down into a windsor chair and cupped her hands over the smooth arm-ends. She could hear his firm footsteps pacing away down a flagged passageway to reach the taproom and then the sounds of greeting at his reappearance after a long absence. She ran her tongue over her lips. No man but John had kissed her mouth since the first kiss they had shared together. It was wholly through her own choice, for over the years other men as well as James had let her see she was an extremely comely woman in their eyes.

Yet nothing she could have done today would have stopped James Esdaile's show of passion. She had seen desire in his gaze from the first speech they exchanged in the herb garden. No matter what he had been saying throughout the tour of the house, whether interesting or mundane, his hooded greenish eyes had been telling her that he would be her lover at any time she should so wish. Such was the dominance of his personality, the thought of husband and family had been absent since the first moment of their initial meeting until now, when she was on her own. She felt as if she had been at the centre of a firework display, but now it was over and the sparks had faded.

James returned ahead of the landlord, who bore a tray with a small mug of frothing ale for her and a two-pint pot for him. "Good day to you, Mrs. Bateman," the landlord greeted her. "It's an honour for the Royal Oak to have Mr. Esdaile back in his parlour again and to welcome you on your first visit."

Hester thanked him. It was obvious the landlord assumed she and James were previously acquainted, both being from the city, and she was thankful for it, because it would stem any gossip. When he had gone, leaving them together, James sat down in a chair turned sideways to the table and facing her. After handing the small mug to her, he raised his own heavy pewter pot in a gallant toast.

"To you and your beauty, ma'am!" As he drank deep, he reflected that there were women and women. Hester was one he would covet for a long time to come.

That evening, while John was mending one of Jonathan's toys that William had broken, she sat sewing a new dress for Letticia and told her husband all that had happened that day. Only an account of the kiss was omitted.

"Is Esdaile still at the mansion?" he asked, having listened attentively as he always did whenever she related her activities and those of the children.

"No. He left on horseback shortly after I came away, but he gave me a key to the side gate and I'm at liberty to help myself to the herbs at any time."

"That was most neighbourly of him."

She lowered her sewing to watch him making the toy as good as new again. In the candlelight he looked much as when she had first fallen in love with him, shadows softening the mature set of hardened bones in his face. Gone forever was that trembling awareness between them that comes from the meetings of young flesh; the possessing and the being possessed that is a kind of miracle as if nobody else had ever known such love before; the tender exploration of all that was new and magically different in a man and a woman. Now there was a richer element in their ardent comings together, the years having added their own quality, as to good wine. Those who mocked the chances of enduring love in marriage could never comprehend what was between this man and her. There in the quiet candlelight, her ardent devotion to him seemed to well up and engulf her from head to toe. It was one of those moments when the very strength of her love for him alarmed her and she was at a loss to know why.

It was not until Hester was going upstairs to bed that she remembered she had left her basket of herbs in the mansion. She smiled and shook her head at her forgetfulness. At least the drying herbs would give a lingering fragrance to the empty rooms, like a reminder of her brief presence there.

Some weeks later wagons arrived at the mansion, showing that James had taken her advice, and a great deal of furniture and boxes were taken away. She thought how individually James's mother, his wife and she herself had all exerted influence over the furnishings of that grand residence. Soon it would be another woman's turn. She hoped it would be done with kindness.

Chapter 8

In spite of John's original misgivings, the manufacture of Sheffield Plate appeared to have created its own market and made little impact in his trade. Orders continued on a steady inflow, and he was able to ask a more realistic payment for his output now that he was beyond the city's restrictions, which made a long overdue difference to the Bateman income. Early on he had acquired a horse on which to make his deliveries, and he kept it in a high-roofed stable beyond the kitchen garden, where there was plenty of room for a carriage, if ever he should be able to afford one.

Not long after their arrival in Bunhill Row, Abigail had met and married a farm labourer with a tied cottage, which she made cosy and comfortable. She was near enough for the children to visit her and came to help at the house when needed. There was no need to replace her, for Ann took charge of the boys. Hester continued to work with John, supervise her household, organise their social activities and spend time with the children as adeptly as moving chess pieces on a board. But there were times when she felt an urgent need for time to be on her own in which to draw breath and revitalise her energies.

Ideally she would have liked to take long, solitary walks in the surrounding countryside, which would have been different from the family rambles with a picnic. She longed to follow some wooded slope, but with the constant demands on her time, she could make only short excursions into the glades and meadows. When even those little outings would have kept her away too long, she snatched some moments of solitude in the Esdaile herb garden where nobody came near. Now and again she sketched the birds there.

Retreat to this peaceful place ended some months after James's remarriage, which had taken place as he had predicted in the spring, when suddenly one morning an architect arrived to make a preliminary inspection. After that there were many comings and goings. The Esdaile carriage was there several times. Hester glimpsed it in the drive, but never once did she see either James or his new wife.

Another lapse of time went by and then the architect was on the spot almost daily, having installed an army of artisans to work outside and in. It soon became apparent that the mansion was to lose its simple exterior lines and take on some Palladian splendour, which was highly fashionable. Hester doubted whether James cared for such drastic alterations, but on one point he had had his way; the mansion remained solidly attached to the wall of the Royal Oak, his door into the domain of good ale undisturbed.

In the grounds, which were being newly laid out by a landscape gardener, only the herb garden was being retained in its original secluded position. Hester, having a special understanding of the reason, was glad about it. The second wife would never know it had been special to the first Mrs. Esdaile. It occurred to her that it was a secret that only she and James shared.

By now her own herb garden was well established. Contrary to her hopes, the country air had not entirely banished John's cough. He would be in full health for months on end and then it would return, usually at night to disturb his rest. It always passed, and he promptly forgot about it, while Hester hoped that the new herbal syrup she had made for him that particular time had been the one that cured it.

No one else ailed, except for the usual childhood sicknesses. These bouts, although they were full of danger and alarming at the time, passed over in each case without after-effects. Jonathan had been the least robust of her children, but even that had been overcome. If he was a little spoiled through his frail beginnings, as well as being the youngest, it was to be expected. He followed William about everywhere and invariably ended in the same kind of trouble, covered with mud or with cut knees and was once rescued in the nick of time from a wooden box that William thought would float the two of them down a stream.

Peter, apart from being older, was too busy to be involved with his younger brothers. He was receiving lessons with other pupils from a retired tutor to whom he went daily in a nearby house in Bunhill Row. Joss's tales of his experiences at the charity school had spared Peter from a similar fate, and John, who watched results, was satisfied that his son was getting a classical education better than that which Joss had received.

"I wouldn't have minded going away to school," Peter confided to Joss, "in spite of the birchings, because it would have been fun travelling to and fro on the stage, but I'm glad not to leave my birds and animals."

That had been his particular dread. Presently he had a lame fox cub that he had rescued from a trap, an owl with a broken wing, a kitten he had found half drowned in a sack and a baby thrush he had reared and was shortly to release into the wild. In the country-side he had come into his own in a different way from his mother. Having always had a heart for small creatures, he was able now to care for any he came across that were injured or distressed. It was why he had never liked visiting the zoo at the Tower. It had seemed terrible to him that those strange and wonderful beasts should be in that bleak place away from their natural habitat.

As the months passed, Joss's twenty-first natal day drew near when his apprenticeship would be at an end, seven years of it be-hind him. He wrote that he had made some important plans that he would tell them about when he came home. Hester released a satis-fied sigh as John finished reading the letter to her.

"How happy he sounds! He must have been promised employ-ment by one of the leading goldsmiths to be in such spirits."

John nodded with a smile. "I should think it's something like that. Well, we shall know at the end of the month."

"It will be hard to wait."

On the morning when Joss would be enrolled into the Gold-smiths' Company, Hester's thoughts were with him. If she and John could have witnessed the occasion, they would have been at the Goldsmiths' Hall. It was a simple business, without ceremony, of signing documents and registering the "touch," which in Joss's case was *J.B.*, and spectators, whether family or friends, were not ex-pected to be present except by official invitation. She drew comfort from his promise to come straight home that same afternoon.

It was barely past midday when she began watching the clock. A good dinner with his favourite dishes was in the final stages of preparation, the table laid, the girls already in their best dresses. The three boys were keeping watch on the road between games. Then, as so often happens when an arrival is long awaited, the moment everyone's attention was diverted elsewhere he arrived unheralded. Hester, half-way across the parlour to take yet another look out the window, paused as the door opened and there he was.

"Joss!"

He was a fine-looking young man now, wide-shouldered, with a tapering long-limbed body, and he was wearing the new coat that he had been told to order at his father's expense for his great day. She rushed to him and he hugged her.

"It's good to be home," he said warmly as he had said so often before. "And this time as a fully fledged craftsman to stay. Nothing shall dislodge me from the Bateman workshop again!"

She stepped away from him, not entirely sure she understood his meaning, and her smile became uncertain. "You're joking, of course," she said, although it was entirely out of character for him to do so. "Don't withhold your good news any longer. Who is to be your distinguished employer?"

"Father. Who else?"

The colour drained from her face with a swiftness that was painful. She said the first thing that came into her head. "But he's not a master craftsman. We only do outwork here. You'd have no chance to put your own 'touch' on articles you had made."

"Neither would I whoever I worked for."

She laced her fingers in and out in her agitation. "But with time you would open your own workshop in the city and employ journeymen yourself." Her dreams for him were being put into words. "You'd be known as Master Bateman, and every piece that left your benches would bear the punchmark *J.B.* for all the world to see."

"I'm not interested in personal fame. All that matters to me is that I do good work, and I like the variety of the orders that come through Father's workshop." While he had been speaking there had come the sound of the others approaching. He swung round to face his father, his brothers and sisters clustering behind.

"My felicitations on becoming a Freeman of the Goldsmiths'

Company, my son!" Jubilantly John shook his son's hand. "It's been a long stretch, has it not? But all worth while."

"Indeed it has, sir."

Then William and Jonathan, who had been held back by Peter's grip on their collars, bounded forward to greet their returned brother, who after a few words with each of them leaned across to kiss both his sisters on the cheek. Hester's voice broke across the family merriment with a harshness of stress that made it almost unrecognisable to herself as well as to them.

"Joss wants to work at the bench with you, John! That is his grand plan!"

"Will you take me on, Father?" Joss said at once.

In helpless frustration Hester saw John's face become transfigured with joy. Instead of advising Joss to look further afield, he shook his hand again as heartily as before. "Nothing could please me more. You shall have a place at the bench and I'll be proud to have you there."

"I thank you. I've never wanted to be anywhere else when the time came. But there is still something more I want to tell you and Mother on your own."

Letticia took the hint and with Ann's help shepherded the boys out of the room again. As soon as the door closed after them, Hester turned away to sink down on the sofa, struggling for self-control; she saw the agreement between the two men as a rejection of all the hopes she had cherished since Joss had shown the first clear signs of being destined to follow his father into goldsmithing. She felt broken inside.

"What is it you have to tell us?" she asked hoarsely, keeping her tormented face averted.

"I've brought someone with me today. She's waiting in the lane. I wanted her to come in with me, but she thought I should have the first moments alone with my family in view of my enrolment today and what it means to you both as well as to me."

"Go and fetch her," John urged genially. "What is her name?"

"Alice Case. I've known her three years. She is the daughter of a drapery merchant whose house is opposite my former master's workshop. We're going to be married."

There was complete silence in the room for seconds that seemed like an age. John spoke with the surprise still lingering in his voice. "You're a man of twenty-one and I knew my mind about your mother and married her before I was your age. If you have found a girl to match her, then I've no objection."

"She does, sir." He looked towards his mother, hoping that she, with whom he had always been in harmony, would give some sign of approval.

Hester, whose spine had jerked rigid as a wand at the marriage announcement, felt as if a faint glimmer had shown itself in the blackness of her present disappointment. If he had really found the right girl, one with the force of character to be ambitious for him as she had been for John, there was every chance that with time Joss would still attain all that she herself wanted for him. She smoothed her fingertips from her temples down the side of her face as if to wipe away any outward signs of the turmoil within her.

"Bring Alice in," she said, twisting around from the waist to look at her son. "It's not right that a future daughter-in-law of this house should have to wait at the gate."

His face suffused with pleasure, and he disappeared from the room. John crossed to where she sat. She had lowered her head at his approach, and he cupped her chin in his hand to look fully into her shattered eyes.

"I know this unexpected turn isn't what you wished for, but remember Joss would not have made his decision to work with us without giving the matter the most serious thought."

"He'll be hiding his light under a bushel!" she burst out protestingly.

John raised her to her feet. "I don't see it that way. Maybe I understand him a little more than you do, my dear."

She pressed her fists against his chest, her expression desperate. "I want so much for him!"

An indefinable change came over John's face, a blend of sudden anger, compassion and love. He seized her by the shoulders and shook her, his fingers digging deep until they brusied. "Let him be, Hester! For God's sake, let the boy be!"

She stared at him for a few seconds before she broke away at the sound of Joss's voice in the hall. "They're coming!" she gasped.

Hastily she glanced into a gilt-framed looking-glass on the wall and touched her hair into place. Her first sight of her daughter-in-law was in its reflection as Joss brought her into the room. The age-old question, common to parents, leapt into her mind. "Whatever can he see in her?" In the same moment that last faint glimmer of hope was extinguished. If she had thought rationally, she would have known that Joss would have fallen in love with a tranquil-faced girl, whose plain features would be beautiful to him, lighted as they were by serene grey eyes. In her he had found his haven. There would be no stimulating conflict between these two, no spurring ahead by this docile girl.

Hester turned from the looking-glass and forced a smile to her lips as Joss proudly presented Alice to her and John. She scarcely knew what conventional words she uttered in accepting her into the family, but they must have been adequate, for the girl looked shyly pleased.

"It is an honour to be received so graciously into Joss's home," she replied, her voice low and melodious. "I hope it is not too much of a surprise for you."

Hester let John speak, her throat too choked at that moment. "By no means," he insisted. "Pray sit down and let us become acquainted."

She took the chair indicated, arranging the billowing folds of her blue silk skirt, which was parted in front as was the fashion to reveal an underskirt, hers being figured with clusters of forget-me-nots. Under a high forehead her nose was long, her brows and lashes sandy-light, echoing the mediocre colour of her hair, her complexion pitted by some past attack of smallpox and her chin small. Yet Joss, who had pulled up a chair to sit beside her and hold her hand, was gazing at her as if mesmerised, stunned with love.

"My parents sent their compliments to you, Mr. and Mrs. Bateman," she said, her smile quick and kindly, redeeming to some extent the plainness of her face. "They hope you will be at liberty to dine with them next Sunday."

"We should be delighted," John accepted promptly. He glanced across at Hester almost warningly. "Is that not so, my dear?"

"Yes, indeed." She was in full control of herself again. Even if she had not been, she would never have spoiled this day for her dear son, whose face was shining with happiness to see his betrothed in his own home. "How soon do you plan to marry?"

Joss answered. "Now that we have your blessing, we shall arrange for the banns to be read for the first time in our respective churches next Sunday."

"So soon?" Hester said faintly.

"We have no need to wait any longer, having waited for three years." He exchanged a sweetheart's look with Alice, whose whole face softened with a devotion to match his.

It told Hester a great deal. Yes, they had waited in every sense of the word. Those who have known each other intimately have more realism and less magic in their glances. At least this slip of a girl had not caused Joss to jeopardise his future, and she was grateful to her for that. "Do you wish to live here?"

"No, Mother." Joss showed that he was highly pleased with what he had to tell. "We are able to buy our own house with Alice's dowry and set ourselves up comfortably."

John raised an interested eyebrow. "You lead us to assume you have found a place to your liking already."

"We have." Joss and Alice exchanged another of those enraptured glances that can shut out the world before he spoke again, his grin broad. "We are to be your near neighbours at Number 85, Bunhill Row. We heard it was for sale a little while ago, and everything is settled."

To Hester it was the final seal on Joss's resolve never to move from the Bateman workshop, for the house was one of a pleasing four-storied terrace with grace and style, large enough to accommodate any good-size family and half a dozen servants. Joss would never have to look for more spacious accommodation, however many children he might have. At the age of twenty-one he had settled his choice on his woman, his work and his place of abode for the rest of his life. Such would have been John's future if she had not crossed his path and disrupted his intention to marry Caroline. Surely a father and a son had never been more alike in temperament and outlook.

At the celebratory dinner, which had been arranged with such thought for Joss's first hours as a Freeman goldsmith, toasts were drunk to the betrothed pair. Over the rim of her glass, Hester looked along the faces of her family on either side of the table and her eyes came to rest on Peter. With his reddish-brown hair and light brown eyes flecked with gold, he was the most like her in looks and in character, her love of birds having taken in him a gentle twist towards all small creatures. He was full of energy and ambition, already looking forward to when he would start his gold-smithing apprenticeship. He was her hope now; he the one to vin-dicate the name of Bateman. For the first time since Joss had broken his news to her, she relaxed and felt the tension ebb from her. She would have to wait longer to see her dream fulfilled, but nothing was lost.

At the head of the table John looked down the length of the board at her and saw she had come to life again. She was laughing as their eyes met. He gave her a look of love that only she could interpret and raised his glass to her. She responded with a smile just for him in the midst of their grown-up and growing children.

Joss and Alice were married at the Cases' parish church. After a lavish wedding breakfast with family and friends, they rode in her father's carriage to 85, Bunhill Row, ribbons dancing from it, and shut the door on the world for several days. Then Joss, who had started work the day after first presenting Alice to his parents, re-turned to the workbench as if he had never been away from it, a quiet happiness in his serious eyes.

He soon showed himself to be the perfect complement to the work-team John and Hester had become, and when disagreements arose, he and his father settled them amicably. Although as a new-comer, he was allotted the mundane workpieces, he knew it was all part of settling in and would change later. Always deep-thinking about spiritual matters, he took a particular interest in ecclesiastical plate and felt well rewarded when given the chance to make an article destined for a church, whatever denomination.

Across from his new home, the alterations to the Esdaile mansion had been completed long since, with still no sign of it being opened for occupation. Hester took up again her quiet sojourns in its herb garden, interested in all news of the Esdailes that reached Bunhill Row. They had had three children in quick succession in the four years of their marriage, and it was supposed locally that the avoidance of travel and the need to remain close to some London physician of high repute for her confinements had kept Mrs. Esdaile from visiting the house that had been completely refurbished to her taste. Hester found the new lay-out of the grounds too formal to suit her liking; it was as though the flowers and trees and bushes had been regimented into place. She was always glad to reach the simplicity of the fragrant herb garden and draw its own special balm into herself before returning to another kind of contentment at the workshop bench.

There was a bunch of recently picked herbs giving a delicate perfume to the workshop one warm and sunny morning when Joss had ridden off to the city to make a delivery of flatware. John and Hester were busy with individual workpieces, bathed by a soft breeze through the open windows, when suddenly their peace was disrupted. Jonathan, wild-eyed with excitement, a gloating look on his narrow face, came bursting in.

"William climbed the tree to get onto the stable roof for a dare. Now he's stuck at the top and can't get down!"

Simultaneously his parents downed their tools without wasting words or time and rushed out. A salver that had been propped at an angle on the bench went on rattling like a settling top. Jonathan glanced around the workshop as he left it. One day he would be a goldsmith and earn lots of money and buy everything he wanted in the way of toys and sweetmeats. Nobody should stop him having anything. One of the reasons he had ceased to follow William in his escapades was that he had discovered retribution was not pleasant; he did not like going without supper or losing the chance of an outing, or being kept in his room on his own for an hour or more. Sometimes through being two years younger and by putting all the blame on William, he had managed to wriggle out of punishment, but his mother's eyes had begun to bore into him at such times, making it hard to keep what he thought of as his "good" look on his face. It was far better to be a spectator to William's ventures and, when the opportunity presented itself, as today, to be the first to report them.

When he reached the stable yard there was no pandemonium and all was remarkably calm. Gone were the neighbourhood boys who had dared William to make the perilous ascent, and Jonathan guessed they had scattered when he had run to raise the alarm. His mother stood quite still, her shaking hands clenched together the only sign of her stress. His father was talking quietly up to William, who sat ashen-faced atop the high thatched roof. It was a sizeable building, and he was as far from the cobbled yard below as a gargoyle on a church roof.

"There's nothing to worry about, William," John was saying reassuringly. "I'll fetch a ladder and get you down in no time."

William gulped. "The thatch is rotten just here. It may not hold a ladder." Even as he spoke, the straw gave way under his right foot and he saved himself from overbalancing by tipping full length from the waist along the rim, clutching hard. Hester clapped a hand over her mouth to suppress a cry and her face, already pale, lost its last vestige of colour.

John, who had felt his heart stop, gave a sharp instruction. "Don't move! I'm coming!"

Diving into the stable to fetch the longest ladder there, he was enraged with himself for not having had the stable repaired and rethatched months ago. It had been in need of new rafters to replace those that were no longer safe when they had first come to Bunhill Row, but he had postponed the expense, padlocking that part of the stables to keep the children out. When he had purchased his nag the repairs had been postponed again, for the thatch had been weatherproof in that section and the beams stout over the hayloft and the stalls below. Underneath William's perch there was a sheer drop down to the unused and still padlocked tack-room with its flagged floor.

Taking a coil of rope from a hook, he threw it over his shoulder and bent to seize the heavy ladder, which he half-carried, half-dragged out into the yard. Hester ran forward to lend her aid by lifting the foot of it off the ground, and together they hurried with it to the sun-baked west end of the stable.

"I sent Jonathan to tell the girls to fetch Tom Cole," she gasped breathlessly.

"Good. I may need his help." He set the ladder against the mellow brickwork and began to climb the rungs while Hester supported it. If he could have trusted the tackroom rafters he would have chosen that route, but it was doubtful whether they would take William's weight, much less his own.

He reached the top of the ladder. It brought his shoulders level with the main beam to which William clung and where the thatch was thin and partly disintegrated. A third of its length lay between them.

"You'll have to edge your way along to me," he told William, "so I'm going to make a noose in this rope for you to put over your shoulders and push down to your waist." The knot formed under his nimble fingers as he talked. "Then there isn't the least chance of your falling even if you do slip."

"I came this far and couldn't get back after I heard part of the roof fall somewhere." William's mouth was set determinedly against giving way, but he could not control its tremulous corners.

"Were you trying to do the whole length?"

"Yes, Father."

"Well, you shall now with me to hold you tight. Now try to catch this rope at first go."

At the foot of the ladder Hester felt it vibrate as John tossed the rope. She bit deep into her lip and closed her eyes in suspense until she heard his exuberant praise for a successful catch. Then came light steps rushing across the yard and Ann was there, lending her weight to the ladder's support, fright dilating her eyes.

"Letticia has gone for Tom," she gasped. "One of the maids is keeping Jonathan indoors."

Hester nodded, beyond speech. It was comforting to have Ann with her. Unable to see what was going on, the seconds passed with agonising slowness as they heard John coaxing the boy along. Then, just when it seemed the situation might be resolved without further mishap, everything changed. William shrieked; John gave a mighty shout and the whole ladder shook as if it had come alive, trying to wrench itself from any support. As Hester and Ann struggled, Tom appeared at a run and hurled his full weight against the ladder to hold it.

"The tack-room," he yelled to them. "Sacks! Hay! Anything to break the lad's fall if Mr. Bateman should lose him!"

Hester tore for the tack-room door. Snatching the key from the lintel where it was kept, she drove it into the padlock. With Ann close behind her she dashed inside and came to a halt, looking upwards, her hand on her heart. A great gap in the roof, showing the blue spring sky above, illumined in brilliant sunshine the broken rafters and the torn thatch with William in his rope harness swinging wildly to and fro like a captive bird amid the dust motes, his sobs echoing against the walls.

"Merciful God!" She seized an old hay fork and began to pitch some dank and smelly straw onto the flagstones that were far beneath him. Rats scuttled out and she ignored them as they flashed past, working as if possessed. Ann had snatched a shovel and worked alongside until abruptly she stopped and grabbed Hester's arm.

"Look!"

Hester let the hay fork fall. William was being lowered slowly and jerkily by the rope being controlled through the gap. Both she and Ann ran forward with their arms ready to catch him. As he came within their reach, they both seized him and collapsed with him to their knees on the straw, for he was a sturdy seven-year-old and no light weight. He wrapped his arms about his mother's neck as if he would never let go, and she hugged him to her, upbraiding and kissing him at the same time.

Ann sprang to her feet and cupped her hands about her mouth to shout up the good news if the slackened rope had not already given it. "William is safe!"

Somewhere out of sight John let his end of the rope fall, and it came rippling down through the sun's rays to lie snakelike across the flagstones. Hester, catching sight of bloodstains on it, pulled William's clasp from her, scrambled to her feet and ran out of the tack-room again as swiftly as she had entered it. She heard John's paroxysm of coughing before she saw him. Letticia, who had returned in Tom's wake and stayed to help with the bucking ladder, stepped out of her way as she approached. Hester almost cried out at the sight that met her. John was leaning against the wall, doubled over by his lung-tearing cough, and he held his hands away from him with elbows bent, each palm a mangled mass of bloody flesh where the rope had scorched it, the fingers torn.

"Fetch a mug of water for your father, Letticia," she instructed. "Put the ladder away, Tom. There's nothing more you can do now and thank you for coming. I'm sure you saved both my husband and son from terrible injuries. I don't think Ann and I could have held the ladder a second longer."

"All's well that ends well," he mumbled, embarrassed by her thanks, and swung the ladder down.

Hester hovered at a short distance from John, knowing there was nothing worse than to feel closed in when in desperate need of air. Letticia returned with the water just as he began to draw breath, and Hester snatched it from her to run forward and hold it to his lips. He took a drink gratefully and then straightened, releasing a ragged sigh.

"That's about the worst attack of coughing I've ever had. It must have been caused by that jolt going through my whole body when William fell. Is he all right? Not too frightened by it all now?"

"Knowing William," she replied crisply, "he is probably boasting to Ann that he all but completed his dare after all." She paused, seeing that a maid had come from the house. "Yes? What is it?"

"There's a gentleman called to see the master."

John sighed. "That will be Richard Clarke, the jeweller and goldsmith from King Street. He's come about an order for watchchains, but I can't see him in this state."

Everything that was business-like in Hester came to the fore. She turned to Letticia. "Wait on him. Serve him tea and don't let him leave. He's a new contact and we don't want to lose him."

"Yes, Mother." Letticia hurried into the house. Hester and John followed at a slower pace, she afraid that any speedy exertion might set off his coughing again. Drops of blood marked their passage indoors and along the flagstones to her storeroom where she kept her herbal remedies. There she bathed his raw hands in a lotion of calendula, suffering with him the pain he was enduring in silence. Afterwards she bound the cleaned flesh in strips of white linen and hoped that no festering would occur. His hands would take long enough to heal as they were without additional complications.

"It's as well that we have Joss to share the workload with me until you are able to return to your bench," she said reassuringly, snipping short the ends of the linen ties to make the bandaging neater.

He appreciated her voicing the thought about Joss's presence that had been uppermost in his mind. "I think we'll find that he will run the workshop well. I'll be ready with advice if he should ask for it, but it will do no harm to let him shoulder some responsibility, because he is well suited for it."

She rolled up assiduously the surplus strips of linen in the basket on her lap. It would be good experience for Joss, even though he could expect to be at least forty-three, the age that his father was now, before John's retirement gave him control of the workshop. Abruptly she lifted her head, for until this moment she had not allowed herself to consider that she might have lost John if he had been thrown from that whipping ladder. Injuries she had faced, but not a fatal result. It would have been beyond her human capacity to bear such a loss if it had come about. The simple truth was that she could not live without him. He was her heart, her life blood, her reason for being on this earth. She had known it from first loving him, and the passing years of marriage had only proved that passion.

John saw the whole of her beautiful face reflect the delayed reaction to shock that was taking hold of her, her grey eyes deepening to ebony as the pupils expanded, a tremor running along the line of her generous mouth. Unable to touch her with his hands, he reached out and rested his wrists on her shoulders where she sat opposite him and by exerting gentle pressure caused her to lean towards him. Guessing her thoughts, he kissed tenderly her quivering lids that were keeping back tears, her brow, her cheeks and then her lips. As her mouth opened to his, she slid from the chair to her knees, the basket of linen rolling away, and clung to him like a drowning woman throughout the long, loving kiss they exchanged.

In the parlour, Letticia was holding Richard Clarke's attention. When she first entered the room, he had been standing with his back to her, looking out the window at Bunhill Row, a tallish man of good bearing with his dark brown hair unpowdered and caught back in a tie-ribbon. He, hearing the door open, assumed it was her father who had entered and spoke with his glance still lingering in the direction of the Esdaile mansion even as he turned.

"Your neighbours have not moved in yet, I see, Mr. Bateman. It should not be long now before—"

"Are they coming then?"

Her exclamation snapped his gaze towards her. There was a moment of mutual surprise. He was younger than she had anticipated, no more than twenty-six or -seven at the most, with a lean, austere face, a fine prominent nose and an attractive, thin-lipped mouth. He in his turn saw a girl of remarkable beauty, her head tilted in fascinated query as she awaited his reply; pale coppery hair framing a heart-shape face, such lambent lights in her huge blue eyes that even her long lashes seemed to shine from them. He found his voice.

"So I have heard. Are you Miss Bateman?"

"I am, Mr. Clarke. Are you acquainted with the Esdailes?"

"I know Mr. Esdaile well on a social and business level. And you?"

"I haven't met him yet. Naturally there is neighbourhood interest in the house. We can't think why so much has been done to it and still it stands empty."

"I believe the second Mrs. Esdaile would have preferred to have had a country house built especially for her instead of having one renovated."

"So that is the stumbling block!" She was in sympathy with the second wife. What woman would want a house stuck to the side of an old ale-house when a new country seat could have been hers? She was about to say as much when he took another glance out the window in the mansion's direction.

"For myself, I'd make that place my first choice any day."

"Because of its easy access to the ale-house?" she asked, tongue in cheek.

He burst out laughing, looking back at her. "No, not at all. The mansion has character and a mellow look to it that I admire."

"In that case, if ale is not your preference, I'm sure you will take a cup of tea with me while we wait for my father to join us after a slight delay."

He glanced at the clock. "That is most kind, but is Mr. Bateman not here? I have to get back to the city by—"

She interrupted him quickly. "My father is in the house but there has been a little accident." With a graceful gesture she indicated that he should take a seat opposite her as she settled herself on the sofa.

"Nothing serious, I hope?" he inquired.

All that was sensual in her noted the way his coattails swung out from his narrow hips as he seated himself and the play of hard muscle in thigh and calf. Her colour rose under his penetrating gaze, as if he had been able to read her wanton thoughts. There were baffling times, coming upon her more and more, when her whole body ached with a hunger of its own that she could neither assuage nor identify. Every look from this man's dark eyes sent fire into her and almost made it difficult to breathe. She linked her fingers and let them rise and fall once in her lap.

"Dire results were averted in the nick of time, I'm thankful to say. I'll tell you all about it over tea."

To her relief it arrived at that moment, one maid bearing the tea-tray and the other carrying the trestle tea-table, which was set up in front of her. She noted that everything was there: the kettle on its lamp, the teapot, the tea caddy as a canister was now called, the cream jug, the sugar vase and its tongs together with the cups and saucers. None of it was silver, not even the tongs, although the china was pretty and the kettle a well-polished copper. She experienced bitter resentment, never more keenly than today, that while an abundance of handsome pieces passed through the workshop, nothing in silver or gold ever reached the family table. Her mother's spoon was the only exception. She knew it had been made by her father as a birth gift after Peter was born; it was used by nobody else. She wished she could have borrowed it today for Mr. Clarke's saucer, for everything about him, from the silver buttons on his coat to the gold fob watch on his waistcoat and the diamond ring on his finger, denoted a prosperous background.

Taking from her pocket the little key she had collected on her way to the parlour, she unlocked the tea-caddy and spooned the required amount of tea into the pot. Then, as she took hold of the handle of the kettle to pour on the steaming water, she winced and put it back on the lamp again to examine her hand.

"What is the matter?" he asked her, leaning forward. "Did you burn yourself?"

She shook her head. "I have a splinter in my palm. Quite a large one."

"Let me see." He sprang up to take her hand in his and bend

over it. "That should be easy to get out. Come across to the window."

She went with him to the light. Again he bent close to her, his long, capable fingers gently pressing the end of the splinter until he could get a grip on it. The clean, male smell of him filled her nostrils, making them flare delicately, and her gaze roved over his hair, his profile intent with concentration on his task, and the breadth of his shoulders. There was such a strange rise of feeling in her that she could visualise his firm flesh beneath the covering of his pristine linen and the smooth cloth of his well-tailored coat.

"Oh!" She experienced a sharp pain as the splinter was jerked from her palm. A globule of blood leaped up bright as a ruby before he pressed the place with his thumb, turning his head to look quizzically into her eyes.

"Where on earth did you get a splinter that size?"

"From a ladder."

He laughed softly, his gaze still deep in hers. "What on earth were you doing climbing a ladder?"

"I wasn't on one. I was holding it for my father. You see, my brother was stuck on the stable roof . . ."

It seemed to her that from that moment everything took a new and subtle turn, she talking and he questioning and then both of them laughing together before getting into easy conversation again. He bound her hand across with his clean handkerchief, which he said he would call for at some later date that was convenient to her; there was no suggestion from either of them that a servant could easily collect or deliver. Over tea she encouraged him to tell her about his business, interested to hear how many journeymen he employed and to gain some idea of the extent of his range in the world of goldsmithing. In any case, as she knew well, nothing pleased a man more than to be encouraged to talk about himself.

"Your father and I follow the same craft in all but name," he commented.

She was puzzled. "I'm not sure that I understand you. Where is the difference?"

"I meant that it's becoming the fashion to divide goldsmiths into two categories. Those who specialise in silver—and I believe that is the metal most used in Mr. Bateman's workshop—are becoming known as silversmiths, while those such as myself, who work mostly in gold, are retaining the title of goldsmiths. It's one of those follies created by laymen who fail to realise that the training is one and the same."

"Oh, that!" She gave her head a little toss of comprehension. "My father said something along the same lines the other day." Tauntingly she raised her arched eyebrows at him. "We're not out of touch with all that comes new in the city even though officially we reside in the county of Middlesex."

He acknowledged her mockery with a grin and answered with gallantry: "I can tell that by your style, Miss Bateman."

It was easy to see that she found his answer satisfactory. He was being thoroughly entertained by her. It was rare for him to be in such a light-hearted mood, which was due entirely to her, for he was of a sober disposition, dedicated to work and still greater achievements.

Shortly after completing his apprenticeship, he had shouldered the heavy burden of an inherited business deep in debt and going downhill fast, a situation he had reversed completely by working all hours of the day and night himself as well as bringing in new and advanced ideas. Since then he had not looked back and was beginning to enjoy his success while keeping a tight control on the business reins. Nothing left his shop or his workshop without his scrutiny, however valuable or simple the piece.

In his personal life he was long overdue for marriage and knew it. Until today there had been only minor diversions, and although as yet he had no defined attitude towards Letticia, gripped merely by the initial spell of violent attraction, there lurked at the back of his mind the conviction that he was going to pursue this new acquaintance relentlessly. She was pouring him a cup of tea and he was describing some of the jewellery presently being made in his workshop when her father arrived, his hands bound up like a pugilist's mitts. Richard stood up at once.

"I was most sorry to hear about your injuries, Mr. Bateman."

"They will soon heal. I apologise for keeping you waiting."

"It has been an enjoyable interlude in your daughter's company."

Letticia displayed her wrapped hand. "You and I are both in the wars, Father. Mr. Clarke extracted a splinter for me." Then she rose from the sofa, shaking out her flowery cotton skirt, and made a graceful move towards the door. "I'll leave you both to talk business." She smiled back at Richard in a certain manner that was never without effect on any man at whom it was directed. "Good day to you."

He hurried across to lean in front of her and open the door wide. As she went through, he looked into her eyes again. "I look forward to our next meeting."

In the hall her mother was coming downstairs. "Did all go well, Letticia? Mr. Clarke didn't get too impatient, did he?"

There was a certain smugness in her daughter's smile. "Quite the reverse. The contact hasn't been lost. In fact, I would say it has been cemented."

In her own mind Letticia was congratulating herself. She had always known she would attract the right man to her when she found him. What she had not expected was to be stirred herself as she had never been before, a disturbing element when above all else she needed to keep a cool and calculating head. Too much eagerness on a girl's part could bring about a loss of male interest, something she had seen happen to friends who had let their hearts run away with them. Richard was older and therefore more astute than most of the beaux she had attracted to her, the exception being a few of the officers from the armoury whose very careers had eliminated them from the start as far as she was concerned, however handsome and well-to-do some of them had been. She wanted a husband who would always be with her, not one dashing off to foreign battles, and it was her considered opinion that Richard Clarke filled all the requirements she had long ago listed for the partner of her choice, which included the ability to support a wife in comfort. Not for her the hard work and scrimping and saving that her mother had known. She intended to have much more from life.

John was well pleased with the order for gold watch-chains that he received from Richard. Many of his contacts had begun with simple orders and had led to much more. As soon as he had seen the young goldsmith off the premises, he went to tell Hester what had ensued.

That same night he had a recurrence of the dreadful coughing that had afflicted him earlier in the day. It racked him until he was bathed in sweat, and twice Hester had to fetch him a fresh nightshirt to put on. Her herbal drink finally worked its soothing effect and he slept, but in the morning he was still tired, as well as aching across the back and shoulders and in his arms from the exertions of the previous day. He rested until noon, coughed a little when he rose to get dressed, and then the worst was over.

"You'll be as right as ninepence soon," Hester said cheerfully when she dressed his hands and saw there was no sign of infection.

"Of course I will," he agreed with equal enthusiasm. He did not tell her that after his spell of noon coughing, he had found specks of blood on the linen rag he had held to his mouth. At the first opportunity he burnt it and hoped that her healing potion would stop such a thing happening again.

He was certainly better in the nights that followed, and gradually under her ministrations the cough faded away even as his hands healed. During this period Richard called at the house several times, once to inquire after John's injuries and on another occasion to collect the handkerchief from Letticia, which had somehow been overlooked on his previous visits. Each time he talked to her for a while, took a stroll with her around the garden or along the lane and again drank tea, but with Hester presiding. Letticia gnawed her lip with frustration every time he left, unable to see that any progress had been made, fearful that he might yet meet someone else more attractive to him and not return to 107, Bunhill Row again. Always demanding, she had never been easy to live with, and the new rise and fall of her moods frequently disrupted the harmony of the household.

Sunk in despair, not having seen a sign of Richard for nearly three weeks, she shut herself in the bedchamber she shared with Ann and failed to join in the interest of everyone else in the arrival of wagonloads of servants and baggage at the Esdaile mansion. Later she did take a peep and saw that indoor shutters had been folded back and windows thrown wide as a bustle of activity made the place ready for the owner's arrival. Remembering what Richard had said about Mary Esdaile's displeasure, she wondered if James would be there on his own. In spite of her own misery, her curiosity was aroused.

Chapter 9

Mary Esdaile arrived at her Bunhill Row residence late one evening in anything but a good mood. A big-boned, boisterous young woman with a round, open face framed with rebellious carrot-red hair that was difficult to keep in order, she strode into the mansion, ribbons streaming from her hat, and turned a thunderous look on her surroundings.

Three sets of double doors stood open, and the illumined rooms beyond gleamed with silk panels and newly covered and gilded furniture, much of the latter from a cabinet-maker James had discovered with the name of Chippendale. All the refurbishing was dazzling, which made everything all the more infuriating. She had hoped to make her wishes for the house's alterations such an outrageous expense that James would abandon it and build more suitably, for almost the same price, where the hunting and shooting were to her liking, for she was never happier than when on horseback or trudging moors with her skirts pinned up and dogs at her heels. Instead he had called her bluff, and this was the result. She and her babies were to be installed for the summer months of every year in a place that was not her idea of the countryside, having the city within easy reach—part of his argument in its favour, since he must be in touch with business matters—and traffic passing the door. If he had not given Great Gains and its estate away to the son of his first marriage, she could have spent the summers there in idyllic isolation.

She hated city life, having been reared in the countryside, and was more at home with farming folk and stableboys than London society, however well she conducted herself there. Everything she had loved had been left behind when her father's parliamentary ambitions had settled him and his family in Clerkenwell. She had seen her sister wed, but her down-to-earth attitude and her fierce independence had kept suitors at bay until James had taken a determined fancy to her.

He had followed her into the house and was handing his hat and cane to a servant. "Well," he asked her, "what do you think of it?" She slewed her glittering amber eyes over her shoulder at him. "It's all perfect," she ground out between her teeth.

He ignored her show of displeasure. Not easily riled, he could tolerate her tempers, for he knew his power over her. The chink in her armour was that apart from being a good-natured woman, she had a rough sense of humour that matched his own, and it was often through bawdy exchanges and rollicking horseplay that he got the better of her. From the start he had intended to have his way over this house, whatever tactics he would have to counter. "I knew you'd like it when you got here," he said cheerfully, pretending to have misread her answer. "Don't I always know what's best for you, my love?"

Rounding on him, she gave him a violent push in the chest. "Oh, if I had a field-gun in my hands now I'd pepper you with shot!"

He gave a great bellow of mirth. She grabbed up her skirts and began to run up the staircase, he in hot pursuit. As she ran, she began to laugh, never able to stay angry for long, and in any case the battle was not over yet. She could raise some new objections before the summer came around again.

Reaching her bedchamber door, she entered, intending to slam it shut, but he was too quick for her, pitting his strength against hers, both of them laughing. She released the door and he bounded in, pitching her backwards with his weight until they fell together amid the cushions and draperies of the Chippendale bed, causing the ostrich plumes on the canopy's dome to sway as if in a high wind.

"I'll get my will over this house yet," she warned riotously, throwing her hat aside, heedless that it went skeetering into a far conrner of the room.

He lay across her, looking down into her amused, defiant face, well aware she meant what she said, her will as stubborn as his own. "Not all the time there's breath in my body!"

She lifted her arms and linked them about his neck. It was tussling with him over endless matters, verbally and physically, that made being married to him such a pleasure. Any other man would have bored her. The difference of eighteen years between them was immaterial to her. With his broad chest and thighs like tree-trunks, he was more attractive to her than any younger man would have been, and none could have challenged his prowess as a lover. Yet if ever she had to choose between his company and the wide hills and woods and valleys of the countryside, there would be no hesitation in her decision.

"You'll never master me," she taunted boastfully, "not in a thousand years."

"We'll see," he replied drily, a wrinkle of high amusement at the corner of his eyes.

By next morning everyone in the vicinity was aware that the Esdailes were in residence, and within days the pattern of their existence became known. He went almost daily to the city in his big rumbling coach, returning to dine at three, while she spent her time playing with her little children as noisily and as uninhibited as if she were a child herself, or went riding on a spirited mare, taking off at a gallop across Bunhill fields and being away for hours on end. Hester had glimpsed her several times but had seen no sight of James when one evening an invitation came. John read it through and made the announcement in the parlour, only the two girls being present with Hester, the boys already in bed.

"We four have been invited to a dancing party and supper at the mansion by the Esdailes."

Hester put the flat of her hands together in pleased surprise. "When is it to be?"

"In three weeks' time."

Letticia, who had showed little interest in anything since Richard had failed to reappear, felt her spirits lift slightly. A new setting and the attention of other men would be some balm to her hurt pride. "Is that long enough to have something new made to wear?"

"It's time in plenty, and I think Ann and I should have new gowns too."

Ann, curled up in a wing-chair with a book, lowered it in dismay. She liked gatherings of close friends, but large parties and balls peopled by strangers were not to her taste. "Do I have to go?"

Letticia scowled across at her impatiently. "Don't be such a mouse, Ann! It would be ill-mannered not to accept. Of course you must go."

Hester nodded endorsement with a preoccupied air. So she was to see James again. He would scarcely remember her. It was obvious that he and his wife had decided to invite the neighbourhood to an informal social occasion out of courtesy. This conclusion was confirmed when Joss and Alice called in half an hour later to say that they had also been invited to the party. But as the days went by, it became known locally that only the Batemans had been singled out for the honour and the rest of the guests would be coming from London and not too distant country estates.

John raised a gently mocking eyebrow at Hester. "You must have made a great impression on Esdaile the day you met him. Joss was still an apprentice then, but Esdaille has taken the trouble to find out that the owner of Number 85 is your married son."

She uttered a little laugh to hide her embarrassment. It was foolish to think of the kiss after all this time, and she was relieved that she had never mentioned it to John. He might imagine it retained some importance for James or, worse still and just as erroneously, for her. "Whatever the cause, Letticia is the most cheered by it. She changes her mind about how to dress her hair for that evening a dozen times a day."

In the sewing room a dressmaker and her apprentice were hard at work making up the fabrics that had been chosen; jade silk for Hester, white ribboned muslin for Letticia and primrose satin for Ann. A fourth fabric of rose satin was for Alice, for Joss felt she should have a new gown too. All four garments, with their own variations, were to be in the current mode of tight bodices with low-cut square or deep oval necklines and elbow-length sleeves. The skirts, which were very full, hung straight back and front and were extended widely over hinged iron hoops at the sides, a quirk of fashion that Hester discarded in the workshop or on country walks, or anywhere else where comfort was more important than this French-dictated mode. She sometimes wondered why her fellow countrymen and women, who generally abhorred France and the French as a result of many bitter years of war, should follow the Parisian fashions so slavishly and buy smuggled wine and lace and

Lyonese silk without the least clash of principles. For herself, she had learned tolerance in many fields since her marriage to John. So much that was good in him had had its effect on her, for he could weigh any situation and see virtues and faults on both sides, even in the latest conflict with France.

There was only one sphere in which she wondered if he had an Achilles heel and that was in her own progress as a silversmith. He was always generous with praise, never tardy with comments on what was a particularly good finished workpiece, and yet there were times when, with that special empathy that existed between them, she sensed an uncertainty in him, as if his male ego was being undermined by her achievements being equal to his. If she really wanted to pin-point its beginnings, she could date it back to the time just prior to Joss starting his apprenticeship when he had praised her little snuffbox on the bench as one of the best his father had ever made. With every nerve in her body she had felt John's recoil, and the sensation was embedded in her memory.

The final stitching of the gowns was done and the last length of hem pressed on the morning of the event, which dawned hot and sunny. The evening retained a balmy warmth enabling the Bateman women, escorted by John and Joss, to wear the flimsiest of silk gauze shawls about their shoulders as they covered the few yards to the mansion.

Ann alone felt cold and shivery, which was due to apprehension, her self-confidence undermined by her apparel. She had chosen the primrose satin against both her mother's and her sister's advice, because it was such a pretty shade and one in which she had felt she could achieve her aim of looking her best, but quite unobtrusively. At the first fitting she had realised her mistake. The yellow hue heightened the sallowness of her complexion, and in her opinion she had never looked worse. Her mother, guessing her disappointment, had suggested changing the matching lace to white for edging the neckline and frothing in a falling cuff from the sleeves.

It had helped a little, but to her eyes she still looked as if she were cut out of old parchment from head to toe, and she disliked the way Letticia had scooped her soft brown hair into the style called Pompadour with crimped curls that did not suit her in the least. The paralysing shyness of her childhood had returned, as it sometimes did in the face of a social ordeal, and her morale was at its lowest ebb as she walked with Letticia past the long line of coaches taking turn in letting the passengers alight at the porch steps of the mansion.

Hester, crossing the threshold and surrendering her shawl to one of the waiting maidservants, marvelled to herself at the complete transformation of the hall while regretting the loss of the old panelling that had given it a quiet charm. The walls were now hung with golden damask, the ceiling richly ornamented and even the staircase changed to a more graceful curve with a metal balustrade of anthemion pattern. As she and John turned towards the ballroom door, she saw that the tapestries originally there had been replaced by panels of an apricot satin ground with a pattern of lyres, baskets and crowns of white roses, which was echoed in the upholstery of the gilded furniture.

Then she sighted James and his wife welcoming their guests just a few seconds before he saw her, enabling her to assess his appearance after the lapse of time. He had put on weight, but his stature was such that he bore it well; his complexion was quite tanned, although that could have been a trick of his snow-white tie-wig, which suited him, as did his ivory silk coat with it gold thread embroidery. As for his wife, she was certainly a credit to him in her evening elegance. Her pearly bosom, the bare mound of the right breast ornamented with a tiny star-shaped patch of black silk, rose alluringly from the rigid bodice, displaying to the full advantage her magnificent necklace of sapphire and diamonds that matched ear-drops in her lobes. Her gown was of silver brocade with panniers twice the width of Hester's, as the height of fashion decreed.

"Mr. and Mrs. John Bateman."

Hester drew in her breath as the announcement of their arrival was heralded out. James turned his head sharply, almost as if he had been waiting for this moment. His smile widened, creasing the sides of his face, and his gaze absorbed her as she approached in her jade silken gown at her husband's side, her burnished hair drawn back from her face, a single strand of pearls tight and high about her long white throat.

"My dear Hester!" he exclaimed as if they were lifelong friends, startling John even more than her by this intimate greeting. "What a pleasure to see you again and to meet your husband." The sincerity in his voice rang through as he addressed John directly. "I bid you welcome to my house, sir. May this be the first of many visits."

John was struck by the genuine bonhomie he recognised in the man. It would be hard not to like such a fellow and he did like him, in spite of the extraordinary lapse of good manners in a greeting to Hester that had been tantamount to an embrace. "You do me honour, sir."

"Allow me to present my wife." James drew Mary's attention to the new arrivals and she responded with a warmth that matched her husband's, her mind lively with curiosity. So this was the silversmith's spouse whom he had talked about. His excuse about wanting to be neighbourly to the Bateman family had deceived her no more than it would have done any other wife with her wits about her. She could tell James was attracted to this lovely-looking woman, probably more than he was prepared to admit to himself. She felt no jealousy. There was no cause. In the circles in which she moved it was easy to spot the women who offered danger, and Hester did not come into that category, except unwittingly in this case.

"Now we are neighbours, Mrs. Bateman," she enthused. "There will be little chance to talk together this evening, so do call on me soon and take tea. Then you'll be able to see my three beautiful babies. Bring your boys at the same time. There's a pony in the stables they can ride and a basket of puppies to play with."

"That is most kind of you." Hester was taken aback by this show of hospitality and wondered if her hostess was lonely away from the city.

"My word!" John muttered under his breath as she moved on with him into the ballroom. "I've a feeling we're going to see more of the Esdailes than we had anticipated."

Hester heard the undertone of unease in his voice and knew he was still put out by the way James had greeted her.

In their wake Letticia and Ann, followed by Joss and Alice, were being received in turn. James summed up each Bateman individually. Letticia was pretty as porcelain with the kind of calculating wiles that would always draw men to her like bees to honey, the virginal white of her gown in itself a veiled invitation. Then Ann—

bright, intelligent eyes in a dull little face. There were depths to this one yet to be plumbed. Now Joss and Alice, a stalwart pair, who reminded him of his own son and daughter-in-law. He hoped his second brood would grow up to match his first, but they would have to withstand Mary's spoiling and her inability to instill any kind of discipline into their lives or her own. Yet he could scarcely blame her for that when he indulged her every whim, the matter of this Bunhill Row residence being one of the few times when he had withstood all her pleas, tempers and feminine tricks. He knew himself to be besotted by her. Why then had that first sight of Hester again after such a long period momentarily turned everything to dust and ashes? It had been a fleeting illusion, for he was a sensible man but, dangerously, it had shown him what he would still pursue if Hester should ever give him the slightest sign. He wanted her as much now as he had that day in the herb garden. The time between had melted away as if it had never been.

As soon as all the guests were assembled, he and Mary started the dancing and the evening proceeded merrily, for both of them liked the formal dances to be plentifully interspersed with jollier measures and country jigs. As host, he would partner most of the women, at least as many as was possible throughout the evening, and after taking half a dozen senior ladies in turn around the floor, he approached the spot where the Batemans had gathered. Hester had just seated herself after dancing with her husband, and James drew her into the music that had struck up once more.

"Where are the tapestries?" she asked him as they danced.

He grinned triumphantly at her. "Safely installed in my London home. You see how I followed your advice. What do you think of the changes here?"

She twirled under the arch of his arm in the measure and faced him again. "Everything I have seen so far is quite beautiful, and your wife is the pearl in the oyster."

"You like her?"

"Yes, I do. She was charming to me. I can see you're a fortunate man."

"I am particularly fortunate at this moment." He pressed her fingers a little tighter within his own. "I've never forgotten the last time you were here."

She raised her eyebrows, smiling in gentle reproof. "Do you have such a long memory, James? Some things are best forgotten."

"But not that day."

She tried to redirect the line of the conversation. "I still have the key to the herb garden. Now that you are in residence, I'll return it."

"No, keep it. I insist."

"But there's no need. I have a well-established herb garden of my own now."

"Have you not been visiting mine then?"

"Oh, yes. It is such a peaceful place. Sometimes I sit and sketch there. But now it will be your wife's domain."

He shook his head, thoroughly entertained by such an idea. "Housewifely pursuits are not my wife's metier. She'll never go near it."

"Nevertheless the cook will, or there'll be kitchen maids sent to gather what is needed for the pot. I would not be alone there anymore."

He wondered if she was afraid he would seek her out in that peaceful corner. "Then continue to go there when Mary and I are not in residence. We shall return to London in the autumn and the place will be yours again."

"Then I'll keep the key," she said gratefully, knowing his offer was well meant. The dance was ending and he swept her down into her curtsey with his own bow. Her face was upturned to his. "I must tell you one thing. I'm so glad that no changes were made to that part of the grounds. The herb garden was a link with your first wife. It is right that it should have remained as it was."

She thought he looked surprised at what she had said. Perhaps it had not been right to mention his first wife on such an occasion, but he would understand it had been said from the heart and would not be put out.

Later James danced with Ann, whose only partners had been her father and her brother, and her pale-faced nervousness dispersed as he talked to her throughout the measure. When he returned her to her seat she sparkled with a rare excitement as she faced her father.

"Mr. Esdaile drew it out of me that I'm a bookworm. He says I may use his library whenever I wish. When he is not in residence, Mother is to have a key and full charge to allow me access."

At her side James gave a nod of endorsement. "My books are being catalogued at the present time, and soon Ann will be able to pluck what she wants from the shelves without any of the confusion that previously prevailed there."

John was beginning to feel overwhelmed by his host's neighbour-liness, which, whatever its guise, seemed to him to be directed towards his wife, who had already told him she was to keep the key to the herb garden. "I accept the privilege on Ann's behalf for her to have the loan of books from your library when you are here, Mr. Esdaile, but otherwise the offer is too generous. I couldn't put such a responsibility on my wife's shoulders."

Hester, who would have voiced the same answer in her own way, saw the disappointment well up in Ann's eyes and, with that special love she had for her younger daughter, she put a hand on John's arm. "I've had such pleasure from the books you have read with me that I know what this chance means to Ann. Let it be uninterrupted. She and I need not come more than once a month into this house. I'm willing to hold the key with the one I already have if you're prepared to reconsider your decision."

He put his hand over hers as he conceded, swayed by her argu-ment. "In that case, the matter is settled."

It was not only Ann for whom the evening had taken a new turn. Letticia, who was used to plenty of partners wherever she went, had taken turn after turn on the floor before she suddenly glimpsed Richard's late arrival. James had gone across to welcome him and they stood together just inside the ballroom door. Excitement, fury and outrage blended to create turmoil within her. She would ig-nore him and concentrate on other partners. If he asked her to dance, she would refuse. Out of the corner of her eye she saw him making his way slowly around the outskirts of the room, greeting acquaintances and pausing to chat longer with some than with oth-ers.

She was dazzling her present partner with her smile, tilting her head prettily and generally playing to Richard, who was never quite where she expected him to be whenever she looked, as if by chance, in his direction, his gaze always maddeningly elsewhere.

She knew a gripping moment of panic when the dance ended and she could not see him anywhere. Had he left again already? Then, as her partner began to lead her back to where her family had seats, she saw that Richard was talking to her parents. He turned as she approached and came to meet her, his eyes full of smiles.

"Thank heavens I arrived in time to have the supper dance with you. There was trouble with one of the horses. How are you? Business took me out of London, but I made a point of getting back for this evening, because I was sure you would be here."

All was well, but she had had a terrible scare. It felt as if her whole body were trembling inside. "Why did you suppose that?"

"Because you mentioned once that your mother and Mr. Esdaile were acquainted." There was a fractional pause. "I have missed seeing you, Letticia."

She looked into his face and saw all that she had ever wanted to discover there.

For Hester the special enjoyment of supper was not so much the food as the sight of such a grand amount of the Esdailes' silver in use. The centre-piece of the long, damask-covered table was of enormous size, standing on scroll feet, its centre oval dish piled high with grapes, its eight circular smaller dishes holding peaches and plums and cherries, the rich colours of the fruit reflected a thousand times over. Then there were salvers, each with the Esdaile crest, on which the glasses were borne; the tureens with domed covers and pineapple finials; the curved sauceboats; the great dishes with engraved patterns that held salmon and pies and game magnificently garnished, beef and suckling pigs and giant hams; embossed stands that supported crystal bowls of syllabub with sugared violets, and the delicate sweetmeat baskets. Over it all the candle glow from some of the finest candelabra she had ever seen touched delicacies and gleaming silver alike with liquid gold.

John, seeing how she took a last backward look at the table as they returned to the dancing, spoke to her teasingly. "Come now, Hester. Tell me your thoughts."

She shot him a laughing glance, looping her hands about his elbow in its grey velvet sleeve. "I was thinking that there'll never by any Esdaile orders trickling through to our workbench at any time. Our host has more than enough silver for his requirements and doubtless cupboards stacked full elsewhere."

"I'm sure you're right."

During supper Joss and Alice had been seated with some young people of their own age, and as they remained with them afterwards, Hester supposed Ann to be in their company. She gave herself up to enjoying the rest of the evening, not knowing her daughter had gone in search of the library.

Ann had been given directions by James. She had no intention of returning to the ballroom, and no one would miss her. As soon as she heard people departing, she would fetch her shawl and rejoin her parents. The second half of the evening ahead of her promised to be far more enjoyable than the first. Her satin shoes made no sound along the downstairs corridor that led to the double doors of the library. She paused in front of a pier glass and, making a grimace at her own reflection, removed the pins that Letticia had used in her hair and combed her fingers briskly through the collapsed curls until her hair hung softly again. With a final smoothing with her palms, her appearance was back to normal. Opening one of the library doors, she entered and closed it behind her.

The size of the room astounded her. It was in semi-darkness, the only light coming from two candles on a central library table on which a number of ledgers stood in a stack, one spread open where it had been left. She remembered that her benefactor had said that his library was being catalogued and she would be careful not to disturb anything. But, oh! So many books! She had not supposed for one moment that there would be such a number. Not only did they reach on shelves from floor to ceiling, but they spread in and out of deeply shadowed alcoves, which by day would offer private corners for reading.

She began to wander along, tracing her fingers along the backs of the volumes and peering at the titles until, becoming impatient when the small letters proved difficult to read in the gloom, she fetched one of the candles from the table to aid her. In an aura of candlelight she proceeded slowly, smiling and catching her lower lip between her teeth in anticipation when she came across a title proclaiming a book she had long wanted to read.

Intent on her exploration, her candle held close to the shelves for the best illumination possible, she moved on into another shad-owed alcove and failed to notice a sprawled foot in her path. Sud-denly she was tripping; a man gave a shout and she sent several volumes tumbling from the shelves to the floor as she scrabbled to save her balance. A hand gripped her elbow, steadying her, and by the light of the candle, which was still in her clasp, she looked into the face of a young man who had sprung out of the alcove chair. He had been sound asleep, to judge by his flushed cheeks and the heavy look of his eyelids.

"Have you hurt yourself?" he asked solicitously, able to judge from her gown that she had come from the ball. Any acquaintance of his employer must be treated with respect.

"No," she replied, still startled. "I didn't know anyone was here."

He released her wrist and stooped to gather the fallen books and return them to their places. Of average height, slim-built, he had a thick fall of yellowish hair that fell across his forehead and shone silkily in the candlelight. His nose was broad in an almost square face that had a brooding quality to it, and his mouth wide with a pugnacious jut to the lower lip, as if he was less than pleased by her intrusion.

"Normally there wouldn't be," he said, "but I was working late and tiredness overcame me. I just took a nap in the chair."

"You must be the librarian who is cataloguing the books."

"That's right." He paused in his task to look at her. "How did you know that?"

"Mr. Esdaile told me. He has given me permission to come to his library and borrow books whenever I wish. I couldn't resist the chance to see what was on the shelves."

He regarded her with a sudden rise of interest. She must be well-favoured by the Esdailes. "My name is Matthew Grant. I hope you will allow me to be of service to you."

"I should be pleased. I'm Ann Bateman."

"Shall you have to come far each time?"

"Not at all. I live in Bunhill Row at Number 107."

"So near." He knew the house, having taken his bearings as soon as he arrived. She was an artisan's daughter, no higher in station than himself, for his beginnings had been humbler than his position nowadays. It was not such a surprise that she was being allowed the use of the library as it would have been in some of the grand houses in which he had worked, for James Esdaile was equally at ease with all ranks of his fellow men, which was one of the reasons for his popularity in the city.

"What sort of books do you like, Miss Bateman?" Matthew eyed her speculatively. She was nothing to look at with regard to her features, but her expression sparkled as she threw her glance here and there at the book-crammed shelves. He was appraising her figure. Her narrow waist rose out of her wide skirts like the calyx of a flower, and her young breasts were full and round. His stare dissolved back to her face as her radiant gaze returned to him.

"History books and nature books and tales of faraway places," she exclaimed.

"Then you'll find all you want here. I'll show you a few of each now if you have some minutes to spare."

"Oh, I have," she replied eagerly. "I'm not going back to the dancing."

He compressed his lips as he turned away to the nature section on the shelves. If the choice had been his, he would have danced the night away. A quiet life out of the city, whether it be London or any other great town, did not suit him, and unfortunately much of his work took him to isolated houses set in rural splendour with nothing in the way of entertainment. With his aesthetic tastes, he had no time for servant girls, except when in dire physical need, and country wenches were no better, for he was repulsed by uneducated voices and rough manners. Occasionally there had been a pleasing widow alone in a house or a wife bored in her husband's absence who had looked in his direction, but these turns of good luck were rare.

There was no chance of such a happening in the present household, although with the age difference between the Esdailes he would take a wager that in another few years their relationship would be less stable. It could be argued that here in Bunhill Row he was near enough to the city to be able to enjoy himself, but he had no transport, and at the end of a long day it was a heavy tramp into town and back again. He had resigned himself to hours of work and no play until the cataloguing was finished, able to look forward to nothing more than an occasional mug of ale at the Royal Oak. But now this girl was to be a frequent visitor at the library. He gave her a smile as he took down a large volume from a shelf.

"This is a book you'll want to study for hours on end."

He opened it for her on the library table after pushing his own ledgers aside, and together they leaned over it. She gazed in wonder at the exquisite illustrations of a mandarin duck, a quail, a strange eagle and many other exotic birds painted by a Chinese hand, every feature distinctive, each eye as bright as if alive. As she turned the pages, he brought her more books, the subjects ranging from ancient Rome to a history of Columbus's explorations and some fictional works by Defoe that included *Robinson Crusoe*. He hesitated about *Moll Flanders,* weighing it in his hand, and then added it out of devilment. It should open those innocent eyes. As it happened, she did not look at it then, having been drawn first to those with illustrations that were new to her, for she had never handled such costly books before.

She exclaimed, admired and asked him many questions. By now they had chairs drawn up side by side at the table, and since, like most people, he found it enjoyable to impart his own knowledge, he answered her readily and was pleased by her appreciativeness. She had the upper hand when together they went through a large volume of English wild flowers and plants. The Latin names meant nothing to her but she was able to give a country name to each, something entirely beyond his ability.

"I've always known that yellow and orange flower as Cuckoos' Stockings. Those wild lilies are Lords-and-Ladies and they do look stately, don't you think? How delicately those Wind-flowers have been drawn and coloured in their pinks and whites, and there's green and white Shepherd's Purse—it really looks like a little purse, doesn't it?" She turned another page. "Oh, here is Traveller's Joy, which is a true name because the blossoms look so pretty in the hedges, and that tiny pansy is one of my favourites. It's called Jump-Up-And-Kiss-Me."

He glanced at her quickly then to see if there was any coquettishness in her face, but her whole expression was absorbed in the book. "I'm impressed," he acknowledged. "You know them all. How is that? I heard your family came from London!"

"So we did, but my mother grew up in the country, and since we came to live in Bunhill Row I've learned the names from her."

"Then they all grow around here?"

"Every one of those I've seen in this book so far, although of course it depends on the time of the season."

"Would you show me where to look for those that are blooming now? Being a city fellow, I should make the most of being in the country area while I'm here."

"Indeed you should." She had no shyness with him. In books they talked the same language, and his kindness to her, his willingness to assist her in her choice of reading in the weeks ahead and the peacefulness of the library after the swirl and whirl of the ballroom gave her a sense of security in his presence. "I could draw a little map and give you clear directions—"

He interrupted her. "No, that isn't what I meant. I should like you to show me, if it wouldn't be too much trouble."

She was glad to be able to do something for him in return for his assistance to her. Had she been more used to attention from the opposite sex, less resigned to her own lack of attractiveness beside Letticia's beauty, she would have realised that his request was not as platonic as she supposed. "It would be no trouble at all. We can settle on a fine day when you're free."

"What about tomorrow?" He loathed the boredom of Sundays. His position in the household was an ambiguous one, for not being staff meant he was free of the commitment of church if he should not wish to attend, and yet by the same token he was not expected to work on the sabbath, which he would willingly have done to alleviate the tedium of time on his hands. To take a walk with a girl of gentle manners and a bright mind would pass several hours pleasurably, and he saw no reason to postpone it.

She considered. "Yes, tomorrow afternoon then. We dine earlier on Sundays. What about you?"

He thought of the countless meals served to him in solitary state, for his position was too high for the servants' hall and too lowly for family dining room. "I can eat more or less when I like. Just say the time and I'll meet you wherever you wish."

The arrangements were made. Shortly afterwards there came the sound of carriage wheels beginning to roll in the direction of the mansion's entrance as the ball drew to its close. She rose to her feet reluctantly, sorry that the evening was over, and looked uncertainly at the books selected for her.

"I can't take all those now."

"Take this one." He gave her *Robinson Crusoe.* "You can fetch the rest in turn when you need them."

She nodded happily. Each book would mean seeing him again, which was a joyful prospect, and in the meantime there was tomorrow to look forward to. "Thank you for showing me those beautiful volumes, Mr. Grant."

He saw her to the library door and opened it for her. She sped away, clutching her book, and fetched her shawl in time to reach her parents and her sister as they bade good night to the Esdailes and no questions were asked.

Both she and Letticia, who shared a room, were quiet while they prepared for bed. It was not unusual for Ann, but after any social event Letticia always had much to tell of romantic encounters and, occasionally, the giggling confession of a kiss allowed. Tonight was different. Letticia was dreamily silent and her gaze abstracted. Ann found that it was she herself who wanted to talk, although shyness about voicing details of her new friendship made her wait until the candle was out and they were both in their beds. In the moonlight pouring through the window, she could see that her sister was lying wide awake.

"Letticia," she said softly, smiling to herself where she lay on her back, "something wonderful happened this evening."

To her astonishment, at her words Letticia bounded out of bed and came to hug her. "Darling Ann. I should have known that you above all people would have noticed, sensitive creature that you are! You read my expression, did you? Or was it that you saw how Richard and I danced far more dances together than we should have done? We couldn't stay away from each other." She snatched up Ann's hand and kissed it in her exuberance. "I've been in a daze ever since those last few minutes before we all left the mansion. I heard Richard ask Father if he might call on him in the morning on a personal matter. There can be only one reason for that! He wants permission to ask me to marry him. This has been the happiest night of my whole life!" Her voice throbbed, and without warning she burst into tears. "I'm in love, Ann. There's no reason to cry, but I'm so much in love. I never knew it could happen like this."

Ann shifted up on her pillows and wrapped her arms around her sister. The moment was gone when she would have told Letticia about her own new friendship, which could not be compared with the miracle of love. "I'm so glad for you. You're shedding tears of joy. May you always be as happy as you are tonight."

In the morning Richard arrived shortly before noon. He was received by John in the parlour, and after a little while the door opened again. Ann, who happened to be crossing the hall, paused as her father beckoned to her. "Ask your mother to come here, Ann. And would you fetch your sister?"

"At once," she said, almost in a whisper in the excitement of the occasion.

Letticia received the summons in the flower garden, where she was waiting on a shady seat. She nodded as Ann approached, no word being needed, and automatically touched a curl into place. As she rose from the seat and went indoors, she realised that in her level-headed way she had never expected the bonus of love in the marriage of her choice, and yet it was to be hers. For the first time in her life she felt humble before the good fortune that had come to her. Well, she would not accept it lightly. It should radiate from her to her parents and her sister and her brothers. Nobody should lose through the bond soon to be forged, least of all Richard himself.

Hester accepted Mary Esdaile's invitation to call and went one Saturday afternoon when the workshop was closed, taking the three boys with her. Mary, with the baby tucked under her arm like a parcel and the two toddlers clinging to her skirts, abandoned the tea that had been set formally for her and her guest in the drawing room and had a nursery tea laid on a table on the terrace, where she and Hester could join the children and sit with them. It was a happy afternoon, enjoyed by all, particularly William, who thought there was no animal in the world to compare with the horse. Mary said he could ride the pony at any time under the supervision of a groom. It was the start of William's association with the Esdaile stables, a privilege he was to use to the full. The climax of the afternoon for all three boys was a choice from the basket of puppies.

In the weeks that followed Hester thought often how right John had been in foreseeing constant involvement with the Esdailes. It was not only Ann having the use of the library and William being forever at the stables, but she and John were invited time and time again to supper-parties and musical evenings and amateur theatricals, Richard and Letticia being included on many occasions after their betrothal had been officially announced. The events were informal in comparison with the elaborate festivities that were a major part of the Esdailes' social life in London and made a welcome change for them both. Sometimes, if a gathering was small, the evening would end in James's own parlour in the tavern, with punch for the women and ale for the men, often the local fiddler coming in from the tap-room to play well-loved country melodies.

As the relationship developed between the Esdailes and the Batemans, John and James sometimes met on their own in the tavern parlour to play a game of chess or enjoy a strong political discussion over a pint of ale. There were no class barriers between them, for John had the natural ease of the well bred in any company, rich or poor, and although he never thought about his antecedents, they were probably a match in every way for the D'Estailes. In any case, he and James were both in trade, and although James was now in a higher world of banking, he made no secret of having retained his financial interests in military accoutrements, which had continued to be a profitable business since England was rarely free of war in one foreign field or another.

Hester's acquaintanceship with Mary remained as from the first meeting. There was pleasure in each other's company, a mutual liking and respect, but an invisible barrier prevented a true friendship evolving, not of Hester's making but of Mary's. Hester could guess that its origins lay in Mary's awareness of James's open affection for her, but since she herself knew that no harm would ever come of it, she simply regretted that she and Mary would never know each other better. Yet nothing seemed to please the Esdailes more than to be invited in their turn to 107 Bunhill Row, where there were always good food, games of cards and plenty of lively conversation.

Ann was only occasionally persuaded to attend these social affairs. Instead she went by day to the mansion's library and met

Matthew whenever he was free from work. For her it was a time of immense satisfaction. With unlimited access to splendid literature and a companionship such as she had never known before, she felt she was being fed mentally and spiritually for the first time in her life. No one could have wished for a better friend than Matthew had proved himself to be, whether on walks or in the library or on balmy evenings when they would sit under a tree somewhere and talk for hours. Her family knew she was seeing him, although it was doubtful whether they guessed how frequently, for they were used to her going off on her own. She was much like her mother in needing a little solitude sometimes, and in her case it was usually to read in a quiet corner. Her two younger brothers teased her about having a beau until her scarlet embarrassment and tear-filled eyes finally quieted William, who cuffed Jonathan into sulky silence.

"I'm sorry, Ann." William was ever quick to own up to his faults. "Letticia never used to cry when we teased her."

She pushed aside his tumbling dark hair and took him by the ears to bring him forward and plant a kiss on his forehead in forgiveness. "I know you meant no harm. It's just that he's not a beau as all Letticia's young men were before she met Richard. Matthew is my friend, nothing more."

Magical words. *Matthew, my friend.* She had come to realise that until meeting him, she had always been lonely in the midst of a large and loving family. Now every morning when she woke it was with a sense of fulfilment and the joyous anticipation of seeing him again. It never occurred to her that she was slipping slowly and irrevocably into love, for she had been long conditioned by Letticia's emotional outpourings into thinking it all began with fiery glances and a tumult of the heart and various other extravagant signs that bore no recognisable connection with anything she felt for Matthew.

The long summer was drawing to its close on the softly scented evening when she strolled with him across the fields until they came to a five-barred gate. Side by side they stood leaning on it, looking towards the fading sunset.

"I'll write to you if you like," she suggested.

He glanced sideways at her. She had her forearms along the top rail, her hands overlapping and her chin resting on them. "What would you write about?"

"The way all the paths we've explored change with the seasons. The latest book I've read and what I think about it. Whether the thrush nests again next year in the tree where you drove the cat away. Oh, everything."

"Would you write that you miss me?" He saw her look down.

"I shall miss you. That doesn't need to be said."

He liked her. She was agreeable company and had whiled away hours for him that would have been tedious spent alone. If it had been possible he would have sought more from her, but she was curiously innocent, seeming to think it accidental if he clasped her waist hard as he helped her down from a stile or his thigh rested against her skirts when they sat side by side. Even if he had persisted, her natural modesty would have defeated him, evidence in her care always to keep her hems in place and in the brooch she wore that hid the little valley between her breasts from his view. Maybe that was why she attracted him more than she would have done otherwise, there being nothing more tempting than fruit that was out of reach. As if finally to challenge that barrier after many long weeks, he put out his hand and cupped her smooth, brushed head before bringing his hand to rest on the soft coils pinned above the back of her neck. The nape looked pale and vulnerable.

"I don't know how I shall fill my life when I'm away from you, Ann." It was a phrase he had used before for other ears, and this time it proved to be more effective than it had in the past, for it was totally believed. She turned towards him, concerned and eager to reassure.

"We'll always be friends, Matthew. For the rest of our lives."

He took hold of her shoulders, looking searchingly into her face. "Do you mean that? It would matter so much to me."

"Of course I do! Don't be sad."

"Dear, sweet little Ann." He enfolded her gently and, not daring to push his luck, kissed her tenderly and chastely. She trembled like a captive bird in his embrace, but she was melting and willing. Her eyes closed and one fluttering hand came to rest against the side of his face. Encouraged, he deepened his kiss, tightening his clasp as she reared to jerk free, alarmed perhaps as much by the hardening pressure of his body against hers as by the seeking intimacy of his mouth. With desire high in him, he wanted to prolong this sensual encounter, hoping to break through her reserve at last to an ultimate conclusion.

"I love you, Ann," he gasped as he lifted his mouth from hers. It was the one excuse acceptable to women when one went too far too soon. "I've loved you since the evening you first came into the library. You're all I want." The lies came glibly off his tongue, spurred by the torment of lust. "Let me show you how much you mean to me—"

She arched her back against his encircling arms to rest her hands against his shoulders and look into his burning face, her own soft and flower-like with the blossoming of long-held love, her eyes shimmering with emotion. "I love you too, Matthew. I have felt all along that you and I are so alike. You have been lonely, too. Now neither of us will ever have to be on our own again."

"Never!" He barely listened to what she was saying, intent only on her softness in his arms, the evening scent in her hair and on her skin. They kissed again, he ready to bear her down onto the grass, but when she drew her lips from his, she startled him by her gush of words.

"Let's go and tell my parents now!" she exclaimed radiantly.

Confused, his whole body keyed for her, he blinked as if he were deaf and had not caught what she had said. "What are you talking about?"

"Our marriage. Oh, I want it to be soon, Matthew." She twirled from his arms and caught hold of his hand joyously. "Let's run all the way."

His first thought was that she was out of her head. Then panic gripped him. He had a sudden vision of her father and James Esdaile bearing down on him to know what he had been about and what promises he had made. Her family's attitude didn't matter to him, but his employer's opinion did. He had done good work in the library and been praised for it, for Esdaile appreciated a job well done. A recommendation from such an important man in the city could weigh the balance for him in the application he had made for a post in the archives of a national museum presently being formed. If Esdaile should hear that he had been footling around with the affections of a friend's daughter, that would be the end of everything for him.

"Wait!" He drew her back to him by their joined handclasp and put an arm about her again, simply to ensure that she did not go darting off on her mad errand, for all desire had ebbed from him. "You're only sixteen, Ann. Your parents aren't going to agree to a speedy wedding when they don't yet know me. We'll have to be patient. In the meantime we can write to each other, as you said."

Her head dropped into the hollow of his shoulder, and her voice was torn. "I can't face a single day without you now that our love has come into the open between us."

"I feel the same, but you know what I've said is true."

She did not need the urgency in his voice to convince her. Her father, who had accepted Joss's decision to marry Alice without protest, knowing his son's steady temperament, had been strict about a lengthy betrothal for Letticia, wanting to be sure her head was not over-ruling her heart. As for herself, he would be even more protective, holding her extreme youth against her and the fact that Matthew was the first man to have shown an interest in her. An interest? Matthew loved her! Nothing should be allowed to stand in the way of their being together. She raised her face to his again and spoke imploringly.

"Let me come with you when you leave. We can be married somewhere away from here and then nobody will be able to part us."

He was momentarily at a loss for words. Quickly he enfolded her against him, looking over her head as he considered what he should say. "You know I have only five or six days' work left. Would you be ready to leave home by then?"

"I would go now with only the clothes I stand up in if that was what you wished."

His conscience smote him. He did not want to hurt her, but the solution she had offered was one that he could turn to his advantage. "There would have to be the utmost secrecy."

She answered fervently. "Nobody will suspect. I promise."

He held her back from him and regarded her with the fond liking that he had come to feel for her over many weeks and that had returned now that the threat of losing Esdaile's reference had been removed. "Then let us make plans."

They plotted every detail. When they parted at an oak tree near her home, she flung her arms around his neck. Under his kisses of parting, which were to be the last until the evening of their elopement, hers lost their previous innocence in a sudden burgeoning of passion. It was as if at last a chord had been touched in her. When he released her, his face was taut and serious at this unexpected response in her and he snatched her back into his arms once more for a final kiss before he let her go from him. Then he watched her as she ran the few yards to her home.

In the porch she paused to look back at him where he stood spectre-like in his light coat in the deepening evening shadows. She did not wave in case of being observed, for already their plan of secrecy was in motion. Instead she directed towards him a look of love that she was sure must travel through the air to him like a tangible caress.

During the next few days she collected together the clothes and few personal items she would be taking with her and packed them in a piece of hand-baggage, which she hid at the back of a cupboard. She wrote a letter of explanation to her parents, ready to leave on her pillow where it would be discovered long after she had left the house. On the evening of her elopement her parents would be at the mansion, and Letticia had been invited with Richard to a ball in the city, chaperoned by his sister, and would stay at her home afterwards. Even the boys would be out of the house, having had a craze that summer to sleep out of doors in makeshift tents. With the servants in the kitchen, there would be nobody to see her leave.

The day of her elopement dawned. Everybody else went about his or her arrangements, and as the evening approached, she felt curiously like a spectator watching a panorama of family life revolve around her as if she were already detached from it. When only her parents were left in the house, she went into the hall to watch them set off for their evening with the Esdailes. It was one of the last they would have this year, for the Esdailes were shortly to move back into London until next summer. As her mother came downstairs, Ann was struck as she sometimes was by the beauty of the woman whose looks she had not inherited. This evening Hester was wearing a gown of iris blue Spitalfield silk. It was not new, but she always had a pristine look about her, whether in her working cottons or in her best attire, as if everything on her was fresh out of its folds.

"Are you all right, Ann?" she asked with a little frown of concern.

Ann felt her colour rise on a sense of guilt. "Yes. Why ever do you ask?"

Hester gave a little shrug. "I don't know. I've had the impression you haven't been quite yourself for the last few days."

It gave Ann the excuse to come forward and hug her mother, something that would have been impossible otherwise. "Stop worrying about me. Go and enjoy yourself."

To her relief, her father consulted his fob-watch. "It's time we were going, Hester, if we're not to be late."

Hester nodded and settled a shawl about her shoulders. She hoped that this evening James would keep his glances more for the other guests than for her. John always noticed. "Good night then, Ann, my dear. You'll be asleep when we get back, I expect. We'll try not to disturb you."

As soon as the door closed after them, Ann ran upstairs to her bedchamber and watched from the window until they passed under the lamp that illumined the gates of the mansion. Now she was safe!

Half an hour later, in her outdoor cloak and carrying a valise, she slipped out of the house and hurried to the meeting-place well past the mansion and her brother's home in the direction of the city. She was early, but that was what she intended. There was a convenient seat on the fallen trunk of an old tree, and she sat down to wait and listen for the gig Matthew would have hired on the quite legitimate reason of having to transport his box of belongings to lodgings in London. Somewhere in the trees an owl hooted. From the direction of the tavern there came odd bursts of noise when the door of the entrance was opened and shut as people came and went. Her heart was beating a happy tattoo.

Two hours later she was frantic. Various vehicles had passed, but Matthew had not appeared. Something totally untoward must have arisen to put their elopement in jeopardy, and there was no way he

could get a message to her. As the minutes continued to tick by
without any sign of him, she could endure it no longer. Time was
fast running out and she had to know what was happening. Suppose
he had been taken ill? Although the hour was late she would call at
the mansion on the pretext of borrowing a book.

When she reached the mansion she hid her valise in the bushes
and ·hurried to the entrance. She was admitted by a manservant,
who knew she would be bound for the library. From the direction
of the drawing room there came a buzz of voices interspersed with
laughter. "Is Mr. Grant still at his work?" she dropped casually.

"No, Miss Bateman. He has gone."

"Gone? How long since? Five minutes? Ten?" She was ready to
fly back out the door, unable to conceive how she could have
missed him.

"He left yesterday morning, shortly after dawn, I was told."

She set her face for the library and hoped her legs would carry
her there. He would have left a letter for her on the library table
telling her where to find him in the city. She had always heard that
shock could make the teeth chatter, and it was happening to her.
Once she was inside the library she rushed to the central table. It
was bare of everthing but a lighted candle. As if she had been let
out of Bedlam, she pulled open the table drawers, quite crazed, and
rummaged in the cupboards, which held only the red leather-bound
volumes of his cataloguing.

Slowly she sank down onto her knees on the floor and pressed
her stricken face against the side of the table, her eyes shut tight on
the realisation of his lies, her mouth hanging open while wave after
wave of anguish crashed through her. She had known as soon as she
heard he was gone that there would be no letter, but the slight
possibility had kept her from bursting into screams of pain from her
breaking heart—there in the hall where she would have brought
everyone running, her parents included. Gradually she became
aware of awful sounds of another kind rising from her chest and
realised that dry sobs were choking her throat. Dear God, she must
not be heard. She put shaking hands over her mouth and struggled
to suppress the noise. No one must know! How well Matthew had
read her character, as she had never learned to divine his. Even
now he must be as certain as if she had told him herself that she

would never divulge the humiliation of this night to anyone, least of all to her own family, for the burning coals of their sympathy would be an intrusion into her most private self that might drive her insane.

Stumbling to her feet, she gripped the edge of the table and set her shoulders back, her torment no longer audible. As she left the library, she took a book at random from a shelf and held it to her as evidence for her visit. In the hall the same manservant on duty opened the door for her, and she went out into the cool night. As if in a trance, she recovered her valise and turned homewards. Indoors, she went up to her room, took her letter from her pillow and held a corner of it to a candle flame until she had to drop the last scrap and stamp it out. She unpacked and put her things away. Then she washed her face in cold water and prepared for bed. In the comfort of her pillow the tears finally came, gushing forth as if some inner dam had burst. She wept far into the night, long after she heard her parents' whispers when they went quietly past her door. As the numbness of initial shock wore off, her agony became steadily worse.

In the morning she pretended to have an inflammation of the eyelids, and her mother bathed them for her with a gentle herbal solution. After that she did not cry again until the day of her sister's marriage. It was a grand affair with a packed church and Letticia was a radiant bride. Ann could not stop the tears running down her face throughout the ceremony, but nobody thought anything amiss. After all, it was usual for women to cry at weddings.

Chapter 10

In spite of Mary Esdaile's continued opposition to spending part of every year at the mansion, three more summers saw them in residence there. During that time the Batemans continued their busy lives, never without work on the benches and drawn into social contact with the Esdailes for three months of every year.

John's only reservation about this pleasant disruption of routine was that James made no attempt to hide his attachment to Hester, which he found increasingly irritating, while accepting in his own mind that it was satisfying to the ego to be married to a beautiful woman whose fidelity was without question. Unfortunately he was often angry with her after an evening with the Esdailes. She was extraordinarily patient with him these days, her temper rare, whereas he flared constantly in a manner that would previously have been alien to him. At times he wondered if it was a symptom of what ailed him, for he was not in good health and tried to hide it from Hester to spare her worry. Whenever his cough troubled him he took the syrup she had made, always with good effect, and on days when tiredness threatened to overcome him at the workbench, Joss always seemed to read the signs and would relieve him of any heavy chore. To his relief, Hester never seemed to notice.

In his home life he had nothing to trouble him, although he wished that Ann would come out of her shell. Nearly twenty, she had never to his knowledge had a beau and had adopted a severe hair-style that even detracted from the lustre of her gentle eyes; her clothes were always plain and without adornment. Letticia had offered her an indefinite stay in London, wanting to pretty her up and find her a husband, but Ann had firmly declined. She seemed to want nothing more than to run the household, leaving Hester completely free for silver-smithing, and to read in whatever time she had to herself, the library at the mansion her greatest source of pleasure.

The two youngest boys now attended a charity school set up in the neighbourhood, and Ann was prompt to extricate William from trouble if it lay in her power, for his schooldays were punctuated by punishments for fights and escapades. She was always sharp with Jonathan, whose devious ways enraged her as never before. "Don't try your sly tricks on me!" she would admonish with a wagging finger. "I can read you as well as any book. Turn out your pockets! There! It *was* you with the catapult! I knew William hadn't broken that window this time."

It was to Ann, to whom he had always felt close, that William confided his ambition to be a goldsmith. Together they were feeding the remainder of Peter's rescued birds and animals that would never be fit to survive in the wild again, a task they had willingly taken on when their brother had left on his fourteenth birthday to take up an apprenticeship with Richard, his brother-in-law, shortly after the wedding day. For a moment Ann was at a loss how to answer and busied herself spooning out the raw meat for an owl. William was virtually barred from the workshop for his boisterous clumsiness, which had caused expensive damage on several occasions. Their mother, who always tried to be fair, had given him some instruction since she had done the same for Jonathan, but her interest had not been there and he must have known it.

"Are you sure that's what you want to do, William?" Ann asked carefully. "I always thought you would like to follow a career in the open air. As a sea-faring man, perhaps. Or training horses to race."

"No." His young face was fervent, the square jaw determined. "It's gold I want to shape, Ann. Silver if and when I must, but it is gold first with me. Sometimes when I see a disc of it on the bench before work begins, my fingers ache to take hold of it and put something of myself into its shaping."

His eloquence did not surprise her. He opened up to her as he never did to anyone else in the family. She took one of his hands into hers and looked at it. Grubby and scarred, with dirt under the fingernails, it would have presented an unprepossessing sight to anyone else, but she observed the strong, mobile fingers and the broad palm.

"You have a craftsman's hands, but can you develop a craftsman's mind? That has to accept discipline in all its forms."

His smile with its charming lift was rueful. "That will be the hardest part." Then his eternal optimism showed through, and he jerked up his chin in a cocksure manner. "But I'll learn."

"You'll have to convince others about that—our parents as well as Joss, whose workpiece you dented two weeks ago, and whomever you want for a master for your apprenticeship."

"I know that. Will you stand by me when the time comes?"

"If you're still of the same mind, I'll do what I can. Take Peter as your example and try to be more like him in the two years left to you."

If he took notice of her words then, they were soon forgotten, particularly one afternoon in late August when he had decided to make the most of the time left to him before starting back at school again. It was some while later that Hester, having just completed an intricate workpiece, came out of the workshop to take a breath of air and rest for a few minutes. It was a stifling hot day, and she pulled off her cotton cap to comb her hair through with her fingers as she reached a garden seat in the shade and sat down on it.

It was then that she heard a distant shout. She straightened, listening intently, and it came again on an unmistakable note of distress. It was William, she was sure of it! What had he done now?

With her apron flying, she rushed down a path at the side of the house to reach the lane. Dust flew up around her skirt-hems as she came to a halt, listening again. Another shout echoed, and she judged it to come from a nearby copse. Had William fallen from a tree? She had a terrible image of him lying with broken bones as she flew across the lane and plunged into the cool shadows of the trees.

"William!" she called out frantically. "Where are you?"

Suddenly the explosion of a gun burst the silence and sent birds flying out of the branches overhead. She gave an anxious cry and rushed out of the trees into the meadow beyond, where a terrible sight met her. James, the smoking pistol in his hand, had just put out of its misery a fallen horse, saddled and bridled, that had broken its fetlock. The culprit rider, the whip still in his hands, lay face downwards, prostrate in the grass, close to the gate that had brought about the fall.

"Oh, William." She shuddered under her breath, knowing now his shouts had been of anguished protest that the handsome animal must die. For a matter of seconds she could not move, knowing what this tragedy would have done to him with his love of horses. She did not have to see his face to know that he was sobbing. Then, just as she was about to hurry forward, James, in a towering rage, strode across to William, snatched the whip from his hand and hauled him to his feet. Then he began to lay the whip about the boy with furious ferocity.

"No!" she cried out, breaking into a run. "Don't, James! Please! It was an accident! My son may be injured too!"

He did not hear her until she was quite close. Then he flung William away and shook the whip at him. "Get out of my sight! Never let me see you near my stables again."

William did not look at his mother. His face was ravaged by grief. "I'm sorry, sir."

"Go home, William," Hester urged. "I'll speak to you later." As he went off at a run, his head down in dejection, she turned fiercely to James.

"You had no right to whip him! You know what horses mean to him. You wouldn't have whipped a groom for a similar accident."

James stepped close to her, breathing heavily, a hard glitter in his eyes. "I would if the fellow had taken the horse against my orders not to ride it."

She was aghast. "You mean William didn't have permission?"

"That is correct. The horse was too strong and wilful for him to manage. I had told him that and so had the grooms, but he took it when their backs were turned."

"He shall be punished on principle," said Hester, "although the horse's death on his conscience will be more than enough, but I still say that beating him was wrong!"

James seized her by the shoulders and thrust his face close to hers. "Don't rile me further, Hester! I've taken all I can endure from you! Why do you think I put up with Mary's tantrums every year about coming here?"

"Don't say any more," she gasped, trying to draw away.

He shook her in his frustration and shoved her backwards against the trunk of an oak, where she was trapped by his tremendous strength, his arm about her shoulders and his hand spread across her breast. His breath came warmly into her face. "I've wanted you since I first saw you in the herb garden and since then I've come to love you! I didn't keep the herb garden as it was through any sentimental memory. The past is gone and what I choose to remember is private to me. During the changes made to the grounds, the herb garden was preserved in its original form for you and you alone! Because you liked it as it was. It was my tribute to you. My silent declaration, if you like."

"Do you think I didn't come to realise that with time?" she burst out. "But I chose to interpret it as friendship. That was what had formed between us and I wanted it to stay that way. Don't destroy all that has brought happiness to us both!"

The appeal in her voice evaporated the anger in him. He let his hands fall to his sides and stepped backwards from her. "I could have taken you here and now in the copse if that was all I wanted from you, but as you said, there is a special feeling between us that I wouldn't want to lose." A dry note slipped into his voice. "After all, lifelong friends are hard to come by."

He turned and walked away from her, back in the direction of the mansion. She stayed at the tree, attempting to put her disheveled appearance to rights. The force with which she had been shaken had caused pins to drop from her hair, and one long strand lay across her shoulder. As she entwined it back into place as best she could manage without a looking-glass, she watched James out of sight, filled with sadness for him. Then with a heavy sigh she set off for home herself.

On the way she recalled her intense anxiety as she had come in search of William and thought bitterly that she should have known that he would emerge unscathed from whatever escapade in which he had involved himself. It was always other people who suffered as a result of his foolhardiness, and in this case a beautiful animal as well. Greatly upset by the whole incident, a long suppressed hostility towards her son rose sharply in her. It was as if the clock had suddenly been turned back. She liked him no more now than on the day when he had been put into her arms for the first time. All that had grown up in between seemed now to have vanished. She told herself firmly that she was in shock and this dearth of maternal feeling would pass, but inwardly she knew some terrible damage had been done that might never heal.

She saw James again two days later at a supper party at the mansion, and they both behaved as if his heated words had never been said and outwardly everything was as it had always been. It was the same during the remaining social events until in September the Esdailes said their goodbyes and left for the city.

When summer came around again, Hester was the only one not surprised to hear that the Esdailes had gone to spend it at Great Gains and that a new country house was being built for them in another county. In contrast to James's absence before his marriage, there was an end to the upkeep of the mansion and its grounds. Tom Cole and his wife were dismissed as groundsman and caretaker; weeds and dust were allowed to have their way.

Hester read into it an ending between James and herself of what he had hoped for and that for her could never have been. He had left her with the key of the mansion that she had had for such a long time, and she retained the responsibility of locking and unlocking for Ann to use the library, even though she knew her daughter to be as reliable as herself. She rarely entered the house, making a habit of returning after an allotted time to meet Ann in the porch. It saddened her to see the beautiful furniture shrouded in dust sheets and silence reigning again where there had been such a warmth of hospitality.

But she had more to occupy her thoughts than the fate of a deserted house. During the past winter John had caught a chill that had taken a long time for him to shake off. Since then he had visibly lost weight and energy. At her persuasion, he had finally consulted a doctor, refusing to let her go with him, and had returned with the information that he had developed a weakness of the chest and with a bottle of physic that she eyed suspiciously. Removing the cork, she had smelt the foul contents and did not dare to think what it might contain. Nevertheless John had drunk it stoically. Afterwards she could see no difference in him and set about her own cures to restore his appetite and strength. It was for that reason she kept the

Esdaile herb garden in trim amid the jungle that was taking over the grounds, for some rare herbs grew better in the soil there than in her own garden. Her conviction that it was simply a matter of time before she discovered the exact blend of herbs that would effect a complete cure became an obsession with her.

"There's nothing the matter with your father that time and my herbs won't put to rights," she replied confidently to Letticia, who had expressed concern about him on a visit home.

"Are you sure it's not consumption?" Letticia ventured, deeply worried by a transparent look to her father's features. She saw stark fear fly across her mother's face before it vanished as swiftly as it had come.

"Nonsense! What an idea!" Hester shook her head chidingly on a little laugh. "Pregnant women get strange fancies sometimes, and you are seeing something far more serious in your father's condition than exists. I've known for years that he had a weakness of the chest."

"You have?"

"Oh, yes. When he first started that little cough, I knew it had its origins in the short time he spent on gilding. As a person gets older, small disabilities take a bigger hold and have to be properly treated. That's all there is to it."

"But Father is barely fifty. If he were well he would be in his prime."

"As he will be again shortly. Goodness me, how you do run on. Put away your needless worries and let us talk of other matters."

Letticia remained unconvinced. A word with Joss and Alice confirmed that they shared her anxiety. Before she left she confronted John and begged him to come into the city with her and see a physician whom she could recommend. He smiled and shook his head firmly.

"I've already seen an excellent doctor and I'm seeing no more. I'm in your mother's capable hands and her medicines are all I need. Stop worrying about me and take care of yourself. That is what's important now."

It was to be her last visit until after her baby was born, since travel was not advised in the last three months any more than it was in the first three. As she journeyed home, she formed the request she would put to Richard, hoping that he would not refuse her.

"Very well," he agreed after she had explained the situation. "The rules shall be relaxed for Peter in the circumstances. He may go home more frequently, but only until such time as Hester is proved right. I've had faith in her skills ever since she cured that poisoned finger for me."

Letticia was uplifted by her husband's optimism. Perhaps she was underestimating her mother's powers. Nevertheless, she was relieved by the thought that Peter, who at eighteen was refreshingly level-headed, would be able to give her frequent reports on her father's health.

Until this new turn of events, Peter had been given no privileges in his apprenticeship, even though his master was his brother-in-law. Both John and Richard had been in agreement that it should be this way, sharing the opinion that those seven years of hard work were good character training as well as a lesson in life. As for Hester, she was thankful every day that Peter was in such a highly esteemed workshop, both for his sake and her own, because after her long wait, he was at last securely on the path that would bring about the fulfillment of her dream for the name of Bateman. Whenever she saw him, they would talk at length together, she eager to hear of the progress he was making and never failing to drop into the conversation some mention of how splendid it would be when he had a workshop of his own in the city. She was taking no chances this time, although she accepted now that Alice had known better than she that Joss would never have been happy in the thrust and drive of London life. They had a baby now to cement their contentment with each other and another was on the way.

Peter was fully prepared to have his own business when the time came. He knew without any false modesty that he was going to become an exceptional goldsmith. There was a kind of liquid power in his hands to which precious metals responded as if recognising their own. Richard was a strict task-master and never praised, but Peter had come to recognise a low-key comment that told him a work-piece had been exceptionally well done. Deeply attached to his family, as all the Batemans were, even Letticia having had bouts of homesickness after her marriage in spite of the social whirl in which she had revelled until her present pregnancy, he had a dual reason now for wanting to return more often to Bunhill Row. He was in love with Elizabeth Beaver.

It was a source of amazement to him that he had known her from the first day of moving in from Nixon Square and yet had not noticed that over the years she was becoming an integral part of his life. A certain awareness came upon him, soon lost in the excitement of the day, when he had been ready to leave to take up his apprenticeship and she had come with the gift of a cravat, which she had sewn herself for him. Then she had stood with his mother and brothers and sisters to wave to him as his father drove him away in the gig. Some while afterwards she had suffered a long illness during which she nearly died. He had written to her several times, and although she replied when she was better, he did not see her, for she had been sent to stay with an aunt at Brighthelmstone in the sea air until such time as she was deemed fit to live inland again.

Her return home coincided with a visit of his to Bunhill Row. Joss fetched him in the gig one Saturday evening, and as they approached their home, she must have sighted them, for suddenly there she was, her bright face freckled from the seaside, her hair flying out like a golden banner and her muslin skirt billowing over her tossing petticoats as she ran to meet him. He stared at her, as once long ago she had stared at him, and was conscious of an awakening in him that must have had its beginnings in the shock of hearing she was ill or even before that, dating back to some time he could not remember. He sat forward in the passenger seat and sprang down before Joss had brought the gig to a halt.

"Elizabeth! Is it really you? After all this time! Are you quite recovered?"

"Completely!" She put her hands into his outstretched ones, and he clapsed them hard.

"Then you're back to stay?"

She nodded joyously, her gaze absorbing him as if she had been long starved. "So whenever you come home now it will be like old times."

His smile spread wider. "Even better, I believe. It's wonderful to see you again." His words brought a marvellous bloom to her face, and he saw that he had made this day a true home-coming for her as well as for himself.

They went hand in hand into his home. Hester, coming down the stairs, saw how they were looking at each other and smiled to herself. It was a development she had long foreseen and one that she welcomed whole-heartedly. Elizabeth was not, and never would be, another Alice. No retiring violet here but a vivacious girl with a quick mind, who had shown the same courage throughout her illness as she had in her childhood days when she competed with the boys in climbing trees and rough games, simply to be near Peter. With her tenacity for life, she would be ready to share his ambitions and encourage him, whatever the initial hardships.

Later that evening Peter held Elizabeth in his arms and kissed her for the first time. It was a moment of wonder for them both, a new discovery of what each held for the other. Even she, who had always loved him, trembled at the strength of tender feeling that had come upon them.

During the months that followed Hester saw in Peter an enormous capacity to love the woman of his choice that was the same in Joss towards Alice, a second son having settled his heart once and for all. She did not think it would ever be like that for William or Jonathan, for their natures were entirely different. More and more her animosity towards William was growing. It was a torment to her, for she reminded herself constantly he was her own flesh and blood, but her tongue became harsh with him as if on its own volition, and at times she, who had never slapped her children, had to struggle not to strike him for some impudence. With John she discussed at length what apprenticeship he should take, for he was approaching his fourteenth birthday and as yet nothing had been arranged.

"I'm afraid no master will keep him whatever trade it is," she admitted. "He's too wild in his ways to conform for any length of time."

"I'll talk to him."

When she heard the outcome of the conversation, her glance of disbelief went from John to William and on to Ann, who had been called in to speak on her brother's behalf. "A goldsmith?" she echoed incredulously. She returned her gaze to William. "But what interest have you ever shown? You are never in the workshop. It is Jonathan who spends some part of each day there."

William gave her a straight look. "You've never wanted me there, Mother."

She could not deny the truth of that. "And for what reason, pray? Did you ever try to work seriously, or resist the temptation to commit some tomfoolery?"

Ann intervened quickly. "William knows his record, Mother. It's nothing to be proud of, but then I'm sure it's not easy for everyone to work for his or her own family. I think William deserves his chance. He confided his hopes to me quite a while ago. This is not an aim that has arisen on impulse."

Hester spread her hands questioningly. "Who would take him? Most masters investigate thoroughly the background of a prospect apprentice. William has gained a sorry reputation for himself in this neighbourhood with his pranks and his girl-chasing."

She saw William turn crimson to his ears. He had not known that certain aspects of his behaviour in recent months had reached her ears.

Ann spoke up again. "Richard will take him. Letticia has already put William's case to him, and he is prepared to give him a chance."

Hester guessed that her son-in-law had not been easy to persuade and it was a measure of his affection for Letticia that he had agreed. "On a certain condition, I suppose?"

"Yes. William must work hard and obey the rules."

Hester turned to John. "What do you think?"

"William should have his chance."

She inclined her head in deference to his decision. "Then I agree." There was none of the excitement in her that she had known when first Joss and then Peter had been accepted as apprentices into workshops of repute. Something of her thoughts must have shown in her face, for William suddenly raised both clenched fists abruptly, like a pugilist in anticipated victory, and shouted out at them all defiantly, "I'll be the best goldsmith ever known!" Then he slammed out of the room before anyone could speak.

Letticia came to fetch him away to his apprenticeship in her coach. She combined the expedition with a chance to let her parents enjoy the sight of her baby daughter, whom they had not seen since the christening two months before. William, eager to get to the city, did not appreciate the lecture she gave him all the way there and tried to look attentive while shutting his ears to her words. His eyes sparkled when they entered the noise and bustle of the busy streets. Before long he would know every inch of London where fun was to be had.

The next day, in order to emphasise all she had said, Letticia took him to an exhibition of Mr. Hogarth's paintings, wanting him to see those that depicted in stages the rise of the good apprentice and the downfall of the bad one. William studied them. He did not say it to his sister, but he thought the bad apprentice had a far jollier time of it, in spite of a miserable demise, than the sanctimonious counterpart with his priggish expression when being beamed upon by his master.

"Now do your best," Letticia cautioned when she relinquished him to the workshop. She had sponsored him mostly for their father's sake, knowing the house would be more peaceful in her brother's absence and hoping that in a new peacefulness John would have a better chance of rallying from the lung weakness that was steadily getting a heavier grip on him. What puzzled her most was her mother's total inability to see or to accept that he was continuing to get weaker. It made her desperately uneasy. If it had been any other woman, Letticia would have suspected her of slight insanity, but there was no one more alert and realistic than Hester. Why then was there the peculiar mental block as far as John's condition was concerned?

It was a relief for Hester to have William away from home. Her conscience had troubled her greatly about the deterioration of her attitude towards him. Now that he was gone, she hoped his visits would be infrequent. Her prayers were for him to do well and overcome the folly in his nature. Richard had rewarded Peter for achievement by letting him come home far more often than had previously been arranged; she wanted William to achieve the same success without being granted the same privileges. It puzzled both her and John that Richard should suddenly have become so lenient.

John did not really approve, and although she was inclined to agree with him, she could not help but be pleased that Peter and Elizabeth should have the bonus of extra time in which to see each other.

Another summer came and went. Richard, visiting with Letticia, gave John and Hester a report on William's first year.

"The boy has goldsmithing in him, there's no doubt of that. When he's at the bench he has no other thought in his head but the task in hand." There was a pause. "When he's away from it, I'm afraid it's another matter."

John looked concerned. "Don't be easy on him."

"I'm not. To date he has received more punishments in twelve months than I expect to mete out to an apprentice in seven years. What brings him most to heel is taking him off the work he likes."

"Pray continue to do that." John paused to turn his head aside, coughing with a handkerchief pressed to his mouth. Then, after a sip from the glass of Madeira that Hester had served to him and to Richard, he recovered. "I want William to achieve his aim to be a better goldsmith than any of us."

Richard raised his glass. "I drink to that. There is nothing more agreeable than to see promise fulfilled."

Nobody ever mentioned John's cough, which now troubled him by day as well as by night. Hester had forbidden it. "I don't want him reminded of it, because it's nothing that can't be overcome. I have a new syrup for him that is working wonders."

She was always proved right, at least for a while. During the lapses Ann, who slept lightly, would hear Hester going downstairs to make camomile tea when, after a severe bout of coughing, John finally slept again. Then, putting on a robe, she would join her mother in the candlelight, knowing her company was welcome.

Joss was sitting in the comfort of his own home one evening when his wife summed up the situation in his parents' house. They had been discussing how he had seen illness in his father's face long before it had made itself manifest and had decided on that day to join the Bateman workshop when his apprenticeship was done.

"I believe it was a revelation," Alice said thoughtfully, a point with which he agreed, for they were both of a strongly religious mind. "What I find strange is your mother's curiously blinkered attitude towards your father's condition. It's as if she were fighting a private battle against it, shutting everyone else out, and the silencing of your father's cough, for however brief a period, is a skirmish won. If anyone remarks on his looking tired, she is quick to say he has worked hard that day and only needs some rest. I have often wondered if consumption was diagnosed by the doctor when your father visited him some time ago after having had such a bad chill. True, John told us it was only a weak chest, but I would not be surprised if your mother suspected that was not the full truth. I have never heard her refer to the cause of his poor health from that day to this."

"Maybe that is the only way she can bear what is happening to him," Joss said quietly, putting into words a long-held opinion. He saw surprise pass across his wife's face to be followed by a rush of compassion. Slowly she turned her head to look long and deep into the dancing flames in the grate. "Poor woman," she said reflectively, almost to herself. "How she must be suffering and how much worse it will be for her if things do not go well."

The new year of 1760 came in on a snowstorm and the frosty weather lasted several weeks. John dressed warmly and, at Hester's instigation, always wrapped a muffler about his neck and chin when going between the house and the workshop or on expeditions out. The crisp, dry air suited him and he did not miss a day at the bench. It began to look as if Hester's strength of will had had effect in bringing him to a better stage of health. In their own private world behind their bedchamber door there was a revival of intense passion on his part. This upsurge of vigour sprang from his desperation to claim all that life could give him before his lungs finally gave way to the disease that he knew had not been banished. Its shadow lay over him, always in wait.

The orchard was full of apple blossom on the day when, at noon, John put down the tools he was using and leaned against his workbench for support. Joss noticed and came to him, alarmed by his pallor. Hester had not seen. She was doing some casting work, making candlesticks, and pouring molten silver from a crucible into the entry funnel of a mould. It was hot and tiring work, for the investment could only be broken away by sudden immersion in cold water, which made the steam billow about her. Once John would have done it, but she and Joss shared all such tasks now, letting him do whatever workpieces suited his interest and his strength. It was as she turned, wiping the sweat from her forehead with the back of her hand, that she saw she was alone. It was not unusual for there to be comings and goings and, unperturbed, she reached for another crucible of molten silver just as Joss returned. He was in silhouette against the sun outside, but she sensed immediately that something was wrong.

"I saw Father into the house. He didn't want me to tell you, but I think he's feeling extremely ill."

It was as if a knell rang through her, but she kept herself under tight control as she whipped off her cap and apron. "Is he coughing?"

"No." He guessed she lived with the dread of hemorrhages, although never by a word or a flicker of expression had she ever shown it. Even now she was totally composed.

"See to those casings for me," she said as she went out of the workshop.

She found John in the room where he did his accounts. He had dropped down into a large wing chair and was hunched in it, his hands hanging limply over the ends of the chair arms. His eyes were closed in his blue-white face, but at the sound of her approach he opened them, the pupils tight with pain, and managed the smile he knew she wanted to see.

"It's nothing," he said reassuringly, keeping up the game of pretence between them. "Just a spasm."

"You'll be all right as soon as it passes." She knelt close to the chair and took one of his hands to cradle it against her breast as she gazed at him, anxiety glazed over by her carapace of calm.

"Indeed I will."

"Don't talk now, my darling. Rest yourself."

Her advice came a fraction too late. His colour rose with the cough gathering in him and then a paroxysm of heaving and coughing seized him until she feared he would choke. Ann, hearing him, came at a run and was sent to fetch the syrup that was kept for bad attacks. It contained laudanum, a last resort when experience had shown that nothing else could ease him. When at last his racked body was granted some respite, Joss was called to help him up to bed, where he fell into a deep sleep.

"He'll be back at the bench again in a few days," Hester said with an optimistic air as she went downstairs again with Joss, Ann having remained at her father's bedside.

"Don't count on that, Mother. There's a marked change in him. It's been noticeable over the past two or three weeks."

She tossed her head. "How can you say that?" she challenged. "He's worked a full day every day."

"Only because he was driving himself. He's a courageous man refusing to give in."

Fiercely she rounded on him. "And he won't give in. Neither will I! Your father and I will continue to fight his illness and we shall conquer it. What has happened today is only a minor setback. By tomorrow he will be on an upward grade again."

Joss opened his mouth to say something and then closed it again. Maybe he had no right to try to undermine such faith in an ultimate recovery. Miracles happened. Who was he to offer doubt at such a time when everything might depend on his mother's strength of will?

John was to remain bedridden for five weeks. Jonathan was always to pin-point his father's collapse as the starting point for his own real development as a goldsmith. By lucky chance for him the gap at the workbench coincided with a spell away from school, for the teacher was ill and since there was no one else to take over, the pupils had been given an indefinite holiday. He was twelve years old, strong and tall for his years with the promise of the Bateman good looks gathering across the bones of his face, but not yet disguising the self-satisfied set of the fleshy mouth or the evasiveness of his eyes if he was confronted with some question not to his liking. Joss, having found he could rely on Jonathan to do a task well, welcomed his freedom from school exactly when it was needed most and brought him into the workshop on the very morning after their father's attack to work a full day as if he were an apprentice already. Jonathan seized the opportunity to learn whatever he could, knowing it would give him an advantage later on.

"I'm going to be rich one day," he boasted to Ann as he waited while she mended a tear in a shirt he wanted to wear. "Then there'll be no more patched shirts for me. I'll have thoroughbreds in my stable and ride the fastest myself."

"Where's all this money to come from?" Ann inquired drily, snipping the thread as she finished her task.

"I'm going to be goldsmith to the King!" He seized the shirt from her without a word of thanks and pulled it over his blond head. Ann put the lid on her sewing basket. She did not dispute his dream. If anyone could achieve his aim she believed Jonathan to be the one, for he would use any means to get his way.

Chapter 11

It had become apparent to everyone except Hester that John would never work again. After his long spell in bed he was thin and weak, able only to sit in a chair in his bedchamber for a few hours a day. Ann was his constant companion, reading to him from his favourite books and others from the Esdaile library. Letticia came home periodically to fuss and try to re-organise the routine that Hester had found most suited John in what she referred to as his convalescence. When John at last was able to dress with her help and get downstairs, Hester was triumphant.

"You'll soon be fit again, my love," she said confidently as he leaned on her for support. "It won't be long now before you and I will be working side by side at the bench again."

The effort of getting downstairs had tired him. She propped cushions for him and lifted his feet up onto the couch when he had seated himself. Through the open window he had a view of the late summer roses.

"In a day or two you'll be able to sit in a shady spot under the trees," she promised, bending to kiss him, and the bouquet of her filled his nostrils deliciously. She was, he thought, still a girl at heart, with the same enthusiasm, vitality and eagerness for life that had first enchanted him. At times he felt that what little strength he had recouped had been drawn from her energy alone, for it certainly would not have come from his wasted body.

To the family's amazement, he was soon able to sit outside as she had promised him. Elizabeth, who came to the house almost daily, often sat with him, which gave Ann time to see to household matters. It was with the two girls on either side of him, ready with supporting arms if they should be needed, that he walked as far as the workshop where Hester and his sons were at work. Jonathan was quick to show him a spoon he was fashioning.

"That's good, my son," John praised, able to see that the right lines had been grasped even though the faults were manifold. Perching on a stool, he explained some finer points to the boy. He stayed quite a time, watching his wife raise a small sugar-vase and Joss in the final stages of a salver. When he left he looked back at Hester, who had paused in her work to watch him go, and she saw in his unchanged Thames-blue eyes a pride in her that warmed her through and through. Then he went out into the sun with the two girls and his shadow passed across her bench as he went past the window.

He never went to the workshop again. It was as if that visit had been the climax of a respite briefly gained before his illness began to wreak its worst on him. Once more the nights became a torment. After a bout of coughing he would lie exhausted against the pillows that kept him propped up while Hester would remove the blood-stained rags from a bowl on the bedside table and change his sweat-soaked night-shirt. Yet she still maintained her constant optimism. Even in a state of exhaustion, when he could barely speak, John attempted to keep up the spirit she lovingly demanded of him.

Nobody knew at what expense Letticia sent her own London physician to see him. Dressed more like a dandy than a man of medicine in burgundy velvet with a satin waistcoat, he made his examination at some length in order to earn his guineas, for he had been able to see at once that the patient was a dying man. When he came out on the landing, Hester was waiting to see him.

"I regret to say I can offer you no hope, Mrs. Bateman. Your husband is in an advanced stage of consumption and all you can do is make him as comfortable as possible. I will leave you a potion that will help relieve his suffering."

She received his statement unblinkingly. He thought her either exceptionally staunch or else quite unfeeling. He was inclined to the latter, for she was brisk and businesslike as she saw him out and thanked him for calling. Joss, waiting in the parlour, went out into the hall as soon as he heard the front door close.

"Well?" He was concerned for her, ready to help her to a chair. "What did he say?"

"Exactly what I expected." Her head was high, her back straight and her face immobile. She went past him into the parlour. There she swung around as he entered after her. "Doctors are the gloomiest of creatures. When they can't effect a cure they think nobody else can. He gave your father no chance at all."

Joss passed a hand across his forehead. Although the physician had only said what he in turn had anticipated, the shock was in its finality, the last destruction of a faint hope that had persisted in spite of all the evidence against it. "Did he say how long Father has left?" he asked hollowly.

Her voice was unusually sharp. "I didn't ask him such a foolish question when I know I can get John on his feet again."

Joss lowered his hand and stared at her. There was a curiously blank look in her eyes, as if she had shut out all the world from herself and the sick man upstairs. "Mother," he began carefully, "I can't wish my father years of the terrible torture that is tearing his lungs to shreds. There's no cure that is known to man."

Her arm came swinging up and she hit him hard on the side of his face. The sound of the slap seemed to hang in the quiet parlour like something tangible. Her eyes blazed with fury. "How dare you! I want no pessimistic talk from you or any other member of this family. You can tell them that! I'll bar the sickroom, and even this house, to anyone who doesn't approach your father's bedside as if on the morrow he will be up and back at work again!"

She swept out of the room and went back upstairs, running the last few steps when she heard coughing commence. Shaking his head, Joss left the house and returned to work. That evening he told Alice all that had taken place.

"She means what she says, I know her. I must warn Peter and Letticia. I had a word with Ann and Jonathan before coming home."

"What about William?" she asked.

"His behaviour in Richard's workshop, or rather his misdemeanours out of it, have barred him from coming home at least for the time being. If there is an emergency—" He broke off and sprang up from his chair to move restlessly about the room. "If only there were someone who could make my mother accept what is going to happen and prepare her for it. I'm sure there is nothing that would give Father greater tranquility. He can't keep up with her eternal optimism any longer. I've seen him close his eyes sometimes almost in desperation."

Alice came across and linked an arm through his. "I think there is someone. I believe Hester would listen to that person as she would to no one else."

"Who?" When she told him he agreed with her, impressed as he had been often before by her wisdom and good sense. "I'll see about it tomorrow."

The following Saturday afternoon when the trees along Bunhill Row were gaining the full autumn hues of copper, gold and crimson, Hester was called from the sickroom by Jonathan, who had seen a coach draw up outside. "Mr. Esdaile has come, Mother!"

She received the announcement with surprise and some uncertainty, turning in the doorway to pass the news to John, who sat in his dressing-robe in a wing-chair near the fire. It was an achievement for him to be sitting out of bed again, and she was greatly encouraged by this good sign.

"Shall I bring him up?" she asked.

"By all means," John replied. "I should like to see him."

Going downstairs, she found that James had been shown into the parlour. On the hall table was a basket of hot-house fruit for John that was typical of their visitor's generosity. As she entered the parlour, James came forward to greet her, seeming to make the room vibrate with his handsome height and powerful presence, an illusion aided by the shivering of the ancient oaken floorboards under his purposeful stride.

"Good day to you, Hester. It's been a long time." He kissed her hand and then stepped back and regarded her steadily. There was no laughter lurking at the back of his eyes today; neither was there any bitterness such as she had seen when they had quarrelled in the copse. Instead there was merely concern, which she interpreted as being solely for her husband. "How is John?" he asked her.

"He is making progress again," she replied confidently. "How are you? And Mary and the children?"

"All in excellent health. You and I have much to talk about after all this time, but first of all am I permitted to see John?"

"Indeed you are." She dropped a hint. "I like him to be cheered at all times, so your good company will be welcome. Please take your kind gift upstairs with you. John will appreciate it."

She led the way. In the bedchamber James concealed his dismay at the change in John's appearance, greeted him warmly and presented his gift, for which he was heartily thanked. He seated himself in a chair placed conveniently for conversation.

"It was good of you to drive out of London to see me," John said to him.

"I'd have come before if I'd known you were ill." James shook his head sympathetically. "This is a hard turn, John. I would wish to have things different for you."

Hester, who had remained near the door, intending to leave them on their own as soon as James had settled, bridled at his frank speaking. If he was going to harp on John's state of health in spite of what she had said, she would turn him out. Since her ultimatum, nobody had referred to John's present physical weakness as anything but a mild disposition. She was about to intervene when the conversation took a turn towards business in the city and some news of the Goldsmiths' Company that interested John immediately. Relaxing again, she stayed no longer and shut the door after herself.

Twenty minutes later James left the sickroom. He met Ann on the stairs on her way up to her father and was pleased to hear that through her reading sessions John had also benefited by her use of the mansion's library. In the parlour he found Hester waiting with tea.

"The tea can wait." He made a restless gesture as if feeling enclosed by the confines of the room. "Get your cape and let's take a stroll together outside."

"Very well." She extinguished the lamp-flame beneath the copper kettle, fetched her cape, and they went out of the house together. He took her firmly by the elbow as they set off along the road and turned down a side lane away from any passing traffic. By his brooding, meditative expression she concluded something was troubling him and was prepared for some confidence such as could be exchanged between friends. Cushioned as she was by her conviction that John's lungs could be healed to a certain degree, she did not immediately grasp the significance of what he said to her.

"I said my farewell to John, since I shall not be seeing him again." There was sadness in his voice. "I admire his courage. He's a brave fellow."

"Are you leaving London then?" she asked innocently.

"No."

"Then what should keep you away?" She hesitated only briefly. "I hope that nothing from the past—"

He broke in on her. "I could call again if I felt it were the right thing to do, but I happen to believe that the last weeks of a man's life should belong to his wife and family."

Her breath shuddered in her throat at the shock of what he had said. "I told you I don't allow pessimism. It destroys!"

"As it happens, I agree with you. But pessimism must not be confused with acceptance of reality. Hope should be sustained on all counts until there comes the point of no return, recognised both by the sick and those who care for them. That day has come to your house and only you are standing out against it, Hester."

"What have you been saying to John? And he to you?" She was paper-white, and even her lips had lost colour as she faced him at a standstill.

"We talked in friendship and parted in friendship, shaking hands in the knowledge that we shall not see each other again this side of the grave."

Anger flashed through her. She would have jerked herself away if his hand had not been like a manacle on her arm. "I'll never let you back into our house again! Heaven knows what gloomy thoughts you've put into John's mind. He is going to recover, I tell you. He may never be fully fit again, but he has many years left to him yet."

He seized her other arm and held her trapped before him, unable to throw him off. "Count those years as weeks or days and you'll be nearer the truth."

"No!" She shook her head wildly. "I won't listen to you."

He thrust his face towards her. "John is going to die soon, Hester. Not all your love and care are going to keep him much longer on this earth."

Her taut lips drew back over her teeth. She looked frightened and at bay, not far from panic. "Who are you to say so? You're not as well qualified as I am to know the true situation and what can be achieved."

"I'm better qualified than you think. I saw my first wife die of the same disease. In the last weeks of her life she looked exactly as John looks now." His face was full of sympathy and pain. "Do you suppose I didn't go through all that you have been enduring? In the end I had to accept that I was going to lose her."

"I'm not going to lose John!" She heard the rising note of hysteria in her own voice and bit hard into her lower lip as if to retain self-control.

"Face facts!" he urged fiercely. "You'll kill him before time if you don't! Set him free from the pretence he is struggling to maintain for your benefit alone. He is tormented by anxiety for *you!*"

She was trembling violently, although no longer from rage. Her desperate whisper came strangled from her throat, her lips barely able to form the words. "I can't go on without him. He is my life."

He gripped her still harder, as if to transmit some of his own strength to her. "He can still be your life. You'll take the same pride in your silverwork as if he were there to praise it. Your skills are his skills. Let him know you have the courage to go on as head of the family in his place. Grant him peace of mind in the time that is left to him."

He saw her eyes grow bleak as finally she drew into herself all he had said, and she sagged as if she would have fallen without his support. Then, as if in a trance, she straightened again and brushed aside his grasp even as he released her. She took a few steps away from him to stand motionless, her hands clasped in front of her waist, and gazed unseeingly before her for a considerable time. He waited in silence, half expecting she would break down into tears when she had fully adjusted her thoughts and come to terms with the inevitable. Her face was gaunt with strain when eventually she turned back to him, but she was composed, only the exceptionally heightened grey of her irises showing that an ocean of tears had been narrowly dammed. She spoke in quiet, controlled tones.

"I thank God for what you have said to me today. I've been cowardly and afraid, thinking of myself and how much I needed

Rosalind Laker

Rosalind Laker

John. It must have put a terrible burden on him, because whenever he tried to talk to me about a future without him, I've refused to listen. You've opened a door for both of us. I'll always be grateful."

Stepping forward, she kissed him on the cheek, rested hers briefly against his, and then went from him back towards the house. There the tea remained forgotten in the parlour. He left by a side path and did not go indoors. The touch of her lips seemed to linger on the side of his face. The long absence had made no difference to the love he felt for her. Had he kept the mansion as a country home and remained in the neighbourhood, instead of building that extravagance for Mary so far away, he would have been able to help Hester before now and been at hand in the darker days ahead. At least she had a good son to stand by her in Joss, for he would carry on in his father's place in the workshop without change or disruption.

Upstairs, Hester found that John, exhausted by the visit as he was by anything in the least untoward, however pleasant, had been helped back into bed by Ann, who had left him on his own to sleep for a while. His lids were closed, but he never failed to hear her light step or sense her presence, and a smile touched the corner of his lips before his eyes opened. He stretched out a hand to her.

"Has James gone?"

"Yes." She sat down on the edge of the bed and held his hand in both of hers. All her feelings showed in her face. "I've always loved you, John. I shall go on loving you until the time comes when we'll meet again."

Relief was liquid in his eyes. Then her own tears came. She lay down on the coverlet and rested her head on his shoulder as he put his emaciated arms about her. He kissed her streaming eyes and her cheeks and her mouth. She wept almost silently until there were no more tears in her. He stroked back some disordered tendrils of hair from her brow.

"You have been the best wife any man could have had," he said tenderly. He had been unfaithful to her only once, when a distraught woman had appealed to his senses, displaying her half-naked body in wild abandonment. It was many years since he had given Caroline a thought, and even now it was a passing reflection without the least importance since Hester had never known of it.

He cupped her face gently, looking into her eyes. "It was a lucky day for me when Jack Needham broke his watch-chain and I was sent to collect it from the Heathcock tavern."

Quietly they reminisced about their courtship. It was safe ground and a preparation for all that would be said between them in the days ahead. Outside dusk had fallen. She did not light the lamp until she stirred from the bed at the sound of Ann's step on the stairs, Jonathan's voice in her wake. John's supper was being brought on a tray.

It might have seemed as the next few days went by that John had regained a measure of strength out of his new contentment, for he talked to each one of his children in turn on their own without any apparent tiredness, even William being allowed home with Peter at this time. Hester, all scales gone from her eyes, was able to see it was the last bright flare of the candle-flame before it flickered out.

Then the nights set in worse than ever before in hours of tormented coughing that did not ease when morning came. He coughed even when drugged with laudanum. As Hester tended to him, wiped blood from his lips and bathed into coolness his skeletal body that had been the giver of so much physical joy to her in the past, her love for him reached a new dimension of the spirit. She seemed to know his thoughts even as he knew hers, sparing him any attempt at communication, the disease having taken possession of his throat.

He lingered until November. Then, mercifully, restoring her faith in prayer, he was spared the last terrible indignity of a fatal hemorrhage and died quietly in his sleep, his heart having given out finally under its constant strain. She was alone with him, seated at the bedside, his hand resting in hers, and she felt him go from her.

"John!" His name burst from her in a last cry of love.

The hour was two o'clock in the morning on the sixteenth day of November, 1760. He was fifty-two years old. At midday, after the doctor had called to sign the death certificate and the funeral arrangements had been made, Hester took John's will from his desk, and at her request Joss broke the seal and read it out to her. They were on their own, away from the family who had gathered in the parlour, Letticia having arrived with her husband and brothers as soon as the message had reached them. It was a short will, for John had made only one bequest.

"To my beloved wife, Hester," Joss read out in his deep steady voice, "I leave my entire estate, including the tools of my craft, it being my belief that she will come to use them in skills beyond anything I have been able to teach her."

Hester raised a stunned face. It had not been a surprise to learn that the workshop, as well as all else, had been left to her, for John had told her and Joss in turn, knowing that their teamwork would continue as it had during his illness before his needs as a patient had kept her from the workbench. What she had not known was that she was to receive his treasured tools. She had assumed they would go to Joss, who was a qualified goldsmith, and no craftsman gave his tools to anyone but his equal. John had paid her the highest compliment possible in that special bequest and had added encouragement for the future beyond anything she could have imagined.

"When was the will written?" she asked hoarsely.

Joss looked at the date. "August, 1750."

"Ten years ago!" Her thoughts raced back to a time even earlier, when Joss had praised a snuff-box she had made, not knowing it was her work, and she had seen John's expression change. Then, and often afterwards, she had supposed his male ego had been put out by her ability. Instead, that shift of expression had simply portended a new awareness of her as a fully fledged silversmith. He had probably made up his mind then that the workshop and the tools should become hers if he happened to be the one to die first. "Joss, I had always thought your father would leave his tools to you."

He came across to rest his hands on either arm of the chair in which she sat. "I'm not disappointed. You deserve the tools, Mother. I don't think you've ever realised your own talent."

"Thank you," she whispered, looking down as she struggled with the wave of emotion passing through her.

He touched her on the shoulder to help her avoid giving way. "Are you ready to go to the lawyers?"

She straightened her back and nodded firmly. "The sooner the will is proved the better. I have been thinking we can't risk delays or the loss of customers, because everything depends on our maintaining credit and orders. It's what your father would have wanted us to do."

From the parlour window Letticia watched them drive away together in the wagonette. She was red-eyed with grief. "How can Mother be so practical at such a time?"

"Be thankful for it," Alice said crisply. "It's not long since that Joss and I feared she would lose her mind completely when this day came."

Many people attended the funeral at St. Luke's Church, for John had been well liked by friends and neighbours as well as those in the goldsmithing trade. It was a cold and blustery day when he was laid to rest in the churchyard. Hester had made the silver plaque on the coffin and Joss had inscribed it. As the wind billowed her cloak and drove a misty rain into her face, she knew her own heart would lie forever beneath that plaque.

Chapter 12

Peter and William came home for Christmas. It was a concession by Richard in view of his mother-in-law's recent bereavement, because, unless Christmas Day fell on a Sunday, it was the same as any other day in a working week, with shops open and workshops busy. Hester, apart from cooking a dinner of roast goose with mince pies and a plum pudding set aflame with lighted brandy, made it a day of rest, closing the workshop. She and Joss both needed a respite, for since John's funeral they had worked all hours to catch up with delayed orders and other matters that his illness had meant putting to one side. She was not prepared for the shock that Peter gave her when they happened to be alone together for a few minutes.

"Father's death has changed everything," he said firmly. "As soon as my apprenticeship is finished, I shall join you and Joss in the workshop."

"No!" She was aghast. "That's not for you. I won't have you tied to this place through some misguided sense of responsibility. Joss and I are managing well and are more or less shipshape now, all orders under control again. You have to make your own way in the world." She caught hold of the front of his coat in her agitation. "I'm relying on you to be the greatest silversmith of all."

"So you are using the new term to describe those of us who prefer to specialise in silver, are you, Mother?" His eyes smiled at her. "You always were up to the minute. That's why I want to throw in my lot with you. Why should I work for another master when I could work for you?"

"But I'm not a Freeman of our craft's Company any more than your father was and I never can be. That would always be a disadvantage to you as it is to Joss. You would be classed as an outworker with us. Your achievements would never be given the acclaim due

251

to them. Take warning from Joss's position. He has his own registered punch-mark that he can never use, since the workshop is mine."

"That doesn't mean it has to be the same for me. I've always had more ambition than Joss. I can go ahead from the Bateman workshop as well as from any other."

"Elizabeth would object." It was a last endeavour to persuade him.

"No, she wouldn't. She thinks my chances would be good from here. Too many masters keep their most promising craftsmen under a dominating thumb for years on end."

In spite of her protest, his line of argument had sent new possibilities tumbling into her thoughts. She pressed her fingertips to her temples as if to sort out the confusion, a light dawning in her face. Peter was right. Why not? What better start for the fame of the Bateman name than John's own premises? Changes would have to be made. Money would be needed to expand. Suddenly a whole new challenge was presenting itself. She would have to think everything out very carefully, but not today. This was a family day and must be devoted to the present and not to the future. She linked a hand in Peter's arm.

"We'll talk of this matter another time. You've nearly three more years of your indenture to serve. Let's rejoin the others."

That night she could not sleep for the activity of her brain. She rose from her bed and paced the floor until the first step to be taken became clear to her. Then she went downstairs to make camomile tea, and Ann, hearing the stairs creak, followed down after her.

"Is anything wrong, Mother?" With her hair loose and hanging in its soft waves, she had thrown off the look of being ten years older than her age, which her plain dressing and severe coiffure induced by day.

"Nothing at all. I couldn't sleep." It was always a comfort to her to have Ann's presence.

Ann took the cups and saucers from a cupboard. There had been many times in the cosy warmth of the kitchen by night, and over countless nocturnal pots of tea, when she could have shared a confidence with her mother and poured out some of the old pain that had withered her inside. Many times she had wanted to, feeling there would be healing in it for her, but Matthew's name had always jammed in her throat, impossible to mention, and now she did not even try. She continued to love the family from within a shell of her own making. Her grief for her father was immense, but nobody had seen her cry. She had become a listener to others, sympathetic and understanding through the lesson of her own experience. It was natural that when the tea was poured, Hester, full of the plans she had made, should tell Ann of it when she would have told no one else.

Ann considered carefully and nodded approval. "You must wear your best clothes for the occasion," she advised wisely. "The coppery silk that sets off your hair would do well without being too noticeable. It would mean no disrespect to Father, who was against your wearing mourning in any case. The last thing you want is to appear as a weak widow playing for sympathy in your black weeds."

"I don't think James has ever thought me weak," Hester commented drily.

"That's beside the point. You must look what you are—a determined woman ready to do business at a man's level and make a success of it."

"I'll do everything you say."

In the morning Hester took a long look at her reflection for the first time in months. Her skin was still good, the lines faint, and she had kept her figure; her narrow waist was still that of a girl. Admittedly there were some threads of grey in her hair, but it had retained its strong colour and a tincture of marigolds added to the rinse when she washed it would bring back its highlights. On no account must she look worn down and weary, but there was no need for pretence either. Confidence was high in her.

She drove the old gig herself into the city when the day came. It was a crisp morning with frost on the road and frozen puddles, but her cinnamon cloak was warmly lined, her coppery silk gown long sleeved, and she wore a wide-brimmed green hat that tied under her chin with ribbons to match.

In Lombard Street she drew up outside the building from which James conducted his business affairs. Inside there were a large number of clerks seated at high desks with their pens scratching. She was shown into James's office after a short wait. It was a high-ceilinged room, comfortably furnished, with a number of fine oil paintings on the walls, mostly seascapes. James came forward to greet her, and her heart warmed anew towards him for what he had done for her and John at their last meeting.

"My dear Hester. This is a most welcome surprise. What brings you to London?"

"First, are you sure I'm not interrupting your appointments? Perhaps I should have made one?"

"Not at all. Today is remarkably free, as it happens. I hope you will stay and dine with me. Let me take your cape and hat. Come through into the adjoining room. It is there that I entertain my most distinguished clients."

Going through the double doors he had opened for her, she could see why. The walls were panelled with crimson silk, the couches, sofas and chairs upholstered in rich brocade. In a marble fireplace coals glowed brightly, and she went across to warm her hands. There were crystal decanters on a side table and, as he exchanged news with her, he poured Madeira into two long-stemmed glasses. Bringing them across to where she stood, he handed one to her and raised his own in salute.

"Your good health, ma'am."

"And yours, sir."

They drank to each other, smiling. Then he invited her to sit down and took the seat beside her on the sofa. "Now tell me to what I owe this pleasure."

"I'm here on business."

"I thought as much. You would have called at my house otherwise. What is it you require?"

He was feasting his gaze on her. Last time she had been thin and taut as an archer's bow. Grief had taken its toll and she had not yet regained much weight, but her vitality had returned and there was a purposefulness about her that boded well for her future. As for himself, her beauty held its same powerful spell over him as when it had been first cast in the herb garden. Again, as had happened many times before, he was dangerously stirred by her nearness. The thought uppermost in his mind was that now she was a free woman without marital ties to another man. Since he and Mary were virtually going their own ways, she residing permanently at their country house and he for months on his own in London, he was equally free in one respect.

"I'm going to register my own 'touch' at the Assay office," she disclosed, "which is the legal requirement if I am to set up on my own. It's time I released my own designs instead of being hide-bound by other people's in the outwork, which so often follows a mediocre pattern. I am also going to cater to those who have been unable to afford silver before now. Thin silver lends itself well to many articles, particularly spoons, and this would bring down the cost considerably. It's not only the rich who will buy from my workshop."

"What lies behind all this?" he questioned perceptively, able to see she was in the grip of something more than self-ambition.

She leaned towards him eagerly. "I intend to make the name of Bateman known." Her voice rang with determination. "I used to think that I had to rely on my sons to do it, but now I believe I should do it in my own right, and that means more to me than I could ever explain."

So that was it. She wanted to pay honour to the man she had loved. His hand clenched on the stem of his glass in an involuntary spasm of jealousy, acute and painful. How odd that he should be jealous now when he had never been jealous of John Bateman in his lifetime. Against his will he felt angry with her.

"How would you go about achieving your ambition?"

"I should have to step carefully at first, proving that my standard is as high as anything that came out of the workshop when John was in charge." She had it all worked out. "Most of all I need a loan to see me through the start of producing silver bearing my punch-mark."

"I see." He took her empty glass from her, since she had declined a refill, and put it aside with his own.

In her enthusiasm she failed to detect the slight coolness in his attitude. "There is nobody else to whom I can turn, James. You know my background. You've seen my work. Say you will advance the money I must have if I'm to expand my business in this way."

"And if you're successful in your venture," he asked uncompromisingly, "will you bury yourself away in the workshop and never emerge again? When should I see you?"

She uttered a little laugh. "Often, if you returned to Bunhill Row."

"Maybe I will one day. But seeing you today makes me want to take up again from that day in the copse. What I said to you then still holds good today. My feelings haven't changed."

She became intensely conscious of how he was looking at her, and the fierce desire in his eyes touched a long dormant chord in her. She had always found him attractive, liked his striking looks, the laughter in him, and admired his fine build as she had admired John's in times past. Added to that was the new depth of feeling that had come with his previous kindness towards her. It was not love as she understood it and never could be, but it was a bond of deep affection enriched and enhanced by the passage of time and all that had taken place in sorrow and joy. Nevertheless, she did not intend to submit to the pressure he was putting on her. She was her own woman now, subject to no man, and she would fight to retain that status.

"Are you bargaining with me?" she demanded steadily, facing him out.

For several timeless moments he held her gaze and then slowly shook his head and sighed regretfully. "No, my dear, I'll not do that, however great the temptation. I'll grant what you ask. You shall have your loan."

"Oh, James!" Her voice broke on the rush of gratitude that combined with her fondness for him to illumine her whole face. He could no longer hold back from her and scooped her to him, arching her spine as he lovingly claimed her parted lips in the most ardent of kisses. She made no protest, her arms going about his neck, her own response a natural expression of happiness in this hour and what he had promised her. What she had not anticipated was that her flesh should threaten to betray her. John's illness had long deprived her strong, healthy body of its needs, and she had believed her desire for physical love lost with his as his health had declined. Now James's tender, travelling caresses were reawakening urges within her, but he was not John and that was his misfortune. Gently but forcibly she drew back from him and extricated herself from his embrace before sheer passion got the better of them, something that had no place in her life anymore.

Disappointment weighed down his face. For a few intoxicating minutes he had believed he was about to possess her at last. He could guess what lay behind her withdrawal, and jealousy gripped him again. He would have given everything he owned to have been loved half as much by her as John Bateman had been in his lifetime and even now when only a memory. His hands continued to fondle her arms as he held her facing him.

"You know I'll love you to my dying day."

Her eyes softened to a mist. "I know."

They kissed again fondly, without their previous fervour. If he wished he had never made a second marriage and waited instead for her, he did not say so, and she thought it all for the best.

When he ordered dinner it was brought in from a neighbouring tavern to be set out on damask by the waiter supervising the minions in their white aprons, who carried the covered dishes. After the wine was poured, she and James were left on their own and they talked over many topics as they ate, her plans in particular.

"Dine with me again whenever you are in town," he invited when helping her on with her cape when she was ready to leave.

"That would be most pleasurable, dear James."

On the sixteenth day of April she drove again into the city. This time she went to the Assay Office, where her name was registered in the list of those craftsmen in precious metals who were not Freemen of the Company and she was shown where to set down her entry. She took the pen firmly, having practiced daily over the past week for this moment. For a second or two there was the threat of nausea that always accompanied the holding of a pen under stress. Her hand shook slightly but the strokes she made were firm if not perfect. *H.B.* There! It was done!

If all the church bells of London had been pealing when she emerged into the street, she would not have been surprised. Anything could have happened that day. After all, it felt as if her feet were not touching the ground.

As she had foreseen, there was no swift path to the progress she wanted to make. Goldsmiths continued to treat her workshop as a place for outwork and her new status went unnoticed. At least orders had never been withdrawn after John's death and she had Joss to thank for that, for due to the personal contacts he had made in the trade during his collecting and delivering of orders, he was as well liked as his father had been and the standard of his work appreciated. She had some trade discs made, bearing her name and trade and address. These were a current novelty and on being handed round brought attention to the trader concerned. Hers resulted in some independent orders in which she dealt directly with the customers and the pieces produced from her own designs bore her touch of *H.B.* for the first time. Encouraged, she put into action her plan to produce a sideline of reasonably priced small articles for ready sale and this outlet proved profitable, her spoons in constant demand, although the bulk of her income continued to come from outwork.

Then a benefactress of St. Luke's Church wished to present a pair of candlesticks in memory of her late husband. The vicar, knowing Hester well, suggested that the commission be put to the Bateman workshop. Hester was invited to call at the lady's house with designs, and one was selected. Although the design was Hester's own and the finished candlesticks would bear her hallmark, she let Joss make them, for ecclesiastical work continued to please him best.

Afterwards the same woman ordered a chocolate pot for a wedding gift, which Hester made herself, and it led in turn to a gradual buildup of commissions that could be fitted in with the outwork, for both she and Joss worked long hours whenever it was necessary. Jonathan, who had been a help to them, had gone to Richard's workshop, the third of her sons to take up an apprenticeship with her son-in-law. Hester looked forward to the day when Peter would join them, convinced there would be good prospects by the time his apprenticeship was done. Busy as she was, it seemed no time at all before that day came and with it his marriage.

By now her business was on a steady footing. She had seen James quite a number of times since the day when a seal had been put on what had been, and always would be, between them. In addition to his original loan, she had received another when her neighbours

moved from Number 108 and she bought the premises for a new
and improved workshop. James had accepted the invitation to Peter
and Elizabeth's wedding, but Mary would not be coming. It seemed
as though nothing could tempt her away from her country environs
and outdoor pursuits.

All the family gathered for the wedding day, including William,
who was close to his nineteenth natal day, with the looks of a bucca-
neer and a jauntiness about him that drew the glances of all the girls
and some of the young married women as he acted as usher in St.
Luke's Church directing the arriving guests. One girl in particular
caught his eye. She was about seventeen, small-breasted and slender
as a wand with a fey will-'o-the-wisp air about her. She had moon-
fair hair and dark eyes slanting and mysterious under winged
brows, her mouth soft and moist and rosy. She cast him a shimmering look from under the brim of her leghorn hat, before following
on up the aisle. He nudged Joss in the ribs.

"Who's that? That girl in the green dress."

Joss glanced after her. "That's Sarah Thorne, niece of Mr. and
Mrs. Thorne."

"She's new here, isn't she?"

"She moved here with them about two years ago. With no children of their own they took on guardianship of her when she was
orphaned quite young." He saw how his brother was continuing to
stare in the girl's direction as she took her place in a pew with a
staid-looking pair. "Stay well away from her, Will. Those people
are strict Dissenters and have only set foot in this church today
because they are related to the Beavers. I know from what Elizabeth has told us that Sarah is allowed no outings except religious
services, and if you start playing the fool with her at the wedding
breakfast they'll whisk her home at once."

"There's no need to worry. I'll not spoil her day." "Far from it,"
he added silently to himself. In fact, he could probably supply her
with a little extra fun!

Hester, believing that nothing could go wrong on this day so
long awaited by both Peter and Elizabeth, considered it to be one
of the happiest occasions she had known. She loved Elizabeth as her
own child and could not have wished for any other bride on her
son's arm when the ceremony was over and they came down the

aisle together, Elizabeth in cream lace with a garland of rosebuds on her golden head, Peter in dark blue velvet, joy in their faces.

William did not attempt to sit near Sarah at the wedding breakfast, which was held in the Beavers' home. Instead he chose a place opposite and some distance from her, where he could look hard at her unobserved by the Thornes, who were seated on the same side of the table as himself. His stratagem worked. She glanced, blushed, went white and glanced at him again. The Thornes had seated her between two elderly people and failed to see that when she smiled or laughed it was for the benefit of someone else at the far end of the table. When he judged the time right, William bribed Jonathan, who would never do anything for nothing, to pass a note to her. Then he slipped away to the orchard at the back of the Beavers' house.

She came, as he knew she would, darting between the trees and looking about for him as she hurried along. When he stepped into her path and pulled her into the shelter of a bush, she gave a startled yelp that he silenced with his hand over her mouth.

"Beware!" he teased. "You'll have those two gorgons after you."

She laughed deliciously as his hand fell away, her eyes wild and dilated with excitement. "This is wicked! I shouldn't be here. What was it you wanted to see me about that you declared urgent in your note?"

"I wanted to know when I could see you again. Do you ever go to a Dissenters meeting in London where you could slip away?"

"That's quite impossible!" she exclaimed. "Dissenters meetings are never held without a watch kept on the doors, because often fanatics of the established Church of England try to break up our gatherings just as Catholic services are invaded at times." She shook her head vigorously. "I could never get out unnoticed."

"What about here then? Somewhere near your home? You live in the lane that runs from the stable entrance of the Esdaile place, don't you?"

"Yes, I do."

His eyes twinkled conspiratorially. "I happen to know a secret way into the stable yard that I used to visit the horses when, after an accident, I was banned from going there by Mr. Esdaile. Surely you could leave your home unnoticed in an evening hour and meet me there?"

She gasped at the audacity of his plan, thrilled and awed by it, tempted as much by the thought of freedom for an hour or two as she was by the companionship that would go with it. Since living with her aunt and uncle she had twice suffered spells of melancholia during which she had been locked in her room, even being force-fed when unable to face eating, and they had feared she would die. Just being in this orchard with someone in high good humour was worth any amount of punishment if she should be discovered. To live with daily disapproval and constant correction was a terrible burden to one who had only known loving kindness before. "How would you get to the mansion? You're apprenticed in London, aren't you?"

"There are ways and means." He was eager. "What do you say?"

She tossed up her chin provocatively. "I say that I'm not at all sure that I do want to see you again."

He played along with her, giving ridiculous reasons why she should that brought forth peals of rippling laughter. Once they scampered in a game of chase and capture in which her forfeit upon being caught was a kiss, which he took with relish.

"Now," he said with satisfaction, his face within an inch of hers, "give me the hour and the date when we shall meet."

Her chest rose and fell breathlessly under her high-necked, unflattering gown. "On Saturday evening my aunt and uncle go to advanced studies on religious matters in the preacher's house, and they are always late home."

He was jubilant. It was the best evening of the week for him, although it would be odd to find himself within spitting distance of his home without being able to visit his family. "Next Saturday it is!"

By the time he had told her where to find the hidden entrance into the stableyard, music had struck up on the lawn where the bride and bridegroom would be starting the dancing. She became nervous.

"I must go back now or I'll be missed."

"Until Saturday then." He watched her run off through the trees. When he returned to the wedding party his mother was dancing with James Esdaile, both of them in a light-hearted mood. He hoped to speak to Hester on her own later when the evening celebrations were over, for his pockets were empty and he would need money to hire a nag to get him to his tryst with Sarah and back again. He glimpsed Sarah only once before her guardians took her away. They considered dancing to be sinful and would not stay any longer. This did not lessen his enjoyment of the occasion. There were plenty of other girls to partner. When dusk fell he took another young woman into the orchard for a different purpose than before, and her husband searched for her in vain.

Peter and Elizabeth had left everyone else to the dancing by this hour and escaped hand in hand down the street to Number 86, next door to Joss and Alice's home, which they had rented for themselves. Inside he slammed the door shut and bolted it. Then he turned to draw her to him, taking the garland from her hair and throwing the faded blooms aside as he looked down into her radiant, upturned face.

"I've had to wait five years for this moment," he said, marvelling that it had come at last.

"I've waited much longer, dearest Peter. And we'll be happy together for ever and ever!"

Kissing her, he picked her up in his arms and carried her upstairs in a tumbled flow of lace. She was as light as a feather, and he was reminded briefly of the fledglings he had rescued in the past. That night she reached the conclusion that no woman could ever have been loved with more tenderness and adoration.

The party ended at midnight, and after coming home from it, William sat on the terrace for a while. The family, as well as guests with far to travel, were being accommodated in every bedchamber under his mother's roof as well as in the home of Joss and Alice and that of the Beavers. A light in one of the windows of the Esdaile mansion showed that James was in residence for the night, for a coach as splendid as his was a natural target for highwaymen in the darker areas of Bunhill Row after dusk.

"Aren't you tired, William?" Hester asked, stepping out on the terrace.

He had been waiting for her, knowing that ever since his father had had to give up doing a last round of the house at night it had been her task. "Not yet," he answered as she came towards him in a rustle of coral silk, still in her finery of the day. "It's such a perfect night. Sit with me for a while. I want your company quite apart from a favour I have to ask."

It was only too easy to guess what he wanted, and she thought how William could always sweeten any pill. But she was in a lenient mood. It was not the time after such a happy day to reprove him for failing to manage on the apprentice wage he received from Richard, although his father had existed on much less. She did not sit down, being more than ready for bed, but she inclined her head benevolently. "There is no need to ask me for what you have in mind. I had intended to give you a guinea before you left in any case."

He sighed with exaggerated relief for her amusement, and the wry twitch of her lips was not lost on him. "Thank you, Mother. Money melts away in London."

"So it seems," she remarked drily. "Good night to you. Sleep well."

On his own again, he hooked his thumbs in his waistcoat, grinning to himself and stretching out his long legs in satisfaction. A guinea! That would cover transport for a long time to come. There was something about Sarah Thorne that was elusive and intangible, intriguing him, and he was always ready for a new challenge. He looked forward in high anticipation to the time he was going to spend with her. There was every chance he would still be enthralled when the present last flare of summer faded into chillier weather, and he intended to make preparation for that.

As soon as he was sure his mother had gone upstairs, he went back indoors and made his way to what had been his father's office, where Joss now kept the books. Opening a cupboard where his mother kept her designs and other items exclusive to her in the business, he took two keys from a hook, one to a padlock on the side gate that led to the herb garden in the grounds of the Esdaile mansion and another to the residence itself. Holding his breath, he listened to make sure nobody had heard the creak of the cupboard door, and then he went out into the old workshop where he made an imprint of both keys in melted castingwax. After this task was done and the keys returned to the cupboard, he hid the hardened wax tablets in his travelling bag and went to bed to sleep soundly.

When Saturday evening came he arrived at the mansion long before he was due to meet Sarah in the stableyard. Knowing the district as he did, he had approached by side lanes and bridle paths in the gathering darkness. He left the nag tied up in the copse and under cover of the trees reached the side gate used nowadays only by his mother and Ann on their visits to the herb garden and the library. His newly minted key clicked open the padlock at once. He entered quickly and refastened the gate after him. The grounds were familiar enough to him, but he had not been many times in the house. He had expected to reach the entrance under the cover of overgrown bushes, but it appeared that after James Esdaile had spent a night in his old home again he had set gardeners to work once more and everything was in a state of being cleared, trimmed and re-dug. At least there was no chance of that gentleman taking up residence again with winter ahead, for he always spent that time of the year in London.

Everything in the mansion was covered in dust sheets, and in the yellowish light given by his lantern it looked as if every room was inhabited by spectres. He made a lightning tour to get his bearings, the shutters over the windows preventing his lantern-glow from being seen from outside, and he only paused in the Esdailes' own bedchamber. There he stood gaping, never having seen such a bed with its carnation-coloured silk draperies, fluted canopy and tinted ostrich feathers rising from a gilded dome almost ceiling-high. There were no dust-sheets here. His guess was that due to a muddle of servant-instructions it had not been properly closed up again after James's sojourn on the night of the wedding. Some idiotic maid had even put clean sheets on the bed. He grinned, running a hand over the fine linen. Maybe luck was going to be with him all the way.

Sarah was so late in arriving that he had begun to think she was not coming. He shone the lantern for her as soon as he heard the crackle of dry twigs as she began to crawl through an ancient duct in the thick wall that might have been there since Roman times. He bent down and grabbed her by the upper arms to pull her through and on to her feet as if she had been a fish on an angler's line. He had expected her to be shy and terrified, but there was a curious, almost hysterical exhilaration in her.

"I did it!" she exclaimed in an exuberant whisper. "I got away from *them*. It shows they can't keep me boxed up with their rules and regulations for ever."

"Well, that's good." He felt somewhat deflated. She had not come entirely to see him but mainly, or so it seemed, to fulfil some obsessive need to prove herself against her guardians. Perhaps she had been waiting to break out in some outrageous move and he had all unwittingly presented it.

"Have I torn my skirt?" She looked down anxiously at the drab garment.

He shone his lantern over it. "Not that I can see." He helped her to brush away the leaves and cobwebs. "I have a better way for you to get in next time."

"Not crawling on all fours again, I hope." She giggled, letting him take her hand to lead her through some undergrowth into the stableyard.

"No, I've a key for each of us that unpadlocks the side gate. Were the gorgons late going out this evening? I had begun to think you weren't coming."

"For once they didn't go out!" Her voice quavered on a rising note of triumph. "It means I was able to get here on the most difficult evening ever! It will always be easy from now on."

"What happened?"

"The preacher had cancelled the meeting for some reason. I had to wait until nine o'clock before getting away, because that's the hour the whole household has to go to bed to save candles. After saying good night, I climbed out of my window onto the roof of the scullery and down to the ground by way of an old barrel that stands there."

He burst out laughing. "I used to leave our house by the same sort of route. You're a girl after my own heart."

She laughed with him, sparkling-eyed and impish, but when he linked his hands at the back of her waist to hug her to him in celebration of her daring, she stiffened away from him instinctively, and he accepted that for all her boldness in meeting him she was also wary. It made him decide not to take her into the mansion until he could be sure she understood she was not exchanging one trap for another. This was a girl to have fun with of every kind, and his impression was heightened of a dancing, evasive trait in her that was going to lead him on and on along a path that would be new to him.

They spent their time that evening learning about each other. She had had a happy childhood until one of the strange fevers that frequently hit cities in summertime took both her parents from her in a matter of days. She had had no other relatives except her late mother's brother and his wife, who had considered it their Christian duty to crush out of her what they considered to be wayward ways brought on by too much leniency and lack of discipline. Sensitive, fragile and lonely, it was no wonder that twice she had almost pined away.

"That will never happen again," he told her, moved by her plight. "You have me now."

"I have, haven't I?" There was wonder in her voice, as if she was only just beginning to comprehend her change of circumstances. It gave him the chance to kiss her, not in laughter as when they had first kissed in the Beavers' orchard, but softly and experimentally in a discovery of each other's lips that was entirely romantic.

He gave her one of the two gate-keys when they left the grounds together and he locked up again after them. Under the trees they kissed once more before they parted, she to get back into her home in the same manner in which she had left it, and he to return to London where he had his own secret way of getting back into his apprentice quarters after hours.

At their third meeting he decided to tempt her into the house. It was a cold wet night, which was in his favour, and he led her towards it saying he had a surprise for her. Her eyes gleamed as he set a key in the lock of the mansion's entrance and turned it. Entering swiftly, he pulled her in after him. To his astonishment, she rushed into the middle of the hall and laughed shrilly in triumph, throwing out her arms as if to the whole house.

"I always wanted to come into this place! Now it is ours! Yours and mine, Will. A playground safe from all the gorgons in the world. Nobody shall ever find us here."

There were times when he felt some faculty was missing in her.

When he expected questions she never asked them. She had shown no more curiosity as to how he had obtained keys to the gate than she had now about the greater achievement of getting into the mansion itself. What had become obvious, and about which he had no questioning doubts, was that she had become strongly attached to him. It was what he wanted more than he had ever wanted anything before. She haunted him when he was not with her. If he had not been absorbed daily in the work that meant so much to him, he believed he would have been unable to think of anything else but her elfin looks and slim, snake-like body that tantalised his own whenever he was near her.

"I'll show you over the place," he offered. "I've explored before."

"No!" she exclaimed, her eyes glittering. "Give me the lantern. I want to see for myself."

He handed it over and ran with her to skid ahead and fling wide doors to let her go rushing through. The beam of light danced from the wildly tossing lantern to send their shadows shooting high to the ornamental ceilings and down across the floors again. She squealed with delight as they went from room to room and skipped ahead of him down to the basement kitchen, where the copper pans on the walls blazed briefly in the lantern's glow as she passed by. In the hall again, she raced ahead of him up the curving flight of stairs with such speed that in his own mind he compared her again to a will-'o-the-wisp with all its teasing elusiveness and he was darkly excited by the strangeness of her.

Once she hid from him and he found himself alone. "Sarah! Where are you?"

There was such silence in the mansion that he felt a sense of eeriness. He called her name again, and when she did not answer he felt the hair rise on the back of his neck. Suddenly she giggled at a distance and there was the bang of a door followed by the muffled clatter of footsteps as she took the servants' staircase up to the attic. By the time he reached her in the cramped quarters under the eaves she had opened the shutters of a small window and released the latch to let the rain come pattering in.

"Come away from there!" he ordered in alarm.

Deliberately she leaned out dangerously, mocking him. "Nobody tells me what to do in this house. Not even you, Will."

He seized her by the shoulders and flung her back into the room. Then he banged the window and shutters closed before he faced her in a fury. "If you want to be seen and put an end to our meetings, that's one thing, but I'll not let you risk your life again in that stupid manner."

She was in too buoyant a mood to be dashed by his rage. Mischievously she laughed, setting down the lantern on a chest of drawers as she came towards him. "I frightened you then, didn't I? I wanted to test whether you really care about me."

"I care for you," he admitted huskily as she came close to him.

She peered into his face as if trying to read what was there for her own satisfaction. "If that's true, then you're the only person in the world who does."

"I'm in love with you."

For a moment she looked as if she might faint under the impact of what he had said to her. Then, in a single movement, she wrapped her arms around his neck and strained her whole body against his. His control snapped. He bore her down on the nearest bed, and her kissing and embrace were as frantic as his. He wrenched her skirts up to her narrow hips but as he thrust himself into her she screamed out in innocent terror and ignorance.

"You're hurting me! What are you doing?" In panic she beat against him with her fists, but he was beyond speech. Then abruptly her spine arched and she threw her arms back above her head, her mouth agape as she climaxed, and he held her as the sweet violence of her body welded with his until he withdrew from her in the nick of time.

It was a long while before she spoke afterwards. He cradled her to him, using gentle words and caresses such as he would have used beforehand if the situation had not rushed out of hand. She stirred in his arms.

"Now we belong to each other for always, don't we?"

"We do," he agreed without hesitation, full of love for her.

She linked her hands behind his neck, her face eager, her eyes aglow. "Make love to me again. This time I'll know what to expect."

All through the winter and into early spring they continued with their secret meetings. She always became a little wild as soon as they entered the mansion and devised games to play amid the shrouded furniture and in the dark corners of the stately house. On occasions they chased each other in nakedness, two pale forms reflected in the gilt-framed looking-glasses as they darted past the Chippendale bed, only one of the many places where they made love. They picnicked in the kitchen, drinking wine from the cellar. She liked to dress up in the silken gowns she found in an old clothes press; once, for a joke, clad in a fashion worn half a century before, she set their picnic out on the long banqueting table. There they sat at either end until, unable to be apart for even that small amount of time, they moved to neighbouring chairs. The door into the tavern was a constant temptation, he wanting to order ale and bring it to her in the Esdaile room there, but it was too great a risk to take. Danger of discovery was also the reason they never entered the library. He knew Ann to be too keen-eyed and sharp-witted, and if she noticed anything out of place she would report it immediately.

Inevitably their trysts were subject to increasing strain, for the constant danger of being sighted on their way to and from the mansion grounds often had their nerves in shreds before they reached each other, resulting in snappiness and bad temper. They quarrelled fiercely, revelling in the release of tension, and exulted in making up again. At times they could not have been happier; at others the mansion became a prison to them particularly when, like all lovers, they wanted to emerge together into other company. It was not unusual for them to part in anger.

"I'm never coming back!" she would shriek before she ran out into the night to be first through the gate. Then he would regret his own heated words and wait out the whole week in anguish, certain that this time she meant what she had said. In some ways it was her unpredictability that held him. He never tired of her. She was always fresh and intriguing and ever evasive. Often he had to win her all over again, especially when she had suffered a dreary week of petty fault-finding and upbraidings that had taken their toll on her belief that anyone could love her.

He had long since discovered that it had been the rare excitement of attending a normal social event that had fired her bold behaviour at his brother's wedding. It was a measure of her courage that she continued to meet him at all, and he viewed her guardians as his enemies as well as hers, never underestimating their power. His ever-ready fear of losing her was also due to her lack of love-words. She listened but never gave back what he wanted to hear. The nearest she had ever come to saying she loved him had been after their first love-making, when she had wanted to clarify that now they belonged to each other for always.

"Tell me," he would urge in a situation completely reversed for him, for always in previous amorous encounters he had been the one begged to declare love and he had told the woman concerned whatever lie had suited the occasion. "I want to hear you say that you love me." Sarah would tell neither a lie nor the truth.

Ever fey, she would sigh, tease, sulk or otherwise remain at a distance from him however close their embrace. It was one of the many causes of their quarrels and in exasperation he would come close to hating her. But the following Saturday he would be at the mansion long before she was due, pacing the floor and eager for her coming. He had not had a second key to the mansion made for her, for the death of a fine horse was still on his conscience and he could never be sure that she would not smash some priceless vase in a temper if ever he should be prevented from getting there. As yet he had not failed her and he hoped to keep it that way.

It was his constant need to be with her that brought about a change in him that was soon noticed by others. For the first time in his life he considered the consequences of following his own will, knowing that drunkenness or gambling or any such indulgence might hazard his chances of being free on a Saturday evening, for any master had the power to curtail liberty for a misdemeanour. As a result, he devoted himself to work as never before and his standard of achievement advanced by leaps and bounds. Richard began to entrust some of the most intricate tasks to him, and as his general behaviour continued to be beyond reproach, he found himself allotted the gold-work that always held his special interest.

Hester had received somewhat cynically Letticia's first mention of an improvement in Will. She did not expect it to last, but some while later, when Richard said to her that he could no longer fault her son in any way, she shook her head in wonderment.

"So he has become a man of responsibility at last. I could not be better pleased, but what has brought about this change in him, do you think?"

Richard shrugged his well-tailored shoulders. "The result and not the reason is enough for me."

To Letticia, she said, "In my experience it's usually only a girl who can work miracles on a lad like William. I know him. He is probably in love for the first time. I hope and pray it endures long enough to set the mould for the rest of his life."

It struck Letticia that Hester, although she never interfered, had a curious insight into all their lives. Nothing ever slipped past her. Not for the first time Letticia considered her mother to be an exceptional woman in many ways. But she and Richard had not come to Bunhill Row that day to talk mainly of William. Elizabeth had become pregnant, and Letticia, knowing their financial circumstances depended on Peter's wages, had brought a large boxful of exquisitely made garments for the forthcoming infant, her own children having grown out of them.

"I've never seen anything so pretty," Elizabeth exclaimed, taking out the little lace caps, the tucked and embroidered gowns and the fine shawls. There was even a pile of trim dresses that small boys wore until they were breeched, which pleased her as much as the rest. "These will be most useful. Of course if we have a girl they'll just be saved for next time."

She hoped for a boy, for she knew that Peter was like most men in wanting their first-born to be a son and she loved to please him in all things. Since their marriage she had experienced a love such as came to one woman in a million and she found it hard to believe there was a man anywhere to compare with her adored and adoring Peter.

Letticia always found herself slightly irritated in their joint presence. They were both reticent people, who did not in any way flaunt their deep feelings for each other, but the loving bond was there, emanating from them in a kind of ray that lit up the cracks in her own marriage. It had never been the same between Richard and herself as it was between these two, and although she had everything she had ever wanted in a material sense, she and Richard had lapsed into a dullness of matrimony that she feared he enlivened with passing affairs of his own.

She was bitterly ashamed of any jealousy she had felt towards Peter and his wife when early one cold morning Joss arrived while she and Richard were still at breakfast. Fully expecting to hear the good news of the baby's birth, she rose from the table to meet him. Her smile faded immediately at the sight of his drawn expression.

"Elizabeth is dying. The baby—a boy—was stillborn."

"I'll come at once," she said faintly, stricken by what she had heard.

By the time they reached Bunhill Row Elizabeth was dead and Peter had locked himself into the room with her. Hester refused to allow anyone to try to persuade him to come out.

"He has to be there on his own with her for a while. Leave him. He has never denied her anything and he will not keep her from what has to be done."

They all looked askance at her, but she retained her dominance. Did she not know better than any of them what it meant to lose a perfect love? The only way Peter would find courage to go on was from Elizabeth herself, albeit her soul had flown. Wanting to ensure his privacy, she sent everyone back to Number 107 and remained on her own at her son's home, closing doors and sitting on a bench outside the kitchen door to let the sounds of his terrible grief stay with him alone.

All day she suffered his torment with him, shedding her own tears. At dusk, as she had expected, he came downstairs. The straightness of his shoulders seemed more poignant to her than his ravaged face.

"I'm going to see Elizabeth's mother," he said quietly. "The poor woman collapsed, didn't she?"

"It will comfort her and her husband to see you."

His leaving the house was a signal for Letticia to reappear with Ann and Alice. Hester was already on her sad way upstairs. She did not have to be told that there would be nothing more in Peter's life than work from now on.

St. Luke's was packed for the funeral. William knew that Sarah would be there, but sorrow over the occasion kept him from looking for her. It was not until the family mourners had gathered back at Peter's home for tea and refreshment that he was able to spot her. She was with the Thornes and avoided his gaze, either out of fear of their noticing or displeasure with him, for it was a month since he had seen her. Then their evening had not been of the best, both of them quarrelsome, and she had roused his passion until they had made love while still fighting and, glorious though it had been, they had somehow parted in renewed animosity.

As so often happened in the interim of their meetings, she had the pinched, brow-beaten look that came from excessive harassment by her guardians, and he longed to kiss it away. Through a stroke of ill-luck, about which she knew nothing yet, he had just returned the nag to the hiring stables after their last meeting when he had been set upon by footpads, a common hazard in the city streets. Although he had used his powerful fists to fight them off, giving them a taste of their own medicine, he had received a clout on the side of his face from a club that had given him a black eye and a cut cheek. It had led to some close questioning by Richard, who assumed he had been in a tavern brawl; rather than let the slightest suspicion of the truth arise, he had admitted to the accusation, which was why the normal Saturday freedom had been denied him.

As the mourners were encouraged to help themselves from a table of food and accept a cup of tea, William took one and handed it to Sarah, who still refused to look at him, her lashes lowered.

"Go away!" she hissed in panic-stricken fury as he sat down on the vacant chair beside her.

"Your guardians are talking on the other side of the room. Don't be angry. I've been under curfew." He pushed a folded letter into the drawstring purse that dangled from her wrist. "That will explain everything."

He then left her, giving his seat up to someone else, and put distance between them as a precaution. Her relief that all was well again set up such a trembling reaction that her cup began to dance on its saucer. Quickly she lifted it to gulp the hot tea and steady her nerves. She loved him obsessively. It was as if all the love in her, which had been crushed down over the years to the point that twice she had been almost extinguished, had risen and engulfed him at their first union and left her mad for him. Her threats, her teasing and her frequent rages came from an inner part of her nature that she could not control. In the same way she could not voice what he wanted to hear; it was as if she crouched defensively inside herself, terrified to mention her loving in case it evaporated, as everything else she had loved had gone from her in early childhood.

These four past Saturdays she had thought she would lose her mind as she waited in the darkness and he did not come. She had thrown her arms over her head and rocked and wept as if demented, believing that he was staying away to punish her, adding to her life of punishments. Yet not once did she doubt he would return to her eventually. She had absorbed him into herself until he was the blood in her veins and the flesh on her bones and the pulse of her heart. Nothing could sever them.

"More tea, Sarah."

She looked up to see Jonathan holding out his hand for her empty cup. "No thank you," she answered, rising from her chair. It was time she rejoined her guardians. Several times her aunt had glanced across at her.

"It's a long time since I've seen you," he said, taking her cup and putting it aside. "Now that I'm in London I'm out of touch with this neighbourhood. Are you well?"

It was obvious he wanted to talk, and she was willing to linger for a few minutes. She liked him, associating him mainly with the pleasure of her first meeting with William, since it was he who had brought her the message to meet in the orchard. At seventeen he had gained the male Bateman length of limb combined with a virile leanness that she was more aware of than she would have been before her innocence was shattered. He did not have the open looks of his brothers, but the narrow eyes, long well-shaped nose and thin mobile lips were attractive in a foxy way.

"I am," she replied. It was not strictly true. Pining for William had played havoc with her whole constitution. "How are you progressing with your apprenticeship?"

He was doing well and chose to boast a little to her, not only of his standard of work, but of his worldly knowledge of London. Not for him the low taverns and stews patronised by the average apprentice. He chose to save his wages for one glass of wine or a light meal in elegant surroundings and to visit the art galleries, the museums and the historical sites. She was impressed.

"How do you spend your time?" he asked as an opening for what he intended to say next. It amused him that he was the only one to suspect that it was she whom William met on Saturday nights, for he had followed his brother once to a hiring stable and seen him ride off on a nag. Further observations had all added up.

"I have a lot of writing to do for my uncle in connection with his religious work," she replied, thinking how dull it sounded.

"Then it must be a great relief to have my brother's good company to look forward to at the end of the week."

She gasped and looked around frantically, but he had spoken quietly and none had overheard. "How long have you known?"

"For months. Don't worry. I wish you both well. You have nothing to fear from me."

She nodded her gratitude, moving away from him to reach her aunt's side. Sorrow, joy and fright had combined in a single afternoon and she felt exhausted by it all.

Yet there was a further ordeal to come. As she arrived home with her guardians, she was told to go to the study. Her aunt led the way and her uncle followed, closing the door after them.

"Now, Sarah," Mrs. Thorne said icily, pulling off her black gloves by the fingers, "you will read aloud to us the communication that William Bateman passed to you this afternoon. If you refuse," she added, seeing how the alarmed girl clutched her purse defensively to her, "we shall take it from you, read it for ourselves and double your punishment for allowing such a liberty from that notorious young rakehell."

With her mind racing, Sarah took the folded letter from her purse as if obeying them. Immediately, with a sudden movement of her shaking hands, she ripped the letter in half and was about to tear it into smaller pieces when her aunt gave a screech and seized the papers from her. Sarah rushed forward to grab her arm and grapple with her.

"No, you don't!" Mr. Thorne roared, yanking her away from behind and holding her fast. The sudden jerk sent her purse, already opened, flying from her hand, and the key to the garden gate clattered onto the floor.

Mr. Thorne pushed Sarah down into a chair, picked up the key, then, taking the torn letter from his wife, he carefully pieced the papers together. He proceeded to read it aloud:

" 'My darling Sarah,' " he began in a deepening note of disbelief. " 'I have missed you with my heart and body more than words can say . . .' "

Sarah covered her face with her hands, curling up in the chair as if she were being knifed. William's loving terms were poisoned by the salicious undertone that crept into her uncle's voice. The letter made it clear to both her guardians that the meeting planned for Saturday evening followed a pattern of many others shared previously. When her uncle came to the end of the letter, he and his wife turned their heads simultaneously to stare dumbfoundedly at their niece. Her sins went far beyond anything they had expected to find when they had begun their investigation, and they had no doubt the key opened an entrance to the place of assignation. They were momentarily at a loss to know how to destroy the evil in their midst.

When they had banished her to her room they sat down for a counsel of war. There was no fear of Sarah getting out again, for Mr. Thorne had nailed up the shutters of her bedchamber and locked her in. He was all for making a full complaint to William's master, but his wife slapped her pigmented hand down on the table to emphasise the folly of such a move.

"Scandal must be avoided at all costs. Think of your position as a Dissenter and the need to hold up our heads against constant opposition from the old Church. Not a word of this must leak out to harm our cause and pour ridicule on us. Sarah shall write to her seducer, a letter saying that it is all over between them. The tone of his showed that he was trying to win her back to him after a lovers' tiff, and he will think he has failed."

"What if he talks?"

"Nonsense!" she scoffed. "He's not going to risk his future by blabbing when the matter is closed."

They had to beat her and half starve her before she finally wrote at Mrs. Thorne's dictation. She hoped that William would grasp that she was writing it under pressure and know that somehow she would see him again. After her aunt had sealed the letter and taken it away, she crawled into a corner of her bedchamber and sat huddled there with her forehead on her drawn-up knees, not knowing or caring whether it was night or day.

Chapter 13

Producing articles bearing her own punchmark had brought the assay officers down on Hester at unexpected moments. It was their duty to weigh, test and otherwise ensure that articles were being produced up to the high standard demanded by the Assay Office. Since she was honest in all her dealings, their deliberately unannounced visits did not bother her apart from some interruption of work. She was on the circuit of two assay officers, one as pleasant as the other was sour.

Mr. Cockerill was the name of the man she and everyone else liked, a childless widower in his early fifties whose strong jaw showed that he could be ruthless with those who abused the splendour of the gold and silver that they handled. He had grim tales of those who substituted baser metals in the making and the cheats who put their punchmark over those of other craftsmen whose products were pure and better than their own.

"A most enjoyable visit, Mrs. Bateman," he always said before he left. Then he would thank Ann for the delicious tea she had served him. His fellow assay officer never received tea and there was always a sigh of relief when he went. Hester, always busy in the workshop, was never present when Mr. Cockerill was poured his refreshing cup from the full silver tea service that she had been able to afford to make for herself at last. It took quite a time before she happened to discover that Ann always used the best porcelain for him as well. Gradually it became noticeable to her that after his visits, Ann's tight-mouthed countenance took on a gentler look. But as time went on and they never met away from the teacups, Hester came to the conclusion that there was nothing more than friendship between them.

The facilities of the workshop purchased around the time of Peter's marriage were ideal for the amount of commissions being received. Trade orders had also increased as Hester's skills became generally accepted. Silver traders had begun supplying sheet silver as well as ingots, and these speeded up many spheres of work by doing away with hours of preparation involving hammering, beating and tapping to a smoothness before marking out could begin.

An apprentice had joined the workshop a while ago, a willing lad addressed as Linney, and there was every indication that he would stay on with the Bateman workshop when he was qualified. "There must be something magnetic about this place," Hester remarked with a smile.

Linney's artistic talents were put to another use when he painted a new trade sign that Peter had made for her. It was to be suspended over the entrance of Number 108 to replace John Bateman's old sign, which had stood at the side gate of Number 107 until Hester had moved it to her expanded premises. It had become outdated long ago with regard to the work she was now taking in.

"The new sign is ready, Mrs. Bateman," Linney informed her one morning. Outside Peter was hammering in the last nails that would keep it securely in place. He descended the ladder as she went out to look up at the sign, her hands on her hips, the wind billowing her apron and flapping the ties of her cap.

"It's splendid," she declared with a catch in her voice, for all along she had been reluctant to replace John's sign. But the day had had to come. This new sign showed one of her elegant coffeepots, skilfully painted highlights giving it the full look of silver, and above it lettering she knew to be *Hester Bateman, Silversmith.* In choosing to announce herself as a specialist in silver work she was following the new trend, and since her mind was always darting ahead as far as business was concerned, she was prepared to fly in the face of traditionalists now and at any other time. Sometimes she wondered if her trait of being willing to take a chance was the same characteristic that had multiplied itself in William before common sense and an interest in his goldsmithing apprenticeship had finally tamed him.

A clop of hooves on the road took her gaze from the new sign and she saw that Mr. Cockerill had come on one of his visits. They greeted each other, and when he had dismounted and tied up his horse, they went into Number 108 together.

"I shall not be coming on an inspection visit after today, Mrs. Bateman," he said in the hallway. "I have been given a new circuit in York, the city of my birth to which I have always wanted to return. I should like to talk to you about it, if I may."

"By all means." She took him into Peter's office, which had been set up there. Peter had taken over the running of the business from Joss to leave him more time for his family, an arrangement that suited both brothers well. "We are going to miss you, Mr. Cockerill."

He sat forward on the edge of his chair. "Not altogether, I hope, ma'am. I am requesting your permission to ask for the hand of your daughter, Ann, in marriage. I know there is a wide gap between her age and mine, but we share literary and other interests and I have reason to believe she reciprocates my sincere affection for her."

Hester responded with pleasure. It would be odd to have a son-in-law almost her own age, but he had shown himself to be a kindly man and she was thankful that love had come into her daughter's life. "You have my permission. Ann is in the house now."

They returned together shortly afterwards, Ann looking happier than Hester could remember. This time everyone stopped work to go into the house and drink a celebratory cup of tea in the parlour with the newly betrothed couple. "Strange," thought Hester, "this parlour has been the sole realm of their courtship."

The wedding took place a month later. It was a quiet affair as both Dick Cockerill and Ann wished it to be, only her family and a few of his friends present. Ann wore hyacinth-blue, the colour that suited her best, and when the time came for her to leave she and Hester embraced, each momentarily at a loss for words. Since John's death they had drawn still closer together and would miss each other keenly, the distance to York being too far for frequent visits.

"All happiness to you, dearest Ann," Hester said as they drew apart.

"Thank you, Mother." With a final wave to all gathered on the steps of Number 107, Ann preceded her husband into the carriage and they drove away.

When the day was over and everyone had departed, Hester felt the emptiness of the house for the first time. There were servants in the kitchen, but none of her own kin any more under her roof. She braced her shoulders, aware it was a day that every parent had to face and she was more fortunate than most in having two of her sons in nearby houses, quite apart from three dear grandchildren who had inherited Joss's good nature. Suddenly tired after the events of the day, she went to bed.

The Bateman family had another cause for celebration when the hated sixpenny tax was removed from silver. It would stimulate trade and do much to counteract the increasing popularity of Sheffield Plate. Hester gave a party, and several friends in the goldsmithing trade were included.

When it was over Hester settled to routine again. Peter began to come more often to the house in the evenings, as if the loneliness of his own home had begun to be oppressive. Previously he had wanted solitude, finding healing in being alone with his memories. Hester usually sat sketching out new designs in the candlelight, for it was a relaxation for her and never a chore, while he lounged back smoking his long-stemmed pipe, and they talked when each had something to say.

Peter was spending a Saturday evening with her when she completed a new design that gave her a rare satisfaction. She showed it to him from where she sat, and he leapt up immediately to lean over her and study it on the table. "That's one of the best you've ever done! It's like a flight of birds."

"They've often been a source of inspiration to me, and recently I've been trying more than ever to capture the flow of movement in a bird on the wing."

"You've achieved it here."

The design combined her characteristic simplicity of form with lovely sweeping lines. It was for a kidney-shaped snuffer tray that would be hand-pierced with a bead mount surmounting the gallery that had symbolised birds between the railings.

"I'm glad you like it." It meant much to her that he had recognised immediately that she had reached the ultimate stage in her designs. From now on she would be on the solid ground for which she had aimed for a long time. After this night there should be no looking back.

Excitement was still in her after he had left and she went upstairs to her bedchamber. Feeling a trifle flushed, she crossed to the window and opened it for some cool night air. It was noisy across at the Royal Oak as it always was on a Saturday night when travellers and local folk became merry together and soldiers from the armoury swelled the numbers in their scarlet coats. She listened for a while, never minding the bursts of raucous singing that often spilled into the road as people wended their way homewards, for these were the sounds she had known in her girlhood when Jack and Martha had kept the Heathcock, long before the days of their retirement.

From the copse, William glimpsed his mother in the moonlight as her hand, cuffed by the white lace of her pale gown, withdrew from pushing wide the latticed window. He stepped back still further into the shadows, although there was not the least chance of her seeing him, and darted away to the side gate of the Esdaile property. He had long since given up entering the mansion by the front entrance, for with the grounds being kept in trim again the chance of being seen from the main gates was doubled in moonlight as bright as on this night. Instead he had made a key for the rear door that gave access to the lawns, and from the corridor within he could watch through a glass panel for Sarah's coming.

As he reached the door, key in hand, he saw a letter wedged into it. Drawing it out, he guessed with a sickening lurch of disappointment that Sarah was unable to keep their tryst. Yet she must have been here only minutes before, for she would not have risked it being there for any length of time. Not bothering to go indoors, he sat down on the doorstep and, opening the shutter of his lantern, focused its beam onto the letter, the better to see what was written there.

His face became stark as her words informed him that all was over between them. The weeks apart had given her time to reflect and she wanted to be free of him. She had never loved him and as far as she was concerned he could throw away the key to the mansion because she would never visit it again. Hers to the gate had been used for the last time this evening and would be buried where it could never be found.

He crushed the letter in his hand with a groan that tore through him, thumping his fist down on his thigh and shaking his head in refusal to accept what she had written and in despair. The memory of her animosity at the Beavers' house returned to him, her resolute avoidance of his eyes even when he had given her that whispered explanation and his note. He groaned again.

Throughout their long relationship she had persistently refused to say she loved him, and there had been times when he had never been sure if it was due to a strange trait in her or her sheer cunning in keeping him forever on a string. Now it was clear that she had never loved him. She had used him as an instrument against her guardians, an act of defiance to prove herself. Why, then, if she had felt she no longer had need of him, had she looked so drawn when he had last seen her? There was an answer to that: everybody had had the same look on their faces that day through sorrow over Elizabeth and he had given his own interpretation to Sarah's expression, being ever on the look-out in his concern for her. Damnation! What a fool he had been!

He sprang to his feet, extinguished the lantern and kicked it into the bushes. Thrusting the letter down into his pocket, he hurried back to the side gate. He felt bitterly resentful, unable to believe that after all there had been between them she had slipped away as easily as she appeared to suppose. Anger and uncertainty confused his mind. Only one thing was sure: in the meantime he was going to get drunk!

He burst into the Royal Oak. It was crowded, the air thick with smoke, and he had to elbow his way through to the bar. "A tankard of black ale, landlord!"

"Good evenin', Mr. Bateman. You be home then?"

"As you see," he answered with a savage grin, "and with a thirst that you haven't enough barrels to quench!"

"Oho! That sounds like a challenge, sir." There was laughter from those close by and a sudden air of expectancy. The landlord drew a quart tankard and set it frothing onto the bar. "There! Let's see what you make of that."

William took the tankard by the handle and swung it up to his lips. He gulped the ale down steadily. It was strong and potent, the perfect antidote for his wounded spirits. Breathlessly and to applause, he set the emptied tankard down again with a crash, wiping his mouth with the back of his hand. "Fill it up again!"

His last clear sober thought was that he would sleep his binge off in the straw of the stables at his own home and return to face the consequences of a night out later the next day. The ale soon took effect. He had eaten nothing since noon, the picnic he had brought to share with Sarah still in the capacious pocket of his coat, and before long he was a main contributor to the bawdy songs that rent the tavern. In such a jovial atmosphere ridiculous wagers arose as if out of the air. All William knew was that he had been wagered a shilling to walk the edge of the taproom bar without falling off. The landlord protested, shouting words of caution that he did not even hear in the hub-bub. Like a tightrope walker he set off, swaying dangerously, his feet going everywhere but the place he intended, and twice he would have fallen off if willing hands had not pushed him back again. He reached the end and jumped off with flying coattails to collapse on the floor, helpless with laughter, propped against a chair.

"You won, sir! Accept this prize."

A coin was slapped into his hand. He made a mock bow from where he sat. "I thank you for it. You're a gentleman."

The donor's heavy-jowled beery face came down on a level with his with a spread of scarlet jacket. "And you, sir, are in the army! You've accepted the King's shilling!"

In spite of his drunken state, William grasped what had been said to him. With a howl of rage he hurled the coin from him and struggled to his feet. "You'll play no tricks on me. I didn't wager with you!"

"But I reached you first with a shilling and you took it fair and square. It's twenty years' service for you in the King's Colours, lad."

"No!" William's yell of fury accompanied his fist aimed at the sergeant's face, but he was jumped on by several soldiers who had gathered in readiness. Shouting and kicking, he was half dragged and half carried out of the tavern. The sergeant, following behind, slammed the tavern door after them, leaving the whole place in dismayed silence. The landlord spoke first with a heavy sigh.

"I tried to warn him. I had heard the army was out for new recruits and had not yet raised the number they wanted."

"Someone ought to let his family know," one customer suggested.

"I'll go across to Mrs. Bateman myself as soon as I've closed up. Now, gentlemen, next orders, please."

The hour was exceptionally late when the last of the drunken revellers departed. Deciding that nothing could be done until morning in any case, the landlord went to bed and did not knock on Hester's door until breakfast time.

Hester heard him out. "Where is William now?" she asked in shock. It was not the time for less important questions.

"He'd be at the armoury. Probably with other recruits, willing and otherwise, on the parade ground already."

As soon as the landlord departed, she ran as she was without cape or hat to Number 85 and hammered on the door. Joss opened it, surprised to see her at such an early hour on a Sunday morning.

"Take your fast riding horse and go at once to James Esdaile," she instructed as she entered. "William was tricked last night into taking the King's shilling and James is the only one who could possibly help us."

Peter, who had sighted his mother from his parlour window, came from next door. As soon as he heard what had happened, he moved to leave again. "I'll go to the armoury now and try to see William."

"I'll come with you."

Alice lent her a cape. They were overtaken by Joss at a gallop, and he waved encouragement as he went by. When they arrived at the gates other families had gathered there, several more young men having been trapped into recruitment elsewhere the previous night. None of them was allowed admittance. In the distance on the parade ground a ragged bunch of recruits was being drilled, but whether William was among them it was impossible to tell. There was nothing to do but go home and wait.

When Joss returned, having ridden back with James on horseback, he informed them, "James is with the commanding officer now. We must hope for the best."

When James eventually appeared his expression was grave. "I have to tell you that there is nothing I or anyone else can do," he said to Hester and her assembled family. "William accepted the shilling before witnesses and without coercion, which gives the army the legal right to keep him in their ranks for a full score years."

Hester sat stunned. Peter spoke. "Did you see him?"

"I did. He is in a dreadful state of mind. All he can think about at the moment is the loss of his career as a goldsmith. Oh, and one other thing. He says he left a nag he hired from stables near Richard's workshop tied up in the copse and will Peter return the animal."

"When may I see him?" Hester implored.

"I'm afraid you can't. The army gives no privileges to recruits. Your first and last chance to see him will be when he marches out of the armoury gates six weeks from now."

Hester rose to her feet the better to withstand whatever was coming. "Where will the army be sending him?"

James took both her hands and cupped them together with his own, his gaze full of compassion. "He and his new comrades are to join a regiment being sent to the American colonies. Recent troubles there have brought about this present phase of recruitment."

"My poor William," she whispered. For the first time in his life her son was having to face up to his own foolhardiness and in the cruelest way possible. It was as if fate had saved up this special retribution to entrap him when the time was right. "Did he say what possessed him to come home and go straight to the tavern without a word to anyone?"

"He said he felt a need to get drunk." James paused. "He also gave me a message for your ears alone."

"We'll go into the next room," she said, signalling to the family not to disperse. When they were on their own she added, "Pray tell me what he said."

"In confidence, he asked that you let Sarah Thorne know what has happened."

She was startled. "Sarah? He hardly knows her." Then suddenly there registered with her the change in him and the reason she had put on it, his presence in the tavern in a mood of exultation or despair and the secrecy that would be necessary to court a girl as closely guarded and chaperoned as Sarah Thorne, which in itself would be a challenge to him. She spoke on an unhappy sigh. "He appears to have forgotten how well known he is in this district and how well remembered for his pranks. By now every person in that alehouse will have spread the news of his recruitment and in every local congregation on this Sunday morning there will be those eager to pass on what they know. I would have no chance to reach Sarah before she hears from others."

She was right in that deduction. After the Dissenters' service held in a member's house, Sarah overheard William's name and what had happened to him as people talked together afterwards. She pitched forward in a dead faint and took a while to revive. Nobody suspected what had triggered the faint except her guardians. Everybody remarked on the exceptional care they took of the girl, hurrying her home in their wagonette to cosset her there.

Hester thought about Sarah a great deal, wondering how many times she and William had been able to meet and where. Perhaps at the home of a mutual friend? Not at the Beavers, for they had moved away a while ago, Elizabeth's mother unable to live with her memories there. For herself, she had always thought Sarah a strange and subdued girl with those dark sloe eyes that were in such contrast to her exceptionally fair hair. Surely no couple could have been more ill-suited than William and her. Hester experienced an odd qualm and was reminded of moods of foreboding she had experienced when she was younger and that had become mercifully less frequent in latter years. It was impossible not to be relieved that there could be no union for William with the Thorne girl. It was simply a matter of great regret that it had had to be a horrendous turn of events that parted them.

"Oh, John," Hester voiced softly in her own bedchamber as she had on many previous nights since she had lost him, "if only you were here. I can't talk over things with anyone else as I was able to talk to you."

She felt herself missing him more and more. Time was doing nothing to heal, and when a crisis arose, her aching for him increased a thousandfold. Her loneliness was private to her, set deep within her innermost being and away from the normal face she presented to the world. Nobody understood better than she Peter's renewed dedication to his work, for it was the only balm for those like themselves. For her there was the added consolation of every day being another step towards making John's surname one known throughout the land.

Ann made the journey from York and arrived on the eve of William's departure. Letticia brought Jonathan with her early next day. They were met by Peter and Joss with Alice and their children. When the time came, they set off with Hester to join other families gathering in a small crowd at the armoury gates. The Batemans spread themselves out at intervals, the better to make personal farewells. Hester had given Peter a purse of guineas to slip into William's hand, knowing he would have more initiative in passing it to his brother than quiet Joss if difficulties should arise. Letticia had brought William a gold watch that had been donated somewhat reluctantly by her husband. "He'll only gamble it away," he had said. To which she replied, "Not if he's learnt his lesson and I pray to God he has." Now, as she waited, she had given the watch over to Jonathan, who would know better how to drop it into a uniform pocket than she would.

The tall gates began to open. Pipes and drums heralded the approach of the marching men in a cheerful rhythm that had no effect on the spirits of anyone waiting except small children too young to understand what partings meant. The first shock for relatives was the anonymity of the recruits, who marched out through the gates behind the bandsmen as if six years instead of six weeks of service lay behind them. Gone were any beards, moustaches or individual hair-styles. All were clean shaven, neat about the head, cocked hats set squarely, scarlet jackets contrasting with white breeches and gaiters, muskets gleaming on left shoulders.

For a matter of moments there was silence. Scarcely a relative in the crowd had not pictured the recruit they had come to see being on the near side to them, but now there was doubt about recognising him wherever he was. As it happened, no recruit marched on the outside, for the army had had long experience of last-minute attempts at escape and what could happen if families went berserk and fought to regain a son, husband or father. A veteran soldier flanked every line at either end and the threat of dire punishment, combined with the solid discipline already instilled, ensured that without any undue emotional interruption recruits would keep in step, even if their heads did go one way and then the other as they in turn searched for faces they knew, some of which they would never see again.

"There's William!" Ann spotted him first. He was second along from the burly corporal acting as a buffer to his line. He grinned as he picked out Ann's wave and the jauntiness of his marching step increased as if he were determined not to have gloom dogging his departure, whatever his feelings and theirs might be.

Here and there families surged forward in an attempt to get nearer their men, but the mounted sergeants in escort made their horses frisky and alarming, forcing people to draw back. William winked in acknowledgement of the wave he received from Joss and Alice and then made a comic face at their children. A few yards further on Hester came into his view. She stood with quiet dignity on the grass verge. His eyes became as serious as hers in the smile they shared, their parting acute, her courage matching his on this terrible day. It was hard for him to lose sight of her, but he was quick to raise appreciative eyebrows in fun when he saw Letticia in a new and becoming hat for the occasion. She dimpled desperately, waving a lacy handkerchief that she would probably use on her eyes as soon as he had gone past. It mattered to him that every woman in his family had given him a smile and withheld her tears amid all the noisy weeping and wailing rising on both sides of the road. He began to look for his brothers, whom he knew would be there.

Peter and Jonathan had just arranged between themselves that one should create a diversion while the other slipped the money and watch to William when there came an upheaval more dramatic than anything they could have managed. Sarah, hatless and with her hair streaming, burst through those gathered there to hurl herself at William.

"Don't leave me!" she shrieked hysterically. "Don't go! I love you! I can't live without you!"

"Sarah!" He had hoped to see her but had thought the chances slight. Now she was clinging to him like a limpet, her arms clamped around his neck, and with her face squashed to his she was wetting his cheek with her tears. Instinctively his free arm went around her even as the corporal lunged for her. He held her just long enough for their mouths to meet in a frantic kiss before she was wrenched from him and thrown against the nearest bystanders. But it had been a signal for other women to snatch a last contact, and as they rushed forward, several lines were disrupted, which gave Jonathan the chance to push the watch and purse of money into William's hand.

"Good luck, Will!" Then he was gone.

William's marching step had been barely interrupted. He swung on with his fellow recruits, aware of order being restored both fore and aft as shrieking women, some with babies in their arms, were torn from their men-folk. He had not seen Peter from first to last, but it was Sarah who filled his thoughts. Perhaps some of that female screaming he could hear came from her. What a time to recant her letter to him! God only knew what would happen to her when the Thornes heard what she had done today. He felt both saddened and irritated by her folly and hoped she had not seen it in his eyes. Hadn't he brought enough trouble down on himself without her inviting comparable retribution from a home source? Did he still love her? He didn't know. Misery and despair had wrecked his feelings since that night in the tavern. At the moment he could only accept that his senses had been inflamed again by the sight, touch, scent and taste of her during those few brief moments.

But long before they reached the Pool of London other memories came flooding back. He thought of her strange ways, the inconsistency of her behaviour, blowing hot and cold, of her teasing refusal to admit she loved him even in moments of passion and the wretched uncertainty he felt when they were apart. He had never been sure of her and now he never would be. Perhaps it was all for the best.

As the recruits marched away down Bunhill Row, bound for a waiting ship, the small crowd dispersed, many in tears. Only a few had tagged along in the wake of the marching men. Hester, about to turn homewards as the family regrouped, glanced around.

"Where's Peter?"

"I think he went after Sarah Thorne when she ran off," Jonathan volunteered.

Hester's face deepened in distress. "Why? By her behaviour she made William's departure from home still harder for him. It's highly likely he will be held responsible for the uproar that resulted and punished in one way or another." She shook her head. "Oh, my poor William. Trouble never leaves him."

Together the Batemans turned for home. Some distance away Peter, in pursuit of Sarah, thought he had lost her. He had been struck by her distraught face and the blind look in her eyes when she had picked herself up from where she had fallen. He had seen that same look in the eyes of animals ready to die from fright or pain. Dazedly she had stared after the departing recruits almost as if she was no longer able to comprehend what was happening, and then she had turned to push her way back through the gathering of people and leave at a run.

He had called after her, but she went on running, taking a foot-path between houses that led to the fields in the opposite direction to her home. When he reached a stile there was no sign of her and he doubled back to a fork that led off through woods. He was afraid that he knew where she was heading and hoped he would be in time. Charging along, he began to take off his coat and had it in his hand when he came out near the place where a stream fed a deep pond. She was already on the bridge across which farmers drove their cattle.

"Sarah!" he yelled to her. "Wait!"

He was too late. She was in her own world, neither seeing nor hearing him. She threw herself down into the water with her arms outstretched as if to embrace the thick weeds that tangled together below the surface and disappeared from his view.

He thundered onto the bridge, kicked off his shoes and plunged in after her. At first he could see nothing, although the water was full of a curious green light. Weeds entwined themselves perilously about his wrists and ankles, forcing him to shake himself free. He came up for air and went down again. Then he saw what looked like silver strands mingling with the weeds and knew it was her hair. Seizing a handful, he yanked it high and she floated towards and upwards with him. They broke the surface of the water together. Gasping, he drew her with him to the pond's bank and hauled her up on to it. She lay white and still and did not appear to be breathing. Knowing from what he had read that half-drowned sailors were put across barrels, he picked her up to thump her face downwards over the fallen trunk of an ancient tree and began to pump the back of her ribs. Water trickled from her mouth and then it came with a gush. He thought she would choke, such retching emitted from her throat, but as it became a rasping for air and she began to cry, he knew she was going to survive.

"It's all right, Sarah," he said reassuringly, kneeling to draw her shivering frame into his arms and hold her to him. "You had an accident. No harm done."

She turned to bury her face against his shoulder. "Why didn't you let me drown? I have nothing to live for."

"We'll talk about that later. Now I'm going to take you home with me."

He wrapped her in his coat and carried her. She was as limp as if still half-drowned, and water continued to drip from her clothes and the gleaming snake of her long hair. Painfully he was reminded of Elizabeth, for she weighed no more in his arms and he had not held another woman since he had last held her.

By taking one of the lanes he had hoped to avoid his burden being seen, to spare Sarah more gossip than she would undoubtedly have to endure from her earlier action that morning. Unfortunately he was sighted at least twice to his knowledge by the time he entered the garden of Number 107 by the stable-gate and bore her into the house. His mother and sisters came hastening forward.

"What happened?" Even as Hester asked, she was guiding him with a touch on the elbow towards the stairs. Then, her guess confirmed, she turned to her daughters. "Letticia, fetch a cup of tea. Ann, get the maids to bring hot water for the hip-bath at once. We must act quickly or Sarah will have lung fever by morning after a dousing on such a cold day." She swung round on her son again. "The same goes for you, Peter. As soon as you've carried Sarah upstairs, you go home and take a hot bath yourself."

"The Thornes should be informed without delay."

"I'll see to that. Jonathan is taking a look around the workshop at the moment. He can go." Then she corrected herself. "No, it will be better to fetch Joss and send him. He'll be more sympathetic."

It did not take the three women long to get Sarah bathed and to comb out the pieces of weed that still clung to her beautiful hair after it was dried. Wearing one of Hester's nightgowns, she was put to bed and Ann stayed with her when Hester and Letticia went downstairs again.

"What a day this has been," Letticia remarked wearily.

"At least we have seen undeniable evidence that Sarah is not pregnant," Hester stated practically in heartfelt relief. "That was my first thought when I heard she had attempted to take her own life." She paused at the window and looked out. "I would have expected Mr. and Mrs. Thorne to be here by now."

Joss returned alone soon afterwards, carrying a packed valise. "The Thornes aren't coming," he announced. "I've brought some of Sarah's clothes."

Peter, who had returned to the house, grabbed him by the arm. "What do you mean? Why aren't they here?"

Joss set down the valise. "They've shut their door on her. Apparently they were out with Sarah this morning when she ran away from them at the sound of the pipes and drums. They witnessed everything that took place and went back home to pack up her belongings. As far as they are concerned, she is now on her own and must survive by whatever means are available to her."

"Surely they had some change of heart when you told them of the near-tragedy that took place at the pond," Hester exclaimed incredulously.

"If anything, I would say it hardened their attitude still further if that had been possible. In their eyes it added an even greater sin to that already committed." He glanced about at them all. "Did anyone here have any idea that Will and Sarah have been meeting secretly by night at the mansion for months?"

There was a response of astonishment from all but Hester. It was as if she had lost the ability to be surprised by anything said or done by her third son. When Joss had given her a few more details, she sighed heavily. "Then William is wholly responsible for Sarah's present predicament."

Jonathan, leaning a shoulder against a door jamb, mildly entertained by the whole situation, addressed his mother. "Don't put all the blame on Will. It takes two to play that sort of game."

"I'm not allotting blame," she replied sharply, "only responsibility. Since William is not present to shoulder it, I'll do it in his place. Sarah shall have a home with me."

She refused to listen to their protests and warnings. Ann, who had come downstairs to fetch fresh tea, spoke out heatedly. "You can't have that girl here! Whatever anyone says, if it hadn't been for her, William would never have fallen prey to that recruiting officer."

Hester faced her. "I'll not have Sarah turned out on the streets for you or anyone else. Show some mercy and be thankful never to have found yourself in similar straits!"

Ann's eyes fell away from her mother's penetrating gaze. It told her that Hester must have had an inkling, never before mentioned even as indirectly as in the past minute, that she had run after Matthew and that he had deserted her. "It's your decision, Mother," she said tonelessly, jerking up her chin. She had Dick now and Matthew did not matter any more. If her marriage was not exactly what once she had wished for, it was safe and comfortable and her husband cared for her. She did not ask for more. The talk switched away from her as Letticia, less easily silenced, took up the same cudgels about Sarah's permanent presence in the house.

Upstairs Sarah had stumbled from the bed, irrationally afraid of being on her own in an unfamiliar room, and she had reached the landing in time to hear most of what had been said downstairs. She raised a trembling fist and banged it down on the baluster. Someone was screaming her thoughts out and she realised vaguely it was herself.

"None of you need worry! I don't want to stay! Nobody shall ever be troubled by me again!"

Peter moved first. He found Sarah lying prone on the landing beating her head and her hands on the floor and sobbing hysterically. When he attempted to lift her up, she resisted him, clinging to the balusters, her sobs turning to screams. Hester came close behind him, having instructed Ann to bring a bowl of cold water which she applied liberally to the struggling girl's face. This had the desired effect, and in a few minutes Sarah allowed herself to be helped to her feet, although she was still sobbing.

"I can't go on without William and yet he will forget me across the ocean. Today there was a difference in him already." Her voice shook as if again hysteria was about to rise in her. "I don't want to be alone!"

It took some time before they finally quieted the girl with assurances that she would never be alone but would be a welcome member of the household.

That night Hester admitted to herself that her daughters were probably right, and she had considerable doubts about Sarah being an easy addition to her home—doubts that proved only too correct. Sarah was persistently difficult and contrary, no longer subdued away from the tyranny of her former guardians, who had sold up and vanished, nobody knowing where. She appreciated nothing that was done for her and had eerie moods when she stared into space, never seeming to hear anything that was said to her. There were nights when she cried for William in such desperation that Peter had to be fetched from his home to soothe her. It was only with him that she regained a certain equilibrium and the better side of her nature showed through. Hester would have liked to be cheered by this sign of improvement, but there was a hint of obsession in Sarah's attachment to him, all the more sinister since she had not yet lost that which she held for William.

James had warned Hester it would be many months before she could hope to hear from William, and she was still far from expecting news when a letter came for her. Peter, recognising William's handwriting, called Sarah to listen while he read it aloud for his mother, both having agreed that she should be allowed to share in whatever he might have written. The girl sat on the edge of a chair, pale and trembling with eagerness as he broke the seal, her hands restless as birds. Peter read in his firm voice:

My dear Mother,
Owing to a piece of good fortune I am able to send you this brief letter to tell you I am safely arrived in the American colonies. Conditions are tolerable after a most distressing voyage. This evening I was sent with a message to a military office

on the other side of the town and happened to fall in with a kindly woman, the wife of the master of a fast merchant vessel, which will be sailing on the morning tide. She has offered to take a letter from me, which she will see is delivered to you when they reach London. It is agreeable to have two local lads with me, the brothers Hounsom from Stoops Farm, and I should be obliged on their behalf if you would let their parents know they are well. Their talk is mostly of crops and next year's harvest, which makes them wretchedly homesick, but I have put my old life from me. I miss you all more than I can say and try not to dwell on how long it may be before I see you again. Meanwhile I endeavour to make the best of my unfortunate state. Many of the colonists are not pleased by our arrival, but at least there are some pretty girls willing to be friendly with the redcoats and I shall not be lonely here. My sincere regards to you and all the family.

Your devoted son,

William.

Sarah leapt to her feet with a piercing scream, throwing her head and body about as if demented, her face distorted. "No word for me! Nothing! I no longer exist!"

Hester sprang forward, but Sarah knocked her aside and tore out of the room to race for the stairs. Peter dropped the letter and dashed after her. Without pausing on the landing, she took the second flight, her footsteps pounding. Whirling a hand around the newel post on the topmost landing where the maids slept, she rushed through the door to the attic staircase and slammed it after her, knowing he was in pursuit. He reached it but the key was turned. He wasted no breath, simply drawing back and smashing his foot against the lock. The door swung open to the last narrow flight. He found her at the attic window, sobbing hysterically and throwing herself at the window-handle, which was stiff from long winter closing.

"No, Sarah! No!" He dragged her away from it as she struggled wildly.

"I will kill myself! I will!"

He pulled her head against him with his broad hand and stilled her arms with his own. "No! That's not the way to get through this.

I should know. It's how I felt when I lost Elizabeth, but I would have failed her if I had taken that path."

"You're stronger. That letter ended my last hope! William will never come back to me. I can't go on! I don't want to live without him."

He stroked her hair gently and held her until her hysteria passed and she drooped listlessly against him. "Help me," she implored desolately.

"I'll help you."

"Promise!"

"I promise." He could not have refused her. She was frightened and pathetic, much like any of the helpless wild creatures he had rescued in the past, but the difference was that she would be less easy to set free. He was convinced that if she was not thoroughly reassured, she would attempt suicide again, the unbalanced streak in her all too obvious. Maybe, as William's brother, he should be the one to shoulder that burden, for with Elizabeth gone, he would never know love again as he had found it with her. If Sarah continued to trust him, he might well be the anchor that would stop her from destroying herself.

During the next two months Hester saw what was happening and tried to dissuade him. "You'll bring terrible unhappiness down on yourself. Don't let pity rule your heart, Peter. I'll always look after the girl."

He was stern with her. "Let me be. My happiness went with Elizabeth. I shall do what I believe to be best."

Hester looked down at her hands in her lap. How could she make her son understand that life went on, that in the years to come he might find room in his heart for another woman without losing his loving memories of Elizabeth. She glanced at his set face. It was hopeless. He was too young, too inexperienced, still too wrapped up in his bitter grief to heed her pleadings.

Not long afterwards Peter and Sarah were married. He had already moved out of the home he had shared with Elizabeth and he took Sarah to another house only yards away from Number 107 in Bunhill Row. There was no love on either side, simply protectiveness on his and a weird doting on hers that bore no relation to the intense feelings she still harboured for William. Once the ceremony was over, it was impossible for Hester not to experience a sense of regained freedom through having Sarah out of her house.

Hester's meetings with James offered welcome spells of relaxation from family worries and workshop tensions. She dined with him whenever she was in the city to discuss designs or on other matters that needed her presence, for otherwise she left all business affairs to Peter and signed whatever papers necessary with her cross. She dressed in style for these visits to London. Side hoops had given way to simple fullness supported by petticoats, the softer style enhanced by the frills of a fichu. Mostly she favoured sea colours these days, knowing they set off the luxuriance of her hair, in which she had taken pride all her life. The marigold rinse could no longer defeat two broad grey wings that swept back into a gleaming coil, but the lappets of a fashionable lacy cap veiled them to a certain extent. In any case James never saw any difference in her, treating her as though she were still thirty-seven, and twenty-one years did not lie between that first meeting in the herb garden and the present day. He was a little broader and stouter and slightly more ruddy in his complexion every time she saw him, his marvellous good humour still matched by his continuing good health. He was like her in rarely, if ever, catching as much as a simple cold. If his cropped hair was thinning, it neither showed nor mattered, for the white wigs that he wore with a formal curl over each ear suited him well.

She was particularly pleased to see him one October day, having heard of a stroke of fortune that had come his way. They met in the private dining room of a large hostelry where the food was superb and the cellar limitless.

"My dear Hester! How well you look and what a pleasure to see you." He kissed her warmly on the mouth. On their own there was no special pretence between them, the deep harmony in their relationship having long since erased the old emotional conflicts.

"This is a celebration, isn't it?" she said when they were seated at the table.

His eyes twinkled at her. "I thought you might have heard. Who told you?"

"Joss read it out of the newspaper." She raised her sparkling glass to him. "My most sincere felicitations, Sir James! No man deserves a knighthood more than you with your long service to the community, especially as Alderman of the City of London for the Cripplegate Ward."

"I thank you, my dear. I value your kind words above those I received from King George himself!"

"Now you're flattering me." She laughed, although she knew as well as he that he had meant what he said.

As was their custom when together, they exchanged family news before moving on to other topics. She was able to tell him they had had a second letter from William, which had been nearly six months in transit. He had written on a cheerful note, but once again a bleakness of spirit had come through between the lines, something she had detected immediately on both occasions when his letters were read out to her.

"He's in Virginia, mostly on patrol. There's a troublesome element among the colonists, with whom naturally, being William, he is in sympathy," she said smilingly.

"I'm with him there and so is half this country, Hester. After all, the colonists are simply Englishmen abroad, and why should they be subject to impositions there that we would never tolerate here? This is being voiced frequently by notable members in the House of Commons, and I hope that reasoning will prevail or greater trouble will come."

"I hope it doesn't." She sighed fervently. "Because William will end up in the thick of it."

"Does he know of Peter's marriage?"

"Peter wrote himself to tell him. In this letter recently received William wishes them both well."

"How did Sarah react?"

Hester frowned unhappily. "In the worst possible way. She kept Peter away from work for three days for fear of what she might do. It has been generally agreed that for her own safety, it is best that she doesn't know in future when a letter comes."

As it happened, that ruse was not to be needed. It seemed that the news of the marriage had had a more upsetting effect on William than anyone had anticipated, for he did not write again. Once Hester received a verbal greeting from him through a soldier in a home-coming regiment, but otherwise nothing more was heard.

Gradually Sarah settled down in her marriage. She developed an interest in gardening, something that was new to her, and was at her most peaceful when planting and tending her flowers. In the winter months she was frequently restless and temperamental, peering out through the windows at rain or snow as if she were caged. Often she would accept social invitations for Peter and herself with neatly written acceptances and then at the last minute refuse to go. He never persuaded her, for she was too unpredictable. When she did attend with him, her behaviour was faultless and she enjoyed herself, giving him an insight into the kind of life they might have salvaged together if some quirk in her nature had not gone awry.

From the first Peter had employed a housekeeper whose duty it was to keep a protective eye on his wife at all times during his absence. Sarah showed no interest in domestic affairs, which in itself was a rebellion against the training her aunt had given her, and with maids to clear up after her, she took delight at times in being deliberately untidy. It was not unusual on days when she could not do gardening for her to tumble everything out of her drawers and clothes-chest onto the floor in an act of defiance against the rigid discipline of the Thornes, wherever they were these days.

Once Peter found her clad only in her petticoats and laughing wildly as she twirled barefoot amid the scattered clothing. "They can't punish me now, can they, Peter?"

"No, never again," he replied patiently as he had done many times before.

Abruptly she stopped her aimless dance and darted across to clutch him about the waist and press herself to him. "Hold me!" she implored, wanting the security of his arms that went about her.

In him she searched always for William, for he was of the same flesh and blood, and any similarity in expression, voice or action was a sudden balm to the ache that was always in her. Since both brothers were built with the same broad shoulders tapering to narrow hips and muscular thighs, it was easy to pretend sometimes that it was William who was coupling with her; at others, when imagination failed, she would begin to sob and shriek, trying to claw and hurt the one person whom she knew stood between her and all that was frightening in the world. She never felt the least regret afterwards. It was Peter's own fault that he was not William, an unbalanced reasoning that remained lodged in her mind.

Chapter 14

It was James who suggested to Hester that she should hold an exhibition. "I'll invite every distinguished person I can think of on your behalf."

She had had a lot of work on his recommendation, and a public display would bring her wider attention in that sphere. Not that she scorned the everyday work that made up the bulk of her output any more than John had done before her. By using thin silver whenever it suited an article, she had brought silver articles into the purse range of people never before able to afford its splendour in their homes. Nevertheless it would be a delight to launch more often into costly and extravagant work. Although she was intrigued by his idea, there was a stumbling block.

"There is nothing I should like more. Unfortunately the financial outlay—"

He held up a hand to check her. "There's no problem there. You and Peter can arrange it between you. Later you may settle your account with me out of the commissions that ensue."

As she had expected, Peter seized on the idea. Even Joss became enthusiastic. To give plenty of time to prepare for the exhibition, a week in December was decided upon and a hall secured in the heart of the city.

"I may be a grandmother nine times over with Joss's and Letticia's little ones put together," she remarked with amusement to Peter, "and I'll not see my sixtieth birthday again, but I have the feeling that this will be a new beginning for me." She put an eager hand on his arm. "Write to William about the exhibition. There's always the chance that a letter may reach him through his last address."

"I'll do that." He knew she hoped that the news would spur

William into writing, but four years had gone by since his last communication and there seemed little likelihood there would be any change now.

Yet the news of her forthcoming exhibition had effect elsewhere. It changed the arrangements Jonathan had been making for his future. Previously the Bateman workshop had had nothing to offer him, in his opinion. All along he had intended to secure a good place for himself in a workshop of renown wherein he could rise financially and in reputation until he was in a position to start up on his own. Goldsmithing was such a lucrative business for the well-known that competition was great, and without an established name it was hard to get the kind of clientele he wanted for himself.

Now, with no more than a few days of his apprenticeship to serve, he had learned that overnight he had a surname that might soon be known everywhere, and his could shine alongside that of his mother's, albeit in reflected glory. Nevertheless, it would still give him a head start. With a place lined up for him in the highly established workshop of Mr. William Dowling, he would have to spin a fine tale to extricate himself and not hazard his betrothment to Anne-Olympe Dowling, daughter of that household and a goldsmith in her own right. She had served her indentures with her father and registered her punchmark a while ago, being a year older than he. He put his case to her first.

"My mother is going to need me at her workbench. I would be failing in my duty as a member of the Bateman family if in view of this new development I didn't join my brothers at their workbench. Would you have any objection to living out at Bunhill Row? The city is spreading that way so fast it won't be a country area much longer."

He and Anne-Olympe were alone in the library of her home in Holborn, only a street away from Letticia and Richard's residence. They had met at one of his sister's musical evenings to which she and her parents had been invited. She was a well-formed, deep-breasted young woman with a swan neck and a good carriage. Her piquant looks, with ebony hair and eyes, were remarkably French, as if in throw-back to her origins, for like Sir James Esdaile, she was descended from the Huguenots, as were many others of a skilled and artistic bent among the banking and craftsmen families of London. She also had a Frenchwoman's flair for dress, able to make the simplest gown supremely elegant. When adorned with the inherited jewels she possessed, some once worn at a French court before the sword of Damocles had fallen across her Protestant forebears, she seemed to take her beauty from their sparkle. She had had many suitors, and it had taken all Jonathan's wits and finesse to convince her father that he would be a suitable son-in-law when his indentures were at an end. Luckily his ability to charm had worked well on Anne-Olympe, intelligent and independent though she was, and it had not been difficult to make her fall in love with him. He was fully prepared to use persuasion to win her round to his new scheme, but she surprised him by agreeing without hesitation.

"I have no objection to your change of plan. In fact, I welcome it. I did not like the idea of starting our married life with the two of us working for my father by day and sleeping under his roof by night."

"Why didn't you tell me this before?"

She eyed him shrewdly. "Because your mind was made up. I know you, Jonathan. When you want something you're determined to have it and you let nothing stand in your way."

He did not care for the penetrating observations on his character she made periodically, but now he only smiled. Time enough to put her in her place when they were married. As his wife, she would be subject to his will completely. He did not intend to be lenient with her. "I know of a house to buy. It's Number 84, next door to my brother's house. It was the childhood home of Peter's late wife and I know it well."

"I'm sure I can rely on your good taste, but I should like to see it before we decide."

He was determined to have that house even if she raised objections. It had a grandeur to its well-proportioned rooms to which the Beavers had never done justice. Out of Anne-Olympe's handsome dowry he could have every luxury installed and its good-size grounds pleasingly landscaped. "How do you think your father will react to my new plans?"

"If you put everything to him as you have to me, he will see your point of view. After all, he is a reasonable man."

It turned out to be as she had predicted. As she had brothers in the business, there was no need for her father to take on a son-in-law and no obstacles were put in their way. She had her first meeting with her future mother-in-law at a formal dinner her parents gave to celebrate the betrothal on Jonathan's qualifying day, and she thought Hester a strong and formidable lady. She would meet the rest of the Bateman family when the invitation was returned, an occasion that was to be combined with the opportunity to see the new house.

Peter left home on his own to meet his youngest brother's wife-to-be, for Sarah was in one of her difficult moods and refused to accompany him. He had to pass Number 84 and he slowed his pace, seeing that the door of Elizabeth's old home stood open and a girl had come out to stand back and view the house from outside. There was something about her looks and her whole being that shot straight to his heart. She was different in every way from Elizabeth, but it was as if some power emanated from her to thaw all that had held him frozen these last years, making his pulse race and his blood go pumping through his veins. He was magnetized by her. She must have heard his step, for she turned and their eyes met in the look that becomes recognition when two strangers each see some quality in the other that compliments their own nature. For Peter it was a revelation, as if he had found the lost half of himself again, and she, guessing by the family likeness that this was Jonathan's brother, was gripped by tension for a reason she chose not to understand. To her intense relief, Jonathan appeared in the porch in search of her and he came down the steps to take her hand and give a cheery wave of greeting to his brother.

"You shall be the first to meet my betrothed. Anne-Olympe, allow me to present Peter to you."

Peter heard himself say all the right things. Afterwards the dinner was a nightmare to him, for her appeal increased every time he glanced in her direction, and his whole body seemed keyed to her every movement and gesture. It was for that reason he avoided any further conversation with her.

"Your brother is very reserved in his manner," she said to Jonathan as they spoke together in low voices on their way home, her parents dozing after the rich food and wine they had partaken.

"Joss has always been the quiet one."

"No, I mean Peter."

"Peter? He is never at a loss for words. Quite the reverse."

"He hardly spoke to me." It troubled her. "Do you think he is averse to seeing his late wife's childhood home occupied by a new-comer to the Bateman family?"

"No, he's not one to begrudge others happiness, even though he has little enough himself these days." Jonathan was enjoying the comfort of the coach. It was one of the first things he intended to buy himself out of her dowry.

"I hope Peter hasn't taken a dislike to me." She did not seem able to let the matter rest.

He picked up her slim hand and kissed the palm. "Who could ever dislike you? Least of all Peter. There's not an unkind bone in his whole body, which was why he acted like a fool in marrying Sarah, as I told you."

"She sounds a sad person. I hope I may befriend her when we are sisters-in-law."

He did not mind how she passed her time as long as she did not interfere with the freedom that her money was going to give him.

Not all the redecorating of their new home was completed by the time they married in April. With paint still wet and some hand-blocked wallpaper yet to be hung, she had much to attend to and supervise in the house until finally all the carpets were laid and the last item of furniture delivered. Full of anticipation, she presented herself at the Bateman workshop. She had donned a plain wool dress and a large apron, and a cap of pleats covered her hair. Her husband, his brothers and his mother were all at work there in what had once been the long drawing-room of Number 108.

"Here I am," she announced, spreading her hands. "Where do I start?"

Only Joss looked pleased to see her. She had had a severe dispute previously with Jonathan, who had no wish for his wife to work, for he thought it was not in keeping with the social position he in-tended to maintain; in any case, he did not want her knowing of any comings or goings he might make in a working day. Peter lowered the tray he was working on, its gallery enhanced by symbolised birds that were fast becoming a characteristic of many of Hester's designs.

"There is no place for you here, Anne-Olympe," he said courteously but with firmness. "As you can see, we each have our own workbench."

"This room is big enough to hold another one."

"I think not. We need the space."

She was keenly affronted and looked to Jonathan for support, but he kept his attention riveted on the bowl of the punch-ladle he was raising. Linney, coming from the packing room next door when the Batemans' voices reached him, gave her a sympathetic glance, having no authority to speak for her. She made a direct appeal to Hester.

"There are other rooms in this house. May I not have a workbench elsewhere?"

"You would still have to use the facilities here," Hester pointed out.

Anne-Olympe flushed painfully. "Am I to be treated as a pariah in this family? I'm a qualified craftsman and believe myself to be the equal of anyone here, saving you, ma'am. Gold and silver are in my blood as they are in yours, and since we are both women, I fail to see why you do not want me here."

Hester was full of pity for her, but she had to side with Peter, even though he did not suspect why she should be his ally in this matter. On the evening of the dinner she had given for the Dowlings, she had inadvertently witnessed an unguarded look he had directed at Anne-Olympe when believing himself unobserved. His whole face had given him away, and if she had had any doubts about the meaning of what she had seen, they had been reinforced by his avoidance of Anne-Olympe whenever possible, his decline of an invitation to view the alterations at Number 84 and his deliberate indifference whenever she was near. It would not be fair to let him suffer her proximity daily in the workshop until time and reason had given him the chance to subdue a passion that could never be fulfilled.

"It's not a question of not wanting you," Hester began as tactfully as she could, "but as Peter has said—"

Anne-Olympe rounded on Peter then, striding across to stand challengingly at his workbench. "I know you don't like me, although to my knowledge I've done nothing to offend you, but you have no right to let your personal bias bar me when I could do so much towards helping with all the work waiting to be done."

He appeared to weigh her words. Then he inclined his head, hardening his jaw. "There are articles waiting to be polished. You will find the polishing machine upstairs."

She took a step backwards, drawing in her breath in outrage. He had offered her an apprentice's first task, but if he imagined he was going to make her retreat from the workshop by that insult, he was much mistaken. Fury made her voice shake. "Very well. I'll start there. If I have to serve a second term of indentures to please you, I'll do it, but the day will come when I'll make you admit that I'm a goldsmith of the highest order!"

"We have taken to using the term silversmith in this workshop," he said evenly.

She clenched her fists at her sides. "Damnation to you!"

Her heels flashed as she stalked from the workshop and upstairs in search of the polishing room. A minute later the machine's wheels and treadle could be heard rumbling with a speed that showed she was venting her anger on it. Peter took up his work, aware of Joss's puzzled regard, before he also continued with what he was doing. It was the first time real hostility of any kind had penetrated the Bateman workshop. Hester resumed the saw-piercing of a serving slice, a skill in which she excelled, and she felt apprehensive. A fiery relationship was potently more dangerous than a passive one with the same roots. She would do anything she could to make sure that nobody, particularly Jonathan, ever suspected why Peter had acted totally out of character this morning in a manner she would long remember.

As time went on, she half expected Peter to relent, knowing what it must mean to him to deny a talented woman her full potential, but he remained totally unbending in his attitude. Anne-Olympe polished meticulously day in and day out, as well as carrying out other minor tasks that any apprentice could have done at the end of his first year. She polished the articles made for the forthcoming exhibition and, having no quarrel with silver, took immense pride in making every piece look its sparkling best before it was wrapped in chamois and placed in its own rosewood box.

"Your exhibits will excel above all the others, ma'am," she declared enthusiastically. She could not bring herself to address her mother-in-law in any other way, for there was a barrier between them that quashed a more familiar term. It was as if this great craftswoman and her second son had joined forces against her for a reason entirely beyond her comprehension. Frequently Hester was at least communicative, but Peter avoided speaking to her except when necessary. When she had made the announcement that she and Jonathan were expecting a baby, he actually turned away and went from the room as if he were deaf and wished neither to know or hear what she had said. Sarah, who had been present at the time, had stared after him with one of her eerie looks before coming forward to offer her felicitations. Anne-Olympe's efforts to make a friend of Sarah had not been successful, but at least Peter did not stop his wife visiting Number 84 even if he never came himself.

The long-awaited exhibition drew near. Peter would handle all enquiries and deal with the business aspects, which would keep him in London for the week. Sarah, nervous of being without him, was to stay with Letticia and Richard at their home. Letticia, who never had patience with anybody's moods, was determined there should be no temperamental nonsense under her roof.

The workshop was left to Linney's charge, and on the eve of the exhibition Joss and Jonathan unpacked the articles Hester had chosen to show. Stands draped with velvet stood ready. She had either made or worked on almost every piece, only the large tureens, coffee urns, dishes and wine-fountains coming from her sons' hands.

As the articles were unpacked, all but the heavier pieces were handed to her and these arranged at her direction. The rest she placed herself. First came an epergne. Entirely hand-raised, it was a splendid centre-piece for any table, the baskets on each of the branches petal-fluted with a band of hand-piercing, festooning on the central base and legs. There was a set of goblets that relied almost entirely on their lovely lines for impact, their only decoration a bead mount on the base and a complimentary mount on the top of the stems, another characteristic that was fast showing itself in her work. Teapots had become larger since drinking tea had first become fashionable, and she was showing several sets in the octagonal style that she also favoured in mustard pots and cruets. Her coffee-pots were belly-shaped, with their own cream jugs and sugar vases, often on trays, and the beautiful curves of the handles of her pairs of sauceboats spelt out her name to those already familiar with her work.

She set her favourite small articles out on tables by themselves. They made up the type of work she had always preferred and showed her versatility. A shell snuff-box with a flush lid took its place among several other charmingly fashioned boxes. There were handsome little salt cellars, some oval in shape, and all fitted with glass liners that showed off with a sapphire glow the pierced decoration at which she was a master. Beside a range of wine labels was a wine-strainer with a gadroon border that was unusual for her, but she was experimenting with it while continuing to use feather-edge decoration on her flatware, as a range of her spoons, knives and four-pronged forks showed, together with narrow scoops and the soup ladles with the round bowls that were typical of her. Taking pride of place was a snuffer tray, similar to the design that had been all-important to her as the climax of years of work, and she had given it an extraordinary flow of the motion for which she aimed in all her pieces. With the wing-like theme of its gallery, it looked as if it might take off into the air from the crimson velvet on which it lay.

When all was ready, she stood in the middle of the chamber and rotated slowly to view it all. Her thoughts went back to that day long ago when Jack Needham had taken her to the Goldsmiths' Hall and her eyes had been opened to the full beauty of silver for the first time.

As she had anticipated, James was the first to arrive at the exhibition next morning. He came through the open double doors, which were flanked by strong-armed beadles for security, and beamed all the way across the chamber as he approached, olive-green coattails swinging, his cream brocade waistcoat well expanded.

"What a day this is!" he greeted her, pressing her hand fondly as he kissed her fingers.

"I'm glad that you of all people should be here."

They strolled together as he viewed the displays. Between praising certain pieces he liked best, he outlined something to her that he had been considering for quite a while.

"I'm thinking of reopening my old home again in Bunhill Row. I need to relax more than ever these days at the week's end, and the journey to my other country seat is long and gets more tedious every time. What say you to my idea?"

"It's excellent!" She felt that the house needed its rightful owner again, apart from the pleasure of seeing James more often. The last time the mansion had breathed with movement, the closed and shuttered windows had kept a secret. She had had to tell him of the Thornes' disclosure that William and Sarah had made use of his home. For her sake, he had been remarkably tolerant over it, but he had been thoroughly displeased. Although he had waived aside the responsibility she felt on her part for leaving the keys where they could be borrowed and duplicated, she had insisted on paying for the repairs to a chair that had been knocked over in a romping game and the replacing of a cracked pier glass. Her own servants had laundered the bed linen and put other matters to rights. "I shall look forward to your return, James."

"Then everything is settled."

Not long after Christmas when the roads were hard and frosty, a band of servants returned to the Esdaile mansion to put it to rights and take up residence in preparation for their master's coming. When James arrived he did not know how he had been able to live away from it for such a length of time, particularly since his quarrel with Hester had long since been healed and enriched into a loving friendship that he valued above all else. Irritated by much of the mansion's artificial splendour, he installed workmen to restore the old rooms again to their original state. When it was done he invited Hester for supper, and there began for them a pattern of peaceful evenings in each other's company during which they played backgammon, chess or cards.

These times with her were in sharp contrast to the busy life he led in the city, where civic responsibilities were ever with him, and he went less and less to his other country seat, for his sons by Mary were now in business with him and she never missed him in the least. It was a totally amicable arrangement. Whenever he and his wife met they were always pleased to see each other and invariably had a jovial ale-drinking session together. When they parted again it was always without a backward glance.

As Hester had foreseen, fame came quickly to her as a result of the exhibition. The Church, with its long tradition dating back to early medieval times of commissioning beautiful silver, became her patron. Joss was soon in his element, producing chalices and salvers, candlesticks and other altar pieces to his mother's designs. Although Hester made some of the pieces herself when these ecclesiastical commissions came in like a flood-tide, she continued with her policy of letting her sons do the work they liked best. As was to be expected, Jonathan always elected to make the most ornate dinner services or anything else of elaborate design when Hester had to comply more with a client's wishes than she would have wished. Yet her fluid lines carried those pieces through and retained an honest beauty that a less masterful designer would not have managed to achieve.

Anne-Olympe gave birth to a son who was named after his father. Not even able to polish during the last month of her pregnancy, she made her own plans as to how it should be in future. On the north side of the house was a large garden room, little used for its poor location in relation to the sun, and in a *fait accompli* when Jonathan was in London for three days she had it made into a workshop. It had everything she needed, from benches to a charcoal hearth. Unable to touch any money of her own, all that was hers having become Jonathan's upon their marriage, she had called on her father to finance her. His opinion of his son-in-law had deteriorated somewhat, and he was willing enough to conspire against him, letting her have some stumps, stakes and many other items from stores in his own workshop.

"Now you'll be a goldsmith again," he said with pride in her as they viewed the finished workshop together. "I'll send you all the work you want."

"No, Father," she declined firmly. "I could never work in competition with the Batemans, not even for you. This is to be an extension of their workshop. Here I shall do whatever work they allow me while at the same time I'll be near my baby. It is how Hester managed when she was my age."

"Do you want me to stay here until that husband of yours returns?"

"No. I'm not afraid of him."

"Does your mother-in-law know why workmen have been here?"

"She may have guessed from the hammering and banging, but she never comes here uninvited."

"That's a mercy! I could never have lived next door to your mother's mother, because her nose would have been into everything."

Jonathan came home with a nosegay of flowers for Anne-Olympe, full of smiles and more satisfied with the social aspect of his time in London than with the business he had conducted. He had enjoyed his escape from the domesticity of married life and hoped that Peter, who ran the Bateman enterprise with keen efficiency, would send him again when the need arose.

"I've something to show you," she said, inhaling the scent of the nosegay as she led the way to the rear of the house.

His jaw dropped at the sight presented to him. "What the devil—!"

Then, as she explained, whatever anger he might have felt quite evaporated. Already burdened with the sense of guilt that most men experience when they return home after being unfaithful to their wives for the first time, he felt almost bound to give in to her in this matter. "Well, I don't approve of what you've done," he stated heavily, "but I accept that you will never be completely happy if I don't support you in this move. I'll see you get all the work you want from the commissions received."

She threw her arms around him in a kiss, scattering petals from the nosegay, the flowers' perfume hiding another that clung to his clothes. In his own mind he began to see that her dedication to work could be to his advantage and he grinned as he swept her up in his arms, his desires renewed.

Hester was relieved when shown the new workshop. It was the perfect solution to keeping Peter and Anne-Olympe apart. They need hardly see each other anymore. She admired her daughter-in-law's bold action, for it came close to what she might have done in similar circumstances, but she could not quell the hostility in herself that came from knowing what this young woman had done, all inadvertently, to Peter. He was a changed man. Even in grief his good nature had stayed open and kindly towards others, but now he could be quickly irritable and was intolerant towards Jonathan at all times. Only with Sarah did he retain the same endless patience that she had never managed to destroy.

"I insist on Peter seeing my workshop." Anne-Olympe's mouth was set determinedly. "He has made it clear he doesn't want to visit my home socially, but he would force himself to go to an enemy's premises if business made it necessary, and that is my claim to half an hour of his time."

Not all her bitter words were repeated to Peter, but he agreed to go anyway, choosing a time when he was sure Jonathan would be at home. Instead, he found himself alone with her. In her triumph at getting him there, which seemed a kind of victory to her in the mostly silent battle that was waged between them, she almost danced ahead of him around the workshop, her lovely profile showing this way and that as she indicated what she wanted him to observe, the tangle of her jet-black curls spinning about in a measure of its own. In her pride in her new possessions, she was not aware that he looked only at her. The last thing he expected was that she should stop dead in her tracks and turn with a swirl of her striped silk skirt, almost catching him unaware. He hardened his face in the nick of time.

"I forgot to show you an old chasing hammer hanging by the door. My father thinks it dates back to the twelfth century and he has given it to me."

"What a magnificent gift. I should like to see it."

She darted across to take it down from the wall and hand it to him. "It has a good feel to it."

He nodded, weighing it in his hand. "Centuries of our skill have become absorbed into this tool. Would you allow me to use it one day?"

"Keep it as long as you wish."

He shook his head quickly. "I'll not take it from you before you've had a chance to use it."

She took it back from him and held it to her. "Then you're going to give me work. Did Jonathan persuade you?"

"There was no need of persuasion, and in any case I always make up my own mind on anything that concerns the business." He nodded at her surroundings. "You have the space here and the facilities you need without overcrowding the main workshop. In the morning I'll send Linney across with the material you'll need for an inkstand."

"Thank you, Peter."

He almost looked back at her. For a fraction of a second he was tempted to gaze again on the face of the woman who enthralled him more and not less with every passing day, but he had almost given himself away once already and he dared not risk it a second time. "Good evening to you," he said over his shoulder and went off down the road in the direction of his own home. She felt rebuffed anew, hurt and angered by him.

When Hester's design and the material came the next morning, Anne-Olympe was aware he had presented her with a challenge. No easy task here, but a grand inkstand with three wells, flush lids and fine beading, complete with a pen-tray and a candle-holder and snuffer. She set to work at once, singing under her breath. In spite of Peter's churlishness towards her, she felt she was making the inkstand for him, and although their shared animosity was unabated, it gave a certain excitement to the project.

The inkstand was magnificent when finished. Hester was generous with praise and so was Jonathan. Peter only gave a nod. Anne-Olympe's Gallic temper flared, making her long to throw the inkstand at him.

"What do you want me to do next?" she hissed.

"Tell me what you prefer."

"Trays!" She knew she would be taking away from him the work that he liked best.

"Very well. The designs are on the shelf."

She took the one that offered the most intricate work. He unlocked the chest where the materials were kept and gave her what she needed. She stalked away.

For all Jonathan's penchant for the luxuries of life, he had the Bateman dedication to work and took immense pride in the articles he made. Hester knew only too well that he also felt that his wife's extension of the working premises had given him a larger stake in the business than his brothers, and he tried to use this against them on occasion. Unfortunately for Anne-Olympe, he was more careless in his marriage bed than he would ever have been at work, and she became pregnant every year. Hester's respect for her daughter-in-law grew. No matter how unwell Anne-Olympe was feeling, she never shirked the silversmithing she had taken on and once collapsed with labour pains at her workbench. It was as if she were driven at all times, not in competition with her husband, but by a need to prove to Peter that she could match any one of the Batemans and him more than the rest.

With such an excellent team of workers at her benches, Linney having elected to stay on as a journeyman with her, Hester concentrated much of her time on designing. Yet she let no one use her workbench and took up her place there to continue making the small articles that were always her choice.

All three of her sons benefited greatly from her prosperity, which had become firmly established during the first half of the decade that had passed since the exhibition, and neither did Linney's wages fall short, he being entitled to the same bonuses as the Bateman brothers. Anne-Olympe received the same benefits as her husband, for Hester had never been able to understand why a woman should be penalised by her sex in the matter of pay.

She found her soaring financial status faintly amusing. It had no importance for her beyond the thriving of her business, for she had always known the true values of life and wealth had never been on her list. Yet inevitably she now had her own coach, as did her sons, and there were thoroughbred horses in her stables. Silk drapes adorned the windows of her home, and much of the replacement furniture was from Mr. Chippendale's shop in St. Martin's Lane. In the matter of jewellery she had sought Richard's advice, for none could judge a precious stone better than he, and from him she had purchased a few beautiful and quite simple pieces that she wore on special occasions.

She chose to wear an emerald brooch and a velvet gown of the same hue on the Sunday evening when she felt a need to confide in James. They sat by the fire in the mansion after having had supper together. She had brought him a tincture made from boiled dandelion root for his minor digestive trouble, and he enjoyed her con-

sideration. Mary had merely slapped him on the back and told him
to ride to hounds more often in the fresh air.

"Peter and Anne-Olympe are more hostile to each other than
ever." She lifted a hand, letting it drop into her lap again despair-
ingly. "Jonathan never takes either side. Sometimes he seems to
enjoy their sparring. He has a curious sense of humour. Who
would ever have thought that a feud between his wife and his
brother would have lasted so long?"

"It's not surprising if what you believe should be true."

"That she is as drawn to Peter as he is to her? Oh yes, as I have
said to you before, underneath all that open hostility there is a bond
between them. She doesn't recognise it, of that I'm sure, but it is
always his approval that she seeks, no matter what show of indifference she puts on. In the same way she is completely loyal to Jonathan, who neglects her shamefully for his pleasures in town."

James kept a tactful silence. It was well known in city circles that
a certain married woman, prominent in society, was Jonathan's mistress, and there had been others before her. The young man had
charm and money, a combination that opened any door. As if reading his thoughts, Hester leaned forward in her chair and tapped
him sharply on the arm with her closed fan.

"Don't suppose I'm ignorant of Jonathan's paramours! I have
ears in my head, too, you know, James. So you may speak freely to
me as an old friend."

"In that case," he answered candidly, "it's a pity that Anne-
Olympe chose the wrong brother and that Peter didn't wait awhile
before remarriage to see what was over the horizon."

"I agree, but he was much younger then and, as we know, the
young never listen to advice. Added to that, we Batemans have
always been a headstrong bunch."

"Even the other Ann in your family?"

Hester gazed pensively before her. "Even Ann in her own quiet
way," she conceded. She would regret to the end of her days those
heated moments when she had let a long-buried and never fully
formed thought about Matthew Grant burst to the surface. Ann's
momentarily stricken face had confirmed the truth of it. Somehow
that had severed a link, putting a longer distance between her and
her daughter than stretched from Bunhill Row to York. How easy

it was by a single unguarded phrase to alienate one's own offspring. There was not even a grandchild to heal the breach, for Ann and Dick's marriage seemed destined to be childless, just as there continued to be no sign that Peter and Sarah would have a family.

"Is Joss back at work again?" James inquired.

Hester broke out of her reverie. "Yes, he was only away a few days. Neither he nor Alice has any idea what ailed him, but he has lost weight and needs to regain it."

"I wish him well. No news of William, I suppose, now that the American colonies have finally rebelled?"

"None. The only consolation with a son in a fighting force is that no news can be good news."

"I agree. The military authorities would notify you if anything fatal occurred." He saw her shudder, and she suddenly hugged her arms. "Are you cold, my dear?"

She managed a bleak smile. "Not really. Perhaps someone walked across my grave. Let's talk no more of death."

"Indeed not." He lifted himself up from his chair to boot a couple of the glowing logs into the leaping flames. "Shall we play backgammon?" he suggested cheerfully. "You beat me soundly last time and I want revenge."

The rosy light danced over her lifted expression and she clapped her hands together in agreement. The rest of the evening passed in good form.

He walked her home to her door as he always did, holding a large umbrella over her, for it was raining a little. They exchanged a good night kiss out of their fondness for each other, although there were still times when he would embrace her as heartily as if they were still as young in their bodies as they were in their minds.

"Good night, James."

"Sleep well, Hester."

She let herself into the house and closed the door behind her. A candle-lamp was always left on the sidetable in the hall for her on these evenings, for she saw no reason to keep the servants up late. Even as she reached for it, someone moved out of the shadows at the stairs and seized her about the waist from behind, clapping a hand over her mouth at the same time. She almost fainted as William's voice whispered in her ear.

"Don't be afraid, Mother. I just don't want anyone else in the house to know I'm here. When I release you, pick up the lamp and go into the parlour. I'll follow, and whatever you do, don't cry out when you see me. I'm not as you last saw me."

His hand left her mouth. As she released her cape, he took it from her and she heard it fall across a chair. Obediently she picked up the lamp. He followed her quietly, but she caught what she thought was the tap of a cane. When she reached the parlour she set down the lamp and then turned as he came from shutting the door after them.

She pressed fingertips to her mouth to keep back the cry he had feared. He was greatly changed. A scar gouged his forehead over the right eye from brow to hairline, and it was not a cane that supported him but a crutch, one leg seemingly useless. As for his clothes, they were tattered and filthy, as if he had slept in them for months, a pervading odour coming from them was suggestive of a ship's hold. Yet the cheerful grin on his unshaven face was unchanged, the same mischief in his eyes as if surprising her had been no more than one of his boyhood pranks. She burst into tears of joy at their reunion, rushing forward with her arms outstretched. They hugged each other for several minutes, she unable to control her weeping and he also moved to a wetness of the eyes that he quickly wiped away when eventually she stood back from him.

"Have you deserted?" she asked fearfully.

He threw back his head and laughed. "I can tell that you don't believe that even eleven years in the army could change me! No, I've not scarpered. They invalided me out and sent me home on a ship with a number of other wrecks they could no longer keep on the march." She had pushed a chair forward for him and he dropped into it, close to exhaustion. "I've had to beg my way here from the Pool of London where I disembarked, and it has taken me more days than I bargained for to make my way to Bunhill Row. Fortunately I was able to slip into the house just before your servants locked up for the night."

"Did the army send you home penniless?" She was indignant at the thought of such military callousness.

He shook his head wryly. "No, but you should know my luck, Mother. I was robbed on board ship, not being able to defend myself as once I could have done. It was being set upon by footpads in a London street that started the chain of events that eventually landed me in the army, and so it's no surprise to me that a similar attack should accompany my leaving it."

"How were you wounded?"

"Not on the battlefield, although I did get this scar in a skirmish." He grinned ruefully. "A runaway army wagon knocked me down and crushed my leg. Mercifully the surgeons didn't cut it off and it has healed."

She put a hand to her head in bewilderment. "Why am I standing here asking you questions? You must be starving!"

"I haven't eaten since yesterday. But tell me first—are all the family well?"

"Yes, I'm thankful to say. Joss is the least fit at the moment but he was back at his bench today."

"And what of Sarah?" He spoke deliberately.

"She and Peter live a few doors away. They have no children."

"Not even mine?"

"No. Did you think that might have happened?"

He shrugged. "I thought it unlikely, but when Peter wrote that he had married her, I did wonder if it had been to give a child of mine a name."

"Is that why you wanted no one else to know you were here?"

He gave a nod. "I didn't want to arrive like a spectre from the past to spoil their lives until I knew the situation. It's why I stopped writing. I know it must have been hard on you not to have a word from me, but I was faced with what seemed to me to be a lifetime in another land and I never expected to see my own country again."

"Why should you suppose Sarah might still care for you after all this time?"

"I've not forgotten what she said to me when I marched away."

"And you?" She almost held her breath in trepidation. "When you wrote after the news of the marriage you made it plain it was of no importance to you that she had wed."

His pain-worn face changed subtly, as if she had touched a nerve. "I daresay if she had not married my brother, I should have tried now to win her back to me."

Her mind was racing. Whatever happened, they must not meet.

Peter and Sarah had put their lives together again, and if that was disrupted, however unintentionally, it would leave Peter more vulnerable to Anne-Olympe and immeasurable trouble there. "Come into the kitchen," she urged, needing time to think. "You look ready to drop, and there's plenty of food in the pantry."

He ate at the kitchen table, wolfing down bread, pickles, cold potatoes and the slices of beef that she had cut from a joint. As she heated water on the range and brought a tin hip-bath that the servants used, she gave him news of the family and friends, for he had received none of the letters written to him for over three years, having been constantly on the move. After he had demolished an apple pie and drained his tankard for the third time, she sat down as she asked him if he had made any plans for his future.

"I have only one and that depends on your helping me, Mother."

"I'll do anything I can. Money is no barrier now. I can let you have a good sum to set yourself up in the business of your choice—"

He held up a hand palm-outwards to show that was not what he wanted from her. "Money doesn't come into this. What I'm asking is that you will let me finish my interrupted apprenticeship with you."

"That's impossible! You can't pick up where you left off. Those past years wouldn't count. You would have to begin indentures all over again."

"I think not. After all, Joss changed masters when the first one died."

"That's a different case altogether. It is no fault of an apprentice when his master dies."

"Neither was it mine being tricked into recruitment. That should count as being beyond my control. I know Richard would never be persuaded to take me back in view of my past record, and you are my only hope." To her dismay, his voice faltered. His face crumpled grotesquely, tears springing from his eyes, and he thumped both fists on the wooden table in desperation. "For God's sake, don't refuse me! Don't bar me from the goal I've craved all these years. I've been spared my hands."

He opened his fists and stretched his fingers wide until they trembled. "I'm begging you to give me a second chance to use them in the work for which I was born!"

She rose from where she was sitting opposite him and went round to draw his head against her, and he clutched his arms around her, his shoulders shaking, his physical pain and mental torment finally taking their toll. "I'll help you, but the cost for you will be high."

"Anything!"

She drew back from him and cupped his face as he looked up at her. "It means keeping your return to England a secret and cutting yourself off from us all again. Nobody must know you were here."

He understood. "So Sarah would leave Peter for me," he said, meditating slowly.

"It's a risk that can't be taken. Too many other people are involved. Is it a bargain?"

Reaching for his crutch, he dragged himself to his feet and held out a hand to clasp hers. "I agree. May I see you sometimes?"

"How should that be managed? You must never come here, and I would be unable to read any note you sent me. Then there's always the danger of our being seen together if you should be fairly near. London can be like a village sometimes, and many people there may well remember you. No, I'm afraid we must let a few more years pass before we meet as we would wish and you come here again." Then she turned to deal with immediate practical matters. "Get those filthy garments off you and I'll burn them later. The bath water will be ready now. I'll fetch some towels."

When she returned with them, he was already in the tub and using the soap she had left ready. Upstairs again, she knelt to open a chest in the box-room. Somehow she had never been able to bring herself to get rid of John's clothes, and now it was as well that she had kept them. She took out a neatly pressed and cleaned coat, a pair of breeches, a cap and a waistcoat; then a shirt, cravat and undergarments with a pair of white knee stockings. It did not matter that there were no shoes, for William's feet were a size larger, but Peter had forgotten a pair of riding boots in the porch a day or two ago and they would fit well. Last of all she took a night shirt and a dressing-robe, for he would have to sleep the night here, although she intended he should leave again as soon as possible.

After leaving the day-clothes in her bedchamber, she went to her sewing box, where she kept an old razor of John's that she used for nicking stitches when unpicking. It could be sharpened on the knife board and rid William of that unsightly stubble.

She emptied the bath water while he put on the night clothes. When he had shaved himself, relieved to have a smooth chin again, they went up to her bedchamber, where she gave him her bed.

"I'll sleep on the couch here later. In the morning I'll keep the servants out of this room and you must stay in it all day. There's a closed stool in the closet when you should need it. Now I'm going downstairs to remove all trace of you being here."

He was sound asleep when finally she returned. Once in the night he rolled onto his back and snored loudly, waking her up. She went across and gave him a shake. The last thing she wanted was for the servants to suspect she had a man in her room, for she had never snored in her life.

At an early hour she was up again, beating the servants to the kitchen by half an hour. On a tray she took up some breakfast for him and enough food for the day. As he sat up in bed and tucked in as if he had not eaten the night before, she sat on the edge of the bed.

"Today I'm going to the city to see what I can arrange. Do you want me to bring any of your old books to read?"

"I'd rather have some newspapers and the older the better. I'm starved for what has been going on in England while I've been away."

There were stacks of them in one of the rooms of the workshop. She fetched him a pile and, after warning him not to rustle them if he heard the stairs creak, she locked him in and took the key with her.

"I want nobody to go near my bedchamber today," she instructed the servants. "I have left my designs all over the table there and I don't want them disturbed." It was not the first time they had been barred from her room for that reason and she was satisfied that she would be obeyed. She drove herself to the city in a wagonette, which she liked to do sometimes, and on this occasion she did not want anyone else knowing where she went.

It was a long day for William in spite of his enjoyment of the newspapers. He exercised his leg rigorously, hoping to dispense with his crutch for a cane before too long, and sat for a long time at the window, feasting his eyes on the greenness of Bunhill fields that stretched away beyond the roof of the old stable where once he would probably have broken his neck if it had not been for his father's timely intervention. He had had a lot of time in which to think about the past during the bouts of homesickness that had afflicted him overseas, and in reflection he believed he had activated his father's illness by the jerk he had caused on the rope that day. Whether his mother held the same conviction he did not know, but long-held resentment had burst forth from her after the shooting of the horse and she had never been quite the same to him after that. If that was the case and she had struggled with herself not to blame him for it, it made what she was doing for him now all the more important. He believed there was forgiveness in her at last.

It was close to four o'clock in the afternoon when he saw Sarah. She must have come up the side path, for suddenly she was there, crossing the lawn slowly in the direction of an archway that had been made in the garden wall to give easy access to the workshop next door. Through the half-open window he could hear her singing to herself, almost tunelessly like a child, and she was holding out her skirts and swinging them absently as if in her own world. It was all he could do not to call out to her. He even started up from the window seat where he sat, but restrained himself in time. His gaze followed her hungrily. She was as enchanting to him as he remembered, with the same fey, elusive air about her. Maybe that was the secret of her spell. She was the only woman who had ever kept him on a string, for he had never been sure of her, always tantalised and forever in pursuit.

Although he watched avidly, she did not return by the way she had come. He was still sitting there when Hester returned with the good news he had hoped for.

"I have taken Richard into our confidence, and because you are Letticia's brother he has agreed to grant you the support you need. A former journeyman of his, a Mr. Glazebrook, established himself recently as a master goldsmith in his native city of Chester. Richard will give you a letter for him and vouchsafe that you were recruited against your will and that he has no vacancy for you at the present time in his workshop. When Mr. Glazebrook first returned to Chester, Richard was of considerable assistance to him, and there seems no doubt he will be willing to allow you to serve the remainder of your apprenticeship with him. Letticia will not be told of what her husband is doing, and I have his word that no one shall know of your return or whereabouts."

William thanked her, impressed by how she had managed everything. "How am I to get there?"

"I shall drive you myself tomorrow in the wagonette. While it is still dark you'll go down to the stable and wait in hiding. I shall come myself to put the horse in the shafts. I have bought you a wide-brimmed hat today, such as drovers wear, and you must pull it well down to shield your face. We often give neighbours a lift into the city, as you may remember, and nobody is going to question me about a man at my side, provided you do nothing to awaken recognition. I have also arranged a banker's draft that will keep you in pocket until your indentures are fulfilled. As soon as you have received the letter, which Richard will have ready for you in his workshop, you will be driven immediately to catch the Chester mail coach."

In the morning everything went as she had planned until she was about to put the horse into the shaft. Then, without warning, a shadow appeared under the arch of the coach house. It was Joss.

"What are you doing here at this early hour?" he asked her in surprise.

She had completely forgotten that he was also going in to the city that day. Before she could answer him, William, whom he had not yet noticed in the shadows, spoke to him. "I am the cause, Joss. The bad penny has turned up again to get sorted out once more."

"Will, of all people!"

The two brothers embraced in joyful reunion. Later she was to be thankful for the most poignant of reasons for Joss's appearance just then. After her brief explanation, he offered to drive William in to London himself and she accepted, glad that they should have some time together. Joss could be trusted completely to keep his own counsel.

"You'll not regret what you've done for me," William assured her as his brother gave him a helping hand up into the wagonette and slid his crutch out of sight. There he adjusted his hat, giving a debonair tilt to it, but the old mischief was lacking in his eyes and his smile was serious as he raised his hand in farewell.

She could not go out into the road to wave him off. Instead she whipped off her straw hat as she crossed the lawn and rolled up her sleeves in readiness for an early start in the workshop on some snuffer-scissors she was making. Concentration on her work had always helped her through times of crisis.

Chapter 15

Hester sat working at her design table in the room next to the workshop, the February sun making pale squares across the paper and gleaming on the black silk of her mourning attire. Although she had just entered her seventieth year she worked as hard as ever, her energies only mildly tempered by time. It was grief that made her feel her age as nothing else could do, not even a stint at her workbench. The passage of two years since Joss's death had done nothing to ease the rawness of bereavement, for it became acute with every ecclesiastical commission she received, and they came frequently. Joss had given such spiritual dedication to that branch of his work, and now, when her designs for religious regalia were allotted out in the workshop, she was always wrenched anew by his not being there to have first choice. It was for this reason that she found it impossible to bring herself to make any of the innumerable small articles commissioned by the Church, those that in the past Joss had always set aside for her in the knowledge that they were her particular forte. She still could not bear to see anyone at Joss's bench, even when it was only to fetch a tool from the rack there.

Quick in all her movements, she raised her head alertly as a maid came from Number 107 to announce a visitor.

"Mr. Glazebrook from Chester has called to see you, ma'am. Shall I bring him here?"

"No!" She did not want her sons asking questions about him. "Serve hot chocolate and ratafias in the parlour. I'll come immediately."

It was a while ago since Richard, having been notified by this man, had informed her that William had completed his apprenticeship and duly registered. Nobody else except Richard, who had written to him, had known that William was at Joss's funeral. He had sat at the back of the church, and outside he had stood apart under the trees, the same black hat shielding his face, a cane instead of a crutch for support, when Joss had been laid to rest beside his father. Towards the end of his life, Joss had prepared her for William never being able to join the family circle again.

"William saw Sarah that day he came home," he said, lying wearily on his bed, having fallen victim to a prolonged and wasting disease not long after he had driven his brother to London. "I think I may tell you now, because you must understand he will always be attracted to her."

"I never thought William could love so committedly."

"I don't know that it is love as you and I understand it, but she has a magic for him. Nothing is going to quell it, not even old age."

Hester's step was brisk as she covered the distance between the two buildings. She knew it had been a disappointment to Joss that neither of his sons, who took after their mother's side of the family, had wanted to go into goldsmithing, but they were established in good apprenticeships for other trades and should do well. Without rhyme or reason, her hopes for the future were pinned on Jonathan's second son, Bill, a lively six-year-old, whose full name of William came from his maternal grandfather and not from his once-errant uncle.

In the hall she paused to touch her hair into place and tuck back a tendril displaced by the March wind. Grief had drained all but a few bright threads of colour among the grey. After settling a displaced frill on her fichu, she entered the parlour where Mr. Glazebrook, a portly man in a dark brown wig, rose to bow and greet her.

After she had poured the chocolate and they had discussed the inclement weather, he came to the point of his visit. "I had some recent news of your son, William, and as I was coming to London on business, I thought I should like to call on you to pass it on in person."

"It is most sociable of you."

"Your son is in Kent somewhere. He had no need of my recommendation when it came to employment. His work was seen by a goldsmith's widow, who offered him charge of her late husband's workshop. I know no more than that."

If her visitor had been James or someone related to her and knowing the situation, she would have rolled up her eyes at the part a woman was playing in William's life once again, but that would not have been suitable with Mr. Glazebrook. "I think it was ungracious of him not to give you more information, in view of what you did for him."

Mr. Glazebrook inclined his bewigged head tactfully. "Forgive me, ma'am, but I believe his intention was to save me the embarrassment of having to withhold his whereabouts from your family if anyone should ask."

Practically Hester hoped the widow was comely enough to make William immune to Sarah's bewitchment, in spite of what Joss had forewarned. "I appreciate your bringing me news of my son, Mr. Glazebrook," she said, extending her hand as he prepared to leave.

When she returned to her work, Anne-Olympe came for a design from one of the folders on the shelf. "I'm about to start on those newly commissioned toddy ladles, ma'am. Have the wooden handles for them with the rope twist been delivered yet from the cabinet-makers?"

Hester looked up. With her thoughts still full of William and, inevitably, Peter and Sarah, there was coolness in her eyes. If only Peter were not drawn to this woman, he could have been told first of his brother's return and then of William's continuing passion for Sarah. Peter would have been the last one to wish to stand between them, and Sarah could have made her choice. As it was, Anne-Olympe was a constant threat and a barrier to the reunion of the family. For the first time ever Hester fired at her in sudden pent-up rage.

"Why must you always address me as if you were a stranger in my household? *Ma'am*, indeed! Always ma'am! If 'Mother' or 'Mother-in-law' sticks in your gullet, then for mercy's sake call me Hester. I'll take no more of your insolent subservience."

Anne-Olympe's face took on a strained and angry look. "I have never held you in disrespect. Quite the reverse. Maybe if you had made me feel less of an outsider almost from the first time I came here, things would have been different between us."

It was rare for Hester to lose her temper, but this time it was a
heady outlet that she welcomed, and she could have had no better
target in her present state than the young woman who stood before
her. She swung herself up from her chair. "I have been more tolerant of you than you could ever know!"

"I fail to see how that could be. You shut me out of your workshop, and when I installed my own, your relief was as obvious as if
you had shouted it from the rooftops. If you had wanted to show a
real hand of friendship towards me, you would have suggested I
take up my work at Joss's empty bench instead of making me stay
where I am."

"Never!"

Colour surged into Anne-Olympe's pale cheeks. "You don't dis-
appoint me, because I knew how it would be. The only kindness I
have received in this family came from Joss, whom I miss as sorely
as if he had been my own brother, and Alice before she moved
back to London in her widowhood. Letticia I rarely see and Ann I
have met only at Joss's funeral. As for Peter, you have no need to
hear me speak of his attitude towards me. His courteous indifference is hardest of all to bear."

"I notice you don't list your husband with regard to kindness!
He is most generous to you, and is he not always extolling your
work?"

Anne-Olympe, although stricken by this new attack, stood her
ground. "Are you determined to claw me to shreds this day? Your
wits and your ears are too sharp for you not to have learned long
ago that Jonathan prefers his rich whores to me. His ostentatious
gifts are to salve his own conscience for destroying our marriage,
and my work keeps me from inquiring too closely into his affairs.
He has never loved me as I had hoped always to love him."

"There are ever faults on both sides. Have you inquired into
how you may have failed him?" There had risen in Hester in her
present heated state the common maternal defence of the youngest
child in any family at whatever age he or she happened to be. "He
married you with the best of intentions."

"How little you know your own son!" The retort was bitter and
full of pain. "He became betrothed to me in the first place because
my father could give him the start he wanted with family influence

to back him. I knew it, but it didn't matter then because I believed he cared truly for me as well. Then at the first sign that you were likely to rise high on the horizon of fame, far above anything my father could hope to achieve, he switched his allegiance but married me for my dowry, which amounted to a small fortune, far more than he could have expected to gain elsewhere. Jonathan loves himself and money in that order. I and my children are sops to his vanity and social position." She stepped towards the door. "Never speak to me of kindness again. I have forgotten how it can be."

As she left the room, Hester, further enraged by having been bested in the quarrel, snapped in two the design pencil she had been holding all the time and hurled the pieces across the table. One half bounced off onto the lid of the box of polished wooden handles about which Anne-Olympe had inquired. Hester stalked into the workshop and summoned a new apprentice to carry it across to her daughter-in-law's domain. She did not want to see her again for several days.

Sarah was playing Oranges-and-Lemons with Jonathan's children and some of their little friends on the lawn of their home when she saw their mother returning from the main workshop, a design in one hand and the other across her eyes as if in some kind of distress. Around her the children tugged at her skirts as she paused in the game, but she watched warily, ready to go if Anne-Olympe should stop to speak to her. She did not know why, but over the years she had become afraid of Jonathan's wife, a fear that deepened and grew for no reason that she could fathom. She did not fear the other Batemans, although she disliked them all except Peter. William was not to be counted because she loved him, which put him in a category of his own somewhere in the recesses of her heart.

"Come *on,* Aunt Sarah! You know the words. 'Here comes a candle to light you to bed and here comes a chopper to chop off your head! Chop! Chop! Chop!' "

Bill was shaking her hands up and down in his as the other children filed underneath the archway of their arms, each of them giggling and hoping to be caught, except the toddler bringing up the rear with little idea of what the game was all about. Sarah did not like that line about the chopper. It held shades of the old axe and block on Tower Hill in by-gone days, filling her mind with dreadful images if she allowed her thoughts to dwell on it. There! Anne-Olympe had gone into the house. She relaxed immediately and the game continued to its hectic conclusion of a tug-of-war with everyone falling about on the grass and losing woollen hats and gloves in the mêlée. Her laughter echoed with theirs. She loved little children and was at her happiest with them. Many times she had longed for a baby of her own, but she had always had a curious moon-cycle that could be absent for months or a year at a time and it seemed to be the reason she did not conceive.

Once she had stolen one of the children's dolls and taken it home to cuddle it on her own. But it had been a favourite with its rightful owner and the resulting hue and cry had frightened her. She had not known what to do with the doll and had hidden it. Then Peter had found it. Before returning it, he had bought her another in its place and she had not been left bereft. There were long periods when she forgot about the doll. These were what she thought about as her good spells, when she and Peter went out socially or had his friends to dine, for she had no friends of her own and did not want them.

When the afternoon games with the children were over Sarah set off homewards. It seemed to her, now that she thought about it, that it was a long time since she and Peter had danced or listened to music in somebody's house or in a hall. There had been Christmas, of course, when they had all gathered at Hester's home for roast goose. She would have enjoyed it with the children if Anne-Olympe had not been there. It was as if some instinct told her that her sister-in-law spelled danger as far as Peter was concerned. Perhaps it came from having witnessed their faces when they clashed over some matter. To her, their faces always registered disagreement while their bodies spoke another language that had no animosity in it. Once she had run to Peter in front of everybody and clung to him to remind him of her presence, for Anne-Olympe seemed to block out everything else for him. Then mentally he had returned to her, cupping her head in his hand, and as he looked at her, she had had the satisfaction of seeing his eyes clear themselves of Anne-Olympe in a smile directed only at her.

Whatever happened she must never lose him. Without him the

Thornes might return to beat her or shut her up again in a cupboard, as they had done in her childhood. There were other name-
less terrors from which he protected her that lurked glimmering
like pond water or swirled about as if viewed from a great height.
Many times he had given her the same reassurance.

"You are my wife, Sarah. Nobody shall ever harm you again. I
have promised you, and nothing can change that."

Yet when her spirits were low she felt compelled to go along
several times a day to the workshop, as she had done twice that
afternoon in the middle of the games on the lawn, to look in on him
at his bench. The others there had given up greeting her, for she
never answered them and they knew she had not come for their
conversation. However busy he was, Peter would always look up
from his work and glance across at her with a nod of acknowledgement, and then she would leave again. On one occasion the new
apprentice had given her a sly look and sniggered. Peter had leapt
forward and given him a clout that had knocked him to the ground.
He had never sniggered since then.

Perhaps she would have felt more secure if she could believe that
Peter loved her as he had loved Elizabeth. She came to a halt on the
impact of the thought, wondering why she had not grasped it before. Yet she knew why. It had been enough that he liked her and
was kind to her at all times, often tender almost beyond belief. It
had become rare now for William to intrude on their marital life,
and even if she could not return the love she aimed to arouse in
Peter, her reward would be in having him enthralled and under her
control.

When Peter came home from work that evening he found his
wife wearing one of her best gowns of lilac sprigged muslin with
green ribbons entwined in her soft pale hair. "You're looking very
pretty this evening." It had become automatic for him to constantly
reassure, strengthen and comfort her. Then, as he made for the
stairs to wash and change out of his working clothes, she blocked
his way by swinging around to sway out her skirts.

"Let's make a picnic of our dinner on the floor in the firelight,"
she suggested, remembering how she and William had lolled on
cushions and giggled as they fed each other with whatever food
either of them had managed to bring along.

Peter, inured to the unexpected, considered his answer quickly. He was tired and hungry and had smelt saddle of mutton upon entering the house. The idea of coping uncomfortably with dripping mint sauce and all the rest of it appalled him. He wanted a broad chair and his feet under the table.

"I think not, my dear. Wait until the warmer evenings when we can take a basket of food out to the Bunhill fields."

When he came downstairs again the table was laid as usual. A twinge of foreboding remained with him. He had pleasured her many times before the fire, and although her suggestion of the picnic might have been a preliminary, there was something subtly different in her attitude towards him.

It did not take long before he understood her aim and what lay behind it. He was immensely saddened by her waif-like hopefulness and foresaw complications that he had never anticipated arising after fourteen years of marriage to her. It proved to be worse than he feared. Throughout the ensuing months she tried all the tricks on him that she had played on William, associating them with the happiness of love and trying to relive those adolescent days. When nothing that she did resulted in wild chases and tumbles and extraordinary things being done to her, she became increasingly bewildered and confused. Worst of all, as far as Peter was concerned, her resentment against him for not being William was reawakened and it was apparent that all the good ground he had gained with care and patience and even fondness to make their lives together worthwhile was slipping away again.

In the workshop Hester had drawn Jonathan into the designing of a gift she was making. A great honour lay in store for James. In November he was to take office as Lord Mayor of London, and she wanted to make him something that would be both ornamental and useful. She had learned, from the innumerable inscribed snuffboxes, tankards, salvers and goblets that passed out of her workshop, how little imagination people showed when it came to presentation pieces, and she knew James would receive more than enough of those items during his year's service to the City. Knowing there was nothing he hated more than hot food gone cold, she had decided on a special dish-cross with a lamp to keep warm whatever dish was placed upon it. There were plenty in his silver cupboards, but this was to be one of permanent sideboard splendour. With Jonathan's engineering skills, it should be able to adjust to whatever size dish was in use.

"Now let me have a look at your drawing," Jonathan said, resting the flat of his hands on her design table as he studied her preliminary sketches. Good living had played havoc with his figure. He had put on an enormous amount of weight, and his jowled face had a beetroot tinge that deepened unattractively whenever he lost his temper or was out of breath. His tailor cut his coats to emphasise his shoulders and disguise all faults as far as possible, but when he was in his shirtsleeves and working apron, the bulges of his once-slim body could not be hidden. Always fastidious, he changed his shirt twice a day in the workshop hours if it was soiled by sweat or dirt, and there was a fresh linen aroma about him as she leaned close to point to one and another of the ideas she had set down.

"I thought that where the dish-holders enclose the central cross piece, you could fix spring pieces of some kind that would expand or contract to need."

"Yes, I can do that." He enjoyed a challenge in silver as much as in a woman. Conquest was always enjoyable and then on to whatever next came his way, whether on the workbench or in a bed. He had no regrets about marrying Anne-Olympe. She was a good wife with regard to keeping his house in order and also an excellent mother. After some initial trouble in the first years of their marriage, she no longer questioned him about his leisure time away from her. After the birth of their last child he had continued to sleep in another bedchamber, which did away with the need to explain absences, and without discussion she had accepted the arrangement. He knew her to be a passionate woman when roused and supposed she found fulfillment these days in her work and in raising their children.

"How soon can you work out the details?" his mother wanted to know.

"I'll have them ready by tomorrow." He tapped the drawing. "Sir James is going to be mightily pleased with this dish-cross when it's finished."

Hester enjoyed every moment of working on her gift. She had made articles for James before, but those had been commissioned and paid for, which was different altogether. Much thought had gone into the decoration, which enhanced every part of the dish-cross, while at the same time the clear simplicity that characterised all her pieces was retained. Both Peter and Jonathan had a flair for design themselves, but Joss, a superb craftsman, had been content to execute and had rarely if ever offered any ideas of his own. When the time came to retire—and she had no intention of thinking about that yet!—her business would be in good hands. Since joining her, Jonathan had never mentioned any thought of setting up alone, although he had long been in a position to do so, and she guessed it was because he thought he had only to wait awhile longer before the full fame of the Bateman name fell across his and his brother's shoulders. He was going to have a long wait if the matter lay in her hands.

When November came and the retiring Lord Mayor was preparing to relinquish his honourable post, Hester made a special trip to see James. She wanted him to receive her gift when others were not present. In the salon adjacent to his office he opened the rosewood box and saw the masterpiece within. He shook his head, marvelling at what was revealed.

"You have surpassed yourself, my dear Hester." He lifted it out and his reverence turned to chuckling delight as the purpose of the spring-pieces became clear to him. "What a gift! What ingenuity! There'll be no more excuses in my household about a dish being too large or too small to keep the food warm!" After setting it down on a polished table, where the reflection doubled its shining splendour, he embraced and kissed her heartily. "I thank you from the bottom of my heart."

She saw him next when he was installed as London's new Lord Mayor at what was known as the silent ceremony, which had already been in existence for five centuries and was so named because not a word was spoken throughout. Her allotted seat in the great chamber of the Guildhall by his invitation gave her an excellent view of the whole procedure, the bowing of James to his predecessor and his acceptance of the civic insignia handed into his trust for the twelve months of faithful duty that lay ahead. Pervading the air was the scent of the posies of sweet herbs and flowers that the civic dignitaries carried at all times in crowded gatherings to keep away infection and—in the past—the plague. It was unlikely that she would ever be able to recall this great day for James without the fragrance in her nostrils of lavender and rosemary, dried clover, mint and honeysuckle as well as the faint perfume of winter-pale rosebuds plucked leafless from sheltered places. It was strange how herbs had patterned their friendship.

She did not try to speak to him after his investiture or attempt to draw near in the crush of aldermen and well-wishers, for this was his wife's day as well as his and Mary had taken her place at his side. She had come from the country to be present at the silent ceremony and to wave him off from the Mansion House next morning when he would ride in state to the Law Courts to swear allegiance to the King while asserting the independence of the City of London to govern its own affairs. This visit was combined with a processional tour of the city to let the people see for themselves the man they had chosen for the office. Mary had grown thin and leathery with the years, lacking completely the curve of bosom and hip that could always bring a twinkle to James's eye in the past. There was a mannish cut to her clothes, as if she had wanted her outfit to look as much like a riding habit as possible, and her only jewellry was a horseshoe of pearls.

Hester did not stay overnight with Letticia and Richard in readiness for the next day as she would otherwise have done, because Sarah had expressed a wish to view the Lord Mayor's procession with Jonathan's children while at the same time refusing to accompany Anne-Olympe. Since neither Peter nor Jonathan could spare time from work to go on the outing, Hester returned home especially to be able to escort her. Always she had encouraged Sarah into family occasions and did not want her to miss this one. In the morning two of the Bateman coaches set off from Bunhill Row. Young Bill had elected to ride with his grandmother and his aunt, while his brothers and sisters rode with his mother. He was wildly excited and bounced up and down on the seat, his bright russet hair the same hue as Hester's had been in her younger days.

"Isn't this fun, Grandmother! We're going to London, Aunt Sarah!"

James had hired a large room on an upper floor for Hester and her family. It was close to St. Paul's Cathedral, where they would be able to see to advantage and view one of the highlights of the procession. When they arrived Alice was there already, having been invited to join them, and Letticia came soon afterwards. As with Alice, Letticia's children were grown, the daughters married, the sons at work. She did not miss them unduly, for her social life was full and, as an unexpected bonus of middle age, she and Richard had mended the rifts in their marriage. As a result, she had regained much of her lost happiness and was more amiable to others than she had ever been.

"I think we should take our seats now," she suggested after they had enjoyed the light repast that James had ordered to be served to them. "We shall soon hear the military band."

"I can hear it now!" Bill was leaning precariously out the open window, and Hester quickly hauled him back.

There were three windows, and the adults divided themselves up with the children, Letticia sitting with Sarah, who had two of the youngest with her. Below in the street crowds had gathered on either side, particularly dense on the steps of St. Paul's where some of the recently formed Bow Street Runners were keeping a passage open to the great door. Through it the Dean, his clergy and the choir had appeared to descend and group themselves on the lower steps, a verger with his silver wand in attendance.

Now the merry lilt of the pipes and rattle of kettle drums rose clearly above the noise of the crowd, announcing the close approach of the new Lord Mayor. Behind the marching band came coach after coach of aldermen and other dignitaries until, with a jingle of harness, cavalry rode in escort to the long-awaited magnificent red and gold coach, the six matched horses driven by a coachman in scarlet livery. A crescendo of cheering rose from below the windows where the Batemans sat. Made by London craftsmen two decades before to be the Lord Mayor's personal equipage during his term of office, the coach shone like a brilliant jewel and swayed on its straps as if weighed down by the gilded encrustations of its glittering ornamentation.

"There's Sir James!" Alice cried excitedly.

They could all see him now, his broad face abeam with joy at the rapturous acclaim he was receiving from the city that he had served and would continue to serve in some capacity after this year's duties were done. In his scarlet robes, his gold mayoral chain agleam, he was waving his tricorn hat exuberantly through the open windows of the coach in acknowledgement of the deafening cheers. As the coach drew level with the Batemans' windows, the whole procession halted. James was to alight here to approach the cathedral steps humbly on foot, and for that reason he had selected those particular viewing windows for Hester and her party. For no more than the few seconds he could allow himself at this stage of the events, he looked up to where he knew she would be sitting. She raised her hand in a little wave of greeting and he returned her smile with a bow. Then he walked for several yards, a lone figure, to kneel with bowed head before the Dean and receive his blessing, which rang out in the crisp autumnal air.

"God bless you and keep you in your going out and your coming in. May this be a year of service and happiness for you and London. Amen."

The choir burst into song. A Bible was presented to James and he held it before him as he returned to his coach. The procession moved on, many people clustering in its wake, others dispersing to return to whatever business they had left for the grand sight they had witnessed. Hester, about to relax back in her chair, grew taut and leaned forward to rest a hand on the sill. A face had turned upwards to her in the mingling throng. It was William!

She pressed her hand to her heart on its thump of joyful surprise. Then, instantly, she remembered that Sarah was in the room. Glancing across, she saw to her relief that her son's wife was busy with the children. The cautionary turn of her head must have alerted William, because when she searched for him again he had drawn a few paces away. A woman about his own age was with him and, after tucking his cane under his arm, he took something from her arms to hold up for Hester to see. It was a very young baby, pink ribbons on its cap, and she gave an involuntary gasp of pleasure, making a motion of applause. William handed the child back and whatever he said to the woman caused her to look up at the window in her turn, her face freckled and vivacious, deeply dimpled as she bobbed a curtsey.

At that moment Bill rushed across to Hester, exclaiming about the soldiers, and William hurriedly turned the woman away with him, his arm across her shoulders. Yet as they began to be lost in the mingling crowd, he could not resist one last fleeting glance up at his mother. Then they were gone. Behind Hester there came a rising wail, thin and piercing.

"That was William!"

Hester sprang up from her chair, but she was too late. Sarah had rushed for the door. "Wait!" Then as she disappeared from the room to go pounding down the stairs, Hester turned in appeal. "Stop her, for mercy's sake!"

It was Alice who moved first. There was a hub-bub with the children, one of them crying, and neither Alice nor the other two women had heard or seen what had taken place. She simply supposed that Sarah, in one of her quirks of eccentricity, had taken it into her head to follow the Lord Mayor's coach, with every chance of getting lost in streets she did not know. Outside there was no sign of her. Alice began to dart this way and that. Surely Sarah, bare-headed and capeless, in a crimson gown, should be easy to sight. The trouble was that with the extra number of people about it was not easy to see far in any direction.

Ten minutes later Alice returned, having searched in vain. Hester sat sideways on a chair, her arm resting on the back of it, and upon seeing Alice on her own she let her forehead sink wearily onto her hand. Letticia and Anne-Olympe looked grave. With the need for secrecy gone, Hester had told them of William's return and his wish that Sarah should never know of it since she was now Peter's wife. What she had not disclosed was her own private fear about the situation with regard to Anne-Olympe, but even that danger had been averted now it was apparent that William had married the widow whose workshop he had taken over. After all the trouble he had caused her, Hester knew he would never have flaunted a bastard. William was well and truly wed.

"Sit down, Alice," Letticia advised, releasing a sigh. "There's much for you to hear."

They all took turns in the next hour to look for Sarah, taking her cape with them in hope. The children, tired from the excitement and increasingly bored being confined to the room, began to get restless and quarrelsome. Just as Anne-Olympe was thinking she must take them home before any damage was done, Bill having made a lord mayor's coach out of chairs on the floor, the door reopened and Sarah entered. She was ashen, her eyes huge and staring, and her hair, which had become loosened from its pins as she had pushed and shoved to get through the crowd, hung in disarray down her back. She fixed her eyes on Hester as she crossed the floor, her movements agitated and unsure.

"I couldn't reach him!" she exclaimed frantically. "I glimpsed him once in the crowd and lost him again."

Hester's voice was husky with sadness. "It was for the best."

"How can you say that?" Sarah drove the fingers of both hands into her dishevelled hair and shook her head wildly. "Tell me how long William has been back in this country! I demand to know."

"Long enough to have finished his disrupted apprenticeship and to shoulder the responsibility of a thriving goldsmithing business outside London."

Sarah's cheeks hollowed and then she made an unsteady gesture of accusation. "You have kept us apart because of Peter, haven't you?"

"It was William's own decision made a long time ago. Have you forgotten why you married Peter? Everything was over with William then."

"It was never over for me!" She threw her arms over her head and rocked with despair. "And it never will be."

Her abject misery touched everyone, the children standing silent, the younger ones frightened. Bill, who was attached to her, went forward and hugged her. He did not understand the situation, but he knew it was something bad. "Don't cry, Aunt Sarah. Please!"

She lowered her arms and took his head between her hands, looking down at him. "You're like my William. Did anyone ever tell you that?" Gently she put him to one side and raised her voice at his grandmother on a curiously hysterical note. "I want William's address. I must find him and tell him everything. Then he and I will never be parted again!"

Hester's pity suffused her whole face. "It's too late. William is married with a child."

Sarah's pallor became sickly white and her colourless lips began to quiver uncontrollably. Although she swayed she did not faint as the others expected, Alice and Letticia having drawn near. Her blurred eyes gazed beseechingly at Hester as if wanting what she had been told to be denied. Since her own vocal cords had apparently ceased to function, she made several small helpless movements with her hands. Hester caught them in her clasp.

"You can make a new start to your life with all of us to help you. We are your family. Think how Peter has become your mainstay. He will always be there."

Sarah did not appear to grasp what she was hearing, simply closing her eyes and nodding as if to ward off anything more being said to her. She was still nodding without meaning when Letticia put her cape about her shoulders and her hat was given to her.

"You should go home now and rest," Letticia said as she patted her comfortingly.

Sarah put out a hand to Bill. "Take me down to the coach. I don't remember where it is."

He looked questioningly at his mother and grandmother. They both indicated he should do as she wished, Hester adding, "Tell the servant in the entrance hall to summon the coaches for all of us and wait with Aunt Sarah there."

It took a little time to get the children into their outdoor clothes as well as to accomplish their last-minute trips to the closed stool in the adjoining anteroom. They were about to leave, Hester fastening the cape of the youngest child, when Bill reappeared, looking puzzled and put out.

"Aunt Sarah took the first of our two coaches and told the coachman to take her home. She wouldn't let me go with her."

Immediately there was consternation. A glance from the window showed she was already out of sight. Letticia tried to calm her mother's fears about Sarah going off alone.

"She wanted to be on her own for a little while, that's all. And when she gets home the housekeeper will look after her."

"That's just it," Hester exclaimed over her shoulder as she headed everyone downstairs. "Sarah and Peter were going to dine with me this evening to allow the housekeeper and the servants to have a whole day off. It's so rare for Sarah to be out of the house. Peter will still be at work and there'll be nobody there!"

Hester had never known a longer or more crowded journey: she and Anne-Olympe with five children in one coach. They came to Peter's house before reaching either of their own homes and she and Anne-Olympe alighted there. Instructions were given to the coachman to see all the children into the care of their nursemaid and to get a message to Peter at the workshop to come at once.

Hester hastened up into the porched entrance and hammered the brass knocker. She could not bring herself to voice the terrible fear that was in her, but she supposed her daughter-in-law guessed. There was no reply to her knocking and she tried to call through the door, pressing herself against it. "Sarah! Let me in!"

"I'll see if there's a window open at the back." Anne-Olympe had already examined those at the front of the house. She did not find an opening anywhere. Without hesitation she took up a stone from the garden and smashed a pane. Putting in her hand, she released the latch and, after gathering her skirt and petticoats, she climbed in. She ran first to admit her mother-in-law into the house and then had time to see that a kitchen knife lay where it had been dropped on the black-and-white chequered tiles of the hall. Nearby was Sarah's hat, it's bright blue ribbons forming a pattern of their own. On the stairs was her discarded cape.

"Pray God we're in time!" Hester gasped, following her up the flight.

It did not take them long to find her. She was curled up in the darkest corner of a large linen cupboard, her face buried in her arms. Hester dropped to her knees and spoke softly to her.

"Let me help you to bed, my dear. You've had a great shock today. A little sleep will bring you comfort." There was no response. Gently she slid a hand under her daughter-in-law's chin and tilted her face. Sarah blinked, her gaze empty and totally vacant. A shiver of horror ran down Hester's spine. "Oh, no! Oh, my dear girl! Have we failed you after all?"

Anne-Olympe, helping Hester to bring Sarah to her feet, realised that oblivion must have come to her sister-in-law's mind in time to save her from the wrist-slashing that the knife downstairs had indicated. Sarah stood motionless to be undressed and put in a night-gown as if she were a life-size doll. Hester, to whom tears were rare, wept uncontrollably as she brushed the beautiful hair while Anne-Olympe tidied up and put everything away. They were just drawing the covers up over Sarah in the bed when there came a knocking on the front door.

"That can't be Peter," Anne-Olympe observed, "because I'm sure I left the bolt drawn."

"I had better go down anyway." Hester dried the wetness of her eyes as she descended into the hall. She opened the door to the coachman.

"Mr. Peter wasn't there, ma'am. He had to go and see a client earlier today, but Mr. Jonathan will tell him to come straight here when he returns."

She closed the door and leaned against it, reaction setting in to the twists and turns of the tragedy that had occurred. Her usual abundant energy had deserted her and her legs felt ready to give way. Determinedly she straightened her back and went slowly across to remount the stairs. That dreadful knife had been cleared away with all else. Although she wanted to hope that Sarah would come out of that deep shock to resume normal living, her common sense told her that it would never be. Something had snapped in Sarah's mind. It would have been easy to give way again to tears of pity and sadness, but she must be strong as she had always been in times of crisis. She was in John's place as head of the family and must carry her duty well.

Anne-Olympe was sitting at the bedside. "Sarah has gone to sleep."

"That's good." Hester sat down herself more wearily than she had intended. She was aware of her daughter-in-law's understand-ing gaze. Unexpectedly it touched her. She and this young woman had come through a terrible time together in the past hour. "I don't know what I would have done without your help, Anne-Olympe."

"Alice or Letticia would have returned with you if I had not been there."

"That's not the point. Today no daughter could have been closer to me than you were and still are as we sit here together. There have been barriers between us in the past and angry words exchanged. I hope they are forgotten."

Anne-Olympe looked down at her linked hands in her lap as if pondering her answer and then raised her head again. "I have known you feared Peter's love for me and its possible consequences. My anger has been a passing thing."

Hester drew in her breath. "I thought I had hidden that particular anxiety as I believed Peter had disguised his feelings for you."

"He did for a long time, probably because Jonathan still held me with the charm that had made me fall in love with him. As that illusion cleared, I began to see Peter in another light. No man in love can guard his glances forever."

"Does he realise that you know how he feels?"

"I'm not sure. I've tried to be as astute in concealing my own emotions from him as he was in keeping knowledge from me for a time."

There was a long pause. "Are you telling me you're in love with him?"

"I am." It was said openly and honestly. "But I'm married to another man to whom I gave a promise of fidelity at the altar, and such is my nature that I must abide by that vow, no matter that he has betrayed me since the early days of our marriage."

"You carry a heavy burden."

"Jonathan is a good father." It was as if Anne-Olympe wanted to cement her reassurance by showing that her marriage still retained an unassailable bastion. "My children are everything to me."

Suddenly Sarah stirred, sitting bolt upright to stare about her blankly. With gentleness Anne-Olympe pressed her back into the pillows, and she slept again almost immediately. Hester rose to her feet, relieved immeasurably that the way had been cleared between her and Jonathan's wife. She had long held Anne-Olympe in respect, and this had now reached new bounds.

"I think I should go downstairs in readiness for when Peter comes. He has to be prepared for what has happened. You realise that Sarah must not be left?"

"I'll stay with her, Hester."

In the drawing-room Hester, heartened by Anne-Olympe's use of her Christian name, took a poker to the damped-down fire and brought forth a cheerful spurt of flame. Then she lighted a few candles to lift the early dusk, as had been done already in the bedchamber upstairs. She had barely set down the tinderbox when the front door was thrown open and Peter burst into the house, his face racked, his greatcoat flying out around him. He tossed his tricorn hat aside as she hurried to meet him.

"What's happened to Sarah?" he demanded hoarsely. "Has she—?"

"No!" She put her hands on his arms, guessing the dread that never left him. "Come and sit with me by the fire before you go upstairs. You should know everything that has happened first."

He threw off his greatcoat and followed her. When he had heard her out about William and Sarah he sat sombrely silent for a little while, his arms resting across his knees, his face deeply troubled. "My poor Sarah," he said at last. "There were times when I hoped she and I would mend each other's shattered lives, but whenever a glimmer of that change appeared there were always setbacks and reversals, never more than in recent months." He did not elaborate, getting up to stand briefly with his back to the firelight, looking down at his mother. "When I have seen her I'll come down again and take you home. I know one should never tell a woman she looks tired, but you do now and I think my remark excusable in the circumstances."

In the bedchamber, Anne-Olympe would have withdrawn when he entered, thinking he might want to be alone with Sarah, but he motioned that she should remain where she was. Sitting down on the bed, he took his wife's hand up from the sheet where it lay and linked the limp fingers with his own.

"Sarah! It's Peter here. I've come home to be with you."

Anne-Olympe watched him with compassion as Sarah opened her eyes and he saw there was no response behind the dark irises. His dejection was almost tangible to her when eventually he gave up his attempt to communicate and turned away from the bed.

"Tomorrow I shall call in the best doctor in London able to deal with disorders of the mind. In the meantime I thank you for what you did today, Anne-Olympe. As soon as I have taken my mother home, I will relieve you at your post."

"It's no hardship. Let me wait until your housekeeper returns to share the vigil. In the morning a nurse can be found."

His return to the house coincided with the home-coming of the housekeeper and several of the servants. Anne-Olympe heard him talking downstairs. It was not long before the housekeeper in her black silk apron came bustling into the bedchamber to take over.

Peter did not hear Anne-Olympe enter the drawing-room where she had come to bid him goodnight. Fresh logs had been put on the fire and they crackled as the flames danced. He stood with his elbow resting on the marble mantel, his head in his hand, an unconscious pose of utter desolation. Although it was not possible she yearned to comfort him with her mouth and her arms and her body. Then he happened to raise his eyes and see her face reflected in the gilt-framed looking-glass above the mantel. All that had never been said between them was suddenly expressed silently with as much impact as if the walls rang with the sound.

He swung round to her and she fell into his reaching arms. The force of his embrace took her feet from the ground and she gasped for a second in delirious joy before his mouth came down on hers in a kiss that she returned with the same ardency, her arms wrapped around his neck. He drew her with him to the sofa where they kissed not once but many times, unable to assuage by the least degree their released passion for each other, murmurs and soft groans of unbearable pleasure mingling as his hand finally defeated the intricacies of her folded fichu and cupped her breast. How she found the strength to halt what was happening between them she was never to know, except that it rose out of her own will-power, the very trait in her that she had spoken of to Hester only a short time before.

"No, Peter. I love you, but no—it can't be. Ever!"

Slowly and reluctantly he slid his caressing hand away from her trembling thigh, kissing her throat and her ears and her eyes and her temples. Then with his own words of love he kissed her mouth again. "I don't know how to let you go, my darling, my love, my life."

"We have the consolation of knowing how we feel for each other."

"Every time you're near me I'll be loving you."

She stroked her fingertips down his face. "Our expressions will be guarded, but not our hearts. Not any longer."

When she was about to leave, Jonathan arrived. He was dressed for an evening at his London club, but had felt bound to call on his brother to express his regrets, having received an account of the trouble from his mother.

"Hard luck, isn't it. Maybe Sarah will recover. One never knows." He glanced at his wife. "If you're ready to go, I'll see you home first."

She looked up over her shoulder at the man she loved. "Good night, Peter."

"Good night," he replied quietly.

When the first doctor was unable to give any useful advice, others came in turn to Bunhill Row. Several suggested putting Sarah in a private asylum, usually one in which they had a financial interest, and Peter immediately showed them the door. She made no improvement whatsoever. Since it was pointless keeping her in bed, she was dressed every day and, when the weather permitted, taken for walks, Hester insisting it was important she have exercise and fresh air. Everybody who cared about her came to see her often with little gifts, all hoping that one day the spark would return. Bill picked her the first ripe strawberry and she smiled at the taste, but it must have been a reflex action for nothing showed in her eyes. Eventually, at Peter's suggestion, William was traced. It was not difficult to find him through goldsmithing circles, particularly since his work was becoming known, and he duly arrived at Number 107, where Hester and Peter awaited him.

"I haven't brought Lucy with me this time or our daughter. It would not have been seemly on this occasion when I'm here to help Sarah if I possibly can, but another time I should like to present them both."

Peter took him home and left him alone in the drawing room with Sarah. William spent many hours with her that day and the next, talking, singing the old songs they had once sung together, retelling jokes that had made her laugh and clapping his hands on his knees in the rhythm of horses' hooves that had once featured in one of their milder games. Finally, faced with defeat, he cradled her in his arms, grieving that in the end her will-o'-the-wisp ways and her elusive quality that had ever kept her dancing ahead of him had finally whisked her away from an awareness of life itself. Utterly docile, she stared ahead as he lowered her back in her chair. He went from the room with his hand over his eyes.

Hester sometimes thought to herself that old age heightened instead of diminished a sensitivity towards love—or at least it did in her case. She could not decide when the realisation came to her, but she was convinced that Peter and Anne-Olympe had spoken of their love to each other. They did not exchange glances, seek to be near each other or snatch any moments of close conversation, but the conviction remained.

She was not in the least sentimental about her youngest son, however unaffected her maternal love might be. Jonathan had been lucky enough to wed a wife in a million, beautiful, talented and loving, but he had thrown everything away to indulge in his own unhealthy pleasures, which had left their mark on him. That streak of luck was still with him, because he could strut about among his friends and gambling acquaintances with the certain knowledge that he would never be cuckolded, unlike many others less fortunate and even less deserving. Anne-Olympe was a woman of her word, and Hester began to ponder how she might show her daughter-in-law her approval in some tangible way. At the moment it was difficult to think about anything except the letter of commission that had come to her from the Dean of St. Paul's Cathedral.

Peter read it to her and talked about the commission. "This is a great honour again, Mother. Out of all the hundreds of gold- and silver-smiths in the city you have been asked to make this wand, for which I see the Dean uses the old word of 'virge.' You should make this piece yourself. It is to be in daily use at services from the date it is received, and you have always said that beautiful silver thrives on wear."

"I'll think about it." It was all she had been able to say, well aware as to why he was encouraging her. He knew there was still that hurdle for her as far as ecclesiastical commissions were concerned. Her hands, wrinkled and age-spotted, were as capable as ever. If there was an aching in her fingers to fashion this newly commissioned piece, it battled with her inability to face having her heart gashed anew by the grief it would evoke.

The design danced persistently in her mind. She could see its silver slenderness, a lovely simplicity to compliment the glory of the great cathedral itself. Many times she took up her pencil to set it down and then turned to other work, shutting it out.

The solution came to her one evening. It was so clear she could not understand why it had not come to her before. In the morning she went to Anne-Olympe's workshop and found her busily engaged on a sugar vase. As was her way, Hester came to the point at once.

"I should like you to work with me on the virge for St. Paul's, if it is agreeable to you."

Anne-Olympe put down the sugar vase slowly, absorbing what had been said. "There is nothing I should like better. Only the preliminary work, though; it should be your piece."

"Nevertheless it would be more convenient for both of us if you were in the main workshop. I know you have been installed here for a long time, but I should like you to consider transferring to Joss's old bench."

"You would do this for me?" Anne-Olympe's head tilted slightly in incredulity.

"It's the least I can do. You're agreeable then?"

"I am indeed." Then Anne-Olympe added as Hester turned to leave, "You must know me as well as I know myself now."

It was an oblique reference to her resolve towards Peter. Hester paused in the doorway and looked back at her. "I believe I do. We are much alike, you and I."

As Hester had supposed, it was not torment but happiness that Anne-Olympe's presence in the workshop gave Peter. It did not alter anything; she was out of his reach as she always would be, but to see her daily, to hear her voice and on occasion to work with her at the same bench gave balm to the domestic tribulation that always awaited him at home. For her it also made her burdens lighter to bear. As for Jonathan, he continued to follow his own selfish path.

Peter made a full-size model in wood from Hester's preliminary design to determine the details of balance, taper and "feel" of the finished article. From it he marked out the exact size and shape of

the wand body onto sheet silver, getting the dimensions by rolling
the wood pattern once across it. When it was cut, Anne-Olympe
filed the long edges straight and afterwards annealed it by heat.
When it was cold again she formed it into a perfect hollow tapered
tube by beating and working the metal until the edges were drawn
together in a close joint. When she had finished soldering it, her
part of the work was done.

Hester gave great thought as to where she should position her
"touch," for the heavy blows necessary to the punching would otherwise have flattened and destroyed the wand. When her decision
was made, a plug of silver was soldered in at a chosen point, after
which she turned her attention to making the caps that would close
either end. Next came the shaping of the decorative ferrules with
their simple bands that would enhance the top, middle and tip of
the wand. For this task much thinner silver was used and made in
three short sections in the same way as the body of the wand to give
conical shapes, carefully sized to fit. Finally it was time to drive
home her touch: *H.B.* The wand was now ready for assay and could
assume its finished title of *virge*.

It was taken to the assay office and brought back the same day.
She set to work to clean away some slight scraping done in the
punching home of the official hallmarks. Then came the polishing
until finally it was done—an article of grace and beauty that was
both functional and sheer pleasure to the eye. In the making of it
she had found healing and peace.

The virge commenced its ecclesiastical life most suitably on a
Sunday. All the Batemans went to St. Paul's that day for morning
service. They filled many seats, for all the grandchildren had come
as well, including the grown-up ones, several with their married
partners, two couples having babies of their own. Ann and Richard
had come from York. Curiously they now looked the same age, as if
she had gained in years and he had lost them in what was obviously
a contented match. Ann had been overwhelmed to see William
again, as he had been to see her.

When the congregation rose at the entrance of the Cross, the
choir, the attendant clergy and the Dean, Hester's eyes went inevitably to her virge. It shone against and seemed part of the dazzling
blaze of gold and jewel-like hues of the cathedral's magnificence.

The tip sparkled like a silver star, reflecting the brilliance from the great windows, and it bridged the years for her. She was reminded of the silver thimble that had once flashed on her mother's finger, awakening her to the beauty of silver and thus to life itself.

She was back at work next morning, but as the days passed, she slipped quickly into an entirely advisory position. A desk was brought into the main workshop where it was set on a raised part of the floor. From it she was able to keep an eye on everything, and although her body grew stouter and slower, her mind remained as alert as ever. No apprentice dared to slack under her eagle gaze, and the family output increased still further. Hester scoffed when her critics accused her of turning out silver with as much speed and abundance as if she were a street magician pulling coloured ribbons from a hat. She had a good working team and that was the secret of success.

Age finally caught up with her, and on her eighty-first birthday Hester retired. Letticia, recently widowed, offered her a home and she accepted, giving Peter the chance to take up residence in Number 107 and to be in full charge of the workshop. The Bateman touch became

P.B.

I.B.

as the brothers worked together, Jonathan not wanting to be confused with his late brother by using his initial and taking the most similar in shape instead.

It proved to be an all-too-short period of only nine months, for one morning Jonathan collapsed and died of a heart seizure at his workbench. He had bequeathed everything to Anne-Olympe. As it was her right to take her late husband's position in the workshop, the Bateman touch changed once again. This time it was

P.B.

A.B.

Not long after her eighty-third birthday Hester dictated a new will. Peter arrived to write it for her, bringing the fresh air of the day into the drawing room where she awaited him, a still hand-

some, grey-haired man of fifty-one. They greeted each other affec-
tionately, and after he had told her the family news and reported
the latest commissions, her interest in the business unfailing, they
came to the purpose of his visit that day.

"So you want to make a new will?" He raised an eyebrow questioningly. In his opinion her previous will, which he had also written for her, had covered all contingencies.

"That's correct. Before we start I want to make sure that the
family know that you are to have the spoon your father made me
after you were born."

"They do, Mother. I promise you that Bill shall inherit it in his
turn after me."

"Good." That pleased her. Bill was soon to complete his apprenticeship with a London goldsmith, and she knew Peter had long
since begun to treat him as the son he would never have. She
gestured towards the table. "Letticia has left paper and pen and ink
for you there."

"So I see." Drawing up a chair at the table, he settled to his task.
He wrote at her dictation. His pen scratched in the quiet room. "Is
that all you wish me to set down?" His hand reached for the sand
shaker to dry the ink.

Her quick smile gave a youthful look to her face. "I have one
more bequest. I'm bequeathing my tools of trade to Anne-Olympe,
just as your father once left his to me. Your partnership with her is
adding prestige to the name of Bateman, and it's my tribute to her
as one craftswoman to another."

He knew what that bequest would mean to the woman he loved
and nodded appreciatively. "You could pay her no higher compliment, although I hope it will be many years yet before she learns of
the honour you have bestowed on her."

After the will was signed and duly witnessed, he stayed on to
dine with his mother and sister. When he left for home, Hester
went to the window to watch him enter his coach and drive away.
There was little doubt in her mind that in Anne-Olympe's widowhood the two of them had become lovers as well as partners. She
was glad of it. Even if poor Sarah in her state of oblivion should
die, they could never wed, because the law prevented a man from
marrying his brother's widow.

As for their work, they had given the articles they made their own characteristics of a lovely thread decoration, and the domed lids of their coffee and teapots were another feature. For their beautiful trays they had introduced a gadroon style of border that proclaimed their touch—always able to give a piece grandeur while never straying from the Bateman principle of motion, simplicity and vitality in silver.

Hester's thoughts turned to Bill. She smiled to herself as she remembered the day when he had come into the workshop and punched his fist on her workbench to demand her attention.

"Which workbench is going to be mine one day, Grandmother?" She had put her fist down in almost the same place. "This one, Bill! You shall have mine when you're a grown man!" They had laughed together and she had hugged him. It was no wonder she was full of hope for the future.